Come Quickly
DAWN

George Patterson has mentored leaders in many countries who have made breakthroughs leading to widespread church planting movements. Much of the wisdom gleaned through his vast experience has been incorporated in Train and Multiply, a "menu-driven" program now used in many languages to train shepherds in church planting movements.

—Galen Currah, DMiss
former adjunct instructor, Western Seminary

George Patterson's instructive fiction is so true-to-life that when I underlined phrases, it bled.

—John Mulholland, PhD
former professor of missions, Colombia Bible Seminary

People love stories. Jesus knew this and so he told stories. Patterson has captured a wonderful way to teach people about church planting. When people learn through stories, it becomes so much easier and more enjoyable and therefore more effective. The principles in it are spot on and the activities at the end of each chapter encourage obedience. This book is a great church planter's manual.

—Pamela Arlund, PhD
director, All Nations

George Patterson is father and mentor to us all. Long a pioneer in church planting and multiplication, both directly and indirectly through thousands of disciples around the world, Brother George is once again pushing the envelope, showing us how the Kingdom is advancing leaving countless transformed lives and discipleship communities in its wake. This time Dr. Patterson has pioneered a new genre in communication: the "training novel." Who knew this maven of church planting could also write riveting prose? Missionaries, pastors, church planters, and every kind of adventurous Christian will be gripped and blessed by George Patterson's *Come Quickly Dawn!* It is a powerful blend of narrative and wisdom that unpacks the secrets of how God is at work redeeming even the most calloused souls for Christ.

—David Garrison, PhD
missionary author, *Church Planting Movements*

Come Quickly
DAWN
A Training Novel

George Patterson

Jeff Rollins, illustrator

WILLIAM CAREY
LIBRARY

Published by William Carey Library
1605 E. Elizabeth Street
Pasadena, CA 91104 | www.missionbooks.org

Kate Kardol, copyeditor
Melissa Hicks, editor
Amanda Valloza, graphic design
Rose Lee-Norman, indexer

William Carey Library is a ministry of the
U.S. Center for World Mission
Pasadena, CA | www.uscwm.org

Printed in the United States of America
16 15 14 13 12   5 4 3 2 1 BP1000

Library of Congress Cataloging-in-Publication Data
Patterson, George, 1932-
   Come quickly dawn : a training novel / George Patterson ; art by Jeff Rollins.
      p. cm.
   Includes index.
   ISBN 978-0-87808-471-5
   1. Spiritual warfare--Fiction. I. Title.
   PS3616.A875C6 2012
   813'.6--dc23
                            2011046135

*Dedicated to Fabio Gutierrez, school teacher,
slain in the night by machete for his faith
in Jesus Christ, following his baptism
in Barranco, Hondura*

Equipping leaders by depicting guidelines that
our Lord Jesus and His apostles modeled,
and that God is using around the
world to revitalize His people
and extend Jesus' reign

Contents

Figures and Charts

Preface

Let's pretend we're sipping Starbucks at a corner table. You glance at your watch and ask, "Why read this book? My time's already maxed out."

"All the more reason. It shows how to face challenges that tax leaders' time and patience as they shepherd God's people. Even experienced leaders will discover blind spots that need fixing; reviewers pointed out an embarrassing number of my own in the manuscript. Want to split a bagel to go with this brew?"

You nod. "But why a hybrid *novel-textbook*?"

"It's to illustrate guidelines for leading. Like in the Gospels, instructive narrative speaks to both halves of our brain. Our intuitive right lobe likes to envision concepts and connect them while the linear left uses exact, linear logic. Overdo left-brain analysis and right-lobe synthesis atrophies—and our churches atrophy, too. Same thing if leaders rely too much on right-lobe insight."

"I wonder if my education left my brain a bit lopsided."

"The double track may stretch you at first, but by the time you've finished three or four chapters you'll be happily rehabilitated."

"Why set the story in a *Hispanic venue* that's foreign to most of us?"

"Many of its vital guidelines derive from events that wouldn't take place in the average American church. Also, we associate God's work with familiar routine in our own culture, which limits our view, and we're unaware of our blind side. Visiting a foreign land to see God working from a fresh perspective has often led to valuable breakthroughs in ministry. Observing churches and cell groups grow in Christ and multiply abroad has helped many serve Him more capably back home. *Come Quickly, Dawn* takes you on this kind of discovery journey."

You thumb through the pages. "Why are some paragraphs numbered?"

"They begin the depiction of a leaders' task. Every task has a number such as **04–c**, meaning *chapter 4, task c*. The task's title also appears within the same paragraph as part of the story. These task numbers and titles appear not only in the story, but also in an *alphabetical index* at the end."

"You said actual events brought out many of the guidelines—how many?"

"Most episodes are authentic; in fact, the more bizarre ones are more likely to be historical. Names and places are fictitious except for historical persons. Fidel Castro's alleged Honduran birth mother and half brother recounted their story in a remote Honduran town as chapter 15 relates. The notorious political assassin El Chorcho pantomimed his prison crises as chapter 3 relates. The striking incidents during the flood and ensuing relief work in chapter 16 occurred when hurricane Fifi devastated Nicaragua and Honduras."

Many thanks to artist Jeff Rollins for his illustrations of characters and episodes in the story. Also many thanks to the reviewers who corrected scads of blunders (blush) in the Spanish and English manuscripts: Dr. Pamela Arlund, Rigoberto Reyes, Yesenia Lopez, Anne Thiessen, Dr. Galen Currah, Dr. Hal White, Nancy Hoke, Luís Matute, Ray Cameron, Drew Severance, Mary Rucker, Brian Hogan, Millie Mosby, and William Carey Library.

This sketch was drawn by a trainee while George was teaching (he thought she was taking notes!). It looks just like him when he ponders serious stuff.

Part I
THE DISCIPLE

1.
An Awakened Church Body Sharpens its Blade Preparing for Battle

"Did that bell clang only twice?" I asked the large, cinnamon-hued dog at my feet in the hastily built night watchman's shack. It smelled of raw lumber, its unpainted sides out of place beside the elegant brick mansion of Simon Alvarez. "This night's endless! Come, Pharaoh. Time for another round." I rubbed my arms to keep warm; night air got nippy on the lap of Mount Silverado.

"Hey! What's up, pooch?" He was growling, ears erect, and I looked around nervously; it was my first night on this job. Across the unpaved street in front of the big house was a grassy square with a few *flamboyán* trees, the heart of the small Central American mining town of Bat Haven. Beyond the square, the lofty twin towers of the church of Saint Muñoz rose in the moonlight; their bell was a blessing, as few townsfolk owned watches. What faith moved Spanish invaders to build those towers so high? Were they climbing to heaven by such works of devotion? I wondered why folks called the town "Bat Haven;" its official name was Saint Muñoz to honor its patron saint, but only Padre Camacho used it.

A scrawny cur was slinking around a trashcan by the courthouse to the south on my left. Its blotches of mange resembled the patchy courthouse walls; whitewash was flaking off old adobes. Pharaoh did not deem the scavenger worthy of attention and led me to the north side of Simon Alvarez' big house where remnants of huge adobes testified that a large dwelling had crumbled long before.

My dog sniffed as I followed it behind the house. The terrain sloped down and I zigzagged amid bushes to where the Rio Furioso rushed by; I heard rapids chattering upstream. It was knee-deep and twenty meters wide, but had deposited flood debris higher than my head. I inspected a path leading downstream and a stench assaulted my nostrils. I lit up a pigsty and envied the serene slumber of the hogs lying in lurid mire. My dog passed them by, still sniffing anxiously.

"Stop fussing, Pharaoh." I patted his back and felt his tenseness. "Get used to the night sounds and smells. Everyone's sleeping quietly—except us." A chilly wind swept down from Mount Silverado, and I hurried back to the guard's kiosk.

"Hey, pooch, you're showing your teeth. Something's definitely lurking in that darkness." The dog trotted toward the river, hair erect on his neck, and I followed quietly. I heard steps. Drawing my pistol, I swung my light toward the sound and suddenly spotted a deer, then two others, blinking at my light, grey statues silhouetted against the blackness. Laughing, I holstered the pistol. Pharaoh bolted, not toward the deer but toward the river. I stole after him, palming the gun. The wind whined suddenly and Pharaoh barked.

"Who's there?" I challenged the shadows. "Speak if you value your life!"

Silence. I shone my light on every bush in sight. Nothing. I waited and shone it again. Still nothing. Turning to retreat, I heard hooves click on rock. "The deer are fleeing, Pharaoh. From what? Let's go see."

Shining my light where the deer had been, I spied a glimmer reflecting off the barrel of a rifle. Dousing my light, I leaped behind a pine tree. The shot shattered the night's silence, and a pinecone exploded inches from my head; a fragment stung my forehead. Before the echo ceased bouncing between the two riverbanks, I heard the raspy voice of Simon Alvarez. "Watchman, did you shoot?"

Moonlight exposed Simon on a balcony. I shouted, "Inside, boss! Out of sight. Now!" Keeping to the shadows, I stole back to the house. Simon was jerking his hook arm in the air nervously, still on the balcony but in shadow. I crept to where he could hear my whisper. "Get inside."

"Who was it?"

"I couldn't see, but I'll capture the intruder. Keep talking as if I were here."

"It's that killer, I tell you."

"Get inside but keep talking." I wondered why he'd said "*that killer.*"

I crept back toward the river in the shadows and spotted the rifleman, crouching as he crept toward the house. Closing my hand around Pharaoh's snout, I stole to a clump of trees where I could ambush and disarm him.

"Shoot the creep, watchman!" screamed Wanda Alvarez, Simon's wife.

The prowler turned and ran. Sloshing his way across the shallow river, he fell and cursed the slippery stones. Steadying my pistol against a tree, I had a sure shot with the sight lined up dead center on his back. Two voices warred inside my head. "Kill the devil or he'll return and kill you!" screamed one. The other countered, "You can't shoot a person in the back—it's cowardly!" I'd been raised to be *macho*—death before dishonor—and nothing was more dishonorable than cowardice. I lowered the pistol and let the rifleman disappear into the night.

As I returned to the house, my hands trembled so that I could hardly holster the pistol. "He's gone," I told Simon.

Lights came on and Wanda joined Simon on the balcony. She shrieked, "You should've shot that slime, watchman! He'll be back."

"He'll be back!" screeched Wanda's parrot inside the house. "He'll be back!"

"Shut up, you fool bird!" Wanda screamed at the parrot.

"Shut up you fool!" rejoined the sassy bird. The more emphatically Wanda tried to hush it, the louder it squawked, "Shut up you fool!"

When I had first heard it, I thought the bird's screech was Wanda's piercing voice. Simon had interviewed me that afternoon for my job, and the hungry bird had repeated its repertoire of complaints, mocking its sharp-tongued mistress.

Adrenalin left my mouth dry and my hands trembled when I got back to the guard's kiosk, but Pharaoh simply flopped down and shut his eyes. That escapade left me doing some serious reflection: had the bullet killed me a month earlier, I'd not have been ready to meet God. I'd not yet learned the difference—the eternal, life-altering difference—between knowing Jesus and knowing *about* Him.

I circled the house again, shivering from shock and cold. Through a front window, I made out a display of rifles, saddles, gear for miners, and a large chart with the word "RIFLE" in big letters. I thought it advertised rifles until I read it; it only used the letters in the word to show phases in developing their mine; shaded spaces indicated it was only two fifths of the way toward production.

Alvarez Mining Co. "RIFLE" Development Progress Chart				
Research	**I**ncorporation	**F**inancing	**L**and acquisition	**E**xtraction of ore
➡	➡			

Alvarez Mine Development Chart

Looking closely, I saw that someone had painted the final phase "Extraction of Ore" over an earlier title to replace it, but it still showed very faintly: "Earning Vast Profit." The moon hid then, and a chill breeze crept down the rocky mountainside, consuming all cheer in its path. On each trip around the house, I gazed eastward hoping for a hint of dawn, but a sulky cloud canopy let no light through. I shuddered, recalling Jesus' warning of "outer darkness." I could handle threats that I saw, but the unseen thing hiding behind the night's ebony robes was unnerving.

I faced the eastern sky and begged, "Come quickly, dawn!" Circling the house, I ducked as a bat flitted nearby, at home in the absence of light. Had I foreseen what that brutal darkness would spawn during the next few weeks, I'd have fled at once from Bat Haven with my family!

<table>
<tr><td>

Task 01–a.

TAKE THE FIRST STEP TO BECOME A LEADER OF JESUS'S FOLLOWERS— KNOW CHRIST.

</td><td>

My hands no longer trembled, and a creepy let-down stole over me, at its dismal worst around 4 a.m. Stupor lured me into perilous apathy, and to stay alert I reviewed in my mind the useless trip I'd made a month before to the States. On that futile journey I'd done only one thing right; God's grace led me to **take the first step to become a leader of Jesus's followers—know Christ.**

</td></tr>
</table>

I had made my way across Mexico a month before to sneak to the border at night, trekking through a desert. I failed to take bearings, lost direction, and wandered around like a dog chasing its tail until I remembered to use the Big Dipper to find the North Star and go that way. I heard a bulldozer coming south—or was it an army vehicle patrolling? I hid behind a bush to watch; the dozer's driver kept looking back furtively. Aha, the illegal traffic was two-way! Following the dozer's tracks, I entered California in the quiet, gloomy early morning hours and felt a foreboding that it held no wholesome future for me.

I got a job loading grapes on a trailer in a Digiorgio vineyard and wired my wife Lucy to tell her where I was. One night a tall *gringo* was leading worship in front of the worker's shack when another came and shouted in Spanish, "Someone here by the name of Tito Garcia?" At first, I did not realize he was calling me; nobody had used my name *Tito* since childhood. Folks had called me "Tiger" because I'd fight at any provocation—stupid of me because as a rule I lost. I asked a worker, "Is that guy with immigration?"

"No, *hombre*. He's from the vineyard office. He's okay."

I identified myself and the clerk handed me a telegram. "RETURN STOP URGENT STOP ADAM DIED STOP MALARIA STOP LUCY SUFFERING SEVERE SUICIDAL MOODS STOP MOTHER."

The world around me ceased to exist, its only reality was the note I held in my hand. I sat to one side dazed, unable to prevent tears. The preacher quit talking, sat by me, and said nothing. I handed him the wire, and when I could control my voice I explained, "Adam, who died, was our baby son—a twin. Lucy's my wife."

"Come with me. Bring your things."

At Roy Watts' home, I met his blond wife, Daisy, and explained my quandary to them. "I spent all I had to get here. Now . . . my wife Lucy! She needs me."

Roy offered, "I'll buy you an airline ticket to return."

"Thanks, sir, but I've always paid my own way. I owned a cattle ranch back home, but a flood wiped out the herd last month. It left our house a mud-filled ruin and the pasture rutted and piled with sand. My dad drowned trying to save the horses. I left Lucy and our three boys—two now—with my mother and came here hoping to earn enough to rebuild. I appreciate your offer, but I can't accept it."

"Tiger," Daisy's eyes reflected sympathy as she spoke softly. "Don't let your pride keep you from doing what's best for your family."

"Do you have a passport?" asked Roy.

"No, sir."

"I'll arrange for you to fly from Tijuana. Stay here in the meantime."

Roy and Daisy showed genuine compassion. They prayed with their children at bedtime, and I watched again in the morning as they read the Bible and talked with the children about what they read. Roy spread out a world map and they prayed for God's workers in places with weird names; they also prayed for me. I remarked to Roy, "You pray directly to God, in Jesus' name. I've always prayed to saints. And your children pray. I admire how you all love Jesus."

"Our risen Savior is the center of our lives, Tiger. He's here with us all the time. He's in this room right now."

I glanced at a small silver cross hanging from my neck. "I'm afraid Jesus has been little more than a religious symbol to me."

They talked about how Jesus Christ died and rose again to grant us forgiveness of sins and eternal life. Their faith in Him was so real! Roy urged me to let God transform my life, but I didn't want anyone, including God, to meddle with it. I struggled with this for three days. Since I had entered the USA illegally, I was technically a criminal, and it took Roy this long to arrange for my return.

Meanwhile, I fought painfully with myself; I was messed up and knew I ought to let God change me, but I was also fond of my corrupt habits. The third day, I surrendered and told Roy, "Sir, I'm ready now to follow the Lord Jesus Christ."

"Then let's confirm it before you leave."

Thus, he baptized me. We all embraced happily, and my words came pouring out—a rare thing for me. "Now I know that God has forgiven my sins! I feel His assurance. It's real! It's . . . it's tangible!"

"Your wife Lucy's condition worries me, Tiger." Daisy had followed Roy and me out to the car. "Promise me that you'll write and let us know how she does."

"I certainly will, ma'am, and I'll never forget what you two have done for me. Never! Someday I will repay you. Count on it."

That was two weeks ago. I'd not yet gotten my night watchman job in Bat Haven and returned to our mountain hamlet of Los Robles. After a healing time of clinging and crying, Lucy climbed out of her dark valley and left its despairing shadows behind. She looked at me, "There's something different about you."

"I hope so. I told you I stayed with a missionary and his wife, Roy and Daisy. They explained how to receive Christ by believing in His forgiveness. I reconsidered—repented, or whatever you call it. Anyway, I trusted Jesus Christ."

"But haven't you always believed in Christ?"

"Ah . . . I guess so, Lucy. Sort of. I had an idea of Him up in heaven among sad-eyed saints and angels flying around. I never thought much about it. I'd never received Jesus by an act of my own faith. I gave more devotion to his mother, the Blessed Virgin Mary, as our priest and my parents did. Now I realize that Mary, like any good mother, would not draw attention away from her son Jesus."

Another long look, eyes opened wide. "Will you go back to California?"

"No, Lu. I'll never leave my family again, even if it means poverty." She hugged me, and I asked, "Are you sure of your salvation?"

"Sure? Can anyone really be sure, Tiger? My folks were not devout. When I was small, mom took me to a spooky séance. I felt something filthy clinging to me after that meeting. I called the medium a witch and mom slapped me hard."

"Oh, I wish I could explain salvation better! Let's go see Jacob Morán." Jacob shepherded Los Robles' only church; there were very few non-Catholic congregations in the mountain villages in those days and they were tiny.

Ears of dried corn hung from round rafters in the thatched, mud-walled house, and Jacob's wife Susan was grinding soaked corn between two stones, as her ancestors had done for generations. "Jacob went to milk the cow." She pointed with her lips to a clearing on the hillside. "Hurry and you'll catch him."

I respected Jacob; his neighbors were poor, but he was poorer since he spent much time shepherding his flock and rarely kept the few coins from offerings for himself. There was always some emergency, and others needed the cash more. He was short, had calloused hands, and seldom wore his one pair of shoes. While he milked, Jacob told Lucy, "A naughty girl crashed a religious guy's party and smeared Jesus' feet with pricey perfume, washed them with her tears and dried them with her long hair. That shook things up. Know what happened?"

"Tell me."

The Guernsey cow chewed loudly while Jacob related how Pharisees had objected when Jesus forgave the woman and changed her life. Since childhood, Lucy had faced her sin more realistically than I, and with a softer heart. By the time Jacob untied the cow, my wife had embraced the risen Christ as her Savior.

We witnessed to our neighbors in Los Robles about what we had discovered, and our exuberance was catching; several received Christ. It had to be by God's Spirit; we certainly had no persuasive eloquence or theological skill. I followed Jacob about like a puppy learning God's truths, and wrote Roy and Daisy Watts that Lucy was well, had received Christ and been baptized, and that neighbors were joining us. I was unaware of the far-reaching effect that note would trigger.

Before long, circumstances compelled me to inform Lucy, "We're broke, the ranch is ruined, and we can't keep staying in my mother's tiny house. We'll move to the city and I'll find work." She nodded and wiped a tear.

We left early and stopped to tell Jacob and Susan goodbye. "You've left me a job!" Jacob drawled in peasant patois. "All them newborn lambs! Let's talk to the Lord about it." We bowed our heads and held hands. "Good morning, heavenly Father. Tiger and Lucy are broke and leaving Los Robles. I ask for kindness; give them and their kids new blessings every dawn, and help me shepherd our many new brothers in Christ. For Jesus' sake and by your grace. Amen."

We turned to go, but Susan said, "Wait." She handed me packets of tortillas, beans, and homemade cheese, neatly wrapped in cornhusks. "It's a long trip."

We trudged most of the day; I toted a gunnysack with effects salvaged from the flood and took turns with Lucy toting Davey, twin to the baby who had died. Lucy asked what work I'd do in the city, and I took a few uneasy steps before replying, "I'll find something."

Would I? I felt the same sharp foreboding as when I'd sneaked over the border into California, the same tension between hope and doubt that impels millions of desperate job seekers to flee to the cities. We stopped on a hill to catch our breath, and our older son Tino raced ahead with our dog Pharaoh; Tino was seven and fully enjoyed the trek as much as his canine protector did.

Arriving in Bat Haven, we learned that the bus to the city wouldn't leave until early the next day, so we visited Lucy's long-time friend Olga. She had recently married Arturo Gomez, and he came home packing a scuffed, bulging, black briefcase and greeted us without smiling—apparently a serious type, all business.

Olga was petite, smiled readily, and a chic navy blue outfit enhanced her striking Mayan beauty; she brought coffee and nodded toward Arturo. "He's Bat Haven's first lawyer; he finished law school a year ago. He also pastors Bat Haven's only church that's not Catholic. My late father started it the year I was born."

I told Arturo how we had witnessed for Christ in Los Robles, and he set his coffee down. "Really?" He studied my face—what was he looking for? His tone became assertive. "Stay in Bat Haven, Tiger. Help us introduce Christ to folks here as you did in Los Robles. Satan's got this town by the throat."

"I have no job here. All I know is cows, and this is a mining town."

"I'll talk with Simon Alvarez. He owns the silver mine half way up Mount Silverado and needs workers. He also runs cattle, but far from town."

"We'll think it over, Pastor Arturo. Your church—what kind is it?"

"Hodgepodge. My father-in-law started it; he was Baptist but others helped who were Reformed, Pentecostal, and Lutheran. The church has folks of all these backgrounds and could go whichever way. We're associated with an interdenominational Evangelical Alliance. I'm not a regular clergyman; all I hope to do is help the church become Christ-centered and biblical again. It's neither now."

Walking to the bus stop the next morning, Lucy looked around and sighed wistfully. "I like it here, Tiger. Can't we stay here instead of going to the city?" We asked God to reveal His will as we waited beneath one of the flowering *flamboyán* trees that bordered Bat Haven's central, grassy square.

Pointing up the road, Tino hopped up and down, excited. "The bus! The bus!"

Lucy gripped my arm. "We have to decide. Does God want us to stay here?"

"Maybe, Lu. I think I'd like to tell folks here what Jesus did for us."

"It has to be for sure, Tiger. Not 'maybe'!"

"Yes! God surely wants us to serve Him here." The bus left without us. Olga was elated when Lucy told her we'd stay, and Arturo came close to smiling.

Mudhole was one of Bat Haven's poorer quarters; my plump cousin, Mouse, lived there, and we went to tell him we were looking for a place to live. He shouted suddenly, "Hallelujah!" and pointed across the narrow lane. "I built that shack over there to rent. You won't need to pay until you're on your feet. Glory!"

We rested in our small, unpainted adobe house, and I told Lucy, "My cousin Mouse jolted me. He shouts so!"

"I know him well, Tiger. We grew up as neighbors and were close. He's always made sure he stood out—loud, excitable, quick to anger, not to mention his imposing bulk, and his religion has always been noisy. Oh, look! Tino's already playing with Mouse's son, Andy. They're the same age."

Simon Alvarez hired me the next day as security guard after he had eyed my dog and I assured him, "Pharaoh won't let a prowler get by him." Thus, I began a second career; some decisions seem inconsequential at the time, but shape the course of one's life. The decision to live in Bat Haven would mold many lives.

> ## Task 01–b.
> ### RESIST LUCRATIVE, BUT DECEPTIVE ALTERNATIVES TO SERVING GOD FRUITFULLY

A soft glow on the horizon jerked me back into the present. Dawn at last! It had been a trying night; I do not normally take pleasure in a rifleman using me as a target. I thought my trials were over for a while, but God still had a tough test for me; one that many new believers fail. Could I **resist lucrative, but deceptive alternatives to serving God fruitfully?**

Stepping out of the guard's shack to start home, I turned to study the craggy face of the higher cliffs on Mount Silverado, lit up by the sun's early rays. I told the dog, "Look, Pharaoh. That mountain's frowning down at us! It disapproves of what it sees in this little settlement in its lap!" For some reason I found it hard to take my eyes off the mountain's brooding, threatening face.

"Wait, Tiger!" Simon was hurrying out from the big house. "That was close last night, I tell you. Oh! Your forehead's been bleeding!"

"A fragment from a tree hit me from the bullet's impact." I wiped my forehead with a sleeve and hoped Lucy would not scold me for staining my shirt.

"You've got guts, man." He pointed his hook at me, which made me nervous. "You take responsibility. You've shown up just at the right time, I tell you, Tiger. Mouse Maldonado says you're experienced with cattle, and I need another foreman for my ranch. It's a ways from town, thirty kilometers beyond Los Robles, but the salary will make up for that. Your family will have a big house with plumbing and electricity. I bought a generator last month."

Our chat seemed about to become profitable when a stocky man with a droopy moustache sauntered over from the square and looked me over. "Good morning, sir. Welcome to Bat Haven. My name's Placido Diaz. Call me Pacho. That's my barbershop on the corner." He turned to Simon, "That new night guard's hut is an eyesore beside your elegant house, and you've hired this gentleman with his gun. Why? The town is calm."

"Calm, Pacho?" Simon jerked his hook up and down, hammering each phrase as he spoke. "You didn't hear the shot last night? Two nights ago, I heard shots at my cattle ranch, and next morning I found the body of my foreman by the door. They meant to kill me, I tell you, but in the darkness shot the wrong man."

"And I need the work," I added. "I think God wants us to settle in Bat Haven; Pastor Arturo Gomez asked me to help him tell folks about Christ."

"A *gunman*?" The barber eyed me dubiously, twisting the end of his long moustache. "Well now! Simon and I are both elders in Arturo Gomez' church. Now, please excuse me." He walked across the grassy square to his shop.

"So what about managing my cowhands?" rasped Simon.

"I'll think it over, sir, and talk with my wife Lucy. She likes it here in town."

"Tell her you'll earn five times more as foreman than you'd get here in Bat Haven as security guard, and she'll have an elegant house, rent-free."

My heart leaped. I'd always dreamed of prosperity; perhaps losing our ranch hadn't destroyed that hope after all! I yearned to go home and sleep, but Simon had to recount the struggles he faced in developing his mine and ranch. He wound down and I started home, walking with my back to the mountain's menacing face. The road to our Mudhole quarter was little more than a wide horse trail, the river to my left and high, forested hills to the right. Arriving in our dusty lane that ended at the river, I met my chubby cousin Mouse riding an aged mule that had cropped ears.

"Hallelujah! I will employ you, Tiger." He spread his arms wide. "I contracted with Simon Alvarez to dynamite rock in his new mine."

"Thanks, Mouse, but I've already been hired on to watch Simon's house. I almost regret doing so; last night an intruder shot at me."

"Really? Hmm. Maybe it was Chuey Ochoa. Did he have a beard?"

"Too dark to see. Who's Chuey Ochoa?"

"He's bad. He'd contracted to handle the mine's explosives, but stole dynamite and Simon fired him. I took his place. Chuey always has a cigar in his mouth—

the longest, fattest cigar you ever saw. He thinks he's another Fidel."

"Fidel?"

"Fidel Castro, the silver-tongued Cuban dictator." Mouse spurred his mule.

Lucy had come out and I loudly announced to them both, "Simon Alvarez offered me the position of foreman of his cowhands with much better pay. Uh . . . regrettably, the ranch is a long ways from town, but . . . "

"Tiger!" Lucy stomped her foot. "You claimed yesterday that . . . "

"Mouse, what do you think?" He halted his mule with a jerk, and I begged, "Help me discern God's will. Does He want me to take the foreman's position?"

"That'd be a step up; Simon's ranch has lots of hands. Let me hear the voice of the Almighty." He faced upward with eyes closed as we waited. "Hallelujah!"

 He leaned toward me in the saddle. "I heard the celestial voice! Accept the job with confidence, cousin." He spurred the mule and it trotted on to his house.

"Baloney!" Lucy stared after him. "Any voice he heard wasn't from heaven!"

"How can you say that? Devout people keep an ear attuned to heaven."

"You don't know your cousin Mouse. One day that voice leads him east, next day west, and south a day later. He never arrives anywhere!"

"That's spooky, Lu. How'd he become such a mystic?"

"A shouting, showman-type preacher came to our town when Mouse was a little older than Tino. Mouse aped him, and folks called him a child prophet. They took him to preach in churches and renamed him 'Moses.' This went on for a few years and he became proud, hot-tempered and obese. 'Moses' became 'Mouse,' and folks stopped listening to him. Don't you listen to him, either, Tiger."

"But God must be providing the lucrative position that Simon offered me."

She gave me an icy stare. "You were sure yesterday that God wanted us in Bat Haven. Which did God do—mistake the location, or forget it overnight?"

"Lucy, please . . . "

"Your forehead's been bleeding. How did you cut yourself?"

"I walked into a branch in the dark." I did not want to alarm her.

"Why does Simon Alvarez need a night watchman?"

"Wealth attracts parasites, Lu, like raw meat draws flies."

"Then I don't envy rich people like him."

"Right. He owns a mine and a huge ranch, but can't sleep calmly at night."

I did not sleep calmly either after that night's work. I tried, but was not used to sleeping during the day, and my mind was disturbed, wavering. Where to work? In town poor but busy in the Lord's work, or on Simon's ranch with a taste of wealth? I gave up and went to the kitchen, hoping the coffee was hot. Lucy poured it, saying, "Tiger, listen, Jesus warned not to crave treasures on earth."

Sleeplessness had left me surly. "Paul also warned that one who fails to support his family is worse than an infidel."

"I see the devil has pierced your soul with a poisoned arrow of avarice!"

"Oh, so you see demons now! And don't try to persuade me with those tears!"

Lucy was still sulking when we went to worship; she held Davey and would not let me help her carry him. We passed the town square and walked up a steep, narrow, twisting lane amid tall pines. The small chapel, built with hand-sawn boards and hewn rafters, stood at the foot of a rocky clearing that extended far up the south side of Mount Silverado. A motorcycle's clamor announced the arrival of the lawyer-pastor Arturo Gomez and his wife Olga. He started toward the chapel toting his black briefcase while Olga stooped to repair her windblown hair in the bike's rearview mirror.

Lucy pointed at flowers around the rustic edifice. "I love those red bougainvilleas, Olga, and the shrubs so neatly trimmed and cared for around the chapel!"

The pastor's attractive young wife sighed. "I wish the lives of those who enter it were as well trimmed and weeded!"

The barber arrived with two grown sons and his white-haired wife, Anna. She pointed to a plant by the door. "I didn't plant that! Pull it up, Pacho."

"No, no!" Olga pulled him away as he bent to obey. "It's a fast-growing papaya. I planted it as a symbol of our church's renewed growth."

"What renewed growth?" jeered one of the barber's sons. "Our church is in a rut deeper than the Grand Canyon!" He wore thick glasses and toted a large book along with his Bible.

"Well, pessimists like you dig the rut, Professor Roger!"

"Roger seems a bit young to be a professor," I remarked to Olga.

"I promoted him to Professor because he loves books so. He and I both graduated last year from university."

Lucy sighed. "Tiger hasn't decided after all if we'll stay in town, Olga."

"What? Oh no!" Olga turned to face me, disappointment marring her beauty. "Tiger, you've got to help us! Lucy, make him stay!" She took Lucy's hand. "I grew up here but when I returned to marry Arturo after my university days, all my childhood friends had moved to the city. Oh, you've got to stay!"

Arturo was waiting for Olga at the door and I told him, "Simon Alvarez offered me the job of foreman on his cattle ranch with a great salary, Pastor."

"Congratulations." No smile. We entered the single-roomed chapel; the pine trees' aroma permeated it like incense, and folks turned to stare at Lucy and me. Olga noticed our discomfort. "Hey, everybody, meet my friend Lucy and her husband, Tiger Garcia. I'm hoping they'll help us tell folks in Bat Haven the Good News about Christ the way they've done in Los Robles."

Lucy greeted them and whispered to me, "Say something!"

I had never spoken in public. "Uh . . . Hi!"

"Ahoy!" sounded a young man's voice from one side.

Olga whispered to us, "That's Julio Diaz, the barber's son and Roger's brother. His twin Nando is at sea and they're close, so Julio acts like a sailor, 'ahoying' folks and using naval terms. He's come only because Pacho makes him."

Arturo told his flock, "I was hoping Tiger and Lucy would help us evangelize, but they might not stay in Bat Haven after all."

"A pity!" giggled Julio. "She's a beauty. Don't you think so, mates?"

"Hush!" Roger slapped his brother's arm with his book.

We sat on a bench that bent under us. Mouse sat next to me and the bench bent even more. Had I known at that time the misery that humble chapel was going to bring us, I never would have brought my family into it.

Young people sat in back where they could whisper and were chuckling at Julio's remark about my wife. I glanced at her. Julio was right; Lucy was a beauty in spite of her frown. Long, intensely black hair, sparkling dark chocolate eyes, and a winsome oval face made her appear years younger than she was.

We sang and Wanda Alvarez' shrill high notes hurt my ears. Our bench creaked as Mouse leaned over to whisper, "She studied for opera in a conservatory but never made it. For revenge she inflicts that voice on us."

Arturo noticed Mouse muttering and stared him into silence. "Today I'm not going to preach. We'll talk over a plan for our church. I want all of you to join in the discussion because it's very important; our future depends on it."

Mouse whispered, "That lawyer thinks anything he says is all-important."

Arturo frowned at Mouse again. "We need revitalization. The town's progressing, but our church is static; most members attend only on holidays, and apathy has sedated the other half. I've tried to awaken our church, spending days preparing sermons, but without effect. Well, I'm making a change, and I hope you all will too. Are you agreed that the church needs a thorough renewal?"

Silence followed until Pacho mumbled, "I guess so, 'Turo. The walls never were painted, these flimsy benches are about to collapse, and . . . "

<table>
<tr><td>

Task 01–c.

LET WILLING
BELIEVERS HELP
PLAN VITAL PROJECTS
AND DO DIFFERENT,
KEY MINISTRIES

</td></tr>
</table>

"No, no, brother Pacho! Not the building—the church body! Now listen, everyone! Olga urged me to consult an experienced mentor and I did. Jethro Mendez, whom you'll meet next week, leads a growing movement in the city of Arenas; he adjusted my spiritual spine and it hurt! I've mainly just been preaching, neglecting my pastoral duty to mobilize God's people, and I apologize. Our church will chart a new course; I'll **let willing believers help plan vital projects and do different, key ministries.**"

Arturo took from his briefcase sheets of paper taped together, unfolded a large, hand-drawn map, and the whispering in back ceased. "This is our area of responsibility before God." He pointed out places on the map. "All these villages need churches and these zones in Bat Haven need cell groups. I want each of you to say where you have friends and family, because that's where we'll start."

Some mentioned places where friends lived; Arturo circled them on the map and added more villages. "We'll carry this out if we can move our church body to do its job, and I mean the whole scope. Tasks that we've neglected include *telling friends about Jesus, making obedient disciples, helping the troubled, serving the needy, forming cell groups, and planting churches.* We'll all use our spiritual gifts vigorously. Now, I'll write down how each of you plans to serve. Who'll begin?"

"So we're to do your job for you, Arturo?" Simon aimed his hook at him. "Don't we pay you to do our church's work? We have our own occupations."

"I have my secular job, too, Simon. Okay, I'll tell you what. I'll put myself on par with all of you. From now on, I'll accept no more pay from the church. We'll all do the work together, making the same sacrifice for Christ. Fair?" All became silent. "Please, let's all take part—young people, women, and children. Tell me what ministry you'll help with, and we'll arrange for you to do so."

"I'll help troubled folks," stated the barber's wife, Anna, with a relaxed smile.

"Thank you, Grandma." Arturo wrote it down.

"She and Pacho have no grandkids," Mouse told me quietly, "but we call her 'Grandma' because her hair turned white prematurely and she takes grandmotherly care of us fouled-up folks."

Lucy nudged me. "Tell Arturo that we'll witness for Jesus to our neighbors."

I remained quiet, but Lucy blurted, "Tiger told me he wants to tell people in Bat Haven about the Lord."

"Social action!" Roger waved his book in the air. "I'll bring justice to Bat Haven's poor and oppressed!"

"Hooray for liberator Professor Roger!" teased a teenage girl behind us.

"Liberate Bat Haven!" shouted Julio and other youths began chanting, "*Liberate*

Bat Haven! Liberate Bat Haven!"

Pacho stood, his stern glare silencing the chanters. "You youngsters would change things too fast! Remember: *Prudence pleas for prayerful patience.*"

"I'll caution women to stop their nefarious affairs!" shrilled Wanda Alvarez; her frequent frown had etched a crease on her high forehead.

"Broadside 'em!" mocked Julio Diaz.

"Smart aleck!" Wanda began to repeat gossip about neighbors, but Arturo stopped her politely. He waited for others to speak, but they sat brooding silently except an older man who grumbled about the church's past failures. I sensed tension mounting—or was it hostility? Lucy squeezed my hand; she felt it too.

Roger's bald grandfather, Gerardo, broke the silence with an aged, trembling voice. "I'll tell my neighbor about Jesus, if I find him sober enough to listen."

"Same for me," Olga said, "and I'll help them be obedient disciples of Jesus."

Task 01–d.
MAKE JESUS A CHURCH'S TOP LEADER BY OBEYING HIS COMMANDS BEFORE ALL ELSE

Arturo nodded. "Obedience is the answer. We **make Jesus a church's top leader by obeying His commands before all else.** Olga, explain this."

She stated firmly, "We enthrone our Lord Jesus as our King only by obeying His commands before all else. I hope you all agree."

Wanda frowned. "The Ten Commandments? Surely, child! Are we pagans?"

Arturo said, "Jesus meant His own commands, Mrs. Alvarez, not the ones God gave Moses. I studied discipleship in books that taught good doctrine but not active obedience to Jesus. As a result, I've failed to make disciples as Jesus said. Obeying Him is the key to revitalizing our church, so I asked Olga to write a song with seven basic commands of Jesus that the first church obeyed from the start, to help us memorize them." Olga sang and a few of us joined her; it listed Jesus' basic commands: 1) *Repent, believe and receive the Holy Spirit,* 2) *Baptize,* 3) *Celebrate Communion,* 4) *Love,* 5) *Pray,* 6) *Give,* and 7) *Make disciples.*

"Excuse me, Pastor," Roger Diaz stood. "Should we emphasize commandments so much now that we're under the new covenant of grace? Isn't it an Old Testament mentality to put such stress on commands?"

"It'd be legalistic if we obeyed out of obligation, but we obey because we love Jesus. He said, 'If you love Me, obey My commands.' Our renewal requires two efforts—God's and ours. Our part is to love and obey Jesus; God's part is to transform us. The two go together like two blades of scissors. The Holy Spirit gives us love to obey and purifies our inner self to bring about a revolution in . . ."

"Revolution?" My employer Simon stood waving his hook menacingly at the pastor. "What do you mean, 'Turo? There's already enough revolution, I tell you! Now I have another matter of greater importance . . . "

"Hallelujah!" Mouse jumped to his feet and the bench sprang up. His outburst startled Pharaoh hiding under our bench. He barked and everyone but Arturo laughed. I shooed the dog outside, however, he soon scampered back in and hid again under our bench. Mouse stepped to the front. "I have experience with powerful revivals. I can start the movement, Arturo, if you let me preach. I'll . . . "

Suddenly Simon swung his hook toward Mouse and roared, "I beg your pardon. I hadn't finished, I tell you. This revolutionary talk has gone on long enough. Now listen, all of you. I need the property that the church owns, to build offices for my mine. I'll pay enough to construct an elegant temple much larger. The church property includes the rocky clearing that extends up the mountain above us, and I need you members to approve the sale right now."

Shocked silence followed. Arturo stepped over to Simon and stood, arms folded, and the two men faced each other for a long, anxious moment. "Why didn't you talk to me about this first, Simon?"

"You get dogmatic about legal matters, I tell you. I announced it publicly so we can deal with it before you confuse everyone with your lawyer talk."

"Well, we'll not deal with it now. You can discuss it with the elders."

"The sale's urgent, and we'll deal with it right now! It'll mean wealth for the church." Simon faced the assembly and raised his hook. "Wealth, I tell you!"

"Hallelujah!" Mouse rose again. "I saw a vision! I'll initiate the movement!" He turned to face me. "Tiger, I'm first elder and treasurer of this church, and I'm experienced in revivals. I've been known as . . . "

He paused for effect, and Julio finished the phrase: "Mouse the Moose!"

The young people giggled and the "moose" turned to face them, stepping on Pharaoh's tail. He yipped and bit Mouse's ankle. Mouse lost balance and sat down abruptly on the bench. It broke and we fell with it. Pharaoh raced outside, and we found another bench. Mouse continued as if nothing had happened. "I'll initiate it with the power that Peter had in Pentecost's renewal!"

> **Task 01–e.**
> SERVE JESUS AND FAMILY RATHER THAN SEEK POWER, WEALTH, OR PRESTIGE

"We'll all initiate it," Arturo replied. "And Pentecost in Acts 2 was not a *renewal,* but the *beginning* of the New Testament church when the Holy Spirit came to live in believers permanently. Mouse, a Spirit-filled believer will **serve Jesus and family rather than seek power, wealth, or prestige.**"

"Power! Divine dynamite!" Mouse bellowed so loudly that neighborhood dogs barked and Davey, our youngest, woke and bawled loudly for a brief moment. Mouse's wife Martha hid her face in scrawny hands; she was his opposite—thin, withdrawn and anxious. Sarcastic neighbors called her "Bones."

Arturo rapped the pulpit. "Enough, Mouse!" "I admire your zeal but we don't move God by the volume of our voice. Renewal does not come from emotion; godly emotion comes from renewal. You have it backwards. 2 Corinthians reveals that genuine renewal is the ongoing, daily work of the Holy Spirit."

"You told us you wouldn't preach at us today, 'Turo," chirped Wanda. "I . . . "

"Any who've not yet spoken," Arturo's voice cut like a razor, "please tell us what you plan to do. We'll all do our part to revitalize our church."

Wanda replied even more acidly, "I'll forbid ladies to use makeup and wear men's trousers!" Giggling erupted and I turned to see a girl sticking her tongue out at Wanda.

"Wanda has a point," Pacho stated. "Holiness is separation from the world."

"Holiness is also positive service motivated by love," declared his son Roger. "It does not consist in negative prohibitions." This touched off a sizzling debate. Some wanted to impose petty prohibitions on believers; others wanted freedom in the Spirit. The more Arturo demanded order, the harsher the furor became, and Olga ran outside sobbing. Lucy tugged my sleeve and we rose to go, too.

"Enough!" Arturo picked up the black briefcase. "We'll finish this next week. I've asked my mentor from Arenas, Jethro Mendez, to come help. We need him!"

We found Olga outside weeping bitterly. "I'm so ashamed! Such bickering the first time you come! I'm just totally humiliated!"

"No, Olga," I replied. "God confirmed Arturo's vision to me with that map. Now I'm sure. We'll stay in Bat Haven; I don't care if we remain in poverty."

Olga hopped up and down squealing in delight, and Lucy hugged me, declaring, "We won't starve, love. I'll raise laying hens and beans!"

Olga wiped her eyes. "The church was really alive when my dad pastored it. How I wish we could return to those wonderful times! They were great, Tiger."

"Looking back won't help, Olga. Let's look to tomorrow and the new movement for Christ that God is igniting today."

"You're just like my father! He told me that folks who pine for the past mire themselves in a swamp of make-believe. When we whined about setbacks, he'd say, 'Just keep sharpening your blade and reaping heaven's harvest!'"

"I like that!" I exclaimed. "Let's do it!"

Olga sighed. "Oh, such a fuss that was!" She turned, pointing at the clearing on the slope above us. "That land is what it's all about. Simon demanded that the church sell it; his new mine is located just above it, half way up the mountainside. I hope the congregation won't give in to him! That'd be a terrible mistake!"

"Why, Olga?" I examined the rocky slope. "Why does Simon want it? There are better lots in better locations. It's worthless except for grazing mules."

"Dad did graze mules on it, Tiger; that's all he used it for. He owned the original mine, deserted now since the silver ran out." She turned and pointed the other way. "Its land was below, from the road here on down to the river. Dad donated only the upper tract to the church. I think . . . "

"Well, I sure blew it today!" Arturo had joined his wife. "Didn't I, Olga?"

"No! Tiger and Lucy are staying in Bat Haven after all, to help us, 'Turo."

A faint hint of a smile. "One can see why others refused to pastor this church, Tiger; they'd heard of its problems. I agreed to shepherd it temporarily; what I'd prefer doing is training new pastors by extension, like Jethro Mendez does for me."

"Is that why you'll accept no pay?"

"No. It's to set the example. Did you know that small churches multiply underground rapidly and win many to Christ where police harass believers? Well, our situation is similar; hundreds of small villages need churches and their pastors will need to be volunteer workers, especially at first. I'll model it. We'll need hundreds of unpaid workers for small flocks. By 'flocks' I mean any kind of church, including cell groups within larger churches."

"Like Pastor Jacob in Los Robles. He proved to us that one who values God's pastoral gift will shepherd folks any way he can with or without pay."

"I made a stupid mistake today, Tiger! I pressed folks to decide too suddenly what ministry they'll help with. The session left me feeling miserable."

"Don't let their indifference daunt you, Pastor. You can't abandon your vision before it bears fruit!"

He looked at me quizzically and Olga laughed. "Don't worry about 'Turo! He'll get discouraged but he'll never quit. He'll change tactics but never waver from seeing a movement for Christ. I won't either, no matter what! We're waging spiritual war, and even if it means my death I'll never lay down my sword!"

I clapped. "True apostolic ardor! Count us in, Olga."

"What made you change your mind, Tiger?" she asked.

"Arturo's map made his vision so clear! Satan had been tempting me to gain power by being foreman of a large ranch and getting the ample income that goes with it, but God challenged me through that map to decide how to devote my life."

Walking home with the boys, Lucy squeezed my hand. "A fascinating bunch! Arturo so solemn, tied to that tired old briefcase, Olga so anxious about that land, your cousin Mouse so noisy, the barber Pacho with his droopy moustache and fear of change, his son Roger hugging his tome on social justice, Simon Alvarez so ambitious, and his tattletale wife Wanda with her strident voice."

"And the young man Julio so enamored of your beauty?"

CHAPTER 1: CONFIRM THE GRASP AND THE PRACTICE OF LEADERS' TASKS

Let these exercises fix tasks in your mind before proceeding to the next chapter. Skip any items that you have already mastered.

01–a. Take the first step to become a leader of Jesus's followers— know Christ. Find four reasons to know Him in His words: *I am the way, the truth, and the life; no one comes to the Father but through Me.* John 14:6

01–b. Resist lucrative, but deceptive alternatives to serving God fruitfully. Mouse said he heard God's voice but would have led Tiger astray. Paul heard God's voice and it led him toward one precise aim the rest of his life. Find where Jesus told him to go: *Go! For I will send you far away to the Gentiles.* Acts 22:21

Notice a way God often speaks: *In abundance of advisors there is victory.* Prov 11:14

God helped Tiger make a decision. Find how God spoke to Elijah to alter his intent when he wished to die: *A great and strong wind was rending the mountains and breaking in pieces the rocks before the Lord; but the Lord was not in the wind. And after the wind an earthquake, but the Lord was not in the earthquake. After the earthquake a fire, but the Lord was not in the fire, and after the fire a sound of a gentle blowing . . . and behold, a voice came to him and said, "What are you doing here, Elijah?"* 1 Kgs 19:12–13

01–c. Let willing believers help plan vital projects and do different, key ministries. Arturo told folks to say how they'd serve before discussing it. Verify what God prefers: *Encourage one another and build up one another.* 1 Thess 5:11

Before visiting Judean villages, Jesus sent His disciples ahead to prepare for His later arrival (Luke 10:1). What should we do to initiate a vital church project?

[ ] Announce it as a surprise.

[ ] Explain it well in advance.

ANSWER: Explain it first, and let participants help plan it.

01–d. Make Jesus a church's top leader by obeying His commands above all else. Note any of these basic commands of Jesus that you or those you lead should give more heed:

- Repent, believe and receive the Holy Spirit
- Be baptized
- Break bread (Communion)
- Love God, neighbor, brothers in Christ, enemies
- Pray in Jesus' name
- Give to meet people's needs
- Learn and obey God's Word

See if you can recall these commands of Christ merely by looking at their icons:

Suggestion: Let someone in your church who can write simple poetry set these basic commands to a tune so that folks can memorize them easily.

Jesus ordered many things and you can sum them up in seven basic commands that the three thousand new disciples in the first New Testament church in Jerusalem began at once to obey. Find them in Acts 2:37–47 (the word "love" is not used, but is evident in their fellowship): *Peter said, "Repent, and each of you be baptized in the name of Jesus Christ for the forgiveness of your sins, and you will receive the gift of the Holy Spirit . . . " Those who had received his word were baptized, and that day there were added about three thousand souls. They were continually devoting themselves to the apostles' teaching and to fellowship, to the breaking of bread and to prayer . . . And they began selling their property and possessions and were sharing them with all, as anyone might have need . . .*

Find whether renewal is *temporary* or *ongoing* work of the Holy Spirit: *Though our outer man is decaying, yet our inner man is being renewed day by day.* 2 Cor 4:16

01–e. Serve Jesus and family rather than seek power, wealth, or prestige. Tiger crossed a border illegally seeking prosperity. Find a danger of grasping for wealth: *What does it profit a man to gain the whole world, and forfeit his soul?* Mark 8:36

Leaders cannot free others from materialism if they also embrace it. Verify what craving money keeps one from doing, in Jesus' warning; *No one can serve two masters; for either he will hate the one and love the other, or he will be devoted to one and despise the other. You cannot serve God and wealth.* Matt 6:24

Find the kind of blessing Jesus gives: *Blessed be God the Father of our Lord Jesus Christ, who has blessed us with every spiritual blessing in heavenly places in Christ.* Eph 1:3

EVALUATE YOUR LEADERSHIP

Underline the number showing the current progress of your church or churches of your trainees, in doing tasks depicted in chapter one.

1=Failing with no plans to improve. 2=Praying and planning with co-workers to improve. 3=Doing it well.

1-2-3   Take the first step to become a leader of God's people—*know* Jesus.

1-2-3   Resist deceptive materialistic alternatives to serving God fruitfully.

1-2-3   Ask willing believers to help plan vital projects and do vital ministries.

1-2-3   Make Jesus your church's top leader by obeying His commands above and before all other rules.

1-2-3   Serve Jesus and family rather than seek wealth, prestige, or power.

2.
A Bold Body Realigns its Agenda to Move in a Healthier Direction

Late that night a truck came slowly with its lights off and pulled in alongside the big house. Strange! Someone with long hair got out and stood looking up at the treetops, barely visible in the starlight. I thought it was a girl, but Simon got out and growled, "Stop gawking at the pines, Sebastian! We've got business."

Sebastian was smoking and walked toward a side door with an unnatural stride, almost dancing, and I smelled marijuana. "You dwell in paradise, Simon." He half sang the words. "My soul synchronizes with this forest-clad mountain!"

"Spare me your infatuation with mother nature! You can become one with the earth after we work out the contract."

"This late? We don't even know yet how much . . . "

"Quiet!" Simon had noticed me. "Abdul, get those blasted sacks inside!" A second man threw two burlap bags from the truck bed and toted one in each hand toward the door. Pharaoh ran and tugged at one; Abdul kicked at him, cursing him in Allah's name, and I called the dog back. Simon stopped in the doorway after the other two went in and pointed his hook at me. "I'm counting on you to take the position of foreman on my ranch."

"I've decided not to, sir. But I appreciate your offer." His malicious glare before slamming the door left me feeling uneasy the rest of the night.

"I can't see the treetops, Papa; it's foggy," Tino said the next day as we neared the chapel; we were meeting to continue planning the church's new course.

Arriving, I overheard Arturo tell Olga, "This meeting will be my final effort to awaken these folks from their apathy. God will make Christ known in this town and all the villages, and if this congregation refuses to serve as the base of operations, then I'll just let them lie in green pastures beside still waters and work instead through a village church. I've had enough . . . " He saw me and didn't finish.

> ## Task 02–a.
> BRING TWO WAYS OF DOING EACH OF THE SEVEN KEY CHURCH TASKS INTO PRACTICAL WORKING ALIGNMENT

Olga had asked parents to bring children early and assigned each child a role to help explain what we needed to plan. Arturo unfolded a star and began, "The star's six points and center enclose seven arenas for vital church tasks. The star enables us to recall them and **bring two ways of doing each of the seven key church tasks into practical working alignment.** I'm hoping the Holy Spirit will use this exercise as the starting pistol that gets us running in the right direction." He pinned the star to the wall and pointed at its center.

"*Church Government* calls for a crown and bylaws. Okay, children."

Olga nodded at Mouse's small son, Andy, and he drew a crown and recited, "The crown is in the heart of the star because we obey Jesus our King above all."

Arturo asked. "Why not use a cross icon here? What did Jesus say about that?"

"It is *finished*!" Roger replied. "It's our risen King who reigns over us now!"

Olga then nodded at our son Tino and he drew a paper beside the crown and wrote "Byloss" on it. Olga corrected him. "Bylaws, B-Y-L-A-W-S."

"Oh." He wrote it again. "Bylaws are man-made rules. Hebrews 13 says to obey our leaders. Axes five says . . . "

"Acts."

"Acts five says to obey God first if man's rule goes against God's rule. Did I remember that close enough, Pastor?"

"Yes." Arturo drew a two-way arrow between the crown and bylaws. "A balanced church body keeps the two aspects of its government in balance. Its authority comes from both God and man, and we'll keep the rules of our God-given human leaders aligned with Jesus' commands. Who recalls His commands?" We hesitated. Lucy started singing the song that Olga had taught that listed Jesus' basic commands and others joined in.

Pacho asked Arturo, "Don't all churches obey these commands of Jesus?"

"Some churches put their own rules above those of Christ. Ours has. Many leaders don't even know His basic commands. They mention love, but fail to provide for the interaction that enables believers to love one another in a practical way. Some replace repentance with mere 'decisions,' while others fail to baptize new believers. To revitalize our church we must make Jesus its actual Head; its true leader by obeying His commands. They're the very foundation for all we do."

Pacho frowned. "Isn't the foundation to know the whole Word of God?"

"Jesus said our foundation is to obey Him. The wise man who built on rock heard and obeyed Jesus; the foolish guy who built on sand only heard. Knowledge alone falls short. Jesus is the rock; our part is to hear and obey Him. Knowledge of the Word is one of the essentials that we build on this foundation. For all eternity we'll be learning more about God."

"*Growth by multiplication* calls for a rabbit and elephant," Arturo continued.

Two girls drew them and one recited, "Rabbits are house churches or cell groups that multiply fast." The other added, "The elephant is a big congregation."

"Thanks, girls. We'll keep little assemblies in proper ratio with big ones. Satan will oppose us, to keep the body lopsided. Here in Bat Haven small cells will enable us to practice the interaction that the New Testament requires and . . . "

"*Cells?*" Roger's eyes had opened wide, accentuated by his thick lenses. "Communists are forming cells all over our country! Are you sure that . . . "

"Relax, Roger. For us, a cell is a tiny church within a larger one. Churches form such groups to keep the family atmosphere that Scripture requires."

Pacho asked, "Won't it cause disunity to have churches within our church?"

"It can avoid disunity. An insecure pastor keeps other leaders from using their God-given gifts to lead a group. This frustrates them, creating the unrest that the pastor fears. The flocks that we start—cells or new churches—must multiply rapidly in order to reach our area of responsibility." I recalled the big map Arturo had taped together of Bat Haven's neighborhoods and the region's many villages.

Pacho pulled on his moustache. "It'll cost more than our budget allows!"

"Relax, brother. Resources multiply along with new flocks. Now, let's hear your plans and suggestions for us to reach out and multiply—anything helpful."

What followed was not helpful. Folks bemoaned past failures and blamed each other. Discord brewed hotter each time anyone spoke, and the children became upset. Lucy put her mouth close to my ear. "Let's leave." Arturo had the same idea; he folded up the star, stuffed it in his briefcase, and slammed it shut.

The door squeaked. "Good evening brothers! God loves you and so do I!" A short man with a cane entered, doffed a hat dyed to look like skunk skin and shed a matching backpack from which a tail hung below the white stripe.

Arturo said, "Meet our advisor, Jethro Mendez. He shepherds a thriving church in Arenas and came to help us—just in time!" He unfolded the star again.

"Sorry I'm late," the elder said. "The bus broke down." He sported snow-white hair and exuded cheer. After shaking several hands, he sat in back.

"Our advisor?" asked Pacho. "He's a city man. Will his methods work here?"

"Jethro works in villages too, Pacho. He had me assess our church agenda with this star, and it shed piercing light on why we've struggled. I've explained the first two tasks, Jethro. Will you explain the rest?"

"No, Arturo. It's too important for an outsider to lead."

"Okay, back to the star. It's to help us discern a good ratio between the two ways of doing key tasks; the ratios vary from church to church and time to time."

"Why different ratios?" Pacho asked. "Won't a task be the same for all churches if it's of God? Just find the better way to do it and stick to it."

"I'm going too fast!"

Roger begged Pacho, "Let's learn this, Dad. For a dynamic church movement, we simply follow these biblical principles—right, Pastor Jethro?"

"Half right," the elderly mentor replied. "Learn the principles, son, but that's just the start. Don't simply work the principles mechanically, work with the folks who apply them. This requires leadership that's firm, loving and prayerful."

"But why two ways to do everything?" Pacho asked. "That's confusing!"

Jethro unbuckled his furry backpack, took out a bread roll and took a bite. "Mmm! My good wife baked this. She mixed the right amounts of salt, flour and yeast. I tried once and guessed. It came out of the oven like a brick and even our dog refused it! Church work is like bread, Pacho. Mix its ingredients in good proportion or it'll go awry, like the tribe of Ephraim that Hosea called an 'un-turned pancake.' For example, worship has two sides. One is serious; we fear the Holy One and approach Him with repentance and tears. Its other side is joyful and spontaneous, with laughter and raised hands. My church once had one-sided worship; we were negative and sour. I scolded and overdid its serious side."

"I see," said Pacho. "I like the way you teach, Jethro, like an Old Testament prophet. Not with the abstract analyses that some preachers inflict upon us!"

"Ouch!" Arturo muttered. He pointed at the rabbit and resumed his court-room tone. "Small cell groups will enable us to obey God's 'one another' commands. *Encourage one another, teach one another, admonish one another,* and more. Pacho, can you help us decide on a healthy ratio between rabbits and elephants?"

"I will, Pastor, but just voicing an ideal ratio won't achieve it."

"It certainly won't, Pacho. The star only gives an X-ray of our church body's spinal column; it doesn't fix the backache."

"Won't false doctrine run rampant if churches multiply like rabbits?"

"I feared that at first, too, Pacho. Has it infiltrated your new flocks, Jethro?"

The white-haired elder shook his head. "Baby churches in a Spirit-empowered movement don't breed satanic doctrine; they're eager to follow Christ. The really crippling 'isms' come from old, sterile churches and apostate seminaries. Oh! What's throbbing?" Something was rumbling overhead, going *po-po-po-po*!

"Helicopter!" Roger ran outside to see, and we all followed; such a bird had never flown over Bat Haven. The fog was too heavy but we heard the craft circle and dart off to land somewhere above the white blanket.

"Satan's sidetracking our planning!" complained Arturo.

"It wasn't Satan," Pacho countered. "It was God, giving us a break before facing another of the star's pairs. It's a lot to digest at once."

"Well, you've had your happy break. Can you endure a bit more now, Pacho?"

"Of course. Am I raising too many questions, Arturo? I don't mean to be rude, just careful. Changing what our church does always worries me."

"You're doing exactly what God wants you to do—make me clarify critical points! Also, everyone pays more attention when you challenge an issue."

I considered that as we filed back in. I needed to learn to welcome challenges.

"*Training leaders* calls for a chain and graduation cap," resumed Arturo.

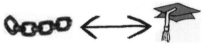 Children drew them and one said, "The chain means training leaders as Paul did; one mentors newer pastors who mentor other leaders on the job, in a chain reaction." The other added, "The graduation cap means academic training."

Arturo added the two-way arrow. "We need a more fruitful ratio between mentoring and lecturing—more group discussion and training leaders the way Paul trained Timothy. Are you with me, Pacho?"

"Yes, but it sounds like you might do away with the pulpit."

"Some folks would cheer if I did."

"Amen!" Julio Diaz shouted.

 "*Support* calls for a tent and salary," Arturo said, and children drew them.

"The tent means self-supported 'tentmakers' like Paul," recited one child and the other added, "The money means paid pastors."

Arturo added the two-way arrow. "We'll need more shepherds who are self-supported than paid ones. I'll set the example, as Paul did in Thessalonica."

Roger asked, "Might having so many lay pastors lower standards for clergy?"

"It could, but we'll give quality training to all who have God's pastoral gift, not just those who can meet a seminary's matriculation requirements and afford the tuition. It's a pastor's duty to train new shepherds, as Paul told Timothy. Roger, help us discern the ratio between 'tentmakers' and salaried pastors that will sustain a movement for Christ in the Bat Haven area."

"Okay, but can it really be so simple to generate a movement for Christ?"

Arturo asked his white-haired mentor to answer this and Jethro explained, "It's very simple to detect the imbalances that stifle a movement, Roger; the challenge is to correct them. Declining denominations all have a pathetically low ratio of volunteer workers to paid ones, too low to sustain growth. Their ratios are often skewed beyond rationality for all seven of the star's tasks."

Pacho remarked, "I thought unbelief caused the decline."

"Of course, but I don't count apostate churches. They're not in decline; they've already hit bottom. They're not real churches—just clubs."

"Liberating!" Roger clapped. "I see now how we laymen and women can take part seriously in a church's life!" Other young people shouted, "Amen!"

"The helicopter!" Julio ran to the door. "The fog's lifted and it's returning."

We ran out again and watched it hover over us, blowing crud all around and dust in our eyes. It then circled the rocky clearing on the mountainside.

Roger wiped his glasses. "It's not a combat craft—no military insignia. Look, it's settling down! They found a level spot up there. I can't see it now."

"Back inside, please!" Arturo was beckoning from the door.

"Wait, 'Turo," Olga was on her toes, straining to see. "I wish I knew what they're doing up there."

"I'll see." Julio ran and climbed a tree. "Ahoy!" he shouted down to us. "Two crewmen are poking around; one's toting a bag. Hey, the 'copter's leaving them stranded!" We saw the craft rise and dart out of sight.

Olga pointed. "They're coming down. That Arab guy was poking around on that slope when I planted the papaya by the door last month. Oh! Simon's going up to meet them. He's in a hurry!"

I told Olga, "They were at Simon's house last night—Abdul and Sebastian."

Pharaoh growled when they drew near and I gripped his collar to quiet him. Sebastian's long, scruffy hair looked like he never combed it; he had a blank grin and clutched a clipboard as he gazed about in a daze. When they got close, Olga asked the Arab, "What did you find up there?"

"Why, hello, young lady! I'm Abdul Hussein. Glad to meet you."

"What did you find? That land belongs to our congregation."

"I'm a geologist," he replied, "and Sebastian is our firm's legal advisor."

Olga kept prying and Simon shouted, "Stop butting into other's affairs!"

The zombie and Arab left with Simon, and Lucy's eyes flashed. "Something's very wrong, Olga. How did Simon ever become an *elder*?"

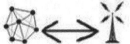

"It was before I came. Yes, something's wrong, and I'll surely find out what!"

"*Evangelism* calls for a network of dots and a transmitting tower," Arturo continued to explain when we were back inside, and children drew them.

"The network," recited one, "means new believers in a loving relationship with friends, whom they tell about Jesus." The other added, "The tower is for evangelism by mass media and big meetings."

Arturo drew the link. "A Spirit-filled body reaches out to the lost as churches did in Acts, in either or both of these ways. Mass evangelism alone, by media or big meetings, normally doesn't sustain a movement, and our ratio has been poor. We'll witness more and help new believers keep loving ties with their friends."

"But Pastor," Pacho whined, doing his job, "one's friends will drag him back into the world if we don't shield him from them!"

"The Holy Spirit in new believers is stronger than the spirit of the world in their unbelieving friends. When friends and kinfolk come to Jesus together, they remain more faithful than individuals who come alone. Without close friends in a body, many believers stop attending. Never extract a seeker from his social network; Scripture shows that God sees him as part of that network, through which the gospel normally spreads. Sustain those loving relationships with friends."

"But what if a friend is providing a new believer illegal drugs?"

"Separate an addict from any false friend who's poisoning him, of course." Arturo then faced the group. "Had enough? Should we continue another day?"

"I haven't drawn my picture yet!" wailed a child.

"Keep going!" begged Roger. "I'm seeing now how to climb out of our rut!"

"I'm glad you value this, son," remarked Jethro. "I hope you all see that to move ahead, you must shift a bit toward the lighter side of each pair of icons."

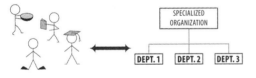

"*Organization* calls for a group of persons with diverse features," Arturo resumed, "and an organization chart." Two children sketched them.

"A small group brings together people with different spiritual gifts," said one, pointing at his scribbly sketch. The other added, "The organization chart means specialized ministries that gather people with the same gift."

Arturo drew the arrow. "We've lacked groups with a mixture of gifts to offset our specialized groups that gather people with the same gift. We'll all serve each other in small groups, doing the different tasks that correspond to our gifts."

"Not everyone's ready for such serious ministry," Pacho replied. "You know the Bible well, Arturo. Can't we just listen to you until we're all more mature?"

"No one will ever be ready to do serious ministry without taking the first step. Jethro, can you clarify the need to have groups that mix spiritual gifts?"

Jethro pointed his cane at Tino. "Walk around like you're blind." Tino groped about, eyes shut, and Jethro said, "This occurs if a body lacks the seer's gift of prophecy." He pointed the cane at Andy. "Walk like your feet were bound." Mouse's son hobbled about and Jethro said, "Let a group run with the 'beautiful feet' of the gospel herald." He asked a girl to serve others with hands tied to her sides, and she acted the awkward role. He asked, "Now what did all this show?"

"We need liberation!" Roger declared. "Don't keep a group from using its spiritual gifts as a body. A group needs folks with different gifts and freedom to use them. We fail if a leader tries to do everything for us."

Arturo hit a fist into his palm. "Too true! I've abused the gift of teaching. The better a pastor teaches, the greater the lure to crowd out other vital tasks."

"But how can good teaching weaken the work?" Pacho wondered aloud.

Jethro explained, "The problem's not with good teaching but failing to integrate it with the other gift-based ministries." Taking a pocketknife from his white-striped backpack, he told Pacho to open his Bible and then angled the blade as though to sever a page.

"Hey!" Pacho jerked the Bible away.

"A monk severed 1 Corinthians 12 on *merging gift-based ministries* from chapter 13 on *love* centuries ago, while inserting the Bible's chapter divisions. Our gifts bear fruit when used with godly love; we help others develop their ministries without doting on our own. Teachers that covet prominence exalt their role above that of others, but Ephesians 4 requires them to equip all believers to build up the body in loving harmony. Only godly love—*agape* love—moves us to give others' ministries equal importance to our own."

"*Knowledge of Christ* calls for a hand pointing up and a book with the title *Truths about Christ*," concluded Arturo, and children drew the final icons.

"Pointing up to the risen Christ means experiencing His Presence," explained one child and the other added, "The book means learning truths about Him."

"I haven't balanced these," Arturo confessed. "I thought the way to lead people to Jesus was to explain His atonement, but now I see that . . . "

"Well, isn't it?" Pacho interrupted. "The way to present Christ to an unbeliever is to explain how His sacrifice saved us."

"The apostles never witnessed to unbelievers that way, Pacho. They simply recounted Jesus' death and resurrection, and told what He'd done in their lives. God receives us because of our faith, not our understanding. Let's avoid both extremes, merely mouthing facts about Jesus and merely feeling emotion without knowing who He is. I need to change my approach and help seekers experience Jesus' power in healing, transformation, and His joyful presence. Okay, we've finished the star. I'm through. Now take a few minutes to think, talk it over, and let me know when you're ready to say how you'll help renew our church."

Olga added, "Let's thank the children." We clapped and stood around talking. Anna Diaz took Olga's hand. "I love how you had the children take part!"

"We'll all learn more if I can get Arturo to yield a minute or two of his precious teaching time during worship to let kids help illustrate his points."

Task 02–b.

AWAKEN FROM

LETHAL LETHARGY

"I've seen my problem," Pacho announced. "I've been the most lopsided of all of us! Let's ask God to help us fry both sides of our pancake!" Several prayed and Pacho concluded, "Lord, heal what made us content with our imbalance—*apathy*. It paralyzed me, and I beg forgiveness. Help us all to **awaken from lethal lethargy**, in Jesus' name. Amen."

"You hit the bull's-eye," Jethro told the barber. "Apathy! It destroys nations and churches! Middle-class churches succumb easily to apathy and plummet into spiritual free-fall. Excuse the irony, but there's hope for your flock; it suffers poverty and insecurity, and God uses both to combat apathy, Pacho."

"If wealth is so perilous I'll close my shop at noon to cut my earnings in half!"

Jethro gripped the barber's shoulder. "You'd see a lot of shaggy men! I'm not worried about you, Pacho, you're solid. But money does turn many from God. *Where your treasure is, there your heart will be also.* Our rich neighbors are often too busy to enter God's kingdom; Jesus likened them to camels squeezing through a needle's eye. Nothing spawns spiritual apathy as quickly as wealth!" He asked an older man, "Do you agree that apathy's been this church's bane?"

The elder shrugged, yawned and left, and Arturo told Jethro, "Only three families agreed to help revitalize our work and reach out: Pacho's, Tiger's, and mine."

"Three are enough." With his cane, Jethro tapped the map that Arturo had used a week before to show where to start churches and cells. "God has given you your *objective*, chief." He then tapped the star. "Also your *strategy*." Gesturing toward the three families, he added. "And your *vanguard*. So CHARGE!"

CHAPTER 2: CONFIRM THE GRASP AND THE PRACTICE OF LEADERS' TASKS

02–a. Bring two ways of doing each of the seven key church tasks into practical working alignment.

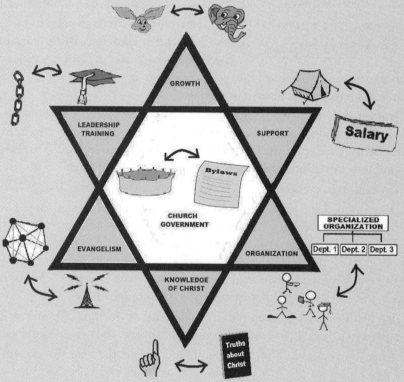

Realign Diverse Aspects of Vital Church Tasks

Evaluate the ratios between each of the two ways of doing a task, and note any that need realignment in your flock or that of your trainees:

[ ]   Obeying Jesus aligned wisely with obeying God-given leaders and men's rules

[ ]   Small assemblies in fruitful alignment with large ones

[ ]   Mentoring in fruitful alignment with classroom instruction

[ ]   Volunteer workers in fruitful alignment with paid ones

[ ]   Witnessing for Jesus in social networks in wise ratio to using media and campaigns

[ ]   Using different gifts in a cell in fruitful alignment with groups that specialize.

[ ]   Experiencing the risen Christ in proper alignment with learning facts about Him.

Arturo had neglected several pastoral duties. Find the result for the church body when godly leaders do their job: *He gave some as apostles, and some as prophets, and some as evangelists, and some as pastors and teachers, for the equipping of the saints for the work of service, to the building up of the body of Christ.* Eph 4:11–12

Find how folks relate to one another in a sound body: *We are to grow up in all aspects into Him who is the head, even Christ, from whom the whole body, being fitted and held together by what every joint supplies, according to the proper working of each individual part, causes the growth of the body for the building up of itself in love.* Eph 4:15–16

02–b. Awaken God's people from lethal lethargy. Detect Jesus' warning: *Because you are lukewarm, and neither hot nor cold, I will spit you out of My mouth. Because you say, 'I am rich, and have become wealthy, and have need of nothing,' and you do not know that you are wretched and miserable and poor and blind and naked.* Rev 3:16–17

EVALUATE YOUR LEADERSHIP

Underline the number that depicts current progress:

1=Failing with no plans to improve. 2=Praying and planning with co-workers to improve. 3=Doing it well.

1-2-3   Decide with coworkers wise ratios between diverse ways of doing vital church tasks and keep the two ways of doing them in practical proportion.

1-2-3   Avoid letting a favorite ministry eclipse other vital ministries.

1-2-3   Awaken God's people from apathy's lethal effect.

3.
The "Old Serpent" Eyes an Awakening Flock, Coils, and Strikes

A bat buzzed past me. I hurled a rock at it and told Pharaoh, "This morbid night is dragging on forever!" Between rounds, I read Mark and formed a routine: read and patrol, read and patrol, read and fix it in my mind as I paced. I came to Jesus' mock trial; its heartless odium added to the heavy nocturnal stillness that pressed in on me like prison walls. The bats left and I felt so apart from all that lived that I even missed them! I came to the crucifixion and thought how those big nails would feel if all my weight hung from them. Oh, the pain! It stuck poignantly in my mind as I scanned the east vainly for a ray of light and Jesus' cry echoed in my mind, "My God, my God, why have You forsaken me?"

Back in the kiosk, Pharaoh flopped down and pressed his nose to the floor. I patted his head and asked him, "Is this hungry darkness exerting its will to abort the birth of a new day?" The tip of his tail thumped the floor, and I thanked him for his terse reply.

On my next round, passing the storefront, I noticed Simon's updated "Progress Chart"; he'd gotten financing for the mine. His next step was "land acquisition."

Alvarez Mining Co. "RIFLE" Development Progress Chart				
Research	**I**ncorporation	**F**inancing	**L**and acquisition	**E**xtraction of ore
➡	➡	➡		

The night dragged on and to stay alert I finished reading Mark audibly; I whispered, but it still sounded loud and out of place in that eerie stillness. Circling the house, I saw no gleam in the east and began reading John. I felt a breeze and saw a leaf flutter down; a dove cooed above me celebrating what I'd just read, "The Light shone in the darkness, and the darkness could not prevent it." Finally!

Going home, a house-front store had opened early, reminding me that I'd promised the boys to bring candy. It was a relief to chat with a human; the storeowner said, "Simon needs your protection, all right. Not that I'd miss him all that much. Miners are fed up and plan to take drastic action. I quit after a cave-in nearly crushed me. Old Hookarm's too tight to shore up the tunnels properly."

My son, Tino, Mouse's son, Andy, and other children were romping in our lane when I arrived and didn't see me. Tino was mocking my chubby neighbor and walking like him. "I'm Mouse the Moose!" He leaned slightly back, palms to the rear, shuffling from side to side while the other children squealed with laughter.

"Ill-bred little devil!" The "Moose" had ridden his mule around the house on his way to the mine and spied Tino spoofing him. Dismounting, Mouse approached my son, walking exactly as Tino had done. Tino ran and hid in bushes.

"Use your belt on him, Tiger. That'll teach him to respect adults."

Behind Mouse, his son, Andy, tickled the mule's rear leg with a stick to make it kick. It brayed angrily, and Andy scurried to join Tino in the bushes. The other children laughed and brayed; Andy had a way about him that made everyone laugh at whatever he did except his parents. Mouse's wispy wife, Martha, appeared at the door and my son, Tino, warned, "Careful! Bones is watching!"

"Andy!" she cried, "Stop torturing that poor animal and bring firewood."

Tino noticed that I was holding something wrapped in brown paper and approached shyly with Andy at his heels. "Candy, Papa?"

"Son, promise not to make fun of uncle Mouse again."

"I promise, Papa."

"And don't call your neighbor 'Bones.' You call her 'Aunt Martha.'"

"Yes, Papa."

"You, Andy, promise not to pester your dad's mule again."

"I promise, 'Uncle Tiger.'"

Martha called again, "I told you to bring firewood, Andy, and clean up those grubby sticks that you and your friends left strewn all over the floor!"

"They're not sticks, mama; they're our swords, and I don't feel like doing all that work now."

"You look healthy to me."

"I don't feel good. My hair hurts!"

Giggles erupted until Mouse pulled off his belt and raised it, his face mottled with rage. He grabbed his son and Martha came running. "Have mercy! Andy was only playing. We suffer enough things without pounding on each other!"

Task 03–a.
CORRECT CORRECTLY

I told Mouse quietly, "Colossians 3 tells fathers not to provoke our children to anger. We need to **correct correctly.**"

"What do you mean?" He was now angrier with me than with the boys.

"Our anger makes a child angry. Let it pass, then kneel down to his level, look him in the eye, and explain in a gentle voice why you're punishing him. When a child does something bad the first time, warn him that you'll punish him if he does it again. If he does, then punish him as you warned, but not with anger. Do it in love and let him know you love him. Don't shout, that only makes it worse; he'll scream too, to get your attention or to wear you out to get his way."

"You're too soft. Your way spoils the brats!"

"Don't call them brats, or they'll fulfill your expectations. And it's not softness, it's self-control; it has worked for me to correct even tough cowhands."

"It won't work with my employees. Since I subcontracted with Simon to blast the rock, I've hired laborers to handle the explosives, and they're lazier than this old mule after stuffing itself with grain on a hot afternoon."

"Treat them like mules and they'll act like mules." I had to practice what I'd advised Mouse sooner than expected. Hearing chortles behind me, I turned to see Tino waddling behind Mouse in violation of his promise. "Hey! You go in inside and stand in a corner facing the wall until I release you." Roy Watts had punished his children that way with good effect when I was in his California home.

I followed Andy inside and received a shock. Lucy rushed to me, eyes wide with fear, clinging like a terrified child. "It was only a dream but it . . . it . . . "

"A dream? What about?"

"Awful! A black shadow flowed down the mountain and covered the houses! It hissed, 'You'll never escape my dominion over this wretched town.' Oh, Tiger, I still hear it! I'm afraid! Something bad is going to happen!"

"What a morbid nightmare! I felt something during the night too, Lu. The darkness was uncanny—not the absence of light but the presence of . . . I don't know . . . something evil! Its murky gloom kept penetrating my mind."

Stepping back, she looked at me, surprised. "You've never feared the dark."

"I still don't—not mere darkness. It's what came with it, Lu."

"Aren't we being a bit superstitious to personify darkness as an evil spirit?"

"We would be if we attributed spiritual power to mere lack of light."

"But why do people associate evil with it, Tiger? Is there a spirit of darkness?"

"Jesus warned of the power of darkness. He meant Satan and his demons, fallen angels that God threw out of heaven. So did Paul, in his letters."

"Papa," Tino begged from his corner, "can I have it now?"

"No candy until you quit pouting. You're learning to respect adults."

Tino began screaming and Lucy screamed back at him. I took her to one side and said quietly, "Careful. I've been reading about this; shouting at kids makes things worse. And don't give in to him; talk to him softly about what he did."

We discussed this awhile, and Lucy knelt by Tino at his eye level. "Do you know why your Papa's punishing you?" He shrugged. "I'm waiting for an answer, and don't shrug your shoulders at me, or you'll stay in this corner twice as long.

I know you want the candy, and that's okay. We want you to have it too, but for now, something's more important. Tell me what you did."

"I disobeyed Papa. I can't be good all the time, mama. I'm just little."

"Of course, I was little too. But you're not a tiny baby, so it won't do any good for you to cry like one. That just makes you unhappy, and others too."

He stayed in his corner a few more minutes before desire for candy surpassed desire for sulking. He showed respect to adults after that—when I was watching.

I was exhausted after the night's taxing vigil and slept soundly until the din of a motorcycle and panicked chickens roused me. I rushed to the door and saw Arturo and Olga dismounting in a cloud of dust and feathers. I quieted Pharaoh while Arturo dusted off his bulging black briefcase. Olga tossed hair out of her eyes and laughed, "Arturo does everything in prudent moderation except when riding this noisy old machine! It puts a hex on him, a 'speed spell.'"

> **Task 03–b.**
>
> BIND THE AGREEMENT IN A TINY GROUP AS JESUS TAUGHT, TO LAUNCH A SERIOUS PROJECT

Lucy brushed crumbs from chairs where Tino and Davey had devoured the candy, then blew on the fire in our earthen stove to heat coffee. I covered a yawn, resenting the interruption of my sleep and unaware that we'd soon **bind the agreement in a tiny group as Jesus taught, to launch a serious project.**

Arturo paced back and forth, pounding a fist into his palm. "What'll we do, Tiger? Only a few members want to serve the Lord. Some just want to impose petty rules; others only want entertainment. We can't go forward without unanimity. How'll we achieve a movement for Christ if all are not in agreement?"

"Don't wait for everyone to agree, Pastor; you'd wait forever! And don't expect perfection from us silly sheep!"

"You're right. Jethro told me that three families were a sufficient vanguard."

"Jesus promised that if two or three agree in His name on what we ask then God will bind it in heaven. A large group rarely agrees unanimously on anything. Can we let God bind a firm agreement right now?"

Arturo stopped pacing and looked at me, his head tilted. "Ah . . . Okay!"

Lucy brought the coffee, but set it aside while we prayed. Arturo finished, "Lord Jesus, we covenant in Your name to bring about the movement for Jesus in Bat Haven and the villages. Bind this agreement in heaven as You promised and grant us the valor to persevere, no matter what Satan does to prevent it. Amen."

Olga clasped our hands. "Oh, thank you! You've heartened us." Arturo joined his hands to ours and added, "God will work in Bat Haven! I'm sure now."

A flash of anxiety interrupted Olga's moment of joy; I missed it, but Lucy remarked, "Something's bothering you, Olga. Do you want to talk about it?"

"I have to be careful; I might get innocent folks in serious trouble if I say everything I suspect. Arturo said not to accuse people without proof. Actually, there's a bit of history behind my concerns; it would probably bore you."

Arturo suggested, "I'm sure they'd like to hear about your dad."

"He owned the original silver mine, abandoned now, and started our congregation with his employees. The church did not flourish and before dad died, he told me he should have tested his pastoral methods in the villages first."

This bewildered me. "Why test methods in backward villages, Olga?"

"Dad and Jethro Mendez started congregations later in Los Robles where Pastor Jacob Morán serves now, and in other villages. They could compare the results of different methods easily, as there were not so many outside influences."

"So what methods did your father discover?"

"He told me seven, and the New Testament confirms them all. *One*, obey Jesus' commands above all; *two*, let churches give birth to new churches; *three*, evangelize entire families; *four*, baptize the repentant without needless delay; *five*, mentor new shepherds until their flocks are doing what God requires; *six*, balance key ministries; *seven*, mobilize many, many volunteer lay-leaders."

"They learned all that in villages? I thought village life bred ignorance!"

"They followed the rule for valid experiment. In the university chemistry lab, I learned to test a process: one controls the amounts of components, pressure, temperature, agitation, and catalysts. Ignoring any factor annuls the experiment."

"Of course, Olga, but churches aren't normally concocted in a chemistry lab."

"But the principle applies. You can test pastoral methods quickly where there are few unknown factors. In Los Robles, you deal with a single culture in a certain way and soon see the results, but city churches are influenced by folks of many backgrounds, TV, and such. One thinks growth comes from using a certain method when it's due to other factors, such as population moving into the area."

"Methods that work in rural areas won't work elsewhere, will they?"

"The seven that I mentioned do, Tiger."

"Okay, I'll test our methods in towns without TV." I yawned. "Please excuse me; my bed's calling. I combated darkness all night and I'm bushed."

Mechanic Shop Proprietor Timothy Caballeros

That afternoon I ventured up the road to talk to my neighbor about Christ. A crooked sign on an unpainted lean-to alleged that the cluttered establishment was a mechanic's shop. The young owner, whom folks called "Gadget," lay beneath a rusty Volkswagen Beetle that slouched to one side. A young lady was smoking as she wiped the car's cracked windshield; her bright pink shorts and halter with big orange polka dots were hardly the town's most conventional fashion. She eyed me and smiled. "Tiger Garcia! I teach your son Tino. He's really sharp."

"Oh? Well, how do you do, teacher! Tino mentioned you; he likes his new teacher because he learns more from you than from his teacher in Los Robles, who only had elementary school herself. But I'm surprised you knew who I am."

"Bat Haven's a tiny town. Call me Evita. I inherited this elegant sedan from my late uncle. I'll sell it cheap. Buy it, my lucky friend. Bargain of the year!"

"Thank you, *Señorita* Evita, but I have a family to feed." I tried to tell her what Jesus had done for my family, but she blew smoke at me and turned to wipe the car's dusty hood. I tried to talk to the mechanic, but grew tired of addressing the two mute feet protruding from under the car and turned to go.

"Wait," she caught my shirtsleeve. "I paint and plan to bring culture to this backward town. Stand still! I might do your portrait; let me see if you're worth painting. An artist's eye captures what others miss. Hmm. Don't move!" She gripped me to immobilize me. "That's better." She stepped back. "Aha! Robust! Turn sideways." She pulled me around and I felt silly. She embraced me to adjust the pose. "Ah! Profile of firm decision! Come to my room and I'll paint you."

I pulled my arm away. "Thank you, Evita, but that would be imprudent."

Task 03–c.
STANCH SATAN'S SNEAKY UNDERCURRENTS OF FINICKY CRITICISM

Gadget emerged smudged with grease, glanced up the street and smirked. I turned to see why; Wanda Alvarez stood jotting something in a notebook. She saw us watching and hurried back up the street. The mechanic snickered, "Uh-oh! 'Wanda the Wasp!' She noted what she seen, Tiger." I asked him what difference that made, and he said, "She lists the sins of us reprobates, and will tell the town you and the pretty teacher was embracing affectionately! Wanda's a sniper and keeps up a barrage of gossip." What ensued would show how urgent it is to **stanch Satan's sneaky undercurrents of finicky criticism.**

"You look uneasy, Tiger." Evita flipped her cigarette away. "Why fret about that hag! Who pays any attention to the rubbish that Wanda the Wasp spews?"

Who indeed. I didn't foresee the infernal blaze that Wanda's tongue would ignite, or I would have fled town with my family. I recalled what Jacob Morán remarked once about believers who liked to criticize: "Some wild beasts turn on their own when it's bleeding; in God's flock it is Satan's cruelest weapon."

Back home, I told Lucy, "Our indifferent neighbors won't listen. How can I evangelize them? Bat Haven is smothered under a cloud of spiritual darkness."

"Oooo, the pessimist! Don't forget our agreement, love; it's bound heaven. The town's passing through a dark night but dawn is coming."

"Then come quickly dawn!"

We heard clatter outside; Gadget had arrived in the Volkswagen with Evita and bellowed over the engine. "Look, neighbor! I purchased this elegant automobile. Bat Haven now has a taxi. The steering was broke, but I fixed it with old parts. It needs a muffler and other stuff but it'll help me do my second job. I'm an owl like you; I work at night as Bat Haven's police chief—at least that's my title; I'm the only cop. A few soldiers stationed here help when they feel like it."

The starter barely turned the motor, but the engine coughed and ran, and Gadget put it in gear with a jerk. While turning, he hit a rut and swerved. Evita screamed and he twisted the wheel, but not before smashing a wooden gate that closed off our tiny yard. He stopped and lifted the hood. "Oops! Didn't tighten them bolts." He took a greasy wrench from a bulging side pocket, bent under the hood, and then left in a blur of acrid blue exhaust.

While dragging the smashed gate out of sight, I heard angry voices up the street. Mouse, on his mule, was arguing with Roger walking alongside. The young scholar read something from a book, and I told him, "We have something in common. I love reading, too. Arturo loans me books on the history of our faith and pastoral work, and I peruse the Bible at night. I'm learning tons of stuff."

"Listen," Roger replied. "The SRE will meet tomorrow in Los Vientos up on top of the mountain. They promote social justice. Go with me, Tiger."

"What's SRE?"

"Don't go!" Mouse reined in the mule. "They're *Social Reconstruction Engineers* and seek revolution like Fidel Castro in Cuba. Communists! All atheists!"

"Not all of them," Roger slapped Mouse's mule to keep it moving. "In Cuba many Catholics and Protestants seek justice and cooperate with the revolution. Fidel Castro closed gambling casinos and outlawed prostitution that was so rampant in Havana, remember? Now he redistributes the wealth, which creates controversy. Some Cuban Christians call that stealing; others support Castro."

Mouse halted the mule again. "They're as misled as the SRE. Right, Tiger?"

"How would I know? I'll go, Roger, if I can get away. I plan to take the gospel to the villages and need to make friends there."

"Hallelujah!" Mouse spurred the mule. "I'll go, too, to see what they're up to."

Task 03–d.

KEEP ALERT TO OPPORTUNITIES THAT GOD GIVES TO WITNESS FOR JESUS

Roger brought me a horse the next morning and the three of us started out to the SRE meeting on Mount Silverado. Mouse warned that the SRE were all violent rogues and I replied, "That's all the more reason to **keep alert to opportunities that God gives to witness for Jesus**."

We rode uphill along the rim of a cliff parallel to the river. Mouse's mule slowed and he spurred it; it trotted briskly a few paces and slowed again, heaving under his weight. Mouse broke a limb from a tree and whacked the mule. It took a quick step and faltered on a loose rock that rolled over the edge, loosening other rocks that hit larger stones, accumulating in a small avalanche. I stopped to watch; white rapids in the Rio Furioso were so far below I couldn't hear them.

"Wow! I hope nobody's down by the river below those falling rocks!" I traced the stream's serpentine course south until it vanished behind a mountain wearing a broad-brimmed cloud sombrero. The mule stopped huffing and we rode on, turning west away from the river, climbing. To our left, a carpet of lush foliage stretched down the mountainside, ending at the large rocky clearing above the chapel. I turned and pointed up at a broken cliff high on our right. "Look! There it is! The frowning face overlooking the town!"

Mouse's mule wheezed and we stopped again. Pharaoh chased an iguana into the brush and three huge macaws flew up, squawking loud protests; they glided over the abyss, showing off dazzling blue plumage. Pharaoh came strutting back with the live iguana and failed to dodge Mouse who grabbed it. "Supper!" He fastened its legs behind its back, using one of its claws as a needle; he pushed it through membrane on the opposite leg and then broke the claw at its base to form a T that would not slip back through the membrane.

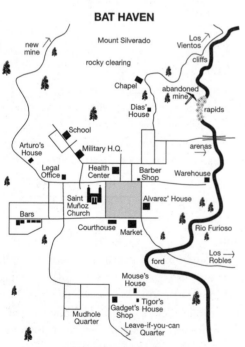

BAT HAVEN

Roger's Map of Bat Haven

Climbing higher, we came upon a man resting beside the path, his shirt soaked with sweat, and I reined in my horse. "Going to the SRE meeting?"

"Yes, sir."

"Get on." I got off and began to help him mount, but he jumped onto the horse in one fluid, relaxed movement—the cat-like motion typical of a seasoned athlete.

"Hey, look!" Roger wiped his thick lenses on his shirt and pointed. "The town! You can make out our houses!"

The view was grand. Flaming orange *flamboyán* trees accentuated the square across from Simon Alvarez' house; opposite it, Saint Muñoz' twin towers dominated all. To the east, on our left, cattle crossed a wooden bridge on the Arenas road, trudging toward execution at the slaughterhouse. A yoke of oxen tugged a top-heavy cart into the market, and children in front of our house on the south side of town, tiny dots this far away, kicked a ball—probably a dried grapefruit.

Roger made us wait while he sketched Bat Haven's first street map.

We continued up the mountain and Roger mentioned our plans to evangelize the villagers. Our new companion had quit panting and said, "You're very kind, sir, and you're believers. I'm Ricardo Solórsano. Papers call me 'El Chorcho.'"

"No!" Roger jerked around to face him. "El Chorcho! The infamous assassin, the criminal most wanted by the State?"

"At your service, gentlemen. I'm a believer, too."

"Wow!" Roger stared, agape. "Are you in hiding?"

"Not from the government, young man. I was in prison, but after the last *coup d'état*, the new president pardoned me because I was the one who'd exterminate the thugs of the prior regime. When I was in solitary confinement, I heard a preacher that came Fridays. I needed God's forgiveness since I'd committed wicked crimes, so I received Jesus Christ as my Savior right there in my cell."

Roger remarked, "You're unarmed, sir. Have you no enemies now?"

"Plenty, son—kin of *politicos* that I liquidated. So I stay in these hills."

"With so many enemies, how'd you survive in prison, Chorcho?"

"Well, they almost got me. A guard sold me a Coke that gave me cramps in my belly." He seized his stomach, writhing, groaning, and twisting. "An inmate told me lemons would neutralize the poison and got some. Well, I recovered. Later, the guard had me lick stamps and stick 'em on envelopes. Well, them lethal cramps hit again." Another demonstration of writhing, groaning, and grimacing. "But I'd stuffed lemons under my shirt. Well, I settled accounts with that guard. I got work in the tailor shop and got some scissors."

Roger stared at him again. "You killed him *after* becoming a Christian?"

"Well, I still had a few bad habits. I'd worship with you folks in town, but I can't show up there; they'd inform my enemies."

I asked, "Can we come to your house and have worship?"

"Oh, please do!"

I rubbed my arms as we rode into Los Vientos; the breeze was chilly. Twisted pines, tortured by the wind that swept the large mesa crowning Mount Silverado, framed a tiny hamlet on the far side. Rocky teeth of a narrow ridge scraped the sky, shielding the few stone houses from the wind. We rode past grazing sheep toward the one house of normal size. Empty beer bottles, corncobs, and horse plop littered the ground in front of it, and men stood eying our approach. I saw a light inside. "Electricity! How do they get it here, Chorcho?"

"Well, that windmill over by the rim generates it; wind always blows here."

A white dog dashed from a shack and attacked Pharaoh. A tall, wide-shouldered man and an ugly scar on his cheek ran and grabbed the smaller dog. "Stop, Popcorn! Sorry, gentlemen, my pup's a bit over-protective."

Chorcho introduced us. "This giant is Benjamin Medina, or 'Mincho the Monster' as we say. He built the windmill and he organizes unions. Well, I envy his skill; treat him civilly because he executes his enemies with his bare hands!"

I dismounted and a ragged young man told me, "Chorcho wasn't kidding. Mincho the Monster did tear a guy apart with his bare hands. You're new. Welcome, comrade. I'm Aaron Ortiz." Aaron was thin, unwashed, and barefoot; his breath stunk and I wondered when he had last bathed or combed his hair.

We entered the house; its front room housed a store and had the ripe smell of sweaty bodies. The giant with the scarred cheek bought us cokes and an aged storekeeper slid the beads of an ancient abacus to add up the purchase. He inserted the coins in a slot in the wooden counter to drop into a box and returned to a shabbily constructed rocking chair. I looked around. Flyspecked walls held old calendars; one had the Virgin's picture, labeled "Saint Mary." Another displayed a voluptuous dancing girl and "Saint Merry" scribbled by it. Unpainted shelves held cartridges, batteries, cans of sausage, women's underwear, and cigarettes. On the counter stood a rusty scale and a big jar of hard candy. Another held sugar; ants were packing off spilled grains. I sat on a sack of corn among the SRE men; some wore mended trousers with patches sewn over patches, others had guns. I heard rhythmic thumping; a man in a back room was working a primitive loom. A short, barefoot lady carrying a nursing baby entered, but upon seeing the armed men, turned abruptly and left.

Three short men with curious, grim expressions on swarthy faces appeared outside an open window, and I asked Chorcho quietly who they were. "Tribals. They avoided Spanish domination by keeping to themselves in these mountains. Well, they still distrust outsiders. Oh, here's the Commandant."

The SRE leader strode in rapidly. "To business!" He held an unlit cigar, the largest one I'd ever seen, and a rifle in the other hand. His beard was heavy, he had fire in his eye and wore crisscrossed cartridge belts. I guessed it was for show, striving to fit the Latin American revolutionary's stereotype. "Welcome, visitors. Friends call me Chuey—Chuey Ochoa. Enemies call me "El Diablo" but not for long; this *diablo* rewards them with a short life span!"

Aaron laughed; he sat by me and said, "He's the devil all right, and my hero."

Chuey took a knife from his belt, flipped it spinning in the air and caught it deftly; his quick, nervous manner reminded me of a hungry fox. He suddenly hurled the knife at the wall inches above my head, piercing the President's photo between the eyes. "I live for one cause—to purge Bat Haven of capitalism and capitalists. Now, comrades, I want to know who these bright-eyed visitors are."

A grizzled miner gave his name and a gaunt man said that he share-cropped on Simon Alvarez' land. I gave my name, adding, "I work for Alvarez, too."

Chuey sneered. "How much does old Hookarm pay you guys?"

"A few miserable coins," snarled the gaunt man. "He treats us like beasts."

Mincho the Monster raised a giant fist. "So unite against his exploitation!"

Chuey pointed his cigar at a tired-looking man smoking in a corner. "You're a share-cropper. How much do you have to give to the landowner? Do all the work and the rich pig gets all the benefit! Is this just? Answer, men! Is this just?"

"Hallelujah!" Mouse stood. "We're the Almighty's strong arm, to conquer a perverse world! We'll invoke celestial hosts and triumph! Hallelujah! We . . . "

"Quiet!" The cigar pointed at Mouse. "Mouthy slob! Who do you work for?"

Aaron answered for Mouse, "He's a subcontractor at the mine, licks Simon Alvarez' boots." Chuey walked up to Mouse and spit in his face.

Mouse reddened; for a moment, I feared he'd strike the bearded leader. He shouted instead, "Satan's among you! I'm escaping before fire rains from heaven!" He strode out, picked up the iguana, and mounted his mule.

Aaron told Chuey, "That overstuffed sack of lard took your place handling the mine explosives, comrade. I work for him and he treats me like horse manure."

The cigar poked Aaron's chest. "Know why? As subcontractor he profits from your slaving like a beast, doing two men's work." The cigar then turned and pointed toward the sound of the mule's retreating hoof beats. "Someday I'll have an understanding with that little boy." His twisted grin gave me chills.

Chuey's tiresome "socio-economic orientation" was a tirade of exaggerated reasons for revolution, geared to trigger hate and envy. He finally wound down and I hurried out. While untying my horse, I started to tell Aaron how Jesus had cleaned up my life, and someone spit behind me. I turned; Chuey had come up to us quietly. "Comrade, the only religion we deal with here is righteous revenge."

"Revenge makes things worse, sir. Justice comes only with God's help."

"Correction!" He raised his rifle over his head. "Justice comes through the people's voice spoken with hot lead bullets. They alone form our vocabulary!"

We started back down the mountain with Chorcho sharing my horse, and Roger commented, "Looks like the SRE seeks justice by stirring up envy and hatred. What do you think, Chorcho?"

"Well, I think they replace a foul error with a fouler one. And you, Tiger?"

"I think some of them want justice. I plan to return and tell them about Jesus."

"Well, then don't mess with Chuey. He's a cold-blooded brute, a demon with a knife, fatal with a rifle, and he has a crazy love affair with explosives. He'll wipe out all his foes if he doesn't blow himself up first. Don't cross him, Tiger."

"That giant Mincho with the hideous scar seemed even more intimidating."

Task 03–e.

WAGE SPIRITUAL WARFARE STRATEGICALLY, PREPARED ALWAYS FOR MARTYRDOM

Gadget saw me returning home. "Wait, Tiger. Olga Gomez just sent word; she wants me to come and bring you and Lucy." The police chief's car battery was dead, but had a manual transmission so we could start it by pushing it. Evita went with us, and Gadget parked the car facing downhill near Olga's house in order to start it again by coasting. We found Olga peering nervously out a window, and I'd soon learn why devout followers of Jesus **wage spiritual warfare strategically, prepared always for martyrdom.**

"I'm still not sure," she told Gadget. "A rough-looking guy's been stalking me." She blushed. "I think he's an assassin and . . . and they want to kill me."

"Kill you!" He shook his head. "Olga! Surely you have no enemies!"

Lucy took Olga's hand. "He was an admirer. You're the prettiest girl in town."

"That's what I told her," Arturo said. "Mountain men can be crude."

"Why would anyone want to kill you?" Gadget asked. "And who are 'they'?"

"It's complicated. Maybe I'm just jumping to conclusions."

"Your imagination is creative," Arturo replied, and she bit her lip.

"Oh, look!" Olga pointed out the window. "He came down the street, but I think he saw your car, Gadget, and hurried back. Oh! I don't know! I think he's an assassin hired by an international conspiracy that's after me."

Gadget and I exchanged glances. "International conspiracy?" he asked. "How do you know this? And who are 'they'? Whom are you accusing?"

"No one yet; I have no proof. But I'm going to get it. I only want protection."

"Then stay off the street, Mrs. Gomez." Gadget advised. Olga flinched at his condescending tone and wiped a tear as we left.

Outside, Evita took a long drag from a cigarette, tossed her head back and laughed. "There's a more likely reason for a guy to tail her. She's a chic chick!"

"That she is," the mechanic chuckled. "She evangelized me and I almost decided to abandon the booze to accommodate the winsome lass."

"Cuidado!" Evita poked Gadget with her elbow. "She's the lawyer's wife."

"Paranoia! The little angel thinks the world's out to get her. I know her type. It's always 'they' who harass the victim who never says who 'they' are."

Gadget and Evita stepped into to a store to buy cigarettes and I told Lucy, "You said Olga was the prettiest girl in town. I disagree; you are. Olga's second."

"How gallant! You didn't get enough sleep this morning."

A boy came running with a note for Arturo. I took it in to him and he read, *"Mr. Arturo Gomez, Come at once. An urgent matter has come up. Placido Diaz."*

"Don't leave me, 'Turo!" Olga grabbed his arm as he picked up his briefcase.

"I'll be right back. Come, Tiger. Let Gadget take Lucy home."

At the Diaz' house, Anna's father Gerardo told us that Pacho and Anna were cleaning the chapel; we walked on, found them weeding, and Arturo pointed at the papaya. "How it's grown! Do you use a magic stimulant on it, Grandma?"

"Sure, Pastor! I'm secretly a witch and address it with occult incantations!"

"They work only halfway; it has leaves but no fruit, just like our church."

"So cynical! It'll bear fruit and so will our church." Anna said as she trimmed a hibiscus. She had an alert manner and a perpetual twinkle in her eye. "That papaya draws its food daily from the soil and climbs toward heaven, just as we draw energy from the river of grace that flows from God's throne."

"Inspiring, Grandma! Hey, Pacho, why'd you send me this note?"

"I did not send any note, sir."

Arturo gasped, dropped his briefcase, turned and ran. "Olga! Olga!"

I followed him. He entered his house and I heard him scream, "No! No! No!" He was embracing Olga's body on the kitchen floor in a red circle of blood, her head battered, her beautiful face mutilated, and her scull crushed beyond hope of life. "No, no! Olga! Why didn't I protect you? Olga! No!"

I felt faint. Pacho and Anna had followed and stood in the door gaping in disbelief. I told him, "Get Gadget." I had to repeat it three times before the barber recovered enough to go for the police chief.

Anna wet a towel and wiped up blood that we had tracked on the floor and then the soles of our shoes. Gadget arrived, looked at the gory sight and grew pale. "Dear God! I'll find who done it, Arturo. Be sure. Whom do you suspect?"

Arturo did not answer.

"Pardon, sir, but to find who done it I gotta move fast. Was she into politics?"

Arturo shook his head.

"Here, Tiger!" Gadget kneeled, pointing. "Cigarette ashes!"

"Or cigar ashes?"

Arturo was sobbing and I sat by him. Suddenly he leaped up. "Olga, I will avenge you! I will, I swear! I swear! Justice demands revenge." He shook his fist toward heaven. "I will certainly avenge you, Olga."

Anna told him gently, "She'd not want revenge, only love for Jesus."

Arturo looked at her, then beyond her, dazed, and sat silently for a while. He then clenched a fist and stood again. "I will get revenge! Justice requires it!"

Pacho sighed. "Thus ends our project to reach the Bat Haven area for Jesus!"

Anna took Arturo's arm. "Wait until your mind clears; blind fury only serves Satan. Then you'll do what Olga wanted with all her heart—win folks to Jesus."

Saint Muñoz' bell sounded. "Oh!" I headed for the door. "Time to go home and get ready for work." On the way I wired the tragic news to Jethro, and back home I told Lucy what happened, adding, "I didn't believe her! I'm a moron!"

Lucy wept as I checked the cartridges in my pistol; I put a few extras in my pocket. She cried, "Oh, this town scares me! I wish you wouldn't leave me tonight! Your job's risky; I had that horrid dream, and now Olga. Please, Tiger, let's go back to our village where it's safe!"

"But we covenanted with God to serve here. He bound it in heaven! Oh, Lu!"

Throughout that night's watch, I was edgy, and the next morning I hurried to see Arturo. He was telling Anna, "You're right, Grandma; revenge is wrong. Hatred blinded me. For Olga' sake, I'll dedicate myself to bring people to Jesus." He stood looking up, a hand over his heart. "Olga, I swear before Almighty God, nothing will deter me! I'll do what your soul desired. I promise, forever!"

I gripped his hand. "I'm with you, Pastor; it's my promise, too."

Jethro Mendez conducted the burial leaning on his cane; following tearful eulogies he concluded, "Thousands of believers suffer persecution. It's rarely reported because oppressors charge them with false accusations that have nothing to do with their faith. Persecutors can't admit publicly that their motive is hatred of Christ and His goodness. Revelation 20 promises martyrs *a privileged reign of a thousand years*. He closed his eyes for a moment. "Picture he

r. Olga, beautiful queen Olga, crowned and seated on her throne beside Jesus!"

"But why Olga?" Roger dried his eyes. "She was an inspiration to all, the spark that ignited our resolve to revitalize our church. Why, Jethro?"

"Spiritual warfare often gets physical, son." He nodded to poll bearers who began lowering the casket. "Courageous fighters drive back the old dragon, and he counterattacks with such frenzied hatred that he whips his scaly tail into a painful knot and lashes out at the most godly—the prophets, Stephen, a myriad of martyrs. It's been the same down the ages. For Olga, he has only prepared the way for a *precious, glorious gem to be added to her crown*. Hollow thuds punctuated his words as soil from Arturo's hand fell on the pine box.

CHAPTER 3: CONFIRM THE GRASP AND THE PRACTICE OF LEADERS' TASKS

03–a. Correct correctly. Find in what way fathers are to be pastors: *Fathers, do not provoke your children to anger, but bring them up in the discipline and instruction of the Lord.* Eph 4:6

Identify the correct motive to punish a child, following God's example: *Those whom the Lord loves He disciplines . . . God deals with you as with sons; for what son is there whom his father does not discipline?* Heb 12:6–7

03–b. Bind the agreement in a tiny group as Jesus taught, to launch a serious project. Find how many this takes: *Whatever you bind on earth shall be bound in heaven, and whatever you loose on earth shall be loosed in heaven . . . If two of you agree on earth about anything that they may ask, it shall be done for them by My Father who is in heaven. For where two or three have gathered together in My name, I am there in their midst.* Matt 18:18–20

03–c. Stanch Satan's sneaky undercurrents of finicky criticism. Find what an untamed tongue causes: *The tongue is small part of the body, yet it boasts of great things…how great a forest is set aflame by such a small fire! And the tongue is a fire, the very world of iniquity; the tongue is set among our members as that which defiles the entire body, and sets on fire the course of our life, and is set on fire by hell.* Jas 3:5–8

03–d. Keep alert to opportunities God gives to witness for Jesus. The arch-criminal Chorcho (a historical person) heard about Jesus in solitary confinement. Whom among acquaintances can you, or those you train, witness to this week?

03–e. Wage spiritual warfare strategically, prepared always for martyrdom. Find comfort for one who suffers for Jesus: *The Spirit Himself testifies with our spirit that we are children of God, and if children, heirs also, heirs of God and fellow heirs with Christ, if indeed we suffer with Him so that we may also be glorified with Him.* Rom 8:16–17

Note what Satan does when God's people seek revitalization: *Your adversary, the devil, prowls around like a roaring lion, seeking someone to devour.* 1 Pet 5:8

Find the martyrs' reward: *I saw the souls of those who had been beheaded because of their testimony of Jesus . . . they came to life and reigned with Christ for 1,000 years.* Rev 20:4

EVALUATE YOUR LEADERSHIP

1=Poor. 2=Planning to improve. 3=Doing well.

1-2-3   Correct children, coworkers, and employees without anger.

1-2-3   Ask God to bind an accord, as Jesus said, to launch serious projects.

1-2-3   Stanch Satan's sneaky undercurrents of finicky criticism.

1-2-3   Stay alert to God-given opportunities to witness for Jesus.

1-2-3   Wage spiritual warfare strategically, prepared always for martyrdom.

4.
Demons Come Riding into Town, Mounted on Foreign Dollars

"Poor Arturo!" Lucy gasped. "He's gotten so thin!" We were on our way to worship and saw the pastor coming. A diesel truck pulled up, its cab bright orange and "*The Caribbean*" written above the windshield. The driver smiled engagingly; he was tall, broad-shouldered, and had the dark skin of the Garífuna tribe that peopled the Caribbean coast. He was one of the few who had tired of fishing mornings in a dugout canoe and migrated inland.

"Hi, Pastor 'Turo." The lanky black's pleasant baritone voice boomed as he strode to the door. "I don't see sister Olga. Is she well?"

Arturo shook his head, hurried in, and sat to one side. The trucker started to follow, but I stopped him. "There was a tragedy, sir. Some fiend murdered Olga."

His mouth fell open, and I held out a hand. "Tiger Garcia. My wife, Lucy."

"What a gaffe I made! Pleased to know you, Tiger and Lucy. I'm Colombo Estrada. I've been on the road nearly a month. You said Olga was . . . *murdered?*"

"Someone beat her to death."

He shook his head and was silent for a moment. "Oh, when will Bat Haven get phones? We're half a century behind the rest of humanity! A wicked back pain has kept my wife Hilda out of touch, too; she hasn't left home for days."

Lucy asked, "Can we visit your wife Hilda and pray for her back, Colombo?"

"Oh, please do!"

I sat by Arturo and he dried his cheeks with a handkerchief. "I ought to handle my grief, Tiger, but I can't shake it. Without her, life's a burnt-out candle."

Po-po-po-po! The familiar throb interrupted, thundering over us. Arturo leaped up and shook a fist. "I hate that noise! I don't know why. I just hate it!"

Mouse and Martha arrived then and she replaced a soiled cloth on the altar with an embroidered one. "It's beautiful!" Lucy praised her, "Exquisite, Martha!"

"I made mistakes if you look closely. I never do anything right."

Hearing the tap of a cane, I turned. Jethro hung his skunk skin cap on a nail by the door and Anna took two grinning young men to meet the elderly mentor.

"I asked God to prepare my nephews' hearts to receive Jesus and when Roger and I saw them, they were ready to listen. It's their first time here, Pastor Jethro."

"Joyful faith in Jesus is more contagious than measles!" The old man shook their hands. "Come, Pastor Arturo. Receive the first fruits of your harvest!"

This jerked Arturo out of his despair and he welcomed the youths. Pacho then beckoned Arturo, Jethro and me aside. "Arturo, you work hard to shepherd us and deserve pay. I'm going to recommend it during worship."

> **Task 04–a.**
>
> RECRUIT MANY
> BI-VOCATIONAL
> LEADERS WHO ARE
> MOTIVATED BY
> LOVE, NOT MONEY

"Thanks Pacho, but to bring Christ to our area we must **recruit many bi-vocational leaders who are motivated by love, not money.** In Acts 20, Paul ended his tearful farewell to Ephesian elders whom he'd never see again by urging them to follow his example of supporting himself and co-workers with his hands. To him this was extremely important. He set the same example in Thessalonica for lazy leaders. I'm doing likewise."

"But the Apostle Paul lived in different times."

"Times differed, Pacho, but not the conditions that moved Paul to set an example; the need is just as pressing now in most parts of the world. Churches in our poor, tiny villages need self-supported leaders, our cell groups too."

"But isn't it biblical to support pastors? Pastor Jethro, doesn't your church in Arenas give you a salary?"

"Yes, but this region needs Arturo's model and someone of influence has to set the pace. Do you recall the star with diverse aspects of vital Christian tasks? What was its main point, Pacho?"

"Ah . . . Each task has two ways to do it and we need good alignment between the two. I guess we need a feasible balance between paid and unpaid leaders."

"Exactly. Wherever God has produced a movement for Jesus, *revival, renewal, awakening* or whatever folks called it, there's been a high ratio of volunteer leaders. They, too, have been called by different terms such as 'teaching elder,' 'lay pastor,' or simply 'leader.'"

During worship Arturo exhorted us, "Olga's passion was to take Jesus to our friends. Anna and Roger have done so; let's all do it for the love of Olga's memory. I'll help you get started. I'll go with you to your friends' homes. Just tell me when . . . Oh!" He covered his ears; a piercing squeal had sounded outside.

> ## Task 04–b.
> ### DETECT SATAN'S TREACHERY AS HE STRIVES TO STIFLE REVITALIZATION

That screech heralded another challenge, to **detect Satan's treachery as he strives to stifle revitalization**. Julio ran to the door. "Aha! Bat Haven's luxury taxi needs brake linings. Our meticulous mechanic, ingenious inventor, and fearless police chief is on his way to become a pious Protestant!"

Mouse jeered, "It'd be easier to convert a jackass."

Gadget beckoned to me from the door and handed me a note. "For the preacher, neighbor. Urgent."

Arturo read it and his face turned to stone; he waved it at Gadget. "Wait, sir— I'll send a reply." He turned to us. "A Mr. Jones offers to buy our chapel and its land. He offers a fabulous price, many times its worth. He wants to know at once if we will consider his offer, as his helicopter has to leave soon."

"Glory!" Mouse faced the assembly. "A gift has fallen from heaven! We'll build a new church with a steeple higher than the bell towers of Saint Muñoz!"

"It didn't fall from heaven," countered Colombo the tall trucker. "It came up from hell. I know 'Panther' Jones, and that *gringo* has earned his nickname!"

Gadget motioned to me again and I went to him. "Tell Arturo that, as police chief, I recommend waiting until I investigate recent events a bit more."

Simon heard him. "You're not a member of the church! Keep out of this!"

Pacho repeated a pet maxim: "Prudence pleads for prayerful patience."

"All you ever do is throw cold water on progress, I tell you!" Simon bawled.

Colombo advised, "Panther's bullying us into it, rushing us. That's his style."

Wanda's voice rose to a pitch that rivaled the taxi's screeching brakes. "We'll build a grand cathedral beside my house!" Others agreed and debate grew heated.

> ## Task 04–c.
> ### MAKE CRUCIAL DECISIONS PRAYERFULLY AND CAREFULLY WITH OTHERS' HELP

"Quiet!" Arturo rapped the pulpit sharply with his knuckles. "Elders, stay afterwards to settle this. Jethro and Tiger too; your opinions may help." It's vital to **make crucial decisions prayerfully and carefully with others' help.**

"I'll hang around too, sir," Gadget told Arturo, "to take your reply to the rich *gringo*. He's at the courthouse yakking with the mayor."

We could not keep our minds on worship after that, and Arturo gathered the elders. "Do we sell our land?" They all began talking at once and Arturo turned to his elderly mentor from Arenas. "What do you think, Jethro?"

"I once hiked near the edge of a high cliff in the dark without a light; the moon was bashful that night and had hid behind a cloud. So, rather than taking blind steps in the dark, I waited until the old lady ventured out again."

It took a moment to digest this, and Mouse bristled. "You're not our bishop, sir, and you don't belong to this church. No outsider should interfere with a local church. Certainly no bishops! A church must be self-governed, independent, and free from meddling hierarchy."

Pacho twisted his moustache. "I don't agree, Mouse. Jethro's like a bishop for us, the only one here with white hair and experience as a church leader."

"No!" barked Simon, pointing his hook at Pacho. "It's a matter for us elders."

Arturo turned to Jethro. "Who does Scripture say should decide such things?"

"You won't like my answer."

"So let God's *two-edged sword* do its job."

"On guard!" Jethro thrust his cane like a sword toward Arturo's heart and we laughed. "The New Testament has examples of all three classic forms of church government: by bishop, elders, and congregations. In general, elders led the flocks. They didn't just sit in sessions to make rules; they *shepherded* the people. As a mentor, I don't make rules for my trainees' churches; I equip them to lead. Gentlemen, Arturo's your appointed overseer; help him decide the issue."

Simon rose and faced the group. "We're wasting time. Who favors the sale?"

Half did so and Arturo told me, "Break the tie, Tiger. What's your opinion?"

"Our police chief cautioned that you let him investigate some things first."

"Out of order!" Simon shook his hook at Arturo. "Tiger's not an elder!"

Arturo called to Gadget. "Go tell that Panther guy we won't make a rushed decision. We'll talk it over calmly and pray." The elders rose to leave.

Task 04–d.
SHOW NEW BELIEVERS
HOW TO EVANGELIZE
THEIR FAMILY AND
FRIENDS

"Wait!" Arturo begged. "Tiger, while you're here with the elders, explain the way you showed new believers how to present Christ to friends and relatives in Los Robles. Our elders will also **show new believers how to evangelize their family and friends.**" Simon groaned, but they all sat back down.

"I invited folks in Los Robles to meetings at first, but no one came. They had not felt the love of friends who knew Jesus. Then Lucy and I prayed for the sick and told what Jesus did to save us, avoiding doctrinal issues. Some received Jesus and we went with them to talk with their friends, witnessing in a way new believers could easily imitate. Soon they went on their own."

I expected Pacho to object and he didn't disappoint me. "You didn't teach doctrine? One must know basic doctrinal truths to receive Jesus."

Jethro rescued me. "God reveals His Son in many ways: the Word, prayer, pals, sacraments, visions, dreams, healing, but always with the Holy Spirit's conviction of sin. What makes the eternal difference is that the risen Christ comes to sinners as the Spirit illuminates them; they sense Jesus' presence and repent."

Simon rose. "Arturo, I run two businesses: a silver mine and a cattle ranch. I don't have time to go visit people as Tiger does." He started for the door.

"Wait, Simon! Please!" Arturo said firmly. "I have two jobs too. I thought I lacked time to visit, but Olga's death jarred me into giving priority to . . . "

"Good day, gentlemen." Simon left.

Pacho sighed. "My problem is that I find it hard to talk with people outside of my barber shop. In their homes I lack the boldness that you have, Tiger."

"Then go by twos, as Jesus' disciples did. I'll go with you. The Holy Spirit will give you boldness; He's done it for others who went with me. You can also invite friends to your home to enjoy Grandma's cooking—kitchen evangelism!"

The meeting ended and I told Jethro, "I have questions about those three types of church government."

"I do too," Arturo joined us. "Come to my office, guys."

We went, and Olga smiled down at us in the legal office, radiant in her wedding dress; her photo hung between diplomas and shelves held more books than I'd ever seen. Jethro told us, "Your concern about church government is healthy. Its classic forms, *Episcopal, Presbyterian,* or *Congregational,* all have significant weaknesses if used unwisely. You can offset those flaws if you're aware of them, but if you're unaware they'll stifle the movement that you envision."

Arturo asked, "Which of the three forms of church rule do you prefer?"

> **Task 04–e.**
>
> PROVIDE CHURCHES THE TYPE OF GOVERNMENT THAT FITS THEIR LEVEL OF MATURITY

"It's not that simple. Above all, **provide churches the type of government that fits their level of maturity.**"

Ever the impatient lawyer, Arturo urged, "That's not a very definite answer."

"I'll give a definite answer, but first you must recognize a fact that many leaders close their minds too. No church always heeds one form of rule; influential folk will in time control to some degree, at times in godly ways, at times in ungodly ways, using approved bylaws or hidden power structures. So eventually all three types of rule will exert influence in some way. A church's administration should allow for its level of maturity, culture, field conditions, and relationship with sister churches. I mentor leaders of various backgrounds and respect the structures that they've inherited; otherwise, I'd just create divisive squabbles."

"You haven't answered my question." Arturo probed in his courtroom tone and I wondered if it had been wise to meet in his legal office. "From a lawyer's view, church rule is a question of who has legitimate *authority*. Many churches ascribe it to only one of the three categories you mentioned: bishops, elders, or congregation. So, who has true authority under Christ?"

"A family lives where there are bullies. The tots don't leave home unless dad goes with them; he's their 'bishop,' their overseer, not one of the children's own 'congregation.' New flocks in pioneer fields need such supervision by an outsider, as Titus 1:5 shows, a mature overseer that's not part of their flock—call him Bishop, Regional Director, Superintendent, Synod Chairman or simply 'old Bob.' A flaw in Episcopal rule is that daddy can abuse his authority or lead the tots astray; history recounts abundant cases of hierarchical abuse."

I recalled, "Pacho wanted you to take on a bishop's role for us, Jethro."

"He did. Well, the tots grow and dad lets them go out without him, provided the older brothers protect them; these 'elders' are part of the kids' flock. That's *Presbyterian* rule; a presbyter is an '*elder*,' a mature leader." He tapped the lawyer's knee with the round end of his cane. "Like you, Arturo. The New Testament makes the word plural—*elders*—when denoting a church's leaders. In Acts 15, churches sent elders to Jerusalem to resolve a grave schism. A peril is that the older brothers can abuse their authority, bully weaker siblings and stifle their initiative. History has ample cases of this too."

I commented, "Simon wanted elders to decide the sale in a presbyterian way."

"Yes. Now, the kids grow up, but remain close. They respect dad's advice but decide most things as a group without always yielding to the older brothers. That's *Congregational* rule. The Antioch church in Acts 13 had matured and had several capable leaders. Thus, it could decide as a body to send Paul and Barnabas as missionaries. A flaw in a flock governing itself is that it can become too independent, and a leader lacking accountability to other shepherds can be a tyrant, making a flock depend on one person and out of touch with other churches. Also, uninformed believers make silly decisions; history abounds with dire cases."

Arturo recalled, "Mouse demanded congregational rule in our meeting. Why do churches make such rigid laws, Jethro? Many demand just one type of rule, regardless of a church's level of maturity."

"For legal and historical reasons. One legal cause is that churches register with the state; this lures many to take for granted an administrative system that's more secular- and program-oriented than biblical- and gift-oriented."

"And the historical reasons?" "Emperor Constantine absorbed churches into the Roman Empire in the fourth century, and church leaders took on *Episcopal* rule paralleling the imperial Roman hierarchy. Orthodox and Catholics still do, as do other denominations that date back to the Protestant Reformation. *Presbyterian* government gained impetus when kings lost absolute control, and districts sent delegates to represent them in national councils or parliaments; Christian elders began representing their people and shepherding them locally, instead of one cleric having total control. Later, *Congregational* rule gained popularity with the growth of democracy."

I asked, "Isn't there a kind of congregational rule in Jesus' promise to bind in heaven what two or three gathered in His name agree on?"

"Why, yes! You're perceptive, Tiger!"

"Well, one thing's obvious," I remarked. "Our church can't get broad agreement now to govern itself as a congregation. We just saw how folks bicker."

"It's not able to follow any leader," Arturo griped, "whether a pastor or bishop. It'd be like shepherding a herd of squirrels! And it's certainly incapable of elders' rule; ours clash like fighting cocks! So where does that leave us?"

Jethro grinned and patted Arturo's shoulder. "God will change this, brother."

Arturo clasped Jethro's hand. "I really value your mentoring,"

Task 04–f. DISCERN CONDITIONS THAT CALL FOR TRAINING NEW LEADERS LIKE JESUS AND PAUL DID	"Good. It's vital to **discern conditions that call for training new leaders like Jesus and Paul did.** Have you considered being mentored, Tiger?" "I sure need it! Can I meet with you, too, Pastor Jethro, along with Arturo?" "Your own shepherd should coach you, Tiger. I train Arturo and he trains apprentice leaders in the Bat Haven area. Such mentoring 'chains' do

not limit the number of trainees. Obedient pastors mentor new shepherds, just as Jesus and His apostles did; it's a key pastoral duty, as Paul told Timothy."

"I see. Please, Pastor Arturo, let me be one of your apprentices."

"I'd be honored. You'll learn things you'd never get from my lectures."

"Didn't Paul *lecture* pastoral students in a school, in Ephesus?"

Jethro replied, "The Greek word in Acts 19 was not *lectured* but *dialogued*; Paul was a mentor. The next chapter shows that Paul worked with his hands when he was in Ephesus, to supply coworkers' needs. That training multiplied churches throughout western Asia Minor; its curriculum obviously included *intensive travel, witnessing for Jesus, church planting,* and *serving bi-vocationally.* Such training multiplies churches, urban cells, and secret flocks in hostile fields."

"Then do you oppose Bible colleges and seminaries, Pastor Jethro?"

"No, Tiger, not if their professors are true believers. Seminaries serve well for some, poorly for others, depending on conditions. I thank God for my seminary training, but most leaders need *local* training, especially to lead cell groups, small flocks, or house churches. Arturo's legal practice won't allow him to go away to seminary so I meet with him every two weeks, sometimes here, and sometimes in Arenas with other new leaders that I mentor."

"What do you do when you mentor them?"

"I listen to each trainee report what his church or cell is doing and assign to each one Bible reading and other studies that fit his flock's current need. I mentor a trainee only if he's leading a new church or starting a cell with his family."

Arturo explained, "Jethro doesn't instruct us only during meetings. He gives us a model that we can easily imitate as we visit people together. I'll do the same for you, Tiger, and you'll model skills for other new leaders, investing yourself in them and sharing responsibility for their success as they train others."

"I learned 2 Timothy 2:2. *That which you have heard of me among many witnesses, commit to faithful men who are able to teach others also.*"

"How many links were in that chain?" Arturo asked me.

"Let's see . . . Paul, Timothy, 'faithful men,' and 'others'. Four! Did they train one-on-one?"

"Seldom, Tiger. Jesus mentored twelve, sometimes three, and rarely, one."

Arturo asked Jethro, "So what's an ideal number to meet with a mentor?"

"For me, only three or four. Listen to each trainee and help him make plans for his flock and the flocks of his own trainees. A small group makes it easy to give the attention needed to arrange for each trainee to begin soon to mentor other newer leaders. This keeps the flocks multiplying; Jesus' parable of four soils focused on *multiplication.*"

I said, "Multiplying needs good soil—good people. Right, Jethro?"

"Good soil, yes; good people, no. Good soil is *bad people* who repent, Tiger. *Where sin abounds, grace abounds much more.*"

"If good soil is bad folks, then Bat Haven could yield a substantial harvest!"

"It will. Just let believers and flocks multiply in their natural, God-given way."

"What do you mean—*natural?*" I asked.

Jethro handed us sweet rolls from his skunk skin backpack. "Eat. Now, how did this bread originate? It's a product of the miracle of reproduction, the same as all grains, fruit, vegetables, meat, eggs, flowers, and the wood of this table. Every day, all creation reminds us how our God multiplies His plants and creatures—and church bodies. So don't waste time on bad soil that yields no fruit. What did Jesus say to do when folks fail to respond, Tiger?"

"To shake the dust from our feet, to seek others who are receptive."

"Right. Missionaries who shake the dust to find people that are more receptive rarely change their place of residence; they simply go to a poorer class of people. As Jesus advised, flocks among poor people will multiply much faster."

"You use the word *flock* a lot. Why, Jethro?"

"Because it denotes any Christian group—a church or a cell within a church."

"Such a treasure of truths! I can't wait to be mentored."

"Then let's not wait." Arturo took a pocket-sized study from his briefcase. "This explains mentored training. Most of these small study booklets include *inductive* Bible studies. They tell you where to find answers in the Word so you can mine the gems for yourself. Ah . . . Jethro says I'm to sell these."

"I sure did. I gave them away to poor students until I saw these studies about the Word of God in their outhouses serving instead as toilet paper. But if they pay for them, they'll read them."

<table>
<tr><td>

Task 04–g.

RESIST THE SUBTLE
LURE TO CRITICIZE
TOO MUCH

</td></tr>
</table>

The next day I met Mouse returning from the mine on his mule, and showed him the training booklet. "I'm studying by extension now, cousin. I can carry these studies in my pocket and read them at night between rounds." Mouse leafed through it and scowled. I'd soon find out why Christians must **resist the subtle lure to criticize too much.**

"Cartoons! Ha! Divine truth comes in comics? It can't be serious theology!"

"Don't be such a grouch! Pictures help dumbbells like me understand, and the pocket size makes it convenient to read the booklets any time. Did you know you reek of exploded dynamite?"

"Of course. I've been deep inside that mountain giving it its heartbeat."

On my first round watching the house that night, I heard Wanda screeching inside. "You're letting a fortune slip through our hands!"

"It's not I who obstruct the sale, woman. But I'll take measures, I tell you—any cursed measures that are needed!"

I felt anger. "Oh, Lord, it's hard to love one's neighbor as you say. Help me!"

The next morning I told Lucy what I'd heard and she said, "If there's another seam of silver above the chapel then it belongs to our church? That's why . . . "

Knocking interrupted and I opened the door. "Mrs. Wanda Alvarez! What miracle brings you to our lowly home?"

She walked past me and sat by Lucy. "I've got to tell you the latest. Simon bought a grand piano, and he's going to get me a new sedan with leather seats."

"How nice! How fun to be rich!"

"I'll let you in on a secret, girl, before we get to business. The money Simon invested in the mine was not his; it was mine. Before we married, he owned only an old horse and a few scrawny steers. He's gained a fortune because of me."

Tino and Davey came running into the house wearing mended clothes and Lucy commented, "What Tiger earns does not meet our family's basic needs. Perhaps Simon could give him a salary that's a little more adequate, ma'am?"

"Girl, don't blame Simon if God has not blessed you as He has us."

"You equate material wealth with God's blessing. Well, the owners of those sleazy joints on the west side employ depraved women and get rich, too. Did God bless those owners, Mrs. Alvarez? Excuse me a second while I bring coffee."

I asked, "What is the business that you mentioned, Mrs. Alvarez?"

"I'll wait for your wife so she can help me convince you." Lucy brought coffee and Wanda said, "The foreman Simon hired, Jaime Ordoñez, is an unsociable, uncouth drunkard, and I won't have him around. Lucy, if you want Tiger to receive God's blessing then tell him to take the foreman's job."

I asked, "Is it only through income that we receive God's blessing? Ephesians says God promises *spiritual* blessings to New Testament believers. The Old Testament offered *material* blessings to Israelites. We . . . "

"Don't preach your theology at me, young man! I know your type of Christian. You associate with women who paint their faces, wear trousers, and read depraved novels. You lack convictions."

"Oh, I have deep convictions, ma'am; I believe with all my heart that I should not wear lipstick!"

"You're mocking me."

"Write it down in your little notebook."

Wanda reached into a pocket for the notebook, tore out a page, and gave it to me. "These are the shameful faults and vices that keep our church from receiving God's blessing. Make those you evangelize stop doing them."

Lucy snatched it from me. "No! Tiger! Don't! That's venomous!"

Wanda slammed her cup down sloshing coffee on the table, glowered at Lucy, and left. Lucy's eyes sparked with fury. "Paranoid wasp! Faking faith in Jesus!"

"She irks me, too, Lu, but let's not judge her. We all have faults."

"Faults! You'll see some day that she's false, totally. Oh, Lord, help me! I'm afraid she'll make me lose control and . . . " Lucy held me tightly. "Oh, Tiger!"

I couldn't shake Simon's ominous words about taking "any cursed measures" to get the church to sell its land. I went to Arturo and asked, "Does Panther want that rocky slope because it still contains silver?"

"Maybe." He looked up at Olga's picture. "She thought the ore had run out, but there was something else. I think Chuey Ochoa slew her; Gadget found ashes near her body and Chuey always smokes a cigar."

"He never lights it. Gadget went to interrogate the boy who took the false note that got you to leave your house, but he wasn't home. Let's go question him."

"No, no! Not me. Leave that to Gadget."

Task 04–h.
DISCERN WHEN A LEADER SHOULD RESIGN, AND HOW.

I rose to go but Arturo begged, "Wait. Help me consider my pastoral role with sanity. My mind's a mess; Olga inspired me to shepherd our flock, but now I face bickering, few do ministry, and seekers drop out. I need to **discern when a leader should resign, and how.** Tell me frankly, would I serve our movement better by merely mentoring new village pastors?"

"I think you should just stop trying to be the savior of Bat Haven."

"Savior! What do you mean?"

"You punish yourself for others' failures, as though God's work all depends on you and on how hard you push people to do evangelism. Look at the positive side and relax; the flock's blossoming under your leadership."

"Blossoming? Have I missed something?"

"There are new believers, Pastor, and older ones are growing."

"But most of them just hold the work back. I'll resign if they don't change soon; I never planned to be a senior pastor."

"Don't let Satan stampede you into making decisions in reaction to his attacks. Let the dust settle and consider your vocation calmly. Above all, don't destabilize the work by saying you *might* resign. If you decide to, then say so and do it, but don't leave the flock dangling with indecision. It would lack confidence in you."

"Well now, you've become my mentor!" He clasped my hand. "Thank you!"

I went with Gadget to question the boy who had taken Arturo the fateful message, but we found the house empty and a neighbor told us, "They took off. They feared the killer would come after the boy who could identify him. You're police chief, Gadget, so I'll tell you where they are—with the in-laws up in them mountains to the north. Don't neither of you tell no one else. Take the road to Los Vientos to where it turns away from the river gorge and look for a path going north. It may be overgrowed; few use it. Nothing but savages and hungry mountain lions up there! After three or four hours, maybe more, you'll see a lake with reeds and the house beyond it."

Gadget brought horses when my night vigil ended and we rode up the mountain trail. Pharaoh scampered ahead, tail wagging blissfully as he discovered new scents. We found the overgrown path and rode north, dodging thorns. An hour later, we greeted tribal peasants; they were burning brush and replied in a tribal dialect. Their agriculture was primitive: slash and burn, grow a few crops, then slash and burn again; it was illegal but they knew no law, but tribal custom. A man was planting where the ashes had cooled; he poked holes with a sharp stick, tossed in corn and beans together, and raked soil over them with his bare foot.

The wind shifted, blowing smoke in our eyes, and we spurred the horses. I tried to talk to Gadget about Christ, but he paid no heed. We soon passed another peasant with the splayed toes typical of one who wears no shoes, toting live chickens hanging from both ends of a pole over his shoulder. Farther on, Pharaoh sniffed the air, growled, and vanished into the brush. We heard frantic growling and he returned with scratches on his side. "Look, Tiger!" Gadget pointed at fresh tracks in the path. "A cougar! Big!"

"Those chickens' scent drew it; it's following them. Let's warn that guy!" Galloping back in a clearing, the horses snorted, reared, and Gadget's mount threw him. We saw why. The cougar was chasing a cow and leaped on its back. It bellowed and fell; its neck crushed by the tawny cat's fangs. It crawled under the corpse and dragged it out of sight, in spite of the cow's much greater weight.

"Wow!" Gadget let out a deep breath, "It could've been one of us!"

"That cat won't bother with those chickens now. Let's get back on course."

The horses were skittish as we started back. Gadget's mount came upon a twisted vine that looked like a large snake; it bucked, throwing him off again and he continued on foot. "Oh no!" he pulled up a pant leg. "A hundred tiny ticks are chewing on my legs!" I was prepared, and sprinkled his legs with powder that killed the ticks.

Riding on, we spotted the lake with reeds; we made our way down to it and the horses had to slog slowly through deep mud to get around the lake. At the house, Gadget asked an elderly lady if the boy was home. She turned pale, her eyes opened wide for a moment, and then she squinted at us, studying us before responding. "Well, you don't look too much like murderers. The child's my grandson and he's in danger; he knows who's behind a killing in Bat Haven. He went fishing in the Rio Furioso yonder behind them hills toward sunrise and didn't return. I fear he strayed downriver to visit his friends in Bat Haven where the wrong people might spot him. His father's out searching for him."

CHAPTER 4: CONFIRM THE GRASP AND THE PRACTICE OF LEADERS' TASKS

04–a. Recruit many bi-vocational workers who are motivated by love, not money. Locate the source of Paul's support in Ephesus and how his coworkers benefited from it: *I have coveted no one's silver or gold or clothes. . . . These hands ministered to my own needs and to the men who were with me. In everything I showed you that by working hard in this manner you must help the weak. . . .* Acts 20:32–35

Verify whom a flock should normally support, at least partially: *The elders who rule well are to be considered worthy of double honor, especially those who work hard at preaching and teaching. For the Scripture says, 'You shall not muzzle the ox while he is threshing,' and 'The laborer is worthy of his wages.'* Tim 5:17–18

04–b. Detect Satan's treachery as he strives to stifle revitalization. Satan counter-attacks those who extend Christ's reign. Detect the root of the evils that commonly beset Christians: *Our struggle is not against flesh and blood, but against the rulers, against the powers, against the world forces of this darkness, against the spiritual forces of wickedness in the heavenly places.* Eph 6:12

04–c. Make crucial decisions prayerfully and carefully with others' help. Elders from Antioch and Jerusalem met and reached agreement in a bitter controversy. Choose guidelines that your flock should heed to make decisions, from among these practices of that assembly. Acts 15:

- [ ] All concerned assembled to settle the matter, not just the top leaders.
- [ ] Those who knew the conflict's history recounted it, explaining their opinions so that everybody heard both sides.
- [ ] While one was speaking, the others kept silent, listening with respect.
- [ ] Elders proposed a solution based on the facts of the case and on Scripture.
- [ ] The assembly let the Holy Spirit guide them; He helped them all to consider the solution soberly and express consent.

04–d. Show new believers how to evangelize their family and friends. Find four pastoral tasks that Paul told his apprentice Timothy to do: *Be sober in all things, endure hardship, do the work of an evangelist, fulfill your ministry.* 2 Tim 4:6

04–e. Provide churches the type of government that fits their level of maturity. When elders from several congregations met to resolve a controversy in Acts 15, to which type of government did this correspond?
[ ] Congregational [ ] Presbyterian (elders) [ ] Episcopal (area bishop)
>   ANSWER: Presbyterian administration, in its original biblical form.

Paul told Titus, an *outsider*, to name elders in each town in Crete to deal with what was lacking in new congregations (Titus 1:5). Which type of government serves new churches better in pioneer fields that still lack experienced elders?
[ ] Congregational [ ] Presbyterian (elders) [ ] Episcopal (area bishop)
>   ANSWER: Episcopal administration, in its original biblical form.

The Holy Spirit spoke to the entire body in Antioch and it sent workers to the nations (Acts 13:1–3). Which type of government did this reflect that corresponds to flocks led by mature leaders like those that they had in Antioch?
[ ] Congregational [ ] Presbyterian (elders) [ ] Episcopal (area bishop)
>   ANSWER: Congregational administration, in its original biblical form.

04–f. Discern conditions that call for training new leaders like Jesus and Paul did. Verify what Paul told Timothy to do where God was about to start hundreds of churches: *The things which you have heard from me in the presence of many witnesses, entrust to faithful men who will be able to teach others also.* 2 Tim 2:2

Find a promise that reassures poor, less-educated leaders: *God has chosen the foolish things of the world to shame the wise, and God has chosen the weak things of the world to shame the things which are strong.* 1 Cor 1:17

04–g. Resist the subtle lure to criticize too much. Notice why one is not to judge others: *Do not judge, and you will not be judged, and do not condemn, and you will not be condemned; pardon, and you will be pardoned.* Luke 6:37

04–h. Discern when a leader should resign, and how. One having a pastor's gift should use it any way he can, even if only with his family. Identify how long spiritual gifts last: *The gifts and the calling of God are irrevocable.* Rom 11:29

EVALUATE YOUR LEADERSHIP

1=Poor. 2=Planning to improve. 3=Doing well.

1-2-3 Recruit many *bi-vocational* workers who are not motivated by money.

1-2-3 Detect Satan's treachery as he strives to stifle churches' revitalization.

1-2-3 Make crucial decisions prayerfully and carefully with others' help.

1-2-3 Show new believers how to evangelize their family and friends.

1-2-3 Provide churches a type of government that fits their level of maturity.

1-2-3 Discern conditions that call for training new leaders as Jesus and Paul did.

1-2-3 Resist the subtle lure to criticize too much.

1-2-3 Discern when a leader should resign, and how.

5.
Social Activists Use the Spirit's Sword
Instead of Weapons of Steel

"You didn't touch supper!" Lucy complained. "Did I burn the beans again?"

"My appetite took a day off. Things bother me, Lu. Olga's killer is loose, the boy who took the note to Arturo is missing, and my past keeps stirring up guilt."

"If old sins are festering, then maybe you haven't confessed them to God."

"I have, often."

"Often! Then He's forgiven you. Finish your beans!"

"The bad things I've done haunt me during my night watch. That heavy darkness is a parasite, Lu; it feeds on my guilt, and drains all my soul's energy!"

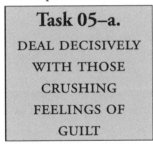

Task 05–a.
DEAL DECISIVELY WITH THOSE CRUSHING FEELINGS OF GUILT

"That's awful! You need to **deal decisively with those crushing feelings of guilt.** How will you help others do it if you can't handle it yourself?"

Lucy's question left me worrying even more about my sins, and when I arrived at work, I dreaded my vigil under the murky skies.

"Come here!" Wanda's cry startled me. "Wait! Tie up that vicious beast first."

"Don't be afraid of him, Mrs. Alvarez. He only attacks evil people." The dog growled and I scolded, "Now Pharaoh, *Do not judge*, says the Lord!"

"Have you come to your senses yet, to take the foreman's job on our ranch?"

"I'm still senseless, Mrs. Alvarez, but I appreciate Simon's offer."

"Did you read the list that I left with you, of the townsfolk's' bad habits?"

"I put it to even better use, ma'am. I started the fire with it this morning."

"Ungrateful buffoon!" Pharaoh snarled again and she slammed the door shut.

Wanda's mother was visiting and was a bit deaf, so they shouted. I heard the old lady's voice: "You kept the Saint Muñoz image that I gave you? Set him on his head and don't turn him right side up until he grants your plea to get that land!"

"Yes, mother, and he'll stay there until I straighten out that arrogant Lucy Garcia. She thinks she's so gorgeous! At her age I was more beautiful than she!"

I patted Pharaoh's head. "People are disgusting; be glad you're a dog!"

A drizzle made sparks in my flashlight beam and an icy breeze chilled me through my homemade poncho—Lucy had taped plastic bags together. At midnight, dim light broke through as the sky's curtains parted for the night queen's royal appearance, along with her winged mammal attendants, flitting about me. Her full, round, lunar face scowled at me, bloodless and brooding. How did poets find her amorous? They didn't have to endure her mute company all night! My pale overseer taunted me, aggravating my aching guilt, recalling my sins. The old *accuser of the brothers* was busy. "Go away, Evil one!" I whispered aloud.

I fell to my knees. "Almighty God, have mercy! Recalling my sin-filled past makes me despair and unholy thoughts infest my mind. Deliver me from the evil one. Put Your hand on me and . . . "

I felt a tap on my shoulder and turned, startled. It was Jethro's cane.

"Hey, I heard you praying. I'm waiting for the early bus to Arenas."

"The devil's after me."

"Don't throw all the blame on the devil. You fight against yourself. Sincere Christians have a conflict in themselves; Romans 7 reveals its root."

I took my New Testament from my pocket, read the passage and commented, "Paul said he didn't do the good he loved, but the bad he hated. He loved God's law, but the law of sin in his body enslaved him. Me, too! Is there a cure?"

"Keep reading."

I did so. "I see. Chapter 8 says there's no condemnation in Jesus and we can live in the Spirit, who helps us slay our evil desires. Oh, your bus is coming!"

My advisor left and I begged, "God, help me put to death my sinful desires and doubts." Assurance came; God had forgiven me and I actually found the night enjoyable! A roosters' choir challenged the silence. Didn't they sleep, either? One crowed and others joined in all over town, trying to awaken the dawn. They succeeded and, as the Psalmist said about the sun, *the bridegroom came out of his chamber, rejoicing as a strong man to run his course.* The bats fled to their dark haven and I hurried home to sleep long and soundly, the first time in days.

Task 05–b.
DETECT AND ARREST GOSSIP BEFORE ITS VENOM SPREADS

I woke refreshed and took Lucy to the market on the south side of the town square. Wanda spied us and cried, "Come here, girl!" Lucy complied and I followed. The Wasp began to divulge a rumor to her about Pacho's errant son, Julio, and I'd watch Lucy **detect and arrest gossip before its venom spreads.**

"I don't want to hear that, ma'am. Please excuse me." Wanda's face contorted, exuding such hatred that I felt a chill. We turned to go.

"Wait, Tiger!" Pacho was running across the square. "Miners brought Mouse to the health center on a stretcher. Someone stabbed him! Come with me."

"Do you have oil in your barber shop? James 5 says to anoint the sick when we pray in Jesus' name." He fetched a greenish bottle and we hurried on.

Mouse's wounds were minor and he was eager to tell us, "I caught Chuey in the mine plotting a strike and he came at me. I enjoy a good tussle. I'm fat but I keep fit doing my share of the heavy work, lifting the jackhammer over my head to remove rock up high—few men can do that. We tangled and I had the best of Chuey until he stabbed me twice. That puzzled me; I'd looked him over to make sure he had no blade and I felt no hidden weapon when we started grappling."

The doctor told Mouse, "Good thing you have all that insulation or the knife would have perforated vital organs."

"Glory to . . . ! Ouch! It hurts!"

Roger mentioned the attack on Mouse as we rode up the mountain together to another SRE meeting and asked, "Think we'll run into trouble too, Tiger?"

Task 05–c.
USE THE POWER THAT JESUS PROMISED, TO SPREAD THE GOOD NEWS REGARDLESS OF BACKLASH OR DANGER

"Could be. Let's **use the power that Jesus promised, to spread the Good News regardless of backlash or danger.**"

After praying I said, "I see you've armed yourself with a book as usual."

"*Social Action.* I'll give it to one of them if I find one who can read. It deals with their error." He pointed down at the town below. "See those folks going in the big door between the towers of Saint Muñoz, Tiger? They'll pray to him and the Virgin Mary. Do they know Jesus?"

"Only God knows. Their catechism and liturgy affirm what Jesus did to save us, if they'll take the Good News to heart."

"Look, Tiger. That vulture just keeps gliding around over the town without flapping its wings. Weird!"

"It feeds on corruption and death, just like *the prince of the power of the air that works in the sons of disobedience*, as Paul said. We might battle him today."

Squawk! Squawk! Fighting cocks were amusing a group of SRE men when we rode into Los Vientos; Aaron bet on a bird that lost and bitterly cursed it. He noticed me and jeered, "God hasn't helped me none, Tiger. I'll mold my own destiny." Others also aired grievances and some, like Aaron, blamed God.

"Glad you're back, comrades!" The giant with the deformed face approached. "We need reliable fighters. Only God knows how Simon Alvarez and other ranchers exploit their workers. Conditions are atrocious in the new mine too."

"Some of these men have strong reasons to be sore, Mincho. I feel compassion for them and want to do something substantial, not just whine about it."

"Really? Just how serious are you?" He looked me directly in the eye.

"Totally." I looked back at him just as directly. "I mean 100 percent serious."

"Okay! Then stay after the meeting and help us make serious plans."

An hour later, I was sitting with the SRE's inner circle as they plotted their next move. Chuey closed the shutters and faced us. "We'll get the rifles we need tonight from Simon Alvarez' store, but this time we won't fail. Who'll volunteer to distract the guard while I . . . ?"

"No, chief," Mincho asserted in a defiant tone. "That'll alert the authorities."

"I said, *who'll volunteer?*" Chuey showed no fear of Mincho the Monster.

"Wait, boss. Let's try at least once to get justice without committing a felony."

"Comrade Mincho, it's my job to plan operations; it's yours to form unions that share our views. You do your job; I do mine. Now, I need a volunteer."

Nobody responded and Chuey poked a man's chest with his over-sized cigar. "You have the honor, comrade. You'll distract the night watchman. Let him see you and follow you down to the river; keep him occupied. We need silence, so shoot that scumbag guard only if you have to."

"I need a helper, Commandant. You told us a while back that he had a big dog; I can't assault them both at once if . . . "

"Valid point. You think like a revolutionary." Chuey poked Aaron's chest.

"Please, not me, chief. I have no gun and that scumbag . . ."

"I'll loan you my spare rifle. Here."

"Please, Commandant. I've never used a rifle. I don't . . ."

"Who let you in to this meeting? Do I have another volunteer?" After a silence, he snarled, "You're cowards! That's what you are! Cringing cowards!"

"No one calls me a coward!" He had irked me and I blurted without thinking.

"How valiant! Good for you, comrade! Have you a rifle?"

"No, sir."

"Take my spare. It's semi-automatic, has a telescopic sight and . . ."

"I am Simon Alvarez' scumbag guard."

Heads jerked around and Mincho the Monster deftly searched me for weapons; I'd left my pistol home. He stood glaring into my eyes and I felt small. I thought he'd choke me with his gigantic hands, but his threatening visage softened. "You've got guts, Tiger. Tell me frankly; now what's your intention?"

They were too attentive, and I begged God quietly for the power that Jesus promised His witnesses. "My intention . . ."

"Spy!" Chuey swung his rifle toward me and those near me slipped aside.

"I'm no spy! I share your hunger for justice, but not your hate. Instead of killing and stealing, let's gain justice in peaceful ways, as our Lord Jesus Christ commands. His methods yield better results—if that's what you really want."

"Garbage!" shouted Chuey. "Don't listen to this religious creep; he just wants to make us grovel." The safety on his rifle clicked. "Move, Mincho!"

Mincho stood like a stone wall between us. Pushing a huge index finger against my chest, he spoke in a booming voice. "Explain those 'peaceful ways.'"

"It starts with your hearts. Resentment drives you and you crave revenge. You need God's love in your hearts to achieve justice and . . ."

"I'm telling you to move, Mincho!" snarled Chuey.

"I want to hear those 'peaceful ways' he's jabbering about. Talk, Tiger."

Task 05–d.
REFUSE TO USE THE DEVIL'S TOOLS TO ACHIEVE JUSTICE

"Jesus modeled practical love for us; He died crucified so that God could forgive us and bring justice. So let's **refuse to use the devil's tools to achieve justice.** Consider history; Jesus' followers have been *the salt of the earth* and brought justice so often that no honest person can deny it. God changes men's hearts and through them transforms societies. He orders us to fight for justice with love, not hate. Our prayers, forgiveness, and compassion will defeat the oppressors; violence only provokes more injustice." I stopped and thought, "All that came from my lips?" It was the longest speech I'd ever made!

Some looked thoughtful; others glared defiantly. Chuey set his rifle aside, took his knife from his belt, and told me, "You're leaving this meeting right now." He tried to step around Mincho, but the giant stepped deftly to shield me.

I begged the men, "Please, let me help you plan more effective strategies."

Shouting erupted and led nowhere. Mincho's finger poked my chest again. "Comrade, it's my turn to give the socio-economic orientation next week and I want you to explain those 'effective strategies' to all our associates, not just this planning group. We have open minds, right, Commandant Chuey Ochoa?"

"We can't let him go, Mincho Medina! He knows too much."

The giant stood close, looking me in the eye. No, he was probing deeper than that. He was reading my heart. "Do you promise before the Most High God not to reveal SRE operations to the authorities?"

"I promise, sir. Before Almighty God, I swear not to inform on you."

The meeting ended. Roger was waiting outside and asked, "Why the yelling?"

"First, let's get out of here." My hands trembled as I untied my horse.

The dog snarled and I turned. Chuey was pointing his jumbo cigar at my heart. "Return, watchman, and it'll be the grand finale of your miserable life."

"You don't frighten me, Chuey Ochoa," I lied.

"Then you don't know me. I've put an end to guys a lot tougher than you! For me, killing a man is the same as squashing a maggot!"

Mincho approached, Chuey sauntered away, and Roger handed the giant the book on social action. "It's from Christ's point of view, sir. It's yours."

"Thank you, comrade. I also have something for you; come to my room. Hold your dog, Tiger, and I'll hold my pooch, Popcorn, or they'll scrap again."

Mincho handed Roger a magazine with the title *Liberation!* "A church I attended once sent me this. It deals with social justice."

Roger analyzed the article through his thick glasses and scowled. "It assumes all rich businessmen are evil. To generalize that way was Marx's fatal error. My uncle owns a large fishing boat and is the most generous person I know. This twists Bible texts to provoke envy, Mincho. We must be careful not to let such propaganda manipulate us. Hatred robed in religious jargon is still hatred."

Mincho studied Roger's face. "I'll read the book you gave me. Go with God." On our way out, he told me quietly, "I like that young man. He's got depth."

Back in town, Roger urged, "Come meet my brother Nando, my younger brother, Julio's twin. He works on my uncle's fishing boat; they're dry docking it for extensive repairs, and Nando has a few weeks off. Mouse already hired him to work with explosives in the place of a worker who's mending from injuries; rocks fell on him where miners had failed to shore up the ceiling properly."

Nando greeted me with a hearty "Ahoy!" At first, I thought he was Julio; both had the same ready smile and roguish look in their eyes. Anna noticed my surprise and told me, "Nando's a mischievous imp, just like Julio. Neither inherited Pacho's cautious spirit. I wish they'd follow Jesus."

Nando rolled his eyes. "Aw, mom, we're not pagans. We know God exists."

"Well, son, He does a little bit more than just go around existing!"

Nando started telling sea yarns and Julio was enthralled. I tried to open conversation about the Lord Jesus Christ and Julio told me, "Me and Nando, we don't believe the Bible like our parents and Roger do. A lot of my pals don't."

"So what?" Roger set his Bible on the table. "I often ran into phony sophistication in the university; arrogant know-it-alls who'd say, 'An educated person knows that the Bible is outdated,' as if saying so made it true. They have no idea of what it really says; judgments based on ignorance are stupid, totally illogical."

Nando held up the Bible. "But would God simply leave us a book of stories about miracles that we must believe for Him to accept us? Is that logical, Tiger?"

"No, Nando, it wouldn't be logical. But it's not the case; God didn't just leave an account of miracles and walk off, and we don't enter His kingdom by human logic. We enter by faith—not blind belief, but trust in a Person with whom we have a loving relationship. He awakens this trust in our hearts if we let Him."

"So what did God leave us besides the Bible?"

"Jesus sent the Holy Spirit to live in us and established His church. I've been reading its history; across the ages believers who've followed the inspired Scriptures have brought the best benefits to the nations and, in spite of human flaws, have always given a witness for Christ through the power of God's Holy Spirit."

Anna put her arms around her twins' shoulders. "Listen to Tiger, and let God awaken your faith."

Nando asked me questions about Jesus and we chatted. Pacho started to argue, but Anna wiggled her fingers at him, signaling him to hold off.

"Do you feel God's conviction stirring in your hearts?" I asked the twins.

Their faces reflected inner turmoil and Nando nodded. "Storm winds are troubling my soul. Is that what you call 'conviction'?"

Talk was taking a healthier tack, and soon the twins asked our Lord Jesus to forgive them and change their wayward hearts. Both tears and laughter followed. Nando lifted up the Bible. "Hey, I see this book in a different light now! Aye! Even God's miracles make sense, once the storm abates."

A searing lightning barrage lit the sky the night before Nando, Julio, and others were to be baptized, and thunder was nonstop. Such relief when dawn brought gentle calm! We gathered in the pine-scented chapel before going to the river. Jethro had come from Arenas and Colombo, the trucker, arrived with his wife Hilda who rushed up to Arturo. "God healed me, Pastor! Tiger and Lucy anointed me with oil and prayed for my back in Jesus' name. For the first time in months, I can walk without pain. I believe in Christ now; I know He's our Savior and I'm going to follow Him. Please baptize me too, Pastor Arturo. *Please!*"

"That's great, Hilda, but I thought you already believed in Jesus!"

"Not really. Not in my heart. I attended church so Colombo wouldn't nag."

Roger, Julio, and their father entered with grim expressions and stood inside the door quietly. Talk ceased and Pacho gasped, "Nando!"

Roger stammered, "Nando! He's dead! He . . . He died last night when . . .!"

He choked up and Julio stammered, "Rock toppled from a mine shaft elevator and hit him; they took him to the health center but . . . He died in my arms."

We were stunned, but managed to pray with them, and Pacho asked Arturo, "Do we postpone the baptisms? Anna can't come; she's staying with the body."

"I came to be baptized!" cried Julio. "Mom insisted on it; she said it's what Nando would have had me do. Nando would have done the same if I'd died."

Task 05–e.

DISINFECT A FLOCK FROM CONTAGIOUS, DISHEARTENING LEGALISM

Dazed by grief, we trudged upriver toward where it was deeper, as Arturo preferred to baptize by immersion. Jethro kept up, using his cane, and I assisted him over rough spots. That jaunt was about to give us a harsh reminder to **disinfect a flock from contagious, disheartening legalism.**

Julio sighed. "Nando was so joyful; looking forward to his baptism!"

"A shame," Mouse answered, "because only baptized people can be saved."

Julio froze, his mouth open, and I embraced him. "Your brother's in God's merciful, loving hands. No place is more secure." He was not listening.

Lucy's eyes flashed and I thought she was going to slap Mouse. "Pharisee! You'd have God send folks to hell for any reason! You malign His grace!"

Julio crumbled, sobbing bitterly. Jethro sat by him and waited for him to recover. "Son, Jesus loves us sinners and doesn't seek reasons to squash us. My sister Carla died giving birth when she was your age. Like Nando, she was awaiting baptism, but her pastor delayed it by imposing non-biblical requirements. I know God forgave her sins; Christ died for her, so He'd never condemn her simply for the error of a foolish pastor. God forgave Nando too, Julio."

"Are you sure?"

"Absolutely. A person's lost because he rebels against God, not because some cleric fails to baptize him. Baptism is God's blessing, to confirm our repentance and trust in Jesus, not a stumbling block to zap any who lack it for reasons unrelated to faith." Julio stood, wiped his eyes on a sleeve, and we resumed walking.

Arturo stepped to Mouse's side. "Any rule that we impose on believers beyond what Jesus or His apostles explicitly stated will lead to hurtful legalism."

"But it takes discipline to follow strict rules. So the more, the better—the more spiritual we are!"

"No! No! Multiplying rules destroys spirituality."

We had to step on stones in the river where the bank was steep, and I steadied Jethro as he stepped from rock to rock. I asked him, "How can we get those whom we lead to do God's work as actively as the members of your church?"

<table>
<tr><td>

Task 05–f.

LAY OUT SHORT
STEPS IN ORDER FOR
VOLUNTEERS TO
REACH LONG-RANGE
GOALS
</td><td>

"Do what someone did with these stepping stones; they located them close together. I'd fall in if I had to jump. So **lay out short steps in order for volunteers to reach long-range goals.** Seeing progress bit by bit heartens them."

"What's the first 'short step,' besides praying, for a cell in Mudhole?"
</td></tr>
</table>

"Let folks obey the foundational commands of Jesus, as the infant church in Jerusalem did. Do you remember them, Tiger?"

"Jesus gave them with *all authority in heaven and earth* so I remember them."

"*Believe in Jesus, repent, and be born again by God's Spirit.* These three go together; like the trinity, you can't have one without the other two.

"*Baptize.* This is more than the water rite; it initiates the new, holy life.

"*Have Communion.* Participate in Jesus' body and blood, and in the life of His body, the Church.

"*Love.* This includes forgiving, caring for the needy, and being good citizens —rendering unto 'Caesar' what is due to the state and society.

"*Pray.* This includes personal and family devotions, spiritual warfare, petitions, signs, and wonders.

"*Give.* Be stewards of three T's entrusted to us: *Treasure, Time, and Talent.*

"*Teach and heed the Word.* We witness, train leaders, and go to new fields."

"Excellent, Tiger! Those are the first stepping stones for your cell."

"Including Communion, Jethro? I've never been approved to serve it."

"You are now." Arturo had been listening and clasped my arm. "You've proven your ability to lead; I approve you, just as the apostles had new leaders serve Communion in their homes, in Acts 2."

"I don't feel very qualified. Don't I need to be ordained? Won't leaders of our churches' National Alliance object? Doesn't your church belong to it, Jethro?"

"I'm on their advisory board. We know a movement for Christ won't spread in the villages if leaders have to satisfy traditional ordination requirements. We don't enforce every detail of the Alliance statutes, only what the Word requires."

Arturo added, "You meet God's requirements to lead, Tiger, if not man's, and we'll lay hands on you to confirm it. We all need the Lord's anointing."

"I appreciate your confidence. Do we need all those little Communion cups?

That would be a hassle in some villages, Arturo."

"The apostolic congregations used one cup."

"What if someone has AIDS?"

Arturo hesitated and Jethro replied, "Just dip the bread in the cup, Tiger. The old liturgical term for that is 'intincture.' No germs migrate to new victims."

"Another easy step! You make God's work so easy for us!"

"Not I. Jesus did away with the heavy traditions and fulfilled the hundreds of commands of the Mosaic Law so that we could live in freedom of the Spirit."

"What do you tell non-believers who attend Communion, Jethro?"

"Don't simply say, 'Don't take this.' Say something like, 'Visitors, please watch closely as we do a most sacred act, because we hope and pray that you'll also receive Jesus and join us in this fellowship.' Some do, in the moment."

Passing below the deserted mine, Arturo pointed. "That hole in the ground gave the town of Saint Muñoz its nickname. Olga's dad called it 'Saint Muñoz of Bat Haven' in jest because so many bats used his mine as their bedroom."

Roger remarked, "The town's changed a lot since then. Our church has to change too, or it'll remain stuck in an irrelevant rut."

"No, son!" Pacho scowled. "Truth cannot change. You read too many books."

Jethro patted the barber's shoulder. "Truth doesn't change, but methods do. Roger won't stray by reading. You've raised him well; he has keen discernment."

"But it's dangerous for a congregation to change how it does things, sir!"

"Truths are permanent, of course. 'A church that marries the spirit of the age will soon be a widow.' But mere methods require change, Pacho, so we seek constant renewal. Serve in the world without joining it."

"Shouldn't Arturo preach a series of messages on renewal?"

"It doesn't come from lectures, or every church I know would be experiencing it. It comes when we let the Holy Spirit move us to love and obey Jesus."

We passed the rapids that I'd seen from the cliff above and Jethro pointed his cane at the white water. "Look, Julio. Jesus compared the Holy Spirit that lives in you to a river of living water. He also likened the Holy Spirit to the wind, and aptly. A congregation raises its sail to go where God wants. 'Winds blow, ships go. Winds abate, sails deflate.' So keep your sails trimmed, Julio."

"Aye, aye, sir!"

Pacho commented, "We can't make the wind blow. The Spirit will move or not move, as He chooses. We're at the mercy of heaven's winds. True, Jethro?"

"Not quite. Look at it from God's view. He isn't the one who holds back; heaven's winds never fail. He's always eager to fill our sails, but we must unfurl them by praying and obeying. What does God do if we don't pray, Tiger?"

"Nothing! Stop praying and the Almighty gets lazy!"

We came upon a knot of people standing around a small body. Gadget was there and told me. "It's the boy we hunted for. Been in the water for days."

"Did he drown?"

"His head was bashed in." Gadget lifted the body and started back to town.

Arturo sat, face in his hands and Pacho whimpered, "No baptisms now!"

"No, dad, no!" Julio grabbed his father's arm.

"It's just as well, son. The new believers were going to be baptized too rapidly anyway. Hilda hasn't even started our newcomer's class."

Task 05–g.

RESPECT BAPTISM'S ORIGINAL PURPOSE AND EFFECT

I begged Pacho, "Don't dishearten the newborn lambs. Satan would take advantage. Let's let the Holy Spirit use baptism to assure them. Let's just obey Jesus and **respect baptism's original purpose and effect.**"

"But they're so new in the Faith! Some might still have bad habits."

"So we wait until they can walk on the water before being . . . "

"Keep moving!" Arturo stood. "Pacho, baptism in New Testament is not a graduation ceremony following a newcomer's class; it is a repentant sinner's response to Jesus' invitation. Let new believers study the newcomers' doctrine *after* baptism, as the apostles had them do."

"But what if they do bad things after baptism?"

"Who doesn't? Baptize newborn believers and bring them into the body where there's love and power. Few leave their vices without this help."

"Do you agree, Jethro?" Pacho asked. "What if we baptize someone and then he gets drunk on the next holiday?"

"Then he'll be a drunken Evangelical! Deal with his sin within the Body where there's pastoral care and grace, and he'll stay faithful; he knows he's 'in.' But he'll leave and never return if you deny baptism and he gets drunk."

"Now that you mention it, last year several left us when we delayed baptism to check out their faith. They lost heart when they committed any peccadillo."

"The apostles baptized as soon as seekers confessed faith in Jesus. Requiring a time of probation tempts them to pretend to be perfect. It's phony because they're newborn babies in Christ and can only fake it. When they're finally baptized, Satan whispers, 'You got in by your merits.' A wise pastor is a good plumber; he unclogs the flow of God's grace, removing man-made rules that obstruct it. Baptism isn't for perfect people; it's for us sinners who repent."

I commented, "John the Baptist drove off those who felt they were good enough for baptism and called them snakes. When we doubt seekers' faith and delay baptism because they have flaws, our doubt becomes contagious and we make 'little ones' stumble; Jesus warned severely against that."

Julio asked Jethro, "You mentioned 'Evangelicals.' Is that what we are?"

"It depends on how you define it, son. Some call themselves Evangelicals and live a lifestyle that imitates Jesus and honors Him. Others wear the label, but preach such a superficial, individualistic, and self-seeking creed that is sickening."

At the pool, Colombo asked permission to speak. "I composed a song on the way; it's for Nando." He sang,

Come quickly dawn! God's glory fills the skies!

Hail the new beginning when with Christ we rise.

Oh joyful hope! God's trumpet gives us wing!

Gaze on Jesus' face and with archangels sing.

"Let's all sing it now." He helped us learn it and then had the ladies sing counterpoint. Hilda suddenly looked up. "Angels! Listen!" Echoes resounding between the lofty cliff walls created striking harmony. Checking her emotion, Hilda told about her new faith; then Julio and others told about theirs.

Arturo baptized the men and Anna baptized the women as Arturo spoke the proper words. He laid hands on them all, saying, "Freed from hell's judgment and risen with Christ for all eternity! Receive God's gift of the Holy Spirit."

We started back down the river path and Hilda pointed up. "Look, Lucy! How majestic these soaring cliffs! So high! Breathtaking! What a grand site for an outing with the children! I'm going to bring them here for a picnic."

"Really, Hilda?" Lucy tilted her head back. "Those crags give me the creeps!"

> ## Task 05–h.
> ### WARN PEOPLE OF
> ### FINAL JUDGMENT

Roger slowed to walk beside Jethro. "Arturo mentioned hell. I'm glad he has the integrity to **warn people of final judgment.** A university professor taught that hell is an archaic dogma; God punishes evil in this life and a loving God would not torture people in fire forever. What's your opinion, sir?"

"To say 'torture' paints God as a cruel fiend, twisting the truth. *Justice* sends men to hell, not *cruelty*. Hell is the place of absolute justice; its scales are perfectly balanced in the highest court of all. Heaven is not the place of ultimate justice, Roger; hell is. Heaven is the place of infinite mercy and unending grace that no one deserves. When hypocritical Pharisees stood in the way of God's grace, Jesus warned them severely of hell's punishment."

"Putting it that way shows why God's grace is so precious, Pastor Jethro."

"We fully appreciate grace when we see it against the dark background of God's just wrath. Men will get what they demand. A rebel once boasted, 'Better to reign in hell than grovel in heaven.' Two worlds will go opposite ways for all eternity: one with happy folk doing God's will, another with rebels doing as they will. Don't fear to offend; to warn of hell is the most loving thing we can do."

Julio told Jethro, "I'm sure glad they didn't delay our baptism, God really used it to assure me."

"That's one of its purposes, son. Acts 2:41 shows that evangelism is not complete until the new believer is added to an active church body by baptism."

"I'll tell my friends what God has done for me, sir. How can I do it without sounding preachy, as though I think I'm better than them, Pastor Jethro?"

> ### Task 05–i.
> WE NEED TO PROVIDE EASY WAYS FOR NEW BELIEVERS TO WITNESS TO THEIR FRIENDS.

"Throw a party, like Levi and Zacheus did. The good news flows best when new disciples tell friends and loved ones about Jesus. Julio; you're a 'son of peace,' one who opens up a new social network to the good news, like Cornelius and Lydia in the book of Acts. **We need to provide easy ways for new believers to witness to their friends.**"

"I'll throw a happy party, sir, after we've mourned Nando!" Julio hugged the old man. "Sir, you're an inspiration to me. You sacrifice to come here from Arenas over that bumpy road. You mentor Pastor Arturo and he's my spiritual father now, so that makes you my grandfather. I'm proud of that, sir, really honored."

"Thank you, son! You've blessed this old fossil!"

"I'll come to your party!" Mouse stepped to Julio's side. "I'll show your pals how to get the fullness of the Spirit. Glory! I'll pray for them with the power of the Almighty. Hallelujah!" He began to command God in an angry tone to demonstrate His power and his bellows echoed in the canyon.

> ### Task 05–j.
> RESPECT THE PLACE OF EMOTION IN A CHRISTIAN'S LIFE AND WORSHIP.

Lucy stepped in front of Mouse to face him. "Cool it! God isn't deaf! **Respect the place of emotion in a Christian's life and worship.**"

"I have power! I am the only one here that has the complete gospel. I . . . "

"I! I! I! Your ego's greater than your girth! If your gospel is so complete, then act it. Normal believers work with the Holy Spirit's power without getting hysterical. You scream demands at God as if He were your slave!"

Mouse walked on sullenly and Jethro chuckled. "Tiger, I admire how Lucy calms Mouse. No one else can. What kind of control does she have over him?"

"They grew up as neighbors and she's always treated him as a little brother."

"Lucy," Mouse whined, "one cannot be sincere without emotion."

"Of course. Emotion is normal; the fruit of the Spirit includes joy. But you take it to an extreme; people who don't know you think you're nuts."

Mouse asked Jethro, "Shouldn't we all be filled with the Spirit, sir? Isn't to feel holy emotion the whole point?"

"'Holy' emotion or 'wholly' emotion?" Jethro spelled the words. "Does the Holy Spirit fill us to get us excited? In Scripture, it was always to serve in some practical way. Acts 4 says, 'They were filled with the Holy Spirit and spoke God's Word with boldness.' Also, the Holy Spirit came on Samson and he tore a lion to pieces. Mouse, we want you to slay the lion, not roar like him."

"Mouse goes to one extreme," Lucy told me when we were alone, "and Arturo goes to the other—hardly any feeling at all except for Olga."

"Then between the two, God might bring balance!"

God brought balance a week later without help from Mouse or Arturo. New believers took friends to Julio's party and celebrated. Spiced pineapple flowed and so did God's sweet grace as several joyfully joined Jesus' royal family.

CHAPTER 5: CONFIRM THE GRASP AND THE PRACTICE OF LEADERS' TASKS

05–a. Deal decisively with crushing feelings of guilt. Verify a promise to repentant sinners: *If we say that we have no sin, we are deceiving ourselves and the truth is not in us. If we confess our sins, He is faithful and righteous to forgive us our sins and to cleanse us from all unrighteousness.* 1 John 1:8–9 Find how to make Satan trot: *Resist the devil, and he will flee from you.* Jas 4:7

05–b. Detect and arrest gossip before its venom spreads. Spot what defiles churches more than most vices: *The tongue is a small part of the body, and yet it boasts of great things. See how great a forest is set aflame by such a small fire! The tongue is a fire, the very world of iniquity; the tongue is set among our members as that which defiles the entire body, and sets on fire the course of our life, and is set on fire by hell.* Jas 3:5–6

05–c. Use the power that Jesus promised, to spread the Good News regardless of backlash or danger. Note what Jesus gives witnesses: *You will receive power when the Holy Spirit has come upon you, and you shall be My witnesses both in Jerusalem, and in all Judea and Samaria, and even to the remotest part of the earth.* Acts 1:8

Learning key Bible verses helps one witness for Jesus. Learn the verse about each of the following topics unless you already know it or a similar verse:

God grants the joy of talking to Him daily, 1 Thess 5:17: *Pray without ceasing.*

We do not save ourselves, Titus 3:5: *He saved us, not on the basis of deeds which we have done in righteousness, but according to his mercy, by the washing of regeneration, and renewing by the Holy Spirit.*

Trust in the only sacrifice for sin that obtains eternal salvation, Heb 9:12: *Not through the blood of goats and calves, but through his own blood, he entered the holy place once for all, having obtained eternal redemption.*

Our participation in Jesus' resurrection is our hope for eternal life, 1 Pet 1:3–4: *He has caused us to be born again to a living hope through the resurrection of Jesus Christ from the dead, to obtain an inheritance which is imperishable and undefiled and will not fade away, reserved in heaven for you.*

God saves us sinners by means of our faith in Christ, John 3:16: *God so loved the world, that He gave His only begotten Son, that whoever believes in Him shall not perish, but have eternal life.*

Saving faith comes with repentance (change of heart), Acts 2:38: *Repent, and each of you be baptized in the name of Jesus Christ for the forgiveness of your sins, and you will receive the gift of the Holy Spirit.*

Assemble regularly with believers, Heb 10:25: *Stimulate one another to love and good deeds, not forsaking our own assembling together, as is the habit of some, but encouraging one another, and all the more as you see the day near.*

Which way are good works vital in salvation, as its **cause** or **effect**: *By grace you have been saved through faith, and that not of yourselves, it is the gift of God; not as a result of works, so that no one may boast. For we are His workmanship, created in Christ Jesus for good works, which God prepared beforehand so that we would walk in them.* Eph 2:8–10

Find three truths that Jesus told witnesses to tell all nations, before He ascended: *Thus it is written, that the Christ would suffer and rise again from the dead the third day, and that repentance for forgiveness of sins would be proclaimed in His name to all the nations, beginning from Jerusalem. You are witnesses of these things.* Luke 14:46–48

05–d. Refuse to use the devil's tools to achieve justice. See why Jesus did not fight in the world's way: *My kingdom is not of this world. If My kingdom were of this world, then My servants would be fighting so that I would not be handed over to the Jews; but as it is, My kingdom is not of this realm.* John 18:36

Civilizations all crumble in time. Verify what can sustain a just society. *Not by might nor by power, but by My Spirit, says the Lord of hosts.* Zech 4:6.

05–e. Disinfect a flock from contagious, disheartening legalism. Churches in pioneer fields often struggle with legalism and petty rules. Ascertain why believers should not count on the old Law to save or sanctify them: *Sin shall not be master over you, for you are not under law, but under grace.* Rom 6:14

Identify who leads us, to avoid "deeds of the body": *If you are living according to the flesh, you must die; but if by the Spirit you are putting to death the deeds of the body, you will live. For all who are being led by the Spirit of God . . . are sons of God.* Rom 8:13–14

Identify the best motive to be holy: *"Love the Lord your God with all your heart, and with all your soul, and with all your mind." This is the great and foremost commandment. The second is like it, "You shall love your neighbor as yourself." On these two commandments depend the whole Law and the Prophets.* Matt 22:37–40

05–f. Lay out short steps in order for volunteers to reach long-range goals. If you have urged your flock to do things in too general a way, then think through and define short steps with coworkers, for your next project.

05–g. Respect baptism's original purpose and effect. Misusing baptism makes seekers stumble. Verify its effect: *All of us who have been baptized into Christ Jesus have been baptized into His death . . . buried with Him . . . so that as Christ was raised from the dead . . . so we too might walk in newness of life. For if we have become united with Him in the likeness of His death, certainly we shall also be in the likeness of His resurrection . . . our old self was crucified with Him, in order that our body of sin might be done away with, so that we would no longer be slaves to sin.* Rom 6:3–7

When should a new brother in Christ be baptized?

[ ]   When he has been entirely sanctified, examined fully, deserving baptism.

[ ]   When he affirms faith in Jesus and wants to turn away from his sins.

ANSWER: The apostles baptized repentant seekers when they believed (Acts 2:41). Valid reasons to delay it include illness, avoiding hostilities, and reaching entire families; such practical reasons do not dishearten seekers.

05–h. Warn people of final judgment. Identify two kinds of people whom Jesus will raise: *An hour is coming and now is, when the dead will hear the voice of the Son of God . . . for all who are in the tombs will hear His voice, and will come forth; those who did the good deeds to a resurrection of life, those who committed the evil deeds to a resurrection of judgment.* John 5:25–29

05–i. We need to provide easy ways for new believers to witness to their friends. Find whom Peter promised salvation when a jailor asked how to be saved: *Believe in the Lord Jesus, and you will be saved, and your household.* Acts 16:31

New disciples share about Christ readily with friends when believers receive both with love. Note whom each of these new believers shared their faith with first:

- *Andrew*: his brother, Peter, John 1:41
- *Lydia*: her family, Acts 16:14–15
- *Prison guard*: his family, Acts 16:31–33
- *Crispus* (synagogue head): his family, Acts 18:8
- *Zacchaeus*: his friends, Luke 19:1–10
- *Levi*: his friends, Luke 5:27–32
- *Cornelius*: his relatives and intimate friends, Acts 10:24

05–j. Respect the place of emotion in a Christian's life and worship. Mouse overdid emotion; Arturo underdid it. Find what believers are to do always: *Rejoice in the Lord always; again I will say, rejoice!* Phil 4:4

Notice what God gives those who love and obey Jesus, John 15:9–11: *As the Father has loved me, I have also loved you; abide in my love. If you keep My commands, you will abide in My love; just as I have kept my Father's commandments and abide in His love. These things I have spoken to you so that my joy may be in you, and that your joy may be made full.*

Choose the most biblical purpose for the Holy Spirit to fill believers:

[ ]   Practical service for God.

[ ]   A trance-like worship experience.

ANSWER: Filling of the Holy Spirit is to serve God in a practical way.

Find joy's source: *Make my joy complete by being of the same mind, maintaining the same love, united in spirit, intent on one purpose. Do nothing from selfishness or empty conceit, but with humility of mind regard one another as more important than yourselves.* Phil 2:1–3

EVALUATE YOUR LEADERSHIP

1=Poor. 2=Planning to improve. 3=Doing well.

1-2-3   Deal decisively with crushing feelings of guilt.

1-2-3   Detect and arrest gossip before its venom spreads.

1-2-3   Use the power that Jesus promised to tell about Him regardless of danger.

1-2-3   Refuse to use the devil's tools to extend Christ's kingdom.

1-2-3   Disinfect a flock from the contagious, disheartening legalism.

1-2-3   Lay out short steps in order for volunteers to reach long-range goals.

1-2-3   Respect baptism's original purpose and effect and practice it accordingly.

1-2-3   Warn people boldly of final judgment.

1-2-3   Provide easy ways for new believers to witness to friends.

1-2-3   Know and practice the place of emotion in worship.

6.
Hell's Fiend Launches an Arrow
Labeled "Cruel Rules"

Task 06–a.

WARD OFF A "WOLF"
BEFORE HE DIVIDES
AND CONFUSES THE
FLOCK

While visiting some newly baptized believers with Roger, we had to **ward off a "wolf" before he divided and confused the flock**. This wolf wore a neon blue shirt with orange flames printed up the front and swaggered, grinning, as he entered Victor Calderon's house.

"I am Lorenzo Guzman and I pastor the most exciting church in town! We will hold our first meeting tomorrow. I hear you folks received Christ. Praise the Lord! Come worship with us and see real power!" He warbled the word "real."

"*Real* power?" Our host mimicked the warble. "What do you do with it?"

"Oh, I do things that Arturo Gomez' church can't do because they . . . "

"You certainly do, Lorenzo!" I stood and faced him. "You rob sheep!"

The phony smile morphed into a wolfish snarl. "Who are you?"

"You can't win people to Jesus. You lack the Holy Spirit's power. To build your flock you have to lure sheep away from other flocks."

"That's a lie! I have the power. I . . ."

"You're a proselytizing predator! Jesus warned about your ilk. You can't deny it; you're trying to do it right now!" Four bright eyes peered around a doorway. I winked at them and heard small feet scampering off as children's voices giggled and bayed like a wolf. Our host, Victor, grinned at me, nodding slightly. Lorenzo turned the same hue as the flames on his shirt and invoked a hearty curse on me as he backed out the door.

Roger wanted to tell his father about that encounter, and I went with him to the barbershop. Pacho snorted, "Oh, yes! I've heard how Lorenzo sneaks around looking for discontented believers. Other wolves are on the prowl, too; two young *gringo* 'elders' wearing ties and white shirts just left; they tried to sell a book by Joseph Smith and invited me politely to a 'social enjoyment' meeting."

"Jesus warned of wolves in sheep's clothing," I told Pacho. Those white shirts were woven from white sheep's wool!"

"Ho! New believers use my barber chair as a psychiatrist's couch and gripe that no one from our church visits them. Wolves take advantage of such neglect."

The Arenas bus stopped at the square across from Pacho's shop, and Jethro got off wearing his skunk skin hat and backpack. Roger and I took him to tell Arturo about the wolves, and Arturo asked Jethro to arm our workers to repel them. A few of us met with Jethro in the chapel, and Roger asked him, "How do we spot wolves when some pose as believers, as Lorenzo Guzman does?"

"Some do believe; Paul warned they'd come from *within* and *without*. Those from within are unethical Christians like Lorenzo who deceive the gullible. Spot these proselytizing wolves by these signs." He bared his teeth, growling. "*Sharp fangs* revile true shepherds, like the words of Joseph Smith." He sniffed the air. "*Big noses* detect discord to lure away discontented sheep, like JW's visits do." He jerked his head about. "*Shifty eyes* and *long ears* detect bleating lambs." He tiptoed. "*Padded paws* sneak around behind genuine leaders' backs." He seized Colombo, who jumped, startled. "*Long, dripping tongues* crave mutton!"

Our laughter quieted and Jethro urged, "Shepherd your flock alertly and it won't seek the greener pastures that wolves offer falsely. To do so, keep your cells small enough to give the care to each member that Scripture requires."

Pacho pulled on his moustache. "I still fear these cells will cause division."

"Only if a leader has a divisive spirit. To avoid this, name leaders who cooperate. Well-led, well-fed cells avoid division. A leader overlooks needs if he's the only one leading a big flock and wily wolves sniff out the neglect."

I recalled my ranching days. "I drove herds where rustlers and four-footed wolves prowled. Each man tended his part of the herd and we lost none, Jethro."

"Exactly! One leader cannot tend every member of a big congregation, so he delegates pastoral tasks to apprentices. A third of the world lives where hostile authorities persecute believers, so they meet secretly and are winning millions to Christ. Folks get intensive, close-up pastoral care in tiny groups that multiply."

"Really?" Colombo asked Jethro in his deep voice. "Then they do a lot more than study the Word. What can we do to keep groups multiplying that way?"

Task 06–b.
FORM SMALL CELLS TO DEAL SPECIFICALLY WITH SEEKERS AND NEW BELIEVERS

"**Form small cells to deal specifically with seekers and new believers**. Don't herd them into Bible study groups for mature believers; let them first attend a seeker's group, meet Christ and, above all, host cells for friends."

Pacho grimaced. "It's not biblical for new believers to host groups, Jethro."

"What about Cornelius, Zacheus, Crispus, Lydia, and Levi? These *seekers' cells* were exclusive, only for folks whom the host invited, folks that could chat with each other easily—no outsiders. They're not churches and the leader, if a new believer, needs a mentor who's more mature. Are you with me, Pacho?"

"Yes, some of those seekers gave parties for friends to hear the gospel."

"Good! Deal specifically with both *seekers* and *seeders*. When folks know Jesus and are baptized, let them gather in a seeders' cell that helps them sow the gospel among friends and host seekers' cells. Seeders' cells, like the group that met in Lydia's home after baptism, are the ones that multiply rapidly to sustain a movement; a new believer can gather friends who won't go to meetings led by us clergy. Such new leaders need a mature believer to mentor them."

Pacho asked, "But how can new believers do what even our elders can't?"

"Easily." Jethro said. "They're free from rusty traditions. A father who receives Jesus can lead family worship and bring in friends; they can pray, encourage one another, and discuss what they've learned. Have you seen this, Tiger?"

"Yes. They do it easily if another believer is mentoring them. That's our job. You've mentioned cells for seekers and seeders. What about mature believers?"

Jethro wrote on the board SEEKERS–SEEDERS–FEEDERS. "Mature believers no longer in touch with seekers or seeders become *feeders* and study the Word to feed not only themselves but also their families and the less mature. Remember these three types of people; we must deal with all three differently. In new movements, the same flock often serves all three kinds of folk, but in older churches like ours, *feeders* pull seekers and seeders into Bible study groups before they've done their job unless a very strong mentor puts on the brakes."

"A *mentor?*" Pacho was twisting his moustache. "Is that scriptural, Jethro?"

"What did my namesake, Moses' father-in-law, Jethro, advise Moses to do?"

"To name leaders of thousands, hundreds, fifties, and tens. The leaders of ten did the shepherding and the others served as administrators. Okay, as 'mentors.'"

"Precisely! To equip them all, God gave the Ten Commandments; they were the foundation of the Old Covenant, but they're not our foundation now, Pacho."

"Now wait! My catechism based much of its teaching on the Ten Commandments; they're basic for our morality and conduct, Jethro."

> ### Task 06–c.
> AVOID LEGALISM, DISCERNING BETWEEN THE OLD AND NEW COVENANTS' TWO VIEWPOINTS

"True, but Jesus and His apostles revealed that a *New Covenant* governs us now. We must **avoid legalism, discerning between the Old and New Covenants' two viewpoints.** How did Jesus say to make disciples, Pacho?"

"Ah . . . By teaching them to obey all the things that He'd commanded."

"Correct. So Jesus' commands—not the Ten Commandments—are the foundation for what we do now, the basic building blocks for discipling. Do you recall how Jesus concluded His *Sermon on the Mount*? Two men built houses. Colombo, you're the wise man who built on the rock. Tiger, you're the idiot who built on sand. Now, go to work, both of you! Okay, Pacho, what happened?"

Colombo and I pretended to build and when Pacho mentioned rain, Jethro poured water on my head and I fell. "What was Jesus' point, Pacho?"

"One must not only hear the Word as both men did, but also obey it."

"Half right. Jesus said '*My words*,' not *the* Word. He's the rock; we build on it when we hear and obey His commands. If we fail to found a new flock on Jesus' commands, then Satan will rush in and fill the vacuum with spiritual-sounding rules and activities, dethroning Jesus as its true Head."

"For sure, Jethro!" Roger agreed. "Our young people and new believers worry so much about petty rules and dogmatic teachers are too eager to indulge them!"

"Help them love and obey Jesus first. Take a few weeks to teach Jesus' basic commands; after that, teach anything they need. Obeying Jesus is the start for all ministry; ground disciples on this rock and wolves can't get to them."

Pacho nodded. "Okay, Jesus' commands come first. But after that, shouldn't we keep Old Testament commands as well as the New? They're all biblical."

"We'll stone you!" Jethro raised his cane as if to strike Pacho. "You cut hair Saturday before sundown! The Law demands your death! Bring rocks, men!"

"Wait! Wait! I didn't mean that."

"No, because the Holy Spirit in you gives you the love that fulfills the Law, as Jesus said. The Ten Commandments are not our foundation now, but they do affirm moral truths. The Jerusalem council in Acts 15 didn't even mention them when deciding how much of the Jewish *Torah* Gentile believers had to obey. The New Testament repeats all ten commands as binding in different contexts except the Sabbath law; in Acts 20 they had Communion the first day of the week."

"So who changed the day of rest, Jethro?"

"No one changed the *day*, Pacho. God changed the *Covenant*. Paul said some believers considered all days equal; it's up to your conscience. Israel's Law had rules for civil, military, and religious life, and Paul revealed two other purposes: expose sin and prepare a nation to receive Jesus. The New Covenant's *Kingdom of Heaven* is for all nations; it differs radically from the Old Covenant."

"But it can't differ so very much," Pacho insisted. "Both are in God's Word!"

Jethro extended his arms. "The *cross* divided all history into two great epochs; one arm pointed back, the other ahead. One special day—the *seventh*—interposed between them; God the Son lay in absolute repose in a tomb, fulfilling perfectly the Sabbath law. On the *first day*, He rose, *first fruits* of a wholly new covenant and creation. By His life, death, and resurrection He fulfilled the entire Law, including the command to rest on the Sabbath. God governs us now, not by laws that condemn to death, but by His life-giving Spirit. See it now, Pacho?"

Pacho shrugged and Jethro opened his backpack with its white stripe. I asked if it was really a skunk pelt and Jethro sniffed it. "Dyed buckskin. Pacho, the New Covenant differs hugely from the Old; look over this *'Chart of Contrasts.'*"

	Old Covenant based on LAW		New Covenant based on GRACE
Duration	Temporary	⇔	Eternal
Awards and punishment	Material temporary	⇔	Spiritual, eternal
God's presence	Behind a veil, earthly temple	⇔	Holy Spirit in believers forever
God's forgiveness	By repeated animal sacrifice	⇔	One eternal sacrifice
Inheritance of the faithful	Brief, secured by relatives	⇔	Eternal, assured by Holy Spirit
Dealings with nations	Separation, conquest	⇔	Reconciliation, discipling
Main rule for conduct	Keep law to avoid punishment	⇔	Live in the Spirit, with love
Normal day of worship	7th day recalled the old creation	⇔	1st day Jesus rose, new creation
Pastoral care by elders	Judges governed with severity	⇔	Elders shepherd with humility

Jethro added, "Some pastors proclaim God's grace, but still inflict legalism on folks by infusing the old legal mentality into the covenant of grace."

"So how does God make stubborn folks obey now," Colombo asked, "since He no longer governs by laws enforced with death?"

Task 06–d.
BECOME HOLY BY NURTURING THE FRUIT OF THE SPIRIT WITH OTHERS' HELP

"The Holy Spirit replaces our hearts' stubbornness with God-given virtues. Jeremiah foretold this long before Jesus' birth; God would write His laws in our hearts. We **become holy by nurturing the fruit of the Spirit with others' help.** Galatians 5 lists it: *love, joy, peace, patience, kindness, goodness, faithfulness, gentleness, and self-control.* These are the very essence of holiness."

"Really?" Colombo asked. "I thought holiness was simply living without sin."

"Is a toad holy? It has no sin. Holiness avoids sin, but does much, much more."

Julio groaned. "Leaping over Mount Silverado would be easier for me than to be holy. I can't live with purity like you guys do."

"You will soon, son." Jethro clasped his arm. "When you were baptized, you died with Christ to sin and were raised with Him to new life. God is working in you, transforming you into the image of His Son. In His sight, you're a saint."

"A saint! Wow! Kiss my ring, guys! I'm a saint, Pastor Jethro? That's crazy!"

"Scripture says you are. You're a spiritual baby and you still dirty your spiritual diapers—a soiled saint, like all of us! Take heart, Julio; you're growing and God watches your faltering steps with joy. Join a group that makes disciples as Jesus said, and you'll grow faster than that papaya out there."

We prayed for Julio and I exhorted, "Let's deal with holiness in small groups just like we're doing now and the Lord will grant victory. There's tremendous power in a cell group that's also a real church."

Colombo asked, "How can a cell group be a *real church*, Tiger?"

"Just let your group do what God requires of a church. What more can God expect of your group if it follows His orders? Call it what you may, *small group, cell, flock, house church, congregation,* or simply *Colombo's Cluster.*"

Jethro sighed. "The word 'church' has been so abused! Define it, Tiger."

"We know it means both the universal church and a local congregation, but the New Testament also uses the word for the closely-knit groups that met in homes in a city or area—the regional body. Church history mentions no buildings used solely for Christian worship until nearly three centuries after Christ."

"Are buildings bad?" Colombo asked. "Have you read about that too, Tiger?"

"No building is intrinsically good or bad; that depends on how people view and use it. Excess institutionalism and professionalism weaken churches, and buildings can reinforce those excesses. Common sense and financial reality forbid forcing all churches to build; it would kill church multiplication in our field."

Roger clapped. "God has given 'professor' Tiger the gift of wisdom!"

"For sure!" Arturo agreed. "Let's name him as a shepherding elder."

"You're joking! Me, a shepherding elder?" A cyclone of doubts assailed me.

"Tiger's new in the faith!" Pacho sputtered. "You forgot that, Arturo!"

"Does mere *time* produce spiritual maturity? Or living in the Spirit, obeying Jesus? Tiger's grown more in a few months than most believers do in a lifetime." Pacho pondered this, agreed, and they prayed to commission me there and then.

"In conclusion," Arturo ordered, "all elders will lead a cell for new believers."

On our way out the door, Jethro tapped the papaya with his cane. "Look, Tiger, how this plant's shooting up! Someone's pushing its 'fast forward' button!"

"That's because it symbolizes our movement. Hey!" I jerked Pharaoh away from it. "Respect the symbol, Pooch!"

Task 06–e.

PROPHESY IN SMALL GROUPS THE WAY PAUL SAID, TO STRENGTHEN, EXHORT, AND CONSOLE ONE ANOTHER

Back in our mudhole quarter, I'd see the need to **prophesy in small groups the way Paul said, to strengthen, exhort, and console one another.**

Lucy met me at the door. "Hey, why the starry-eyed look?"

"I can't believe it! Arturo had them name me as an elder! Was he insane?"

"A shepherding elder? I'm glad!" She hugged me. "It's about time!"

"Arturo ordered all the elders to lead cell groups for new believers."

"All?" She broke away. "He was insane! Those elders won't nourish the new-born, not even Arturo; he serves only heavy meat, not milk!"

"Whoa! Arturo can correct their errors. He's a lawyer and knows the Word."

"He'll correct them, all right! He wields the Word as if in a courtroom! So exact and challenging! To have to be right always is not right—win a debate, but ruin a relationship. You listen to folks, but Arturo's communication is one-way."

"You've honed your blade a bit sharp, Lu!"

"Have I? What will Simon teach? He doesn't respect the Bible and will use his group to carry out his own selfish aims. He's a puppeteer; he manipulates people. And Mouse is a *pulpiteer*; he'll use his group just to preach his wild visions."

"So cynical!"

"No! God will give us leaders who treat new believers with patience, but He'll raise them up from among those who receive Jesus. Just wait. You'll see."

Frantic shouting in the street startled us later that day, and we ran to the door. Mouse had wasted no time to gather his group. "A vision! Blood will run in our streets! Hell's agents will attack our homeland! Glory! Thousands will die!"

"Glory to our merciful God!" Gadget guffawed as he left shaking his head.

"Sad!" I groaned. "Mouse never learned the New Testament purpose of prophesying in a small group. 1 Corinthians 14:3 says believers prophesy to *strengthen, exhort, and console*."

"Not to warn sinners by predicting punishment like Jeremiah and others did?"

"That was a main aim of Old Testament prophecy. Paul was defining how 'all' are to prophesy now. Hear what 1 Corinthians 14:24–25 says, Lucy: *If all prophesy, and an unbeliever or an ungifted man enters, he is convicted by all, he is called to account by all; the secrets of his heart are disclosed; and so he will fall on his face and worship God, declaring that God is certainly among you.*"

Task 06–f.

EXTEND "MENTORING CHAINS" AS THE APOSTLE PAUL TOLD TIMOTHY TO DO

"Ahoy!" Julio called to me across the square that night; he and his grandfather Gerardo came bearing a treat—a bowl of berries! I tried some and they were superbly sweet. The old man used them to illustrate how to **extend "mentoring chains" as the Apostle Paul told Timothy to do.** "Anna planted them and they sent out runners that started new plants. We give the surplus to our neighbors and tell them the gospel." Gerardo drew a plant in the dust with his toe. "Jesus likened growth in His kingdom to that of plants." He drew more plants. "Its creeping runners take root, sprout, and new plants send out more runners. A church sends out runners too, with its God-given DNA."

Julio asked, "Can we multiply churches like this in the villages, Tiger?"

"We can if we train leaders the way Paul told Timothy to do it: one trains others who train still others at the same time. Jethro's church multiplies that way. Leaders break the chain if they wait until every church can afford an academically-trained pastor. There are never enough new leaders then, to keep multiplying."

Gerardo remarked, "Inflated egos also wipe out the runners." He rubbed out a plant with his foot. "I've seen plenty of 'em! Proud leaders won't share real authority with apprentices. They got to run things and loathe letting the work grow beyond their control. They just want their own flock to grow forever bigger and start no new ones. They'd win hundreds more to Jesus if they did."

After I ate the last berry, Gerardo clasped my shoulder. "Tiger, I been watching you. God will use you to extend His work. He gave you the vision. Others are too busy griping to step out, but you will surely lead them out of that darkness."

They left and I puzzled over Gerardo's prophecy that I'd extend God's work.

Task 06–g.

EXTRACT ROOTS OF BITTERNESS BEFORE THEY DEEPEN AND DESTROY BOTH HATER AND HATED

Sharp voices disrupted my musing. A tall dandy strutted beside Evita under the town's one street lamp, wearing a short, black matador's jacket fringed in orange with silver buttons, skin-tight trousers tucked into high, shiny black boots and a gold chain at his waist. She told him, "Boozed and confused you are, my *elegantísimo* friend!" The word oozed with sarcasm. "Thank you, kind sir, but I prefer you not escort me home." The chain of events that ensued would teach me to **extract roots of bitterness before they deepen and destroy both hater and hated.**

"To the mattress, girl! No woman refuses Duke Reyes-Castillo!"

"This one does. Back to your barstool! Good night, you sorry aristocrat." He seized her arm and she jerked away. "Enough of your courtly attentions. *Chao!*"

"Stop your prudish act, woman! Look." He took bills from a vest pocket. "You'll earn more tonight than in a month teaching your brainless brats to spell."

"Ohhh! I'm not a woman for rent, sir! And my pupils are not brainless brats."

He grabbed her and she slapped him. He pinned her arms inside his powerful biceps, trying to kiss her as she jerked her face from side to side. Fury seized me; I sped and pulled him away. For being drunk, he was fast; a fist hit my chin, lights flashed, and I swayed. Another hammered my jaw. When my head cleared, I was lying in dust. He kicked my face and aimed another, but I managed to draw my pistol. Backing off, he strutted away. I rose and lurched dizzily toward my kiosk.

"Poor thing!" Evita supported me. "Let me help you. My valiant liberator!"

"Who'd that arrogant bully say he was?"

"Duke Reyes-Castillo, the spoiled son of an old Spanish family. He runs cattle on a large range to the south. He calls himself a duke, but that stuffed piñata hasn't a drop of noble blood in him!"

"Oh, that one! I've heard of him. He treats his cowhands like serfs!"

Evita steadied me as I wobbled back to the kiosk. I learned later that the Wasp had heard the ruckus, gone to her window, and observed Evita helping me.

The next day, back home, Lucy's sobs woke me. "What's wrong?" I asked.

She kept weeping and I asked Tino, "What's with your mom?"

"I didn't do nothing, Papa."

I found a note with no signature on the table. "*The teacher of your son was embracing your husband as he staggered in the town square last night.*" Oh, no! I tried to tell Lucy what happened, but she wouldn't listen, not even when I pointed to bruises on my face. Blinding bitterness had thrust down deep roots!

I took my hat, intending to escape her accusing looks, but the inquisition began. "So, whom do you plan to see now?"

"Members of my cell group."

"Does your little cell group include an alluring young schoolteacher?"

Angry, I left without replying. As I passed Gadget's shop, Evita was mounting her bicycle; seeing me, she got off. "There you are! My courageous protector! You rescued me!" She rushed to embrace me; I pulled away, but not in time. When I came home a couple hours later, I walked into a tornado.

"I saw you!"

"You saw me what?"

"With *her*, hugging in the street for everyone to see!"

I felt frustrated and grabbed my hat. Lucy cried, "So now where?"

"Oh, the barbershop, I guess. But I'll stay with you if you want."

"It doesn't matter to me. Go where you want!" She ran into the bedroom and flung herself sobbing on the bed. The root of bitterness had deepened even more.

Pacho was out, but Anna was mopping the shop. "Hi, cowboy. How's Lucy?"

"Fine. Well . . . Not really, Grandma. She was crying. She misunderstood something I'd done. I sure don't understand women; I understand horses better."

"Your problem is that you're a man! You should assure Lucy every day in some way that you love her."

"She knows I love her. She's just grouchy, like a stubborn mare."

"She's not a horse, cowboy!" She gave me a push. "Go explain to her what she misunderstood, and read a husband's duty in Ephesians 5." I told her I would, and she added, "Read in chapter 6 how to care for your whole family. Wait. Maybe I can help. What happened? Don't skip any stupid thing you did!"

Meanwhile, as I'd learn later, Lucy heard a car, dried her eyes and opened the door. Wanda toted in a big box and pointed at the new car. "Like it? It has blue leather seats. Listen, Lucy. Simon's going to build me a bigger house with a grand piano and paintings by famous artists. Do come visit me then."

"You're very kind, Mrs. Alvarez."

"And you're very fortunate; your husband's so handsome! The girls are all eying him. Even your son's teacher."

"Why do you tell me this?"

"Oh, I'm sure it's not a serious affair. Now, I saw you admiring a vase that I had on display in our store window last week. So . . . " Wanda opened the box.

"The ceramic vase! Its butterfly designs are gorgeous! And it's large!"

"I'm glad you like my little gift. Say, I saw the loveliest philodendrons up the river by the old deserted mine. Let's go dig one up and put it in the vase."

"Why not? Tino's in school and I can leave Davey with Martha." Two minutes later Lucy was cruising through town on a blue leather seat.

"Wait, Tiger!" On my way home, Evita stopped her bicycle, panting. "I've raced all over to find you! Wanda said a kid got into the old mine and to get you to help me find him since you're their only security personnel and it's too dangerous for me to go alone. I got a flashlight. Hurry, before he gets lost or hurt."

We trotted up the path by the river to the abandoned mine and Evita pointed at the entrance. "It had a safety barrier, but some fool removed it."

I pushed thorny vines aside from the cavity's mouth, crouched, and crawled into the darkness. "Wait there, Evita. These derelict tunnels are hazardous."

Even with the flashlight, I could see little until my eyes got used to the dark. Taking careful steps forward, I passed side tunnels and ducked under rotting beams that sagged under tons of earth. I stopped where the ceiling had collapsed.

Noise behind me gave me a start. "Any sign of the boy?"

"No, *Señorita*, and I've seen no footprints in the dust. Wanda was mistaken. Hey, you shouldn't have come in here; it's extremely dangerous. Let's get out."

"Look! Stalactites are hanging from the rafters."

"Bats, sleeping."

"Oh no! Everywhere!" Evita scampered to the entrance and we crawled out. She laughed. "Look at you! Am I as arrayed with dusty cobwebs as you?" We went back down to the river to wash, and she asked, "Want in on a secret? I'm going to marry your neighbor Gadget. We haven't announced it yet."

"Wonderful, Evita! May God bless you!"

While washing our arms and faces, Evita exclaimed, "Such cheerful rapids! They're alive! Hear the foaming water sing as it dances over the rocks! Oh, it'll make a great background, Tiger, to paint your portrait! Let's . . . "

"Ah . . . I don't think so. It would not be proper."

"Together with your wife, of course, my scrupulous friend!"

"How's your project progressing, to bring culture to our backward town?"

"I'm glad you asked! I formed a Development Committee with other teachers; we leveled a soccer field by the school and made benches so folks can watch or hold public events. We fenced it so players don't have to share it with cows. Wait! Give me your hand to steady me over these slippery stones."

Meanwhile, Lucy and Wanda were coming up the river path; Lucy was toting a spade. "Do philodendrons grow up this high in the mountain's cool air?"

"Why not, girl? I guess they're farther up the river than I thought. Come."

Rounding a bend, Lucy saw me helping Evita over the wet stepping-stones. "Oh! There's Tiger! What on earth is he doing here with . . . with *her*?"

"Why, I can't imagine, dear!" Wanda's voice dripped with sweetness. "There's a nice secluded swimming hole up there—a romantic, peaceful place."

Lucy dropped the spade and ran back toward town, leaving hot tears on the path behind her; the Wasp cackled shrilly.

"Did you hear a weird laughing sound just now?" Evita asked. "It sounded so sinister that it made my blood freeze!"

"I thought it was a bird. These noisy rapids make it hard to hear."

Back home I found a large vase with butterfly designs smashed to bits in our yard and Lucy would not speak to me.

The next day, as I learned later, Evita had come to our house while I was gone. "Tino didn't show up at school today, Lucy. I hope he's not sick."

"He's fine. Did you enjoy your little swim yesterday, *Señorita*?"

"I didn't . . . Just a minute! What are you referring to, Mrs. Garcia?"

"Nothing. Nothing at all. Thank you for your visit, Miss Schoolteacher."

"Wait! Speak frankly, woman!"

"You know what I mean! Don't come lying in my house."

"Good heavens! You're . . . You're trying to create an all-out quarrel!"

"You're no teacher; you're a rotten hooker going after the fathers of . . ."

Evita slapped Lucy and a hair-pulling, cat-scratching frenzy ensued. Neither won; it left only bruised emotions and unresolved hostility, Evita left disheveled, sobbing. The bitter root's malignant tentacles had sunk still deeper! Lucy, her face bleeding and hair tangled, took our two frightened boys to Mouse's house. "Your face!" Martha gasped. "You're all scratched! What happened?"

"Oh, I just want to die! I can't think straight. I . . . Please take the boys."

"Mama!" cried Tino. "I don't wanna stay with Bones. I wanna be with you!"

"Okay, darling. I'll stay with you, but not in that house with your father."

Thus, I found the house empty and no supper. Fear struck, sharp as a snake-bite. I heard Tino and Andy playing at Mouse's house, but was too proud to go and beg Lucy to return and left for work hungry.

The next morning the house was still empty. Agony! I slept without eating until a motorcycle woke me. Arturo entered and paced, hitting a fist into his palm. "The cells are failing except yours. Visitors that don't know the Bible feel ill at ease; older ones make them feel shy and seekers don't return. What's wrong?"

My mind was elsewhere. "Why's Lucy so quick to distrust me?"

Arturo didn't hear either and asked me again why the groups were failing. I forced myself to answer sanely: "They form wrong. Form temporary seekers' cells first; new believers should hold private meetings with friends where they can take part comfortably, like Levi, who gathered his pals to celebrate knowing Jesus. Folks are at ease when they meet in homes of friends or kinfolk."

"You said seekers' cells are 'temporary.'" Arturo stopped pacing. "Why?"

"They're just for seekers and their friends. It's usually a party. When they receive Jesus, the group can become a regular cell for new believers."

"You've said this before, but I guess it never registered. Oh, the inertia of tradition! Will you start such a group, Tiger, for seekers and their friends?"

"I already did, two here in town and one in Los Vientos, but I don't lead them; the owners of the homes hosts them and I mentor the hosts."

"Hey! That's the key!" A rare smile appeared. "You gave me the key, Tiger!"

"Pastor, I don't understand why Lucy's so quick to distrust me, she . . ."

He had rushed out. I could not sleep so I crossed the street and told Martha, "I have to see Lucy. Please. I . . ."

"She won't talk to you, Mister Garcia." My slim neighbor stared at me icily.

Mouse came to the door. "Leave Lucy alone. God's punishing you."

Tino ran to me. "Papa look, my pants are like new! Bones sewed the holes."

I returned to the empty house, and griped to Pharaoh, "A giraffe with a sore throat couldn't be more miserable!" I read Ephesians 5 as Anna had urged; it said I was to love my wife as Jesus loved the Church. I poured out my agony: "Lord, cut the bitter root from my heart, from my family, and from our church!"

CHAPTER 6: CONFIRM THE GRASP AND THE PRACTICE OF LEADERS' TASKS

06–a. Ward off a "wolf" before he divides and confuses a flock. Wolves slander, brag, smile falsely, twist Scripture, and teach false dreams. Find how to deal with them: *Reject a factious man after a first and second warning, knowing that such a man is perverted and is sinning, being self-condemned.* Titus 3:10–11

Verify how to resist satanic attacks: *Take up the shield of faith with which you will be able to extinguish all the flaming arrows of the evil one.* Eph 6:16

06–b. Form small cells to deal specifically with seekers and new believers. Notice why Jesus befriended bad people that Levi had gathered. *"It is not those who are well who need a physician, but those who are sick."* Luke 5:31

Which more commonly causes divisive discontent within a congregation?

[ ]   Forming small groups.

[ ]   Keeping believers who have God's pastoral gift from leading groups.

ANSWER: Stifling the use of gifts causes much more frustration.

06–c. Avoid legalism, discerning between the Old and New Covenants' two viewpoints. Find a vast difference between them: *I will make a new covenant with the house of Israel . . . not like the covenant which I made with their fathers in the day I took them out of Egypt . . . I will put My law within them and on their heart I will write it.* Jer 31:31–33

The Law led to death. Verify what Jesus did with its lethal rules, Colossians 2:14: *Having canceled out the certificate of debt consisting of decrees against us, which was hostile to us, and He has taken it out of the way, having nailed it to the cross.*

Contrast the two covenants' duration: *The ministry of death . . . engraved on stones, came with glory . . . how will the ministry of the Spirit fail to be even more with glory? . . . if that which fades away was with glory, much more that which remains is in glory.* 2 Cor 3:7–11

Romans 3:20 reveals that a purpose of the old Law was to make men aware of sin. Find another purpose: *Before faith came, we were kept in custody under the law, being shut up to the faith, which was later to be revealed. Therefore the Law has become our tutor to lead us to Christ, so that we may be justified by faith.* Gal 3:23–24

The New Covenant does not apply to an earthly nation, but says to obey the state. Notice an exception to this rule: *They commanded them not to speak or teach at all in the name of Jesus. But Peter and John answered and said to them, "Whether it is right in the sight of God to give heed to you rather than to God, you be the judge."* Acts 4:18–19

Find whom God promised Abraham that he'd bless through an heir: *"Go forth from your country, and from your relatives and from your father's house, to the land which I will show you, and I will make you a great nation, and I will bless you, and make your name great, and so you shall be a blessing, and I will bless those who bless you, and the one who curses you I will curse. And in you all the families of the earth will be blessed."* Gen 12:1–3

To avoid confusion of the Old Testament legalistic outlook with the New, use the following list of *"Contrasts Between the Old and New Covenants."* If it still does not convince you, then visit an Orthodox synagogue.

Duration of the covenant

Old Testament: Temporary, Jeremiah 31:31–32; Hebrews 8:13

New Testament: Eternal, Hebrews 9:15; 10:10–14

Means of God's forgiveness

Old: Sacrifice animals repeatedly, Hebrews 9:6–10; 10:1–4,8

New: One eternal sacrifice, Hebrews 9:10–11; 10:9–10

Rewards and punishment

Old: Material, earthly, temporary, Deuteronomy 30:15–20

New: Spiritual, eternal, Ephesians 1:3; John 3:16; Revelation 20:13–15

Main miracle, base of the covenant

Old: God's people escaped slavery crossing through the sea, Exodus 14

New: The Resurrection of Jesus, Luke 24; Romans 6:1–14; 1 Corinthians 15

Initiation by a covenant sign

Old: Circumcision of the flesh, Genesis 17:10; Deuteronomy 10:16

New: Baptism, Matthew 28:18–20; Romans 2:29

Commemorative dinner

Old: Passover lamb, Exodus 12:1–15

New: Body and blood of Jesus (Communion), Luke 22:19–20; John 6:25–68

God's presence

Old: Behind the veil in an earthly temple, Exodus 25:8–9,26; 40:35; Leviticus 16:2

New: Holy Spirit resides in believers forever, John 14:16–17; 1 Corinthians 3:16

Outstanding prophet

Old: Moses gave Law, later prophets applied it, Numbers 12:6–8; Deuteronomy 34:10; John 1:17

New: Jesus gives grace, truth, John 1:1,14–17; Act 3:22–26; Colossians 1:15; Hebrews 1:1–4

Outstanding priest

Old: A High Priest served in the earthly Most Holiest Place, Leviticus 16:1–27

New: Jesus intercedes in glory, Hebrews 4:14–16; 5:4–10; 9:1–14; John 14:2–3

Outstanding king

Old: David conquered nations, Leviticus 20:23; 1 Samuel 18:7; 2 Samuel 7:8–16

New: Jesus deals with all nations, Matthew 28:18–20; Ephesians 5:23; Revelation 19:15–16

Dealings with the nations

Old: Separation and conquest, Exodus 6:6–7; 19:1–6; Deuteronomy 2:31; 4:1–9

New: Reconciliation, discipling, Ephesians 1:4; 2:12–22; 3:1–6; Colossians 1:19–22; Revelation 7:9

Access to God

Old: To see or approach God meant death, Judges 6:22–23; Exodus 19:12; Leviticus 10:1–2

New: Jesus' obedience opened the way to approach God, Romans 5:18–19

Main norm for conduct

Old: Keep laws to avoid punishment, Deuteronomy 6:1–3; 28:15–26; Exodus 20:18–20

New: Live in Spirit, motivated by love, John 14:15; Romans 13:8–10; 2 Corinthians 3:3–11

Prescribed form of corporate worship

Old: sacrifices of animals and holidays, Leviticus chapters 1–7,23

New: In spirit and truth, and with the Lord's Supper, John 4:24; Acts 2:42

Means of sanctification

Old: A person's own efforts, keeping laws, Leviticus 11; Isaiah 55:7

New: Rebirth, transformed by Holy Spirit, Romans 14:1–9; 1 Peter 1:3; 1 Timothy 4:3–5

Basic requirement for justification

Old: Keep the Ten Commandments, Exodus 20:1–17

New: Repent and believe in Jesus, John 3:16; Luke 24:44–49

God's guidance

Old: Laws governed many details of the people's life, Exodus 18:20; 24:3

New: By Word and Holy Spirit's illumination, Ephesians 1:17–20; John 14:26; Romans 8:1–27

Main revelation of foundational truths

Old: Giving laws on Sinai, visions by means of angels, Numbers 12:6; Deuteronomy 1:9

New: God became man, made known in flesh, John 1:1–3; Hebrews 1:1–3; 2:2–4

Purpose of learning God's word

Old: Keep God's Law and be prepared for the coming of Christ, Galatians 3:3–26

New: Be transformed, built up, equipped to serve, Romans 8:23,28–30; Ephesians 4:11–12

Pastoral care by elders

Old: Judges governed severely, Exodus 18:24–26; Acts 15:10

New: Elders shepherd with humility, Titus 1:5–9; 1 Peter 5:1–4; Matthew 20:25–28

Guideline for giving

Old: Tithe (one-tenth of net earnings), Deuteronomy 12:11

New: Give joyfully what one purposes in his heart, 2 Corinthians 9:7; 1 Corinthians 16:2

Inheritance of the faithful

Old: Temporary, protected by kin, Genesis 12:1–2; 17:1–8; Deuteronomy 6:1–3; Ruth 4:13–7

New: Eternal treasure assured by Holy Spirit, Ephesians 1:3–14;
1 Peter 1:3–5

Main day of worship

Old: Seventh day recalled the old creation, Exodus 20:8–10

New: First day recalls Jesus' resurrection, first fruit of new creation,
Acts 20:7

06–d. Become Holy by nurturing the fruit of the Spirit with others' help. New believers often view holiness as heeding petty bans. Find what the Holy Spirit produces in those whom He sanctifies, and note virtues that you will give more attention, Galatians 5:22–23: *The fruit of the Spirit is love, joy, peace, patience, kindness, goodness, faithfulness, gentleness, self-control; against such things there is no law.*

Verify what to do with our bodies and minds, Romans 12:1–2: *Present your bodies a living and holy sacrifice, acceptable to God, which is your spiritual service of worship. . . . Do not be conformed to this world, but be transformed by the renewing of your mind, so that you may prove what the will of God is, that which is good and acceptable and perfect.*

Find what Jesus advised His followers, Luke 9:23–24: *If anyone wishes to come after Me, he must deny himself, and take up his cross daily and follow Me. For whoever wishes to save his life will lose it, but whoever loses his life for My sake, he is the one who will save it.*

06–e. Prophesy in small groups the way Paul said, to strengthen, exhort, and console one another. Paul revealed how prophesying differs now from that of the Old Testament. Find three purposes to prophesy, 1 Corinthians 14:3: *One who prophesies speaks to men for edification, exhortation, and consolation.*

Find God's warning against trusting in illusory dreams: *"I am against those who have prophesied false dreams," declares the Lord, "and related them and led My people astray by their falsehoods and reckless boasting; yet I did not send them or command them, nor do they furnish this people the slightest benefit." Jer 23:32*

Note. Dreams from God like Pilate's wife had are vivid and give vital news. Many Muslims have seen "Isa" in a dream and turned to Jesus.

06–f. Extend "mentoring chains" as the Apostle Paul told Timothy to do. Select biblical guidelines for mentoring chains that you should initiate or improve:

[ ]   Trust God to empower flocks to multiply like grain.

[ ] Let new congregations meet in homes and keep multiplying without stopping the flow of God's grace to build a chapel for every new flock.

[ ] Mentor new shepherds like Jesus and His apostles did.

[ ] Delegate pastoral responsibilities to many apprentices.

06–g. Extract roots of bitterness before they deepen and destroy both hater and hated. Note things that replace discord in a flock: *Let all bitterness and wrath and anger and clamor and slander be put away from you, along with all malice. Be kind to one another, tenderhearted, forgiving each other, just as God in Christ also has forgiven you.* Eph 4:31–32

EVALUATE YOUR LEADERSHIP

1=Poor. 2=Planning to improve. 3=Doing well.

1-2-3 Ward off "wolves" before they divide and confuse a flock.

1-2-3 Form cells to deal with "seekers," "seeders," and "feeders," to keep multiplying.

1-2-3 Avoid legalism; discern between the Old and New Covenants' outlooks.

1-2-3 Gain holiness by nurturing the *fruit of the Spirit.*

1-2-3 Prophesy in small groups to *strengthen, exhort, and console* one another.

1-2-3 Extend mentoring chains as Paul told Timothy.

1-2-3 Extract roots of bitterness before they destroy both hater and hated.

7.
The Serpent's Creeping Spawn Infiltrates an Unwary Community

Arturo had asked the elders to meet at his office the next day and I forced my feet to take me. Arturo told us, "Troubling news. Chuey Ochoa's brother, Torivio, is out of prison. He's more devious than Chuey, so take care. Now, I called this meeting to let Tiger tell how he gathers seekers. Go ahead Tiger . . . Tiger?" I was lost in thought—Lucy and I together was heaven; without her, it was . . . "*Tiger!*"

<table>
<tr><td>

Task 07–a.

USE GOD-GIVEN
SPIRITUAL GIFTS
TO PRACTICE THE
"ONE ANOTHER"
COMMANDS

</td><td>

"Oh! Ah . . . Seekers feel awkward studying what's beyond them, so avoid heavy doctrine until they're ready, and chat with them. Let the group interact; **use God-given spiritual gifts to practice the 'one another' commands.**"

Colombo asked, "How big can a group be and still have everyone interact?"

</td></tr>
</table>

"A dozen or so adults. If folks go passive, the group's too big. Help everyone take part, including kids, and do all the ministries that the apostles required."

"But can a group so small do all those tasks, Tiger?"

"No, not by itself. Plan joint activities with other cells. For instance, Pacho's cell helps folks in mine that need guidance for family problems. Isolated cells become ingrown and ineffective, detached from the larger body of Christ."

"Shouldn't groups form with folks who have a particular ministry? One group cares for the needy; another evangelizes kids and so forth."

"A group doing only one ministry can meet a specific need, but in time it neglects its own members' needs. We serve each other better in a cell with a variety of gifts, and a family with kids should be together in a cell at least once a week."

Colombo asked me, "Does Scripture say to mix the gifts like that, Tiger?"

"Paul compared believers with their various gifts to the organs of one's body; everyone serves the others in love. The 'one another' commands also appear throughout the New Testament: 'exhort one another,' 'teach one another,' 'correct one another,' and the like. We'll develop this interaction in our groups."

"No!" Simon aimed his hook at me. "We elders are to hold sessions to define rules; it's not our job to lead your cells."

Arturo replied, "Yes it is. God tells elders to shepherd His flock; He does not tell them to make rules."

"You're making rules now, Arturo! Having cells will cause rivalry and . . . "

"No, Simon! Rivalry comes when two leaders vie to steer a group at the same time, like two chauffeurs pulling a steering wheel in opposite ways."

"We're not that stupid!" snapped Simon.

"We're doing it right now!" I said. "Simon, a pastor's like your cattle driver. To move a big herd he needs several cowhands or he'll lose cattle. We . . . "

"So now we're a bunch of cows, Tiger?"

"Well, Jesus called us sheep and they're even dumber than cows. A shepherd of a growing congregation needs co-pastors to help care for us dim-witted sheep, in groups small enough to give all the attention we require."

"Now we're brainless sheep!" Mouse laughed and sided with Simon.

Arturo slammed his briefcase shut, rising. "Last one out lock the door!"

"Wait!" begged Pacho. "I'll lead my group, but I need more orientation."

"I'll lead a group, too, 'Turo," Colombo said, "but I need help, too. Please!"

Arturo sat back down. "Okay. Tiger, recap the guidelines for cell worship."

"Before starting, assign things to adults and kids. Help them overcome shyness, but don't rush timid people. To begin, pray to consecrate the time and place. A chapel gives a worshipful aura; but in a home, we sense God's presence in other ways. Excessive informality weakens worship." Simon and Mouse were chatting and their rudeness stung, but I continued. "Do as Scripture says. Break bread, plan work to do during the week, discuss texts dealing with it, and ask for God's help. Let folks ask and answer questions. If gabby folks grab all the attention, ask others to comment. Avoid always having the final word; if you're dogmatic, others will be too, and fellowship will go sour."

Arturo said firmly, "Pacho, let your cell care for people with personal or family problems; Anna has that gift. Mouse, your cell will evangelize the miners."

"I'll evangelize everyone, 'Turo, not just miners. And now that I see what you want your groups to do, I've decided not to lead one—not as you say."

"I won't either, I tell you," snorted Simon.

"This meeting has ended," replied Arturo hotly. He left his office without a word and mounted his motorcycle.

"Wait!" I followed him out. "Don't let those jokers discourage you."

"I thought they'd support the cells if I named them as leaders."

"That's a sorry reason to designate someone as a leader, sir."

"I didn't think. Stupid of me! I have to resign." He revved the motorcycle.

"No, Pastor! One cannot reason well when feeling frustrated. Wait and . . . "

The Caribbean pulled up. Colombo leaped from the cab, shouting over the motorcycle's din, "Pastor, thieves stole my warehouse! Help me! Do something!"

"Slow down! Who? And how did they carry off a building?"

"Help, me! You're a lawyer. Chuey and his brother, Torivio Ochoa, forced me to sell my warehouse for almost nothing. They slit sacks of coffee and came at me with machetes. They'd have filleted me, so I signed a receipt, a formal document; two of them witnessed it. Chuey's in on it; he's putting up a sign, *People's Warehouse*. Do something!"

"Your signature legalized it," Arturo replied, "unless witnesses will testify that they coerced you. I can threaten legal action; I'll do what I can, right now!"

"Don't go alone!" I cried, but he had already sped off, much too fast.

Task 07–b.
APPRECIATE WHY OUR FATHER IN HEAVEN ALLOWS HIS BELOVED CHILDREN TO SUFFER

I arrived at work without supper again. I was learning to **appreciate why our Father in heaven allows His beloved children to suffer**. Wanda hurried out to inform me, "Arturo has a broken leg and it's your fault!"

"My fault? How did he . . . ?"

"They disconnected the brakes on his motorcycle while he was wrangling with your subversive friends in Colombo's warehouse. He hit a tree."

"Oh, no! But why accuse me?"

"You entangled my church with those revolutionaries. Also, Tiger, you cannot lead a group; a church leader has to keep his family in order. Have a good night."

An owl mocked my gloom that night with its one-note song. In the morning, I couldn't face the empty house with its accusing stillness and went to ask Arturo for advice. His plastered leg rested on a stool and he removed crutches from an empty chair for me to sit. I told him, "Sorry about your leg. Lucy left me; she believed Wanda's gossip. I can't lead a cell if I can't lead my own family."

"Not you too!" He hit his desk with a fist. "Satan never relents! He knows how effective the cells can be. Be patient, Tiger, God is greater than Satan."

"I can't live without Lucy."

"Nor I without Olga." He stood, reached for her photo, but fell back into the chair with a groan. "Why does God let His children suffer so much, Tiger?"

"I came to ask you that. It's driving me crazy."

"I'll try to answer sanely. God punishes us to correct our bad ways because He loves us; He also lets us suffer as He did Job, to teach us precious truths."

"Then we must be learning a lot of very valuable stuff now!" I grumbled.

"Don't be cynical, brother. Paul revealed that our suffering doesn't compare with the glory and rewards that we'll receive from our Lord in the resurrection."

"The present pain is still a reality. I've done things that hurt Lucy, but why's she so quick to believe lies about me? I can't sleep; I'm all confused!"

"My idiocy pains me worse than my leg; I told all the elders to lead groups. Jesus prayed all night before naming the twelve, but I acted hastily. Tiger, don't desert your group. God gave it to you to care for."

"Then, don't you desert your flock either, Pastor."

Task 07–c.
EXAMINE MOTIVES TO LEAD AND CONFESS TO GOD ANY SELF-IMPORTANCE

Mouse and Simon entered, voiced sympathy for Arturo's injury and to my surprise Mouse made no loud prayer. What ensued would show why leaders must **examine motives to lead and confess to God any self-importance.**

"I changed my mind," Simon told Arturo. "I'll lead a group of cattlemen."

"I'll lead a group too," Mouse stated, "and meet in the chapel."

"Good, but not in the chapel. The cells are to take Christ into homes."

The two left and I asked Arturo, "Why the change? What are they up to?"

"Simon lets nothing important go on unless he runs it, and Mouse craves an audience. Why'd I asked them to lead cells? I was a fool!" He slapped the side of his head. "Trouble's brewing, Tiger; leaders moved by ambition bring pain."

"Isn't love for Jesus and His people the only true motive to lead believers?"

"Yes. Jesus told leaders to be humble servants. History shows that ruthless egos and greed unite to destroy God's work, trigger wars, and corrupt societies."

Task 07–d.
CORRECT PEOPLE'S BAD HABITS WITHOUT GRUMBLING, GOSSIPING, OR JUDGING

Heels clicked outside and Wanda entered. We were about to see why wise leaders **correct people's bad habits without grumbling, gossiping, or judging.** She screeched, "Mouse is screaming insanely in the chapel! Disgraceful! Folks will think we're maniacs. Stop him, Arturo!"

"Oh no! I told him not to meet in the chapel. Now what? How can I lead a congregation when not even the elders heed me?"

"Precisely!" A crooked smile flashed briefly across Wanda's clouded face.

"I'll go straighten him out!" Arturo took a step without his crutches and fell. Wanda peered down at him. "You let Tiger abet those revolutionaries. I dedicate myself to rectify the town's corruptions, but you give me no cooperation."

"Mrs. Alvarez," groaned Arturo as I helped him to his feet, "simply scolding folks for bad habits doesn't sanctify them. They need the Word and the work of the Holy Spirit. Pardon my frankness, but you must correct your own habit of condemning people. You only say bad things about people. You never . . . "

"Is that so? Well, everyone—absolutely *everyone*—speaks ill of me, lying, and you do nothing! You've said people should not lead in a church if they neglect their family. Well, here's Tiger. Do your duty; forbid him to lead any group."

"I'll make my own decision about that, ma'am."

I left, and in a sleep-depraved daze, followed my dog aimlessly. He growled; Chuey was going to the People's Warehouse, followed by his Doberman. I followed; I'd have it out with that bearded bully. Outside the shed, his dog came at me, but Pharaoh seized its throat and shook it violently. They writhed so that it took a while to grab Pharaoh's collar and jerk him away; by then he'd choked the attacker to death. It occurred quietly, as Chuey's dog could not breathe.

Chuey saw me enter and hurled sacks of corn on top of a bale. Making sure he was packing neither firearm nor knife, I approached and accused him, "You and your thugs caused Arturo Gomez to break his leg."

"Oh, poor boy! I'll send him flowers."

"Yeah, funny! Why don't you just leave us alone? We don't bother you."

"But you do bother me, scumbag watchman. You convince gullible miners to leave us; they become Jesus creeps like you and abandon our noble cause."

> ## Task 07–e.
> ### ACHIEVE SOCIAL JUSTICE BY USING METHODS THAT ALSO ARE JUST

"No! They fight social ills in Jesus' way. Doesn't your cruelty bother your conscience? I'm as eager as you are to help the miners; let's discuss in a civilized way how to **achieve social justice by using methods that also are just.**"

"Your way's for weaklings, Puritan. Scram. I got work to do."

He shoved me toward the door, saw his dead dog, and spoke with tense lips. "Go, meddler, before I cut your guts out. Show up at an SRE meeting and . . . "

"Mincho invited me. I'm going to cooperate with him to help the miners . . . "

"No, Tiger Garcia. Absolutely *no!*"

"Yes, Chuey Ochoa. Absolutely *yes!*"

We stood glaring at each other. "Without a weapon, Chuey, you're just a windbag." His face reddened and I turned to go, adding, "Someday you and I will clash and it'll be explosive and fatal, but God will be my shield."

"Not 'someday.'" He stepped agilely, blocking my path to the door and took his cigar from a shelf. "Right now, I'm finishing you." He pulled the oversized cigar in two; he had hollowed it out to hide a thin stiletto! With a click, the blade extended further. My mouth went dry and fear paralyzed me as the slender tip came nearer, pointed at my navel. "Say your final prayer, creep."

Leaping, Pharaoh seized Chuey's wrist and he dropped the blade, cursing. Holding his bleeding wrist, he backed away. I held the dog back, picked up the slim blade, stepped outside, and hurled it into the river close by. "All right, friend," I challenged, "now that you've played your cowardly little trick, let's get it over with." I took a step toward him and he backed up.

"Tiger, I swear by all the saints and the Holy Virgin, someday I will terminate you and your Christ will not save you. Your dog neither."

I tried to stay calm. "Only Jesus will bring the justice you say you want."

"That's a myth."

"And your golden myth that Marx and his socialism bring paradise? Where has it done so? It's impotent except to bring poverty and death. *Hasta luego.*"

To calm myself, I sat on a bench in the square. Mincho came and joined me. I reminded him why Nando had died in the mine and he growled, "I hate Simon Alvarez. Every cell in my body hates him! I'll see that the miners get revenge."

I asked why he had such a special hatred for Simon and he said, "Nando would be alive if Simon obeyed the safety laws. I read Roger's book; it tells how Christians have led in combating social ills such as cremating widows in India, slave trade, child labor, racial discrimination, and infanticide."

"I hope you pressure Simon into dealing humanely with his miners; he pays no attention to me. I'll do anything to help except violence; just tell me what to do."

"You're not experienced in this, Tiger; you'd get hurt. Just pray and leave the rest to me; I know how to get Simon to treat his miners and cowhands fairly."

Mincho left; I saw Lucy enter the market and started after her, but she saw me and darted into the ladies' room. This hurt more than if Chuey had sunk his blade into my heart and twisted it! Uh oh—Wanda saw Lucy too, and followed her. I returned to the bench, sat beside Mincho, and waited for Lucy to come back out.

CHAPTER 7: CONFIRM THE GRASP AND THE PRACTICE OF LEADERS' TASKS

07–a. Use God-given spiritual gifts in cells to practice the "one another" commands. Find what occurs if "all" discuss truth: *If all prophesy and an unbeliever . . . enters, he is convicted by all . . . the secrets of his heart are disclosed, and so he will fall on his face and worship God, declaring that God is certainly among you.* 1 Cor 14:24–25

Find things that God tells His people to do reciprocally: *Teach one another,* Col 3:16; *Confess sins to one another,* Jas 5:16; *Be kind to one another,* Eph 4:32; *Comfort one another,* 1 Thess 4:18; *Submit to one another,* Eph 5:21; *Forgive one another,* Eph 4:32; *Pray for one another,* Jas 5:16; *Admonish one another,* Col 3:16; *Exhort one another,* Heb 3:13; *Serve one another,* Gal 5:13; *Show patience to one another,* Eph 4:2; *Encourage one another,* 1 Thess 5:11.

Choose small group worship guidelines that need attention where you work:

[ ]   Prepare in advance for adults and children to take part.

[ ]   Consecrate the time and the place with solemn prayer to begin meetings.

[ ]   Break bread. Put the bread and cup of Christ's presence on a cleared table.

[ ]   Pray to praise God, heal, confirm plans, and intercede.

[ ]   Sit in a circle and let all speak to edify, console, and exhort one another.

[ ]   Make plans for what members will do for Christ during the week.

[ ]   Encourage all to talk; do not let attention-seekers or know-it-alls dominate.

[ ]   Prepare children to briefly tell or act out Bible stories, along with adults.

[ ]   Help everyone voice praise in song, testimony, or citing Bible verses.

[ ]   Change postures. Stand or kneel in accord with local custom.

What do believers do as a group, besides obey Jesus' commands, to be a *church*?

[ ]   Specialize in a ministry, in order to do it well.

[ ]   Do all ministries that God requires, in close cooperation with other cells.

ANSWER: Do ministries in harmony and cooperate with other groups.

07–b. Appreciate why our Father in heaven allows His beloved children to suffer. Find comfort for believers who suffer: *We are children of God, and if children, heirs also, heirs of God and fellow heirs with Christ, if indeed we suffer with Him so that we may also be glorified with Him . . . the sufferings of this present time are not worthy to be compared with the glory that is to be revealed to us.* Rom 8:16–18

07–c. Examine motives to lead and confess to God any self-importance. Identify good and bad motives for leading: *Shepherd the flock of God . . . exercising oversight not under compulsion, but voluntarily, according to the will of God; and not for sordid gain, but with eagerness; nor yet as lording it over those allotted to your charge, but proving to be examples to the flock.* 1 Pet 5:2–3

Which person is more likely to develop into an effective shepherd?

[ ]   One who receives the best grades in an examination on biblical truths.

[ ]   One who from the beginning helps his own family to obey Jesus in love.

ANSWER: To shepherd one's loved ones reveals a true pastor's heart.

See what the apostles did when returning to visit congregations that they had started: *They returned to Lystra and to Iconium and to Antioch, strengthening the souls of the disciples, encouraging them to continue in the faith, and saying, "Through many tribulations we must enter the kingdom of God." When they had appointed elders for them in every church, having prayed with fasting, they commended them to the Lord . . .* Acts 14:21–23

Identify a shepherd's qualities: *Appoint elders . . . namely, if any man is above reproach, the husband of one wife, having children who believe, not accused of dissipation or rebellion . . . above reproach as God's steward, not self-willed, not quick-tempered, not addicted to wine, not pugnacious, not fond of sordid gain, but hospitable, loving what is good, sensible, just, devout, self-controlled, holding fast the faithful word . . . able both to exhort in sound doctrine and to refute those who contradict.* Titus 1:5–9

07–d. Correct people's bad habits without grumbling, gossiping, or judging. Find how to avoid judgment: *Do not judge so that you will not be judged. For in the way you judge, you will be judged, and by your standard of measure, it will be measured to you.* Matt 7:1–2

07–e. Achieve social justice by using methods that also are just. Note why believers should obey civil laws and authorities: *Every person is to be in subjection to the governing authorities. For there is no authority except* *from God, and those which exist are established by God. Therefore whoever resists authority has opposed the ordinance of God, and they who have opposed will receive condemnation upon themselves.* Rom 13:1–2

EVALUATE YOUR LEADERSHIP
1=Poor. 2=Planning to improve. 3=Doing well.

1-2-3 Use God-given spiritual gifts in small groups to obey the "one another" commands.

1-2-3 Consecrate the time and place set apart for group worship in homes.

1-2-3 Appreciate why our Father in heaven lets His beloved children suffer.

1-2-3 Examine motives to lead and confess to God any self-importance.

1-2-3 Correct others' bad habits without grumbling, gossiping, or judging.

1-2-3 Achieve social justice by using methods that also are just.

8.
Despair Torments the Souls of the Faithful

Task 08–a.

LET FAITH IN
CHRIST OVERRIDE
FEELINGS, FEARS, AND
JEALOUSIES

While waiting for Lucy to exit the market, I pictured Chuey's warped grin as he came at me with that skinny knife. Wanda left the market. Had she gotten to Lucy again with her insidious gossip? How would it all end? A bitter lesson awaited me, to **let faith in Christ override feelings, fears, and jealousies.**

"MagiKleen!" A blaring loudspeaker jolted me. "Housewife's best friend! New queen of detergents! Buy MagiKleen!" Gadget was cruising in his taxi, newly painted brilliant orange, and a man was barking into a microphone. They stopped and the advertiser switched off the microphone to catch his breath.

I walked over to them and Gadget asked, "Like my new paint job?"

"It's even uglier now." I was in no mood for aesthetics. "Why flaming orange?"

"Paint was left over from Colombo's truck. Why so grumpy?"

"Chuey almost sliced my belly open. My dog jumped him."

"So what did you do to provoke your pal Chuey?"

"He coerced Colombo into selling his warehouse to the SRE. He also disabled the brakes on Arturo's motorcycle; he crashed and broke his leg."

"Oh? Chuey's flouted the law long enough; I'll arrest him. Where's he live?"

"In Los Vientos on Mount Silverado's top mesa—a dangerous, lawless dump."

"Get in, Tiger. We'll run up and bring him in."

"You won't arrest Chuey without a skirmish. He's always armed and he's wily. Besides, you can't drive all the way up there."

"Then I'll go by horse tomorrow with soldiers and sneak up on him. You can lead us to Chuey's house. Them villages don't have no street addresses."

"I couldn't evangelize there again if I showed up with the law. Don't go yet, Gadget; someone will die in vain. Chuey will just deny everything even if you did manage to arrest him. Get hard evidence against him first."

"Okay, pal, but don't get yourself degutted in the meantime."

"Hey, I'm in hot water with Lucy. Can I meet in your house with Victor

Calderon and his friends at six? It's to talk about the gospel of Christ."

"Of course. I'll have the tequila ready for your happy hour."

Meanwhile, as I learned later, the spark of Lucy's beautiful eyes had wilted as a tidal wave of desperation swept her into an abyss of unreasonable despair. Seeing her troubled face, fear gripped Tino and Davey and became panic when she took them to Martha. "I give you my children. I'll bring their clothes."

"No! No!" screamed Tino. "Mama, Bones isn't our mother! Mama!"

Martha noticed Lucy's blank face and lifeless eyes. "I'll watch them until you recover your . . . uh . . . your peace of mind."

I couldn't bear going into the empty house, so I wandered down beyond the end of our lane to pray beneath cottonwoods that grew by the river. A twig broke behind me; I turned and spied familiar black hair ducking behind a bush. "Tino! Why spy on me?"

"I escaped. I'm supposed to be staying with ol' Bones. Mama cries all the time. Mouse says God is punishing us. Are we awfully wicked, Papa?"

"Oh, son, it's a dreadful misunderstanding. Where's your mother now?"

"Home, getting our clothes. Look. Bones sewed my torn shirt; it's like new!"

"Call her 'Aunt Martha.' Go back while I talk with your mother."

I found Lucy stuffing a small shirt into a bag. "What are you doing, Lu?"

"What does it matter to you?"

"Lucy, I can't live alone. You . . . "

"Let your beloved schoolteacher accompany you then."

"Lu! That's not fair! You know I love only you! Let's talk this over and . . . "

"Go away with your lies. I know why you leave the house so much."

"I only leave to take care of the cell group I lead and . . . "

"You only love your sweet little group. Marry it!" She left with the clothes.

"I'll do anything you tell me!" I begged, following her. "Anything!"

"Anything? Okay, I'll tell you. Let someone else lead your dear little group!"

"Lu! Don't keep me from serving God!"

"Oh! You serve God, do you? You don't even serve your family! Look at our gate lying back there. You haven't fixed it since Gadget smashed it and Hilda's goats ate my flowers. You didn't care! Only your group matters to you!"

"Don't force me to leave the work that God has given me to do!"

"You choose, Tiger—between me and your beloved group. *Chao.*" I watched her take the boys' clothes across the street to Mouse's house and my heart ached.

Pharaoh nudged me, and I told him, "I've failed to face issues squarely, pooch, and talk with Lucy instead of taking off in a pout. Jesus said to love Him more than parents, wife, and children. That means if I don't love God with my whole heart, then my love for Lucy will also be hollow. I'm a total failure!"

I decided to repair the front gate to placate Lucy and was looking for nails when Gadget called. "Forget your meeting, neighbor? We're waiting. I'll break out the booze if you're not here in a minute!"

I ran and was surprised to find Evita with the group. I did not feel like leading and asked Victor Calderon to give his testimony. He stammered, then stated firmly, "Grudges corroded my soul; you all know how crabby I was. But I received Jesus and He gave me peace, replacing my bitterness with forgiveness. My good works didn't save me; I didn't have any. God renewed my wife and kids, too. We're all happier now, and sure of our eternal salvation. What a joy!"

"Sure of salvation?" Evita reacted. "Come now, Victor! No one can be *sure*."

> ### Task 08–b.
> MAKE SURE WE KNOW THAT JESUS IS OUR ONLY SAVIOR AND MEDIATOR

"You can, *Señorita*. I can't explain it; it's of the heart. All I know is that we're to **make sure we know that Jesus is our only Savior and Mediator.**"

"Salvation depends on one's virtues," Gadget remarked. "Right, Tiger?"

"Yes . . . I mean no! Nobody deserves God's salvation. We're all sinners."

"For sure! I'll visit your church, Tiger. When's your Mass?"

"No, Gadget!" Evita snapped. "We're Catholics. One does not change his religion! It's your spiritual mother; you can't change your mother!"

No one replied; Victor saw I was distracted and explained, "We're Catholic, too, Evita, but not *Roman* Catholic. Tiger taught us last week that we're 'reformed' Catholics; 'Catholic' like in the Apostles' Creed, meaning the universal church. We're 'reformed' because we trust in God's undeserved grace and no longer pray to saints; we pray only to God in Jesus' name, as He taught and . . . "

"What about the Blessed Virgin? Surely you pray to her, Victor!"

"No more, ma'am. Help me, Tiger. Why don't we?"

I was in no mood for tact. "The apostles' writings show that Mary did not receive worship from them. No sincere mother usurps the attention that her son deserves. And Jesus didn't let His followers use Mary as a mediator; she told Him the wine had run out during a big wedding and He did nothing. She then told the servants to speak directly to Him, and then He turned the water to wine."

"Really!" exclaimed Gadget. "So how do you pray, Tiger?"

"As Jesus taught—in His name, not to saints. 1 Timothy 2 says there's only one mediator between God and men—*Jesus*. Prayers to Mary are not . . . "

"Sacrilege!" Evita's face had reddened. "Your perverse ideology undermines our religion! You Protestants are . . . are . . . termites! Disgusting termites!"

"Let's not discuss dogmas," Victor begged. "Gadget, just think about the pain that the Lord Jesus suffered to save you and receive His grace."

"Not now. I got to straighten out my life first." Gadget left for his shop, Evita stomped out, and the meeting ended.

The sun was setting so I rushed to work without going home. I prayed, "Lord, tell my guardian angel to give me double protection tonight; I forgot my pistol."

Meanwhile, Lucy's mind had cleared enough to regret her ultimatum. "Oh, Martha, I was horrid! I made Tiger choose between God and me. So selfish!"

Mouse pontificated, "The Almighty is punishing you. You deserve . . . "

"I know! I know! Don't rub it in, Mouse! I've ruined my family and my life! It's better if God takes me." She dried her eyes. "I'm going to go see Tiger."

Finding me gone, despair overwhelmed Lucy. She saw my pistol still hanging on the wall, and a moment later, it was pointing, trembling, at her temple. "How will it leave me looking?" she asked herself. "Oh . . . Blood in my hair!"

She shuddered and lowered the gun. "Poison won't disfigure me." Suicide was common then, a quick way to deal with a hopeless mess, even if it didn't make sense. In her heart, Lucy knew that God had a different answer, but she needed someone to help her focus on this truth; she was too tired to face it alone. She leaned against the bed's headboard and stopped thinking; it was too painful. Her eyes clouded over; her face went blank. She was staring into space the next morning when I found her sitting on the bed.

<table>
<tr><td>

Task 08–c.

PREPARE CAREGIVERS
TO HELP PEOPLE
SUFFERING FROM
CONFLICT, PERSONAL
HANG-UPS, OR
ADDICTIONS

</td><td>

"Lu! What's wrong? Why the gun?" No answer. "Lucy?" Vacant eyes focused on nothing. I shook her and rubbed her hands, but she remained a statue. "What can I do?" My heart beat hard as I eased her back and covered her. "Oh, dear God, help!" I'd soon see why concerned leaders **prepare caregivers to help people suffering from conflict, personal hang-ups, or addictions.**

</td></tr>
</table>

I ran to get Gadget to take her to the doctor and came upon Evita and Anna. "Ridiculous!" wailed Evita. "We weren't swimming, Grandma. We were looking for kids in the old mine; that cursed Wasp set us up. Here's Tiger, he'll tell you."

"I'm on my way to your house, cowboy," Anna told me. "Our group gives care to troubled people and I'm Lucy's 'Big Sister.' Wanda's told the whole world that you and Lucy are at war, and I've come to negotiate a truce."

"She's like in another world, Grandma. She won't talk. I'm taking her . . . "

"Let me see her, alone." She hurried to our house. I sat waiting and an hour went by, maybe two; it seemed like forever. I found paper and wrote: *Pastor Arturo Gomez, Thanks for all you taught me. With sorrow, I resign my offices. I am taking my family back to Los Robles to have peace. Gratefully, Tito Garcia.*

I took the note to Gadget for him to deliver to Arturo. Coming back, I met Anna leaving our house, smiling! "'Bye, cowboy. Lucy's waiting to see you."

I dashed inside. "Lu! Lu!"

"Hi." She was washing cups in the kitchen. "Grandma helped me think things through. She was so patient! We untangled the mess about Evita; jealousy had warped my reason. Please forgive me, Tiger!"

We embraced, wept, and talked frankly for a change. I begged, "Forgive me for not helping you get over those moods! I went with Evita to rescue a kid . . . "

"I know. Anna told me. The healing has begun, Tiger, and I'll see the doctor if those dangerous moods return. Anna will meet with me until I can control my anxieties. Since real events triggered my moods, she assured me that I'm not bipolar or psychotic and my brain doesn't have some weird chemical imbalance."

"Oh, thank God! He'll help us both change the way we've treated each other."

That night's darkness tried to haunt me again, but I praised our Lord for Lucy's recovery as I paced and softly sang Colombo's song about eternal dawn. I actually enjoyed my starry vigil and slept soundly the next day. Lucy and I then went to thank Anna and found her sweeping the floor. I praised her, "Grandma, you have unusually shrewd wisdom!"

"It's my white hair, cowboy, it fools people; I had it at twenty-five. She laid the broom aside and handed me a list of simple pictures. "I studied caregiving and drew these eleven icons to help us recall member care guidelines. Learn them. Your group needs caregivers. All the groups do." I read the first two aloud.

1. LET GOD'S LIGHT SHINE ON THE PROBLEM. Ask Him to make His presence known and bring His power to bear. Some ills yield only to Jesus' miraculous touch.

2. LISTEN UNTIL A PROBLEM'S ROOT IS APPARENT. The real issue is seldom one's first complaint, and family conflict is rarely one-sided; hear both sides. If one gripes that a spouse quarrels a lot, find out what provokes the quarrels.

"Listening is so crucial!" Lucy wiggled my ear. "Grandma asked questions until I saw my problem's root—jealousy. Tiger, I saw Evita hugging you and assumed the worst. When I was ten, my dad left my mom for a bimbo; it left a deep, painful scar and I've felt insecure ever since, distrusting even my own husband."

"Oh, why didn't you tell me, Lucy?"

"I didn't realize its bad effect until the Holy Spirit gave me strength to face the truth about myself. God used your patience, Grandma." Lucy hugged her. "You stayed with me until I climbed out of my self-made dungeon of deception."

"You'll be as patient, Lucy, when you help others. At first, troubled folks deny guilt, make excuses, and blame others, but wise caregivers get beyond that."

3. RESTORE COMMUNICATION. Let quarrelers listen to each other, *speaking the truth in love*. Let one repeat the other's complaint, to make sure both hear each other.

"Oh!" Lucy winced and shook her head. "I blocked out our communication! Every time I didn't talk with Tiger, Satan stood ready to supply the answers!"

"I was worse," I admitted. "My stubbornness and unwillingness to talk with my wife only added more bricks to our barrier. Proud egos prefer the pain!"

4. CONFESS PAST SINS AND BAD THOUGHTS TO GOD. *Trust the Lord to forgive* (1 John 1:8–10). To shed bad habits and demonic oppression, confess old sins, occult activity, resentment or grudges, and ask Jesus to free you from them. Don't try to do this alone.

5. FORGIVE AS JESUS FORGIVES US (Eph 4:32). Let an offense be a chance to show God's grace; accept being defrauded rather than getting even, as 1 Cor 6:7 says.

6. GIVE CARE IN A SMALL GROUP IF POSSIBLE. Loving friends help troubled people face the truth. *In many advisors there is victory* (Prov 11:14).

"My dad was an alcoholic," I recalled. "He met weekly in a small group of recovering addicts who held him accountable, and he overcame his compulsion."

"Does an evil spirit penetrate an addict's mind, Grandma?" Lucy asked.

"It might. When drugs, booze, or sex drives him, he must seek help at once from someone he's accountable to, shun false friends, avoid sources of the poison, confess his flaw to God, and stop the habit cold; tapering off won't work."

7. BEHAVE PRUDENTLY WITH THE OPPOSITE SEX. To give care to one of the other sex, have a spouse or other person within sight.

8. SUSTAIN FAMILY TIES WITH LOVE AND RESPECT. Ephesians 5 tells husbands to love their wives as Jesus loved the church and gave His life for it, and tells wives to submit to their husbands as to Christ and to respect them.

Anna joined our hands. "Wives need love; husbands need respect. Tiger, your love helps Lucy respect you and submit. Lucy, respect means to honor; submitting helps Tiger to love you and avoids rivalry. Guys strut around like peacocks, but still lack confidence if wives don't respect them. Comedians create a stereotype of the bumbling husband whom no one respects, which devastates families."

Lucy squeezed my hand, "I did not show respect to you, Tiger! I'm sorry!"

"I made it hard for you to do so. I just walked off!"

Anna tapped her Bible. "Ephesians 5:21 tells both husband and wife to submit to one another. That keeps peace."

9. BE DISCREET. Keep secrets, never reveal confessions and don't repeat rumors. Proverbs 20:19 warns, "A slanderer reveals secrets . . . do not associate with a gossip."

Lucy groaned. "I swallowed Wanda's gossip and it twisted my mind. She knew how to prey on my fears and I believed her rather than you, Tiger!"

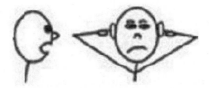

10. HELP THOSE WHO WANT HELP. Some enjoy being victims and stay in chronic crisis to get attention. Don't abet this; help them look out for the interests of others (Phil 2).

11. AVOID ADDING ONE STRESS TO ANOTHER. When compounded, anxiety, fatigue, solitude, and pride bring despair. If an actual painful or stressful event triggers despondency, then one recovers easier. Elijah lost heart when he let these common stresses pile up.

Anna drew simple figures to help us recall despondency's common causes. "Elijah's *mental* reason for despair was *fear*. He boldly faced hundreds of Baal's prophets, but one woman terrified him. Queen Jezebel had supported Baal's prophets whom Elijah had killed and threatened to kill him. Worry seized him and he fled. To calm him, God assured him with a quiet, small voice. We can normally ease such anxiety with prayer and meditating on God's promises."

"Fear paralyzed me," I confessed. "I was sick with worry that I'd lost Lucy."

"Elijah's *physical* cause of despair was *fatigue*. He ran from Jezreel to Beersheba, over a hundred kilometers. God alleviated it by giving him rest and food."

"I hadn't slept well for days, Grandma. Like Elijah, I was drained."

"Elijah's *social* reason for despair was *solitude*. He foolishly left his servant in Beersheba and went on alone into the desert. To correct this, God sent him to Elisha, his apprentice, and gave him work to do with other people."

Lucy admitted, "That was me. I kept to myself and avoided others' help!"

"Elijah's *spiritual* reason for dejection was *pride*. He thought he alone was faithful, but God told him seven thousand in Israel had not knelt before Baal. Pride so easily takes offense! Good caregivers help the prideful deflate overblown egos."

"Oh, Grandma!" Lucy covered her face. "I was too proud to mention my downward spiral to anyone, not even to Tiger. How stupidly arrogant I was!"

"What about severe psychoses like schizophrenia?" I asked. "And demonic oppression? How does a caregiver deal with those, Grandma?"

"Clinical psychosis is not demonic oppression, but they can both be present. Hallucinations, voices, and bizarre conduct can be from a brain abnormality, beyond a non-professional's ability to treat except to pray for healing. But we can free the demonized. If one has practiced the occult, speaks evil or accuses in a strange voice or rages irrationally at the name of Jesus, then pray in His name to free the victim from evil spirits. It's repulsively creepy to be so near them."

"I've been near them." Lucy clasped her arms around herself. "Mother took me to mediums' sessions. I don't like to talk about those filthy, lying spirits."

"Then let's not. Now if these guidelines don't help or if you don't understand a psychological condition, then send a person to a licensed counselor. Last week our cell took up an offering to send a neighbor to a Christian therapist in Arenas."

Lucy picked up the list. "Let's try recalling the guidelines by only seeing the icons." We soon recalled them all and a bit later did it without the icons. I was copying the guidelines when we heard an engine roaring loudly in the street. We ran to the door and Anna covered her ears as the orange taxi braked outside.

Gadget begged, "Pardon the din, Grandma. A rock busted the muffler. Kids put it in the road to mark a soccer goal. Tiger, we was looking for you."

> ### Task 08–d.
> LIVE PRAYERFULLY BY FAITH WITHOUT ALWAYS SEEKING SIGNS FROM GOD TO BOLSTER IT

Arturo with his cast eased his way out of the back seat and shoved my resignation at me. "This is rot." I was learning why devoted followers of Jesus **live prayerfully by faith without always seeking signs from God to bolster it.**

"I don't know, sir. So much has happened! Lucy and I are back together, but I still feel unfit to lead without some sure sign from God that He wants me to."

"You demand signs? Jesus condemned that! He was elated when folks believed without signs. It's not real faith if He forces us to believe with signs."

"Okay, sir, I won't demand a miracle—but one sure would be reassuring."

"Hopeless cowpoke!" Anna stamped a foot. "God restored your family. What greater sign do you want? Celestial trumpets and a visit from Archangel Gabriel? Do you pray to manipulate our sovereign God, or to adjust your will to His?"

I laughed sheepishly at my stupidity, took my resignation, and tore it up.

Anna joined my hand to Lucy's and said, "Now, you whimpering 'Elijah,' you've recovered and so has Lucy, so stop whining! Go take care of your beautiful wife and the lambs that God gave you to look after! Get!" Lucy laughed heartily as we left. What a relief to see her joyful self again!

CHAPTER 8: CONFIRM THE GRASP AND THE PRACTICE OF LEADERS' TASKS

08–a. Let faith in Christ override feelings, fears, and jealousies. Note a benefit of trials: *Rejoice, even though . . . you have been distressed by various trials, so that the proof of your faith, being more precious than gold which is perishable, even though tested by fire, may . . . result in praise and glory and honor at the revelation of Christ.* 1 Pet 1:6–7

08–b. Make sure we know that Jesus is our only Savior and mediator. Verify it: *There is one God, and one mediator between God and men, the man Christ Jesus.* 1 Tim 2:5

08–c. Train caregivers to help people suffering from conflict, personal hang-ups, or addictions. Find two essentials to cure vices and family feuds: *Therefore, confess your sins to one another and pray for one another so that you may be healed.* Jas 5:16

Identify several ways to use Scripture to give care: *All Scripture is inspired by God and profitable for teaching, for reproof, for correction, for training in righteousness; so that the man of God may be adequate, equipped for every good work.* 2 Tim 3:16–17

Review duties of husbands and wives: *Submit to one another in the fear of Christ. Wives, be subject to your own husbands, as to the Lord. For the husband is the head of the wife, as Christ also is the head of the church . . . Husbands, love your wives, just as Christ also loved the church and gave Himself up for her . . . For this reason a man shall leave his father and mother and shall be joined to his wife, and the two shall become one flesh. Nevertheless, each individual among you also is to love his own wife even as himself, and the wife must see to it that she respects her husband.* Eph 5:21–33

Note any family-care guidelines that you should heed better with your spouse:

[ ]   Assure your spouse often of your love, appreciation, and respect.

[ ]   Forgive: *Don't let the sun go down on your anger*, Eph 4:26.

[ ]   Talk over slowly how to correct the children and spend money, Eph 5:21.

[ ]   Do not let in-laws get bossy in your family affairs, Gen 2:24.

[ ]   Pray and meditate daily on God's Word together, 1 Thess 5:17.

[ ]   Avoid any conduct that could cause jealousy, 1 Thess 5:22.

Note children's duties to parents and parents' duties to children: *Children, obey your parents in the Lord . . . Honor your father and mother . . . so that it may be well with you, and that you may live long on the earth. Fathers, do not provoke your children to anger, but bring them up in the discipline and instruction of the Lord.* Eph 6:1–4

Note non-professional caregiver's guidelines that you plan to heed more:

[ ]   Pray and rely on the Holy Spirit's guidance and that of God's Word.

[ ]   Ask questions to detect discord's root, not merely its symptoms or excuses.

[ ]   Help persons who are at odds communicate calmly with each other.

[ ]   Exhort offended persons to forgive as God has forgiven us.

[ ]   Deal with common problems in small groups when possible.

[ ]   Do not give care to one of the other sex alone; let someone else be present.

[ ]   Avoid espousal rivalry: husband love wives; wives respect husbands.

[ ]   Keep secrets; never divulge confessions.

[ ]   Help people who want help and heed advice; avoid those who enjoy being victims.

[ ]   Let recovering addicts form a group and hold each other accountable.

[ ]   Relieve common causes of despondency: *fear, fatigue, solitude,* and *pride.*

Notice how despondent believers can get their minds off themselves: *Set your mind on the things above, not on the things that are on earth. For you have died and your life is hidden with Christ in God.* Col 3:2:3

Find another way to gets one's mind off one's self. *Do nothing from selfishness . . . with humility of mind regard one another as more important than yourselves; do not merely look out for your own personal interests, but also for the interests of others.* Phil 2:3–4

Verify three things that God gives to hearten us: *For God has not given us a spirit of timidity, but of power and love and discipline.* 2 Tim 1:7

Note any of these common causes of despair that you could avoid more carefully:

[ ]   *Worry.* Confess anxiety to God; become occupied in calming activities.

[ ]   *Weariness.* Set apart days of rest; have recreation and get sufficient sleep.

[ ]   *Solitude.* Keep relating closely to friends, family, and coworkers.

[ ]   *Pride.* Humble yourself and confess even the faintest arrogance to God.

08–d. Live prayerfully by faith without always seeking signs from God to bolster it. Find Jesus' view of seeking signs. *An evil and adulterous generation seeks after a sign.* Matt 16:4

EVALUATE YOUR LEADERSHIP

1=Poor. 2=Planning to improve. 3=Doing well.

1-2-3   Let faith in Christ override feelings, fears, and jealousies.

1-2-3   Make sure we know that Jesus is our only Savior and Mediator.

1-2-3   Prepare caregivers to help people suffering from conflict, hang-ups, or addictions.

1-2-3   Live prayfully by faith without always seeking signs from God to bolster it.

9.
Severe Ordeals Mold Tiger's Character

Perched on a rocky ledge on the cool, windy slope above the chapel, Chuey Ochoa calculated the distance, clicked his rifle's sight to match, and buttoned up his jacket. A cloud hid the moon, obscuring his view of the door and he cursed it. Inside the chapel, I told Pacho, "I asked Simon for the night off to attend this meeting for group leaders. He arranged for his new ranch foreman, Jaime Ordoñez, to take my place and docked me two days' pay. I haven't met Jaime yet."

"You won't find him pleasant when you do; he's a surly loner. Jaime's killed at least four men in gunfights and always claimed self-defense. His one asset is his skill with horses; he's tops. Just beware: don't ever cross him if he's drinking."

"Which is his daily agenda!" Mouse added. "I plan to drive the drunkards out of Bat Haven with my powerful preaching! Hallelujah! Hey Pacho! You look like you got indigestion whenever I raise my prophetic voice. Why?"

> **Task 09–a.**
>
> POUND YOUR EGO DOWN DAILY WITH GOD'S HAMMER TO SERVE GOD'S PEOPLE HUMBLY

Smack! Jethro's cane whacked the floor. "Time out! Guys, I didn't endure that bumpy ride from Arenas to listen to you disagree; I came to hear you agree on cell leaders' duties. Start with this: **pound your ego down daily with God's hammer to serve God's people humbly.** Jeremiah called God's Word a sledge that shatters rock. Use it! Now, you need a coordinator to help you agree and work as one for a change. Tell me, what kind of leader leads leaders?"

Pulling up a sleeve, Mouse flexed a sizeable bicep. "One with an iron fist!"

Colombo laughed. "That depends on whom you slug with it! You use it on your allies! I visited your group and you led it like a longhorn bull! Jesus requires a leader to be the humblest of servants in the kingdom of heaven."

"In heaven, yes. On earth you don't get things done leading like a wimp!"

The tall trucker rolled his eyes. "You missed Jesus' point! I grew up in a tribal village where life revolved around an authoritative leader. Our pastor took over that role from a witch doctor after missionaries brought the gospel; he was tough, but a humble servant at the same time. An insecure leader is bossy and stifles initiative, but a confident one delegates pastoral duties to others."

"Bull's-eye!" Jethro gave thumbs up. "Use power to serve Jesus; abuse it to serve Satan. It's neutral, a curse or a blessing, depending on your heart. Tyrants use fear to force people to follow. Mao Tse Tung brainwashed them. Napoleon slew good men who opposed him. Hitler promised relief in a crisis to all who followed blindly. Lying politicians make hollow promises to get votes. Godly leaders avoid all this, share their power, and make it easy for others to lead too."

Roger asked, "Doesn't democratic voting avoid abusive leadership?"

"Only if voters are informed and unselfish. Greedy voters elect whoever promises the most and whoever lies most convincingly. Above all, ego is the prime foe of godly leadership. I've let it run away with me and hurt folks—my nastiest sin."

I pondered this. "*Swollen egos.*" Aha! That fit Simon and Mouse! Whoops! Ouch! The Holy Spirit poked my conscience. It fit me too! I merely hid it better!

Roger asked Jethro, "So what particular technique of leading should we use?"

> ### Task 09–b.
> #### KNOW AND DO THE TASKS THAT THE NEW TESTAMENT SPECIFIES FOR A BODY OF BELIEVERS

"Don't focus on technique, but on what the folks are to do. That's the essence of leadership. Know exactly what God wants your group to do, then what you should do as leader becomes obvious— simply make it easy for them to do it. You're leading well when your folks **know and do the tasks that the New Testament specifies for a body of believers.**"

Colombo asked, "Then what are the tasks that God wants our groups to do?"

Jethro unbuckled his skunk skin backpack. "Use this *Vital Ministries Checklist* to register your group's progress in doing the tasks that God requires of any flock. Don't be afraid to be lazy and delegate the tasks to others. No one person can do them all, but you must know them so you can see that others do them."

I scanned the task titles: *Shepherding, Member Care, Prayer-related Activities, Stewardship, Citizenship and Mercy, Worship, Transformation, Evangelism, Missions, Multiplying Churches, Pastoral Training,* and *Overseeing.*

Jethro said, "You're leading as God wants when a cell's doing these tasks."

"Pardon my fussiness," Pacho begged, "but you want us to go a bit fast!"

"Right, Pacho! Way too fast for a traditional, program-oriented church! However, it wasn't too fast for Paul and it's not too fast for a movement in which the Holy Spirit multiplies flocks." The barber made a bow of acquiescence, and Jethro said, "Tell us, Tiger, how we get a cell to start doing a task that's new to it."

I thought a moment and said, "Don't just preach it; show folks how to do it in a way they can imitate. If you can't do it well, let someone else demonstrate it."

"Good! How do you get members to serve in sync with each other?"

"Talk over what they'll do during the week, who'll do it, and how, until they agree. Help each member plan his part, like Nehemiah, who assigned a span of Jerusalem's broken wall to each clan to repair. Also, don't quit one ministry in order to start another; keep doing them all. To focus on just one ministry at a time is slothful; it neglects people's needs."

"Good!" Jethro said. "Now listen all of you. Your church needs a coordinator to keep your groups serving in harmony. Who among you is a *leader of leaders*?"

"That I am not," sighed Arturo. "How about Tiger?"

"He can't avoid fights!" exclaimed Pacho. "He's a magnet for violence!"

As if on cue, the moon escaped its cloud shroud. Chuey steadied the rifle over a rock, switched off the safety, and lined up the crosshairs on the doorway. Inside, Pacho added, "Also, a coordinator must be one who's been free of vices."

"You're the only one who never had a vice," Mouse replied. "So you're it!"

They approved Pacho as group coordinator and started out the door. Pharaoh, standing guard, sniffed the air, and barked as they passed. On the slope above, Chuey took a deep breath, held it, and caressed the trigger. I asked Jethro, "Was it wise to name Pacho to coordinate our groups simply because he's had no vices?"

"We'll see if he has the grit for it; biblical leaders were resolute. They all had faults, but repented: Abraham lied, Moses slew an Egyptian, and David lusted. They also had strengths: Abraham's faith, Moses' love of justice, and David's courage."

Stepping outside, I stooped to calm the barking dog and the bullet hit where my head had been. We darted out of sight, but Pharaoh tore up the slope. Another shot sounded. I called the dog, but he did not return. I crept up through shadows and saw him lying still, a small hole in his forehead. The moon slipped behind a cloud and I cradled the limp body in my arms, stumbled back down, borrowed a spade, and buried Pharaoh under the pines. I suspected it was Chuey and for some reason slaying my dog embittered me more than trying to kill me.

"Where's Pharaoh?" Tino was searching around the house the next morning.

"Son, someone shot him last night. He's gone."

Tino wept bitterly and Lucy held him. "We'll get another dog just like him."

"There is no doggy like Pharaoh. Why'd they shoot him, Papa?"

"It doesn't matter now." I told Lucy that Pacho was our group coordinator.

"Pacho!" She shook her head and plunked into a chair. "How dumb!"

"He's devout, Lu, the only elder who's not had vices. A godly man."

"He is, but he's negative and lacks initiative. He won't inspire other leaders."

"Look, Lu." I handed her the *Vital Ministries Checklist*. "Jethro wants us to use this chart to monitor each group's progress. It lists what a group should do and has a space for the date when it's doing it. A shepherd leads well only when he knows the tasks that God requires of a flock and helps it do them."

She ran her finger down the task titles. "It has a serious omission."

"What?"

"You figure it out. Now, I also have an oral *Domestic Duties Checklist* for you. Item one: repair our front gate that Gadget knocked down ages ago."

"Oh! Okay. But first, Gadget and Evita need marital advice; they've announced their wedding. Maybe he'll stop drinking for her."

Lucy shook her head saying nothing, and I left to see Gadget and Evita.

"Dynamite." Gadget pointed at a wooden crate in his shop. "Mouse brought it on his mule. Hey, I'm gonna close the entry to that old, deserted mine forever!"

"My idea." Evita sat on the crate. "That hole in the mountain is treacherous. Kids will wander in and get hurt or, more likely, a rabid bat will chew on them!"

"A book on radioactive ores came in the mail, Tiger. Evita sent for it because Olga had suspected something weird about that slope above the chapel. You gotta see what it says about atom bombs! I'll get it." Gadget ran into the house.

Evita lit a cigarette. "Does Lucy still accuse me of trying to enchant you?"

"Not now. That was madness."

"Entirely? You haven't even a spark of fondness for me? I'd hoped our friendship included some affection! Pardon my presumption, Saint Tiger!"

"Oh . . . Yes, of course we're friends. Certainly friends, Evita."

"Did I miss some warmth in those words?" She rose and embraced me impetuously, chuckling, "My beloved, sanctimonious *amigo*!"

"Enough! You know the harm such playing around has caused."

It was too late; Gadget had seen the embrace. He hurled the book down and sped off in his taxi. Following on foot, I spotted the orange cab parked outside a bar. He was staring blankly at two empty shot glasses and raised a third. I told him, "Nothing's going on between Evita and me. I only love my . . . "

"Go 'way!" He called me an obscene name, turned his back, and gulped the drink. I tried again to explain, but he covered his ears and crooned a ribald song.

That night I met Jaime Ordoñez, Simon's ranch foreman. Rain was drumming loudly on my kiosk's tin roof when he appeared soaking wet, unshaven, and shifty eyed. He reeked of whiskey, stale tobacco, and staler sweat. I shook his calloused hand and he squeezed hard, obviously—and successfully—to inflict pain.

"Got a cigarette?" I told him I didn't smoke and he sneered as he ambled off without adieu. I recalled Pacho's warning; meeting Jaime would be unpleasant. Well, that it was and it left me feeling uneasy the rest of the night.

Task 09–c.
PROCLAIM WHY THE RISEN CHRIST IS OUR ONE HOPE FOR FORGIVENESS, ETERNAL LIFE, AND A JUST SOCIETY

The next day I hiked up to another SRE meeting with my pistol in my belt, feeling alone and vulnerable without Pharaoh. I was determined to **proclaim why the risen Christ is our one hope for forgiveness, eternal life, and a just society**. I neared some men and they suddenly stopped talking.

Chuey eyed my pistol and chuckled. "Let's see what this cowpoke can do with that toy. Aaron, put six bottles by that tree."

Chuey aimed, shattered three bottles with as many rapid shots at six paces, and the men applauded. "Your turn, Watchman. Do it that fast."

"My pistol's the old type. I have to insert a cartridge each time."

"Use mine. It has three shots left."

"I don't care to, sir."

Mincho the Monster handed me Chuey's revolver. "Yes, you do." I shot three times slowly and missed every time as "boos" rang in my ears.

"Well, let me." Chorcho, the reformed assassin, loaded the pistol, aimed a bit slower than Chuey, but hit a whiskey bottle with each shot as the men clapped.

Chuey told Aaron to put bottles by the windmill fifty meters away. Aaron had barely lifted his hand from a bottle when it shattered. Chuey handed the rifle to me; I aimed slowly and missed. The men jeered and my face burned. Chuey drew a circle on an outhouse, stepped back and threw his knife; it stuck dead center. He handed it to me. I threw; it hit sideways below the circle and fell. "You won't attend our meeting," Chuey poked me in the chest with the tip of his oversized cigar. "So back down the hill you go, like a good boy!"

I did not move and Chuey tapped Aaron's chest. "Bring my knife."

Mincho stepped in. "You've humiliated Tiger enough today, chief. Tiger, I said you'd explain how to get justice without violence and I'll see that you do if I have to break necks!"

We were too many to fit in the stone house so we met in the open air. I prayed for the power that Jesus promised His witnesses and when Mincho told me to speak, Chuey slid his rifle's bolt. The click made me nervous and I forgot what I'd prepared. I blurted what first came to mind, speaking loudly because of the wind. "What did Jesus do to save us?"

"Well, He died for our sins," answered Chorcho. Big Mincho added in his gruff voice, "And rose from the dead on the third day."

"Yes. His resurrection gives us new life. How long does it last?"

"Forever," affirmed Chorcho, "and that's a fairly long time!"

"Anyone lives forever," Aaron challenged me, "with or without religion."

"Jesus said he'll raise everyone from the dead, either to life or to damnation, Aaron. He's our one door to heaven; trust Him for both pardon and new life."

Mincho, the giant, said, "For God to pardon us, we must do works of justice."

"God rewards works of justice, but they don't earn our way to heaven; Jesus opened that door by dying for us. That's why we love Him and seek justice instead of revenge. You can do this if you get right with God first. God forgives us so we forgive our enemies and achieve more with love than hate. I wrote a Bible verse about this for you to think about during the week." I handed out slips of paper with the verse and Chuey surprised me by accepting one.

A weather-beaten man told me in a shamed voice, "I can't read, comrade."

"I'll go to your home and teach you to read if you want."

"Really? Please do! I live in that shack there with them pigs in front."

"I'll be there. Now, another question. Why should sinners like us fear God?"

"I'll show you whom to fear!" Chuey elbowed me aside and pointed up. "See that buzzard?" He tossed the slip of paper with the Bible verse in the air to gauge the wind, and before it landed a few meters away, the bird fell, turning somersaults in the air. I joined in the applause. I despised him, but couldn't help appreciating such skill, until he whispered, "That's what I'll to do to you—soon!"

The session ended and Chuey hurried down the trail toward town. Chorcho warned me, "Well, don't go back that way, he intends to ambush you."

Aaron heard and commented, "Cliffs on all sides are too steep to go down. That trail's the only way out, so you'll have to face Chuey. Nice knowing you!"

Task 09–d.
FACE THE THE WORLD'S HATRED WITHOUT DESPAIRING

I prayed quietly, "Lord, help me **face the world's hatred without despairing.**"

Chorcho pointed west. "There's another way. A trail leads down over there if you got the guts, Tiger. It's risky; no one's used it for years." I told him I'd try and he advised, "Once you're down, go west. Here, take my water bottle and fill it before you reach Buzzard's Banquet Hall. They named that desert aptly; a prospector died of thirst in it last week and his partner barely made it out alive. It's low and heats up this time of year; creeks are dry. In the desert, go south until you reach the river; a long day's walk."

I searched frantically for the path until Chorcho pointed it out; only a hint of a ledge that dwindled to nothing across some short spans. Jagged rocks below it left me reeling with apprehension. "Hurry!" Chorcho urged. "That bloodhound will return looking for you; he's on a 'Tiger' hunt! I'll be praying." I started down, begging God to calm my panic; a careless step would end me. "Hurry," Chorcho repeated, "or he'll inscribe your epitaph in blood on that rock cliffside!"

Halfway down, the shelf crumbled and I slid. I seized a jagged rock to check my fall; it ripped my left hand and I left red handprints as I inched down. The ledge disappeared and started again a few feet beyond—too risky. I started back up, but spotted movement behind a curtain of shrubs at the rim. Could I leap to the bottom? I looked down. Not yet! I forced myself to jump over the gap. I looked up, saw a hat move close to the cliff's brim, and scrambled downward. My hand, slimy from blood, slipped and I almost fell; Chorcho's glass water bottle jarred loose from my belt and smashed on stones below. A sharp pain stabbed my chest then; I fell and the world blacked out.

I came to under limbs that hid me. I opened my blood-soaked shirt. A raw bruise oozed blood; the bullet had ricocheted and hit sideways. I tried to rise, but my side shrieked with pain. Gritting my teeth, I tried again, but my left leg collapsed; my ankle was sprained. The soil was bloody where I'd lain; broken glass from Chorcho's bottle had lacerated my back. Pressing against my side to stop the bleeding, I crawled, found a forked stick to use as a crutch, got to my feet, and hobbled on. At dusk, fierce thirst hit me; I looked for a creek, found one, and drank. Wolves bayed, but I was too done in to care and slept.

Nothing is eerier than awakening to a wolf's howl close by in total darkness. I felt around for my crutch, struggled to my feet, and limped on blindly amid briars that tore my shirt. The moon came out and shadows moved in the brush. I tried to hurry, but my heavy breathing caused piercing pain in my ribs. The moon hid again and my *Via Dolorosa* led to a cliff so steep that I would have plunged onto rocks far below if dawn's earliest glow had come a second later. I hobbled around the death trap into Buzzard's Banquet Hall—with no water.

How a small mountain range could alter climate! Only cacti grew on its west side, no breeze stirred, and the blazing sun seemed to hover only inches above torturing my brain; I'd lost my hat. Had I gone deaf or was the emptiness that deathly quiet? I knew better than to base faith on feelings, but in that inferno, feelings overrode reason; God could not be present in such a dead wasteland!

At midday, I made out trees far to the south. The river was there, but at my crippled pace I'd never make it over the rough, eroded terrain. Fear poured adrenaline into my blood, stirring my resolve. I gritted my teeth and moved faster, but without water, I knew it was hopeless. My trousers clung to my legs, wet with sweat—or was it blood? Where sand was black, scorching heat penetrated the soles of my shoes. "Have pity, oh God! This oven's roasting the life out of me!"

Chuey's hate-filled face invaded my mind. I detested him and the entire unbelieving world. Jesus warned His followers that the world would hate us and we'd suffer for Him. Peter, James, and John said the same. Now it was upon me! I trudged on, my mouth dry, my legs heavier than lead. "Lord, I beg you, spare me the world's hatred! It's following me! I feel it! Free me!"

Pain triggered fury, goading me to plot revenge. Chuey would feel the same agony that he'd caused me! Oh, yes! I imagined ways of torturing him, each time more atrocious. But wait! Jesus said to forgive as He forgave us! A war raged—

heart *versus* imagination. I couldn't hush my evil deliberations until I reworded my prayer for freedom from hatred: "Lord, free me from *my own* hatred!"

> ## Task 09–e.
> ### PUT TO REST THOSE GNAWING DOUBTS THAT GROW OUT OF DEFEAT AND FATIGUE.

A tumult of past sins raged in my mind; I shook my head, but they clung there, goading me to despair and clamoring, "You deserve to die!" I spied shade under a dry creek bank, pushed stones aside and lay down, telling myself, "**Put to rest those gnawing doubts that grow out of defeat and fatigue.**"

The sun went down and a breeze cleared my mind; it also blew dust in my mouth leaving an acrid taste. I rose and limped toward the distant trees. Too far!

"Take a step," I ordered unwilling legs. "Now another. Never mind the pain."

My ears buzzed. Was it a breeze or the "old dragon" hissing? "Where's your God now? It's over. Give up. Provide the buzzard's banquet!"

Another step. "You're useless. Everything you try to do ends in chaos. What madness to try to renew such an ungrateful church!"

Another step in the growing dusk. "You fool! Every time you speak about your frail faith, you only gain enemies!"

"You lie!" my cracked lips challenged the mocking voice. "You always lie! Go away. In Jesus' name, get out of my mind!"

I came upon a small pool; it smelled like sulfur and I pushed aside scum and dead insects. I drank; it tasted bitter and I vomited. Heaviness hit me and I collapsed in the mud, dazed and unable to will my body to go on. I closed my eyes.

The sun was high when I woke. I had to keep moving or die; crawling, my hand pressed something sharp. I cried out and looked to see what it was—a cactus thorn. Wait! My eyes were focusing now and I made out paw marks in the dust. Rabbits? Fresh water was near! I followed the tracks back the way I'd come to a small spring. I had crawled right past it! Never had water tasted so sweet!

I rested, drank deeply again, and crawled back to my crutch. I got to my feet and trudged on for hours, every muscle in my legs protesting. I came to a grassy lea in a hollow and stepped in a hole; the fall jarred my back and it bled again. I felt the slimy wetness, smelled the blood, and felt nauseous. I hobbled on until a long ridge blocked my way. I had to go around—but which way? My heart sank. Guess wrong and I'd pass another day out there, which would finish me.

A horse whinnied off to my right where a small herd of wild horses was grazing. I limped toward them and they fled, kicking up dust. A large gray stallion led with such speed that even in my semi-delirium I admired him. A roan mare stopped, turned, and took a tentative step my way. Had God sent her or was it a mirage?

"You've had an owner." I spoke softly and approached slowly. "Don't fear."

She snorted and tossed her head, but did not run. She let me pat her neck and

I let her get used to me. Too weak to jump on her back, I led her to the ridge, climbed a rock, and mounted. "Okay, old girl, go where you like."

She trotted in a direction I'd not have gone. Closing my eyes and gripping the mane, I slipped in and out of awareness, for how long I don't know. I recall only the odor of horse sweat, hooves clopping on occasional rock, and gentle swaying.

"Hey, you! That's my mare!"

I forced my eyes open; a man stood in front of a mud-walled house. Where was I? Why was I on a horse? I heard flowing water. A river! My mind cleared then and my cracked lips stung as I answered, "I found her in the desert."

"Man, you're all blood! You've wrestled a she-bear! Come in and recover."

His wife brought the strongest coffee I'd ever tasted and boiled water to sterilize rags; she bandaged my chest, back, and lacerated hand. She rubbed suet on my crusted lips and brought a heap of scrambled eggs and tortillas. "Duck eggs. Eat all you want; we got plenty." I obliged.

The man grinned as I emptied two platefuls. "Two prospectors stole the mare. They passed through a week ago. She must have broken loose."

"They paid for it." I recalled Chorcho's words. "One died in Buzzard's Banquet Hall and the other barely survived. Tell me, where are we?"

"Lone Stone—if a few scattered huts merit a name. It's half a day's ride upriver to Bat Haven on a good horse. Take the mare in the morning and turn her loose in town. She'll return; she knows who feeds her corn."

"A thousand thanks, sir!"

Neighbors came to hear me relate my odyssey and my host exclaimed, "God surely preserved your life!" I told them how Jesus had cleaned up my corrupt life and about His cross, the empty tomb, and the Holy Spirit coming to us. "He'll come to you, too, and assure you of God's forgiveness."

As I left, my host gripped my hand. "Please return, sir, and tell us more."

I arrived home dusty and smelling horsy, but Lucy hugged me anyway. How I loved my precious family and life itself! I recounted my ordeal and added, "It gave me deeper trust in Christ, Lu, and a stronger sense of His presence. I'll never be the same. I plan to go back and evangelize to those folks in Lone Stone."

"Oh, if you only owned a horse!"

"Wake up! The wedding!" Lucy was shaking me. "It's today! Gadget and Evita. I promised to take flowers early. Father Camacho's marrying them."

We arrived at the square, and a man was yelling at a small crowd. "What a backward dump! One mechanic, and he so drunk he forgot to tighten the lug nuts. The wheel came loose and we crashed. My wife's all banged up and our car's pure *pasta*. I went to the police and by all holy saints in heaven, I swear I'm not lying—the same drunken mechanic's also police chief! *Caramba!*"

"Calm yourself, sir." The mayor had stepped out of the courthouse.

"I'm perfectly calm! Who do you think you are to . . . ?"

"I am José Campos, municipal mayor. How can I help you, sir?"

"Mister Mayor Campos, jail that mad mechanic before he kills someone!"

I handed Lucy the vases with flowers. "Go on in. I'm going to see Gadget."

The groom was sitting in his shop with a bottle and flushed face, groaning. "I injured her! I injured her! My fault!"

"God will forgive you if . . ."

"Don't preach at me; I already got enough afflictions! I'm ashamed. I admire folks that follow a religion; to do that you gotta do as it says, but I can't. I'm . . ."

"Listen . . ."

"I'm destroyed!" he waved the bottle in the air. "Disgraced! Dismayed! Dishonored! Dis . . . Dis . . . Discharged! Mayor Campos will fire me as police chief!"

"Stop, Gadget! Promise not to drink any more. Not a drop. Promise."

"I promise! I promise!" He smashed the half-empty bottle on the floor.

"Maybe Mayor Campos will overlook what you did if I talk to him. I'll try."

"It's time!" Gadget was looking at his watch. He groaned and rose.

I gasped when I opened the taxi door. "Filthy! You forget you're bringing Evita back in a white wedding gown!" We scrubbed the seats and sped off.

At the square, I saw Mayor Campos and interceded for Gadget. "I'll mentor him, sir, and hold him accountable. Please give him another chance."

"Well, it's worth a try, Mr. Garcia. But he's finished if he fouls up again."

I joined the guests in the Church of Saint Muñoz. Half an hour passed and the bride did not appear; Father Camacho kept glancing from his watch to the door.

"Tiger!" Gadget had stepped to where Lucy and I sat and whispered, "The ring's on my kitchen table. Go get it." He handed me the taxi's key and I sped to Mudhole and back. Gadget was waiting outside, pacing. He grabbed my arm. "Get me a drink! I'm desperate! Gotta calm my nerves."

"You promised not to drink any more, pal."

We waited a bit longer and Gadget was coming to pieces, so I went with him to Evita's rented room. We found her at a table in her wedding dress and Gadget reached for her. "What're you delaying for, woman? Everyone's waiting!"

"You got drunk and I'm afraid. I need assurance that you'll stop drinking."

"I already told you. I'll change, girl!" He tried to pull her up.

"Don't touch me!" She pushed him away. "You'll never change. You're hopelessly obstinate! Cousin to those stubborn jackasses in that corral!"

"No I'm not, but when we marry, I'll be their brother-in-law." She tore off her veil and hurled it at him; he then dodged a shoe. We left her sobbing.

At the church, I told the priest what happened and he dismissed the guests. As we left, Wanda aimed a finger at Gadget in the wide, church doorway and cried for the town to hear, "A fine police chief corrupts the town with debauchery and sabotages his own wedding! Good thing Evita wised up!" Then she injected her most insidious venom. "Just as well. Everyone knows she visits Tiger at night."

Gadget wilted. He ran back in, assaulted the air with curses, kicked the flower vases scattering blossoms across the floor, and headed for a bar.

<table>
<tr><td>

Task 09–f.

HELP THE ANGUISHED AND DEJECTED FIND RELIEF AND COMFORT IN CHRIST

</td><td>

During that night's vigil, Pacho came running. "Gadget's gone crazy! He drank his supper and packed dynamite off to the old mine. Said he'd end his shameful binges!" We ran and I begged the Lord, "Give me the ability to **help the anguished and dejected find relief and comfort in Christ.**"

"Gadget!" I shouted into the tunnel entrance. "Come out of there!"

"Hard to connect them wires in this black hole."

</td></tr>
</table>

"I'm not going to let you destroy yourself. I'm your friend and . . . "

"Friend? Yeah! My fiancée's friend too. Sneaking around with her at night!"

"Wanda lied, Gadget. Come out of there!"

"Gonna blow myself up. Go 'way or you'll disintegrate with me."

"Wait. I'm coming in."

Pacho backed off, but I crawled on my hands and knees into the darkness; overlooking the pain in my hand, bandaged after ripping it on the cliff.

"Cursed vice!" Gadget slurred. "It's destroyed me and now I'll end it!"

I groped forward, smelled alcohol breath, and tried to speak calmly. "Jesus will forgive you and help overcome your vice. He did it for me. Let Him . . . "

"Get outta my tomb, Tiger. Go 'way! I got the detonator hooked up. I now erase me from this cursed planet. I'll erase you too, if you don't beat it."

I heard faintly Pacho's frantic pleas outside for me to leave, and pled with Gadget, "You can't erase your sins that way. Let Jesus blot them out forever!"

"I've ruined myself. I'm finished with Evita. I'm finished with my job. I'm finished with my worthless life. Worthless! Worthless! It's over. Now . . . "

"Your life has infinite worth, Gadget. Just receive God's love—right now."

"I've thought about God's judgment and I'd try hard to be good—a day or two. I'll only do more sinning if I keep living and God will be even more irate with me. He gets angrier with me the longer I live. No hope! Here goes."

"Come out, Tiger!" came Pacho's faint, panicky shout.

Gadget's breathing was jerky as he held back sobs, and I tried again. "Jesus understands your misery. He's with you right now, even in this cave."

"In my tomb? The King of Kings wouldn't stoop to enter such a morbid place. He knows my misery? Ha! How'd he know, living in royal luxury up in heaven?"

"Listen, Gadget. Jesus suffered and was in a cave much worse than this; He experienced death for all of us. Think of that! Fix it in your mind right now!"

"What do you mean, 'in a cave like this'?"

"Is your mind clear enough to grasp what His death really meant for us?"

"I can grasp anything that you can. I'm not brain dead—yet."

"He died on Friday and lay buried like in here the seventh day, *dead*, and took our sins with him. Tell me what happened on the first day of the new week."

"He rose from the dead."

"Yes. That canceled the devil's power over . . . "

"The devil got possession of my soul. I'm going to . . . " .

"No! Jesus has freed you. By His death, He removed the shame of your sin. Let me pray for you; we can both pray. He'll hear you, even in this darkness!"

"NOW!" I heard a click and Gadget screamed as he fell, "I'm dead! Dead!"

"Calm yourself."

"You come with me to hell, Tiger? I thought you'd go to . . . "

"We're on earth; I unhooked the detonator." I held him, feeling him shake as forlorn sobs erupted with bitter remorse from the depths of his tormented soul.

Task 09–g.

REPLACE FETISHES AND PETITIONS TO SAINTS WITH PRAYERS IN JESUS' NAME

Hours slid by. Gadget wept, mumbled about needing Rosary beads and repeated incoherent prayers to Saint Muñoz. I asked the Lord silently, "Let him **replace fetishes and petitions to saints with prayers to You in Jesus' name.**" Finally, a gentle hint of dawn's glow came from the cave's mouth. "You still with me, Tiger?"

"I am."

"An evil spirit has come to take my soul; I feel movement in the air."

"It's a bat. They come to sleep in the dark during the day."

"Them birds are really weird. They fly jerky."

"They're not birds; they don't have feathers. Membranes on their legs serve as wings. They're more like rats; I've come to know them well—too well!"

"So how do them phony birds find their way in pitch dark, Tiger?"

"They screech and their echo guides them—Sonar."

"I didn't hear no screeching."

"It's too high pitched for human ears."

"Can Jesus hear my prayer to take away my addiction? I mean really?"

"He did for me. Pray in His name. Trust in His forgiveness and His power."

"I'm not a religious type."

"Religious types had Jesus killed. He's a person like you except He never sinned, so he knows what you face. He wept. He's beside you now."

"How can He know what I face? He never was enslaved by no bottle."

"He became a man to share with us all kinds of ordeals and temptations. He feels your sorrow and intercedes for you with God the Father. Let's pray and . . . "

"Father Camacho taught me to say prayers to the Virgin and Saint Muñoz."

"And you know what they've done for you. Jesus told us to pray in His name. Trust Him to save you; He hears the plea of every repentant soul. He'll raise you with Him to new life, starting now. Let your sin be buried with Him."

"Too good to be true. Your church wouldn't receive no scoundrel like me."

"Of course we will! It'll be a joy to confirm your faith."

Silence followed and Gadget muttered a soft prayer. I heard only the last word, "Jesus." A bit later, he told me, "Okay, I'm ready to face the light."

I led him by the arm toward the glow. He crawled out of the hole into the brightness and blinked. "It's like being resurrected from the dead."

"More than you realize. God has raised you with Christ from the dead."

He stood, faced the sun, and shouted with all his might. "Resurrected!"

High cliffs above echoed, "Resurrected!"

I heard cheers. Pacho was approaching with Mayor Campos. Gadget turned, crept into the hole, and crawled back out with the detonator. He reeled out wire as he moved away from the entrance. Pacho backed away. "What are you doing?"

"Closing this cursed door to hell forever. Get back!"

Campos grabbed his arm. "Wait!"

Gadget did wait. When the dust settled, he laughed. "Look! No trace of that miserable tomb! Only a few dead bats! Mayor Campos, you'll see I'm following Jesus now. I'll repair the car that crashed due to my neglect, sir. I'll apologize to Evita. I'll do anything to repair all the damage I've done. Anything!"

I thought of reminding him of our front gate that he'd smashed, but refrained.

CHAPTER 9: CONFIRM THE GRASP AND THE PRACTICE OF LEADERS' TASKS

09–a. Pound your ego down daily with God's hammer to serve God's people humbly. Note Jesus' view of ego: *Rulers of the Gentiles lord it over them, and their great men exercise authority over them. It is not this way among you, but whoever wishes to become great among you shall be your servant, and whoever wishes to be first among you shall be your slave.* Matt 20:25–27

Identify what truly godly shepherds do: *Shepherd the flock of God among you, exercising oversight not under compulsion, but voluntarily, according to the will of God, and not for sordid gain, but with eagerness; nor yet as lording it over those allotted to your charge, but proving to be examples to the flock.* 1 Pet 5:3

09–b. Know and do the tasks that the New Testament specifies for a body of believers. Choose tasks that your flock or your trainees should do better:

[ ]   Provide a checklist of vital ministries that leaders use to monitor progress.

[ ]   Lead others with godly humility without abusing authority.

[ ]   Prepare volunteer workers to be leaders with a servant's heart.

[ ]   Mentor apprentice leaders while they form and lead new cell groups.

[ ]   Recognize publicly and regularly those who do good work for the Lord.

[ ]   Provide edifying activities for children, adults, and entire families.

You can use the complete *Vital Ministries Checklist*, Appendix A, as a menu to select vital tasks that need attention, assign related reading, and evaluate progress.

09–c. Proclaim why the risen Christ is our one hope for forgiveness, eternal life, and a just society. Verify what He did for mortal men by rising from the dead: *Christ has been raised from the dead, the first fruits of those who are asleep. For since by a man came death, by a man also came the resurrection of the dead. For as in Adam all die, so also in Christ all will be made alive. But each in his own order: Christ the first fruits, after that those who are Christ's at His coming.* 1 Cor 15:20–23.

Discover three things that God did for us together with Jesus in His resurrection. *God . . . made us alive together with Christ . . . and raised us up with Him, and seated us with Him in the heavenly places in Christ Jesus.* Eph 2:4–6

Identify to what extent Christ's blood avails to cover sin: *If anyone sins, we have an Advocate with the Father, Jesus Christ the righteous and He Himself is the propitiation for our sins and not for ours only, but also for those of the whole world.* 1 John 2:1–2

09–d. Face the world's hatred without despairing. See why the world hates believers: *If the world hates you . . . it has hated Me before it hated you. If you were of the world, the world would love its own; but because you are not of the world, but I chose you out of the world, because of this the world hates you.* John 15:18

09–e. Put to rest those gnawing doubts that grow out of defeat and fatigue. Satan inserted doubts into Tiger's tortured mind. Notice what Job affirmed about God when he was suffering: *Though He slay me, I will hope in Him.* Job 13:15

09–f. Help the anguished and dejected find relief and comfort in Christ. Jesus healed lepers, freed the demonized, and forgave shameful sins. Count petitions that a believer can make when feeling shame: *Purify me with hyssop, and I shall be clean; wash me, and I shall be whiter than snow. Make me to hear joy and gladness, let the bones which you have broken rejoice. Hide Your face from my sins and blot out all my iniquities. Create in me a clean heart, O God, and renew a steadfast spirit within me. Do not cast me away from your presence and do not take your Holy Spirit from me. Restore the joy of your salvation and sustain me with a willing spirit.* Ps 51:7–12

09–g. Replace fetishes and petitions to saints with prayers in Jesus' name. Note what images fail to do: *Their idols are silver and gold, the work of man's hands. They have mouths, but they cannot speak; they have eyes, but they cannot see; they have ears, but they cannot hear; they have noses, but they cannot smell; they have hands, but they cannot feel; they have feet, but they cannot walk; they cannot make a sound with their throat. Those who make them will become like them, and everyone who trusts in them.* Ps 115:4–8

See what devout Ephesians did with books on the occult: *Many of those who practiced magic brought their books together and began burning them in the sight of everyone; and they counted up the price of them and found it fifty thousand pieces of silver.* Acts 19:18–19

EVALUATE YOUR LEADERSHIP

1=Poor. 2=Planning to improve. 3=Doing well.

1-2-3   Pound ego down daily with God's hammer to serve God's people humbly.

1-2-3   Do all tasks that God requires in the New Testament of a flock.

1-2-3   Tell why our risen Lord is our one hope for forgiveness, life, and justice.

1-2-3   Face the world's hatred without letting it trigger despair.

1-2-3   Put to rest those gnawing doubts that grow out of defeat and fatigue.

1-2-3   Help the anguished and dejected find relief and comfort in Christ.

1-2-3   Replace fetishes and petitions to saints with prayer in Jesus' name.

10.
Passive Hearing and Mindless Emotion
Replace Genuine Worship

<table>
<tr><td>

Task 10–a.

LET ADULTS AND
CHILDREN HELP
ILLUSTRATE THE
WORD DURING
WORSHIP AND CELL
MEETINGS

</td><td>

A small, barefoot boy came running into Pacho's shop with another smaller lad at his heels. "Mr. Barber, I don't have no Big Brother!" This would lead me to discover how to turn teaching into a memorable event—**let adults and children help illustrate the Word during worship and cell meetings**.

The smaller boy echoed, "Mr. Barber, I don't have no Big Brother too."

</td></tr>
</table>

"You got a Big Brother for my cousin Cory," the larger boy told Pacho.

"You got a Big Brother for 'cussin' Cory," parroted the echo.

"I'm bad as Cory," the first one added. "So I need help too, to follow Jesus."

"Yeah! Cause we don't want to go to hell neither when we get dead."

"Well, I should say not!" Pacho lowered his scissors. "Give me your names and where you live. Your Big Brothers will visit you." They gave the information and scampered off with happy smiles.

"Impressive, Pacho! Who are the Big Brothers?"

"Come to the house at four and see. Hey, Mayor Campos noticed the change in your wild neighbor; he said he'll let Gadget be police chief again."

"Great! Maybe he could become a Big Brother and help other alcoholics."

"That'd be the day! That clown's quit boozing, but he still gets wild ideas!"

I took Lucy to Pacho's house to see the "big brothers" and she exclaimed, "It's a beehive, Grandma! And older children are working with younger ones."

"Coordinated chaos! Watch them act out Elijah's contest with the prophets of Baal. They didn't rehearse it. Roger will simply narrate it and they'll act it out without talking unless he says to shout something."

Roger asked Lucy, "Will you be the evil Queen Jezebel?"

"Oh! Let someone else do it whom you'd like to see participate a bit more."

He begged a lady nearby, who flinched. "Me? Oh my! Well, I guess so."

Roger bowed before her. "Then we crown you Queen, your Royal Highness!"

Roger explained how false prophets worshipped idols that were images of the false god Baal, and everyone took part in some way in the noisy reenactment. Smaller tots enjoyed leaping and screaming at Baal to burn up their sacrifice, and we all cheered when fire fell on Elijah's sacrifice. Lucy poked me, laughing. "Look who's King Ahab! Grandma, how'd you ever get Pacho to do it?"

"He grumbled, but I coaxed him out of his shell. Now he loves it and closes his shop an hour early to take part! Kids take it seriously when men work with them and Pacho benefits even more than they do; his inhibitions just roll away!"

Roger recounted Jezebel's vow to slay Elijah and she chased the prophet around the room. I remarked, "Everyone has a part, Grandma. No audience!"

"Why an audience? They're not *performing*, cowboy. They're reliving sacred history, the absolute best way to learn God's Word."

"It's a tremendous way to teach! Does Arturo know about this?"

"Yes. He wants the kids to act out stories, or portions, in a minute or two to illustrate his teaching during worship. Thank God he'll share his time and not rob us of a blessing, especially the kids; they love being part of serious worship."

Queen Jezebel told us, "My husband and I came a month ago to see our daughter act as Ruth and the story touched us. We follow Jesus now as a result."

Roger asked the Princess, the queen's daughter, to tell Elijah's story; others gleefully shouted details that she overlooked. Roger asked the children what idols were and the replies showed a good grasp of the lesson. He urged, "Tell your parents about Elijah and act it out for your friends. Plan that now." Big Brothers sat with Little Brothers and Roger wrote the plans to review at the next meeting.

I told Anna, "I don't suppose adults will act out stories as eagerly as the kids."

"Most adults love it once they try; we're all born with an imagination. As children, we love to pretend we're mothers, cops, robbers, soldiers, and spacemen flying around zapping evil aliens. But we get our childhood imagination educated out of us—a shame! But what fun to reawaken it! Just look at Pacho!"

"I wonder why more churches don't act out stories in this simple way."

"They make it a showy production that's useless as a weekly teaching tool. Keep it brief, a minute or two—no props or costumes and little or no rehearsing. If a story's long, use only part of it. Big kids don't need to memorize lines, only the idea, to say in their own way when a narrator comes to their part in the story. He has little tots shout a word or two, or do some simple act like clap or boo."

"How'd you get the idea to help kids and adults take part this way together?"

"Olga did it and I vowed to carry it on when she died. Cells can easily enable kids to take part, Tiger. It's so wholesome for parents and kids to work together!"

"They're doing so many things at once! How do you and Pacho keep order?"

Task 10–b.

OLDER CHILDREN KEEP ORDER, LEAD, AND DISCIPLE YOUNGER ONES

"We don't. We let **older children keep order, lead, and disciple younger ones.** Some are strong role models. All the kids grow in Christ then and behave more orderly. Oh! You'll see an example now; those two are fighting."

"Monitor!" Roger shouted. "Do your job!"

A larger boy with an armband labeled "M" and two others stopped the scrap. The offenders listened as their Big Brothers used the incident to teach forgiveness and, after boyish threats from the monitor, asked for forgiveness from each other.

"Impressive!" Lucy exclaimed. "I like how you mix kids of different ages!"

"All kids love the attention of older children, Lucy, and try to please them. Some churches neglect this dynamic and they segregate children by age all the time; that's unnatural and weakens discipline. We adults need to get out of the way at times and let older kids lead as we guide them from behind the scenes. Better to guide than to govern. Let young adults guide older teenagers, let them lead younger teenagers, who lead older grade school kids, and so forth."

I asked, "Don't children normally want to be with others of their own age?"

"Of course, but not all the time. They respond eagerly to discipling from the next older age group, as you see. Mingling the ages is vital for a child's wholesome social development. Just make sure the Big Brothers know the Lord Jesus Christ, Tiger, or it'll blow up in your face."

"Can you help our Mudhole group do stories like you do, Grandma?"

"You don't need me, cowboy. Just follow these rules." She handed me a list.

Teach with Stories by Briefly Acting Them Out

1. Act out a story or part of it to illustrate a point in the weekly worship's teaching.
2. Aim to relive sacred history, not to perform, entertain, or seek admiration.
3. Narrate the story or part of it, pausing to let learners act out what you say.
4. Keep it brief; a minute or two is often enough; use only parts of long stories.
5. Avoid props, costumes, and showiness, so that you can act out stories every week.
6. Let adults, at least one man, act with children to add seriousness.
7. Most stories need little or no rehearsal; let a narrator relate a story as others help portray it.
8. Let older kids coach the younger to do their parts.
9. Let older children express ideas in their own words, ad-libbing.
10. Let tiny tots mimic actions or repeat a word or two that a narrator tells them to say.

11.   You usually need no audience; let everyone say or do something in a simple way.
12.   Prepare questions that all can discuss about the story.
13.   Ask what folks plan to do during the week about what they learned.

Anna added, "Get Jethro to show you how to teach a doctrine by linking Old and New Testament stories on which it's based."

That night Jaime came wobbling to my kiosk. "Heard you're a cowboy. Ha! I can rope cows faster 'n you; I'm the best. I can break worse broncos than you can. Do a contest and we'll bet. How about tomorrow morning? Let's bet now."

I declined politely and he ambled off into the darkness. During the boring night, my reckless side regretted not having taken on the haughty challenge and attempted; at least to make Jaime lose his bet and swallow his arrogance.

Jethro was in town the next day and Lucy asked him to dinner. I showed him my *Vital Ministries Checklist*, pointing to the end of it. "Look what Lucy added."

"'*Family Duties.*' Hmmm. No wonder! I forgot to ask my wife to proofread it!"

"Anna told me to ask you how to link stories from the Old and New Testaments to teach a doctrine. We're curious, Jethro."

Task 10–c. LINK A DOCTRINE TO ITS DUTY AND RELATE IS CONCRETE, HISTORICAL ROOTS.

"You'll need a discipline of steel to avoid excess abstraction; use stories to **link a doctrine to its duty and relate its concrete, historical roots.**"

"Might we neglect doctrinal passages if we use stories too much?" I asked.

"Not if you teach like Jesus did; key biblical truths are all based on historical events." Jethro took a chart from his backpack.

Stories (historical events) Underlie all Divine Truths

GOD THE FATHER
Old Testament events showed God's attributes; His laws and events on earth reflected eternal, foundational truths.

GOD THE SON
Gospel stories depict Him working out to perfection God's eternal attributes and decrees as He lovingly obeys His Father.

FATHER   SON
HOLY SPIRIT

Acts and New Testament letters show Him applying Jesus' work to believers, empowering to serve God and neighbor in love.

"Historical events properly linked show how the three timeless Persons of the Trinity work as One to *reveal, fulfill,* and *apply* every vital truth to our lives. Use the stories to link abstract with concrete, doctrine with duty, and Old Testament with New. Linking them is the pastoral approach to systematic theology."

"*Pastoral?* Why do you say that?" I asked Jethro.

"To teach a divine truth fully, we link three vital dimensions: its *origin* in an attribute or decree of God in the Old Testament, its *fulfillment* in the flesh by Jesus in the Gospels, and its *current application* by the Holy Spirit as we work it out in our lives, as seen in Acts, the letters, and Revelation."

"Can you give us an example of linking a truth's three dimensions?" I asked.

"Okay. What's a current need in your cell group?"

Lucy answered, "Holiness. Few of us take it seriously enough."

"Begin in the Old Testament with *God the Father*; He decreed with eternal authority, *Be holy as I am holy.* Can you recall events that showed this attribute?"

I replied, "The High Priest's sons, Nadab and Abihu, entered God's holy presence without the required blood and fire burst out and zapped them—a rather blazing statement about holiness!"

"Right. Then, the Gospels show *God the Son* working out holiness on earth in obedience to the Father. In His agonizing prayer in Gethsemane, the 'final Adam' yielded perfectly to the Father's will, accepting an agonizing death."

"Holiness at its zenith!" I exclaimed.

"Correct. Then, from Acts on, we see *God the Spirit* putting Jesus' holiness into believers. Ananias and Saphira lied to the Holy Spirit in an unholy way and He zapped them, just as He did Nadab and Abihu. Folks feared after that."

"Let me see if I've got it," I said. "All three Persons of the Trinity cooperate to make us holy. The *Father* decrees holiness as revealed in the Old Testament. The *Son* worked holiness to perfection on earth as seen in the Gospels. The *Holy Spirit* transforms us now to be holy, as in Acts and the letters."

"Yes. The three Persons of the Trinity are One and work in harmony to do all the vital works of God. Link Old Testament stories to related events in Jesus' life and the apostolic churches. Lazy teachers merely teach dogma abstractly, Tiger."

"I see, Jethro, but what Old Testament story lays a foundation for *rebirth?*"

"Start with Adam and God's eternal edict decrees: *obey and live; disobey and die.* The Passover account made an earthly application, as did other Old Testament historical events. Recount Jesus' resurrection and His assurances that He, the only perfectly obedient man, shares with us this life, His life; holy, eternal life."

"I see. But what about doctrinal books like Romans that aren't historical?"

"Romans based its teaching on the stories of Adam, Abraham, Moses, Jacob, and David, assuming that readers knew them. To teach Paul's letters recount the background events or you'll bore folks. If a letter doesn't cite a story to clarify a doctrine, then find one yourself; search the Scriptures like the Bereans did."

Lucy clapped. "How refreshing, Jethro, the way you use stories!"

"It's God's way. Our faith differs from all other religions in that it bases all key doctrines on historical events. The Koran, Book of Mormon, writings of Confucius, Buddha, and Hindu holy men all originated from mystic musings and dreams; they used stories, but only to illustrate their meditations. Key Christian truths all originated in the historical events of creation, the fall, the flood, God's covenant with Abraham, and so on. God later added visions and dreams to inspire His writers to clarify the historical doctrinal truths even more vividly. "

Lucy sighed. "It'll take us a year to find all those foundational Bible stories!"

"Not quite. Maybe an hour if you're a slow learner." Jethro took another chart from his black and white pack. "Icons denote events that gave rise to key doctrines. Review the list until you can recall the events by seeing the sketches. Then, go over it again until you recall the events simply by remembering how each one led to the next; the cause-and-effect link mentioned last after each one." We spent the next few minutes studying the *Flow of Sacred History*:

Creation to Babel

1. CREATION, Genesis 1–2. God created the heavens and the earth. Adam and Eve, the first couple, enjoyed fellowship with their Creator. Everything was "good," but . . .

2. ORIGINAL SIN, Genesis 3. Satan entered a serpent's body to deceive Eve; who disobeyed God and led Adam to do so, too. This brought God's curse on creation. Men's sin increased and they grew unbearably evil and violent before God, so . . .

3. NOAH'S ARK, Genesis 6–9. God punished mankind with a huge flood. All people drowned except righteous Noah and his family, whom God kept safe in a huge box-shaped boat. Mankind began again as one race but...

4. BABEL'S TOWER, Genesis 11. Men grew proud and built a city and a big tower hoping to reach the heavens and avoid being scattered. God confused their tongues and many distinct nations were born. These nations soon fell into idolatry, so . . .

Abraham to Moses

5. GOD'S PACT WITH ABRAHAM, Genesis 12–15. God promised the man of faith many descendants, a land for His holy people and a Descendant who would bless all races.

However, Abraham's great grand children in envy sold their brother Joseph as a slave, so . . .

6. SLAVERY, Exodus 1–18. Famine drove the clan to Egypt, the land of pyramid tombs. Their slaved brother Joseph had risen to high rank there and protected them. They multiplied for 400 years. Then cruel oppressors enslaved them, but . . .

7. PASSOVER, Exodus 12–15. God had mercy and sent plagues that forced Egypt's king to free his Israelite slaves. An angel slew all firstborn except where a lamb's blood marked the door. God divided the Red Sea to let Israel escape from Egypt's army. Moses led the newly born nation, which had no laws, so . . .

8. MOSES RECEIVED GOD'S LAW, Exodus 18–20. On Mt. Sinai God engraved ten commands in stone, the foundation for ancient Israel's Torah. They broke His laws and He let them wander in the desert forty years. As God had promised Abraham, He led His people to their Promised Land. It was full of hostile tribes, so . . .

Joshua to David & Solomon

9. JOSHUA LED ISRAEL'S ARMY TO CONQUER CANAAN, Joshua. Brave Joshua led God's army into the Promised Land and divided it among Israel's twelve tribes. Men of the Levite tribe were priests and helped govern. Joshua died and folks neglected God's Law, so . . .

10. JUDGE'S RULE, Judges. God raised up judges—warriors who enforced His Law—to lead His people. When God's people worshipped idols, He let pagan nations oppress them. When they repented, He raised up a judge to free them. They saw that pagan nations had kings and foolishly wanted the same, so . . .

11. RULE BY KINGS, 1 & 2 Samuel. God gave Israel's united tribes kings, starting with Saul and David. They crushed Israel's enemies and brought prosperity. God promised David an heir (Jesus) would rule forever. David wanted to build God's temple but had shed too much blood; God let him gather building materials, so . . .

12. GOD'S HOUSE BUILT IN JERUSALEM, 1 Kings. David's son, Solomon, taxed heavily to build the temple. God blessed it with the glory of His Presence. Priests slew animals as blood sacrifices to cover sins, and Israel prospered until Solomon's son Rehoboam because King and taxed people even more harshly, so . . .

Divided kingdom to foreign domination

13. DIVIDED KINGDOM, 1 Kings. Civil war began; rebel tribes formed a new kingdom, Israel, in the north. Both kingdoms, Israel and Judah, weakened; many worshipped idols. Prophets warned them to repent or become captive, but . . .

14. CAPTIVES TAKEN INTO EXILE, 2 Kings 25. Unjust kings and idolatrous people rebelled against God, rejecting His prophets' warnings. God lifted His protecting hand and let Assyria take Israel captive. Later Babylonia's king took Judah captive. God's punishment brought His people in exile to repentance, so . . .

15. EXILES' RETURN AND RECONSTRUCTION, Ezra. A repentant remnant returned to their land and rebuilt Jerusalem. Malachi wrote the last Old Testament book during this era. They never again fell into idolatry but religious legalism and hypocrisy because rife and God again brought judgement on His people, thus . . .

16. DOMINATION BY FOREIGN POWERS. This era produced no Bible books. From 586 BC on, Persian, Greek, Syrian, Egyptian and Roman empires ruled and gathered heavy taxes. Devout Jews waited for the promised Messiah to free them, thus . . .

Jesus' earthly life

17. JESUS' EARTHLY LIFE, Gospels. Jesus was born a virgin. He defeated demons, illness and sin, made followers "fishers of men," began a spiritual kingdom; Rome ruled politically. People called Him King, angering envious rulers, so . . .

18. CRUCIFIXION, Luke 23. Religious leaders arrested Jesus for blasphemy, as He had let people recognize Him as the Son of God. Roman soldiers crucified Him. He died for our sins and was buried. However, God's eternal law decrees that the righteous will live, so . . .

19. RESURRECTION AND ASCENSION, Luke 24. Jesus rose from death on the third day and promised to raise all who repent and trust Him, and to send the Holy Spirit in His place with a New Covenant. Jesus ascended to Glory and His disciples stayed in Jerusalem as He had told them, waiting for power from on high, so . . .

20. HOLY SPIRIT'S ADVENT, Acts 2. He came as Jesus promised. On the Pentecost Feast, disciples saw flames over them and proclaimed the gospel with power. 3,000 Jews heard and repented. The Holy Spirit gave them boldness to testify for Christ, thus . . .

21. SPREADING THE FAITH, Acts 8–28. Spirit-filled believers spread the News; it multiplied like grain as Jesus said it would. New Testament books were written during this era. Many died as martyrs. The Church spread with vitality for three centuries, but then . . .

Early church

22. CHURCH AND STATE UNITE, (fourth century). In AD 311, Roman Emperor Constantine legalized Christianity. It became popular and pagans came into churches without having true faith. An elite clergy arose as churches organized as an earthly institution. Divisions arose and arguments about theology; thus . . .

23. EARLY CHRISTIAN CREEDS. To refute falsehood, godly leaders codified beliefs that they agreed on. The Apostles' Creed defined the gospel; the Nicene Creed affirmed the Trinity. The Faith spread by the Roman Empire because corrupt, thus . . .

24. FALL OF THE ROMAN EMPIRE, (centuries 6–7). Fraud and selfish rulers let the Roman Empire decay from within; it lost it's power and churches in the East separated from those in the West. Many in Western Europe looked to the Church of Rome for stability, thus . . .

25. RISE OF ROME'S BISHOP (centuries 5–7). The Roman Church and it's head the Pope claimed authority over all churches. Eastern Orthodox churches opposed the Pope and separated from him. Devout believers in both East and West strove to keep the Church pure but could not halt the growing corruption; pagan influence and legalism led to decay, thus . . .

26. CRUSADES Against ISLAM, (centuries 11–13). European armies, supposedly Christian, tried to recapture the Holy Land (Israel) and other lands from Muslim invaders. The church's part in these military expeditions was a shameful error. Greed, power, lust and false doctrine corrupted the Western church, so . . .

Dark Ages to present

27. DARK AGES (AD 600–1000). People neglected God's Word and education declined. Faith grew cold in Europe except in monasteries but kept spreading in Asia. Islam captured the Holy Land and threatened all of Europe, so . . .

28. REFORMATION (1500s). Martin Luther and other reformers translated Scripture, taught salvation by faith and resisted the Pope. The Roman Church's counter-reformation corrected some abuses. Biblical truth spread but churchgoers were not reborn; thus . . .

29. EVANGELICAL AWAKENING (1700–1900). Believers who knew the living Christ urged others to receive Him in their hears and be transformed by the Holy Spirit. Denominations grew out of the revival and missionaries took the gospel to pagan lands; thus . . .

30. CURRENT GLOBAL OUTREACH. Workers are taking the Faith to every culture on earth. The current frontier, where authorities ban evangelism (one-third of the world's population), is being penetrated rapidly, pointing to Jesus' final coming.

31. JESUS' FINAL RETURN, foretold in Luke 21, Revelation.

Lucy and I quickly recalled the events by the icons. Then, sooner than I'd expected, we recalled each event by its link to the prior one. Lucy was ecstatic. "Wow! Now I see how God has worked across the ages, the whole vista!"

"Our cells will love it," I said. "Especially kids, as they role play the events."

"Kneel, Tiger and Lucy." Jethro knighted us with his cane! "I dub you Sir Tiger and Lady Lucy, *Royal Interpreters of the Word!* Teach God's life-giving truths vividly in their historical settings, showing each Person of the Trinity at work, to *reveal, fulfill,* and *apply* each truth in our lives."

We rose, laughing at the old gentleman's dramatic flair. I said to Lucy, "God has raised us to a new level of shepherding skill, and to a graver responsibility." I then told Jethro, "I'm reading Old Testament prophets' censures of unbelief, injustice, and idolatry during my night vigils and it has become tedious."

"Think how much more tedious it must have been for God! Don't forget what I knighted you and Lucy to do just now. How can you apply it to your reading?"

"Oh! I'll mix my reading in the Prophets with related stories in the Old Testament history books, the Gospels, and the apostle's warnings against idolatry."

"Right. That'll ease the tedium and give you healthy fodder to reflect on. But listen. God has a reason for all that censure of idolatry; folks still need stern warning. Popular ideas of life, morals, and heaven replace the fearsome Judge of the Universe with a harmless, indulgent god, or gods of folks' own making. The only difference is they're depicted in books and movies rather than in stone."

I thought of poor Saint Muñoz, upside-down in Wanda's closet. "Some idols of the old painted plaster kind still hang around too."

Gadget came racing down our lane the next day, dodging puddles on Arturo's motorcycle. "Look, Tiger. Arturo's leg is still in a cast, so I improvised this gearshift so he can operate it by hand. I'm trying it out. Get on."

We passed two young elders in white shirts by the square and Gadget plunged through a puddle, splattering mud on them. He started to make another pass, but while struggling with his hand-operated gearshift he hit a rut that flung us sideways, toppling us into the mire. "Ole!" cheered the muddy young men.

We arrived all mucky at Arturo's office and used up his paper towels. He begged, "Tiger, come with me to the mine to talk to Mouse. He plans to preach in the chapel when he gets off work today and I want to see him in time to call it off. He's been telling the world that we lack power; it's divisive and confuses people. I'll make one last try to dissuade Mouse and your presence will help."

Task 10–d.
DEAL WITH EMPLOYERS AND EMPLOYEES WITH RESPECT AND FAIRNESS

I rode behind Arturo up the steep road to the mine that was about half way up the mountainside, holding his crutches. The odor of hot grease warned us to stop twice to cool the straining motorcycle engine. We found Mouse perched on a box of dynamite and what happened next showed me how crucial it is to **deal with employers and employees with respect and fairness.**

"I came about your meetings," Arturo told Mouse. "Folks complain that . . . "

"Come if you want to talk." He put on a miner's helmet with a lamp and handed me a flashlight.

"Grab that dynamite," he ordered a worker; the man was Aaron Ortiz who'd griped in an SRE meeting that Mouse treated him like a beast. We descended a shaft in a noisy, wobbly elevator; little more than a large, dangling pallet. Its lack of safeguards reminded me how Nando had died and I felt anger at Simon who accepted no responsibility. I renewed my determination to see this changed.

We started down a dark corridor with iron rails and Arturo lagged. He shouted to Mouse, "I can't keep up on crutches on this rocky floor, and you knew it." He told me softly, "Go talk to him; I'll wait on top."

I hurried after Mouse past side corridors, stacks of rough timbers, rolls of wire, worn drill bits, and other clutter. I tripped on a loose stone in the semidarkness and fell, but caught up with Mouse farther down where the acrid odor of exploded dynamite made the stale air even worse. "Mouse, your meetings . . . "

"Move!" he yelled at Aaron, who was panting as he lugged the dynamite; Aaron hurried, stumbled, and the death-filled crate crashed onto the stone floor. "Son of Beelzebub!" Mouse cried. "Hug that like you'd hug your bride!"

"Boss, it's heavy, the floor's rough and the air's bad. I'm not a mule!"

"Pick it up and move!"

**ENTRY PROHIBITED
ABSOLUTELY NO
TRESPASSING

INTRUDERS WILL BE
SHOT ON SIGHT**

A barrier on one side had a sign: *Entry prohibited. Absolutely no trespassing. Intruders will be shot on sight.* I asked Mouse, "Why such a lethal warning?"

"I don't ask questions; I do my job. You shouldn't be here. Go back."

Aaron had dropped behind and I told Mouse, "You treated Aaron harshly. That's not wise if you want employees to work conscientiously and respect you."

"I pay that lazy laborer to do what I say, so he better darn well do it!"

"Aaron couldn't support a family on his pay; it's no wonder he resents . . . "

"Mind your business, cousin!"

"Where are the seams of silver?"

"Who knows? My job's to blast the rock. Simon pays me well since I'm the only one he trusts with explosives. Now go back." Mouse ambled on.

Aaron caught up, wheezing, and lowered the crate gingerly. "You can get killed here, Tiger. I heard you tell Mouse how to treat workers; voices carry between these rock walls. I hate that bully! I work for him only to learn explosives. I plan to be as expert as Chuey Ochoa; he's my idol—a great man!"

"I question your choice of a role model, Aaron."

"Join him if you want to end up on the winning side. Simon Alvarez is a fool; he doesn't know how to mine. He hasn't even put in air shafts yet this far down the tunnel." He picked up an empty crate and trudged back up the tunnel.

I sighed and started back, but stopped at the warning sign; its sternness stirred my curiosity and the urge to explore lured me to climb over the barrier. I passed a curve and saw a clipboard and columns of numbers written under "*Magnitude*" and "*Zone*." An instrument lay beside it; I picked it up and read "*Geiger Counter.*"

BANG! A shot deafened me and debris fell from above. Dropping the instrument, I turned. Abdul, the Arab geologist, stood close with a pistol aimed at my heart. It took a while for my ears to stop ringing enough to hear his words. "Sorry to startle you with my friendly warning. Are you swiping my equipment or just being nosy? Please refrain from trespassing or my next shot will be less friendly. Please don't make me keep firing; it pains my ears in this cramped space and this gun gets inconveniently hot."

"Who shot?" Mouse's voice came faintly. "Tiger! Where are you?"

"Don't reply," Abdul ordered. "Just ease your way out and have a good day!"

Back on top, I told Arturo, "I saw a Geiger Counter in a barred passage."

"Well, that could explain some things. Wait . . . *Where* did you say you saw it?"

"Geologists use them to detect radioactive ore. I'm contaminated. Will I die?"

"Oh no! Unrefined ore has extremely low radiation. It needs extensive processing to enrich it enough to use in reactors or bombs. But over time . . . "

"Geiger Counter?" Mouse had emerged and heard. "It must be for routine checks. If it is uranium, Simon doesn't know how to mine it, or wants to keep it secret. Whatever it is, he's going about it all wrong. He should stick to ranching."

"Why keep it secret?" I asked. "It's not illegal to mine uranium, is it, Arturo?"

"The ore is called pitchblende, and it's legal to mine it. Panther's financing it and wouldn't want other mining companies to know and outbid him for the land."

Mouse told us, "Olga's father showed me how to mine, but Simon won't listen to me. He's doing it all wrong. Now I'm worried; exposure to low radiation over time becomes toxic, even lethal. I'll provide protective clothing and masks to filter out dust for my workers, whether or not Simon does it for the other miners."

"We must do more, but what?" I said. "Mouse, why do you haul the waste rock clear up here to the top? Why not dump it out on the rock-strewn slope? Just extend the tunnels out to the mountainside surface. Is Simon hiding his work?"

"Who knows? My crew just drills, blasts, and jackhammers—that's all."

Back in town, Arturo and I told Gadget our suspicions; we discussed for hours how to get both Simon and Mouse to curb their worrisome activities, but came up with no helpful ideas. Arturo bought a padlock and told me, "Please lock the chapel; my broken leg's paining from riding around on bumpy roads."

Task 10–e.
KEEP ORDER DURING WORSHIP WITHOUT DISCOURAGING SPONTANEITY

After locking the chapel door, I stopped for a Coke in a small store down the road. Mouse came with his group, eyed the lock, and bellowed, "Get a crowbar!" A lad ran, returned with a bar, and Mouse yelled, "In the name of the Father, Son and, Holy Spirit!" Off came the lock, and they rushed in shouting. What came next would remind me why leaders must **keep order during worship without discouraging spontaneity.**

"They pray angrily!" remarked a lady who was watching the store. "Religion fascinates me; it's entertaining to watch—from a distance. Hear them carry on!"

"God detests noisy religious celebrations, according to the prophet Amos, unless the worshippers also do acts of justice and mercy."

"Oh! You're one of them! I beg your pardon, sir."

I went to watch from the chapel door; Mouse was looking up, growling, "Lord of Hosts, pour fire on the devil that blocked entry to Your holy temple!"

"I'm the devil that blocked it."

"He came up from hell!" screamed a small girl, darting away from me.

"I locked it because God prohibits worshipping as you're doing, making yourselves all crazy. He orders us in 1 Corinthians 14 to control our spirits, Mouse."

"You quench the Spirit!" He pointed an accusing finger. "Devil's envoy!"

"Do we worship to praise God or to entertain ourselves with excitement?"

"How would you know anything about true worship?" Mouse barked.

"I read. To attract and excite people, some churches spend extravagantly on entertaining productions and lavish equipment that can replace genuine worship. The Holy Spirit's power reaches all the way to the end of their electrical cord!"

"Agent of Satan! My flock is going to grow and be the largest in town!"

"Come down to earth! Some folks leave churches where they're active to go to bigger churches where all they do is shout during worship. Is this your plan? God gives guidelines for worship; Psalms reveal occasions to worship *shouting for joy* and occasions to worship *quietly*. You haven't learned to discern these different times, and your shouting always sounds more angry than joyful."

"Satan's agent!"

"Folks, please leave. Pastor Arturo Gomez sent me to lock the door."

They filed out sullenly, but Mouse kept shouting at empty benches. He finally wound down and followed me out. "My fire will die without these meetings."

"Let it die. The only time in Scripture that worshippers screamed as wildly as you do was on Mount Carmel, and God had Elijah slay them." "God values my efforts to make worship a moving experience if you don't."

> ## Task 10–f.
> EVALUATE OUR SERVICE FOR THE LORD NOT BY OUR EFFORTS, BUT BY ITS LASTING FRUIT

"Get real, Mouse! We're to **evaluate our service for the Lord not by our efforts, but by its lasting fruit.**"

"You and Arturo belittle the gift that God gave me as a child, but you won't stop me. I'll show folks who the Almighty's true prophet is! Hallelujah!"

"Not in our meetings. And we don't belittle anyone's gifts. You forget that God's gifts are to serve others, not to show off."

"God recognizes the efforts I make for Him, Tiger. You'll see!"

"Our ministry gains no value by doing it frantically. Think, Mouse! Don't you see why we should evaluate our service by its results rather than our efforts?"

"What results?"

"What God brings about: concrete things that last, new disciples, victory over vices, and meeting folks' needs. The Apostle Paul thought humbly about his own efforts; he told the Corinthians, *I sowed and Apollo watered; but God is the One who made the plant grow.* Paul's point was that God produced the results. He . . ."

"What's that got to do with how I lead praise? Hey, I worked up an appetite, and a taco vendor's put up a new stand." Mouse veered toward the market.

CHAPTER 10: CONFIRM THE GRASP AND THE PRACTICE OF LEADERS' TASKS

10–a. Let adults and children help illustrate the Word during worship and cell meetings. Note guidelines that you will give more heed:
- [ ] Let an entire family be together during at least one meeting a week.
- [ ] When preparing to teach, find related Bible stories to tell or act out briefly.
- [ ] Let small tots help tell stories, doing or saying simple things.
- [ ] Give children of unbelievers minor parts and invite their parents to watch.
- [ ] Avoid acting arty, showing off, and making dramatizations too complex.
- [ ] Keep it brief; two minutes can be enough; do only key parts of long stories.

10–b. Older children keep order, lead, and disciple younger ones. Which children in your flock might lead younger ones? Plan this with coworkers.

10–c. Link a doctrine to its duty and relate its concrete, hisotrical roots. Notice a reason why Jesus taught with stories: *The disciples . . . said, "Why do You speak . . . in parables?" Jesus answered them, "To you it has been granted to know the mysteries of the kingdom of heaven . . . "* Matt 13:9–13

10–d. Deal with employers and employees with respect and fairness. Find rules for work-related relationships: *Servants, be obedient to those who are your masters according to the flesh, with fear and trembling, in the sincerity of your heart, as to Christ; not by way of eye service, as men-pleasers, but as slaves of Christ, doing the will of God from the heart . . . And masters, do the same things to them, and give up threatening, knowing that both their Master and yours is in heaven, and there is no partiality with Him.* Eph 6:5–9

Verify how to treat servants: *Masters, grant to your servants justice and fairness, knowing that you too have a Master in heaven.* Col 4:1

10–e. Keep order during worship without discouraging spontaneity. Find an exhortation related to emotion in each of these four texts:
Praise Him with trumpet sound; Praise Him with harp and lyre. Praise Him with timbrel and dancing; Praise Him with stringed instruments and pipe. Praise Him with loud cymbals . . . Let everything that has breath praise the Lord. Praise the Lord! Ps 150:3–6

Let the spirits of prophets be subject to the prophets. . . . All things must be done properly and in an orderly manner. 1 Cor 14:32, 40

God is spirit, and those who worship Him must worship in spirit and truth. John 4:23

The Lord is in His holy temple. Let all the earth be silent before Him. Hab 2:20

See how God views sham worship: *I hate your festivals, nor do I delight in your solemn assemblies . . . Take away . . . the noise of your songs . . . the sound of your harps. But let justice roll down like waters and righteousness like an ever-flowing stream.* Amos 5:21–24

10–f. Evaluate our service for the Lord not by our efforts, but by its lasting fruit. Identify the final "bottom line" reason to teach God's people: *All Scripture is inspired by God and profitable for teaching, for reproof, for correction, for training in righteousness; so that the man of God may be adequate, equipped for every good work.* 2 Tim 3:16–17

EVALUATE YOUR LEADERSHIP

1=Poor. 2=Planning to improve. 3=Doing well.

1-2-3   Let children take a serious part in worship, church life, and small groups.

1-2-3   Let older children keep order, lead, and disciple younger ones.

1-2-3   Link doctrine to its duty and relate its concrete, historical roots.

1-2-3   Deal with employers and employees with respect and fairness.

1-2-3   Keep order during worship without discouraging spontaneity.

1-2-3   Evaluate *results* of serving the Lord, not mere *efforts*.

11.

The Faithful Discern God's Way Out of a Maze of Deception

Without Pharaoh, the night's gloom weighed heavier than ever and languor courted carelessness during lethal predawn hours; to stay alert I threw rocks at leaves in the river. Revolting images kept creeping into my mind: Olga's head bashed in, the hole between Pharaoh's eyes, and Abdul's mocking leer as he aimed his pistol at my heart. The next morning I craved sleep and headed toward the bed, but Lucy pulled my arm. "Wait! Tino has a question."

"Papa, why do you and mama drink blood in our meetings?"

"Communion," Lucy clarified. "He's been dying to ask you."

<table>
<tr><td>

Task 11–a.

MAKE IT EASY
FOR BELIEVERS
TO EXPERIENCE
THE DIVINE
MYSTERY OF THE
COMMUNION
BREAD AND CUP

</td><td>

"I'll try to explain it, son, but it's a mystery and no one fully understands a mystery. Spirit-filled worship leaders **make it easy for believers to experience the divine mystery of the Communion bread and cup.** I've read a bit about this; some writers think they can explain it in rational terms, but it's only because they don't accept the invisible, inscrutable work of God."

"Yikes!" Lucy threw up her hands. "You left both of us behind!"

</td></tr>
</table>

"Sorry! I've been reading too much! I'll skip the abstractions. Before Jesus' birth, faithful Jews led a lamb to the temple, tied it on the altar, laid their hands on its head, and confessed their sins. A priest cut the victim's throat and blood spurted all over the altar, like in a slaughterhouse. Imagine the smell and . . . "

"Tiger!" Lucy threw up her hands again. "Now you're being too tangible!"

At least I had gotten Tino's wide-eyed attention. "That's cruel, Papa!"

"It was ugly: the stench of blood, manure, and smoke. They burned the lamb."

"Disgusting!" wailed Lucy. "*That* was worship? It was shocking!"

"Yes, because our sins are disgusting and shocking to God and must be covered by an innocent victim's blood so God can forgive us. The victim was a lamb and this hasn't changed; our sins still require an innocent victim's blood.'"

"Really?" Tino put a finger to his mouth and looked down. "I sinned yesterday, Papa. Real bad! I gave Andy a nosebleed. So I need a lamb to kill. Mrs. Hilda Estrada raises goats and sheeps. Can I get a lamb from her?"

"Jesus is God's lamb now, son. He bled on the cross to take away our sins and we relive His death when we take Communion. When He broke bread and handed it to His disciples to eat, He said. 'This is My body.'"

"My teacher Evita said cannonballs eat human people."

"Cannonballs? What . . . ?"

"Cannibals," Lucy translated.

"They wear bones in their noses, Papa. They poison their spear points to kill *gringo* missionaries and eat them up."

"I guess they prefer white meat."

"Tiger!" Lucy slapped my arm. "Explain why we're not cannibals."

"It's because the Communion bread is Jesus' body in a mystical way, son."

Lucy asked, "Isn't the bread just a symbol?"

"It is a symbol but don't say 'just.' It's much more. Eating it is a 'communion' or 'participation,' in Jesus' body, as 1 Corinthians 10:16 says. The symbol points us to the real thing that we experience—Jesus' presence."

"Why do you call it 'simple,' Papa? For me it's complicated."

"*Symbol*—not *simple*. Like a road sign, it points to something important. When we use a symbol with true faith, trusting God to do what the symbol points to, it takes on the authority and value of the real thing that it symbolizes." Tino cocked his head to one side with his I-don't-get-it frown, and I said, "Okay, son, here's an example. If I sign a serious agreement and later break my word, can I excuse myself by saying 'My signature was only a symbol'?"

"No, Papa! You'd make me stand in the corner if I did that! It's dishonest."

"That's why a symbol used with sincere faith takes on the power of what it symbolizes. The symbol affirms its reality. The Communion bread and wine make Jesus' sacrifice real to us, not only by focusing our attention on it, but also by enabling us to experience His presence. Do you understand this, Tino?"

"I'm not supposed to. You said nobody understands the mystery."

"Touché!" Lucy laughed.

"Son, you've more sense than some learned theologians who write as though they fully comprehend every detail about the Lord's Supper and everything else."

Lucy patted Tino's head and commented, "I know one thing for sure about Communion; it makes me very aware of Jesus' presence, provided Arturo doesn't turn the ceremony into just another teaching session."

"I feel His presence, too, Lu. The original Passover was a moving event, as was Jesus' talk about eating His flesh and the Last Supper; we should share that ardor during Communion and not just analyze abstract Latin terms about it."

"Papa," Tino laid his hand on my arm. "I like you to tell me these things. I won't be bored no more when Pastor 'Turo serves Communion; I know it's important. I won't squirm, like last time when you took me out and paddled me."

"It wasn't for squirming; you sneered at your mom when she corrected you."

"Oh, Tiger! Spend more time with the boys!"

"I promise not to go anywhere today, Lu. Now, let me get some sleep. I . . . "

Bang, bang, bang! Gadget was pounding our door. "Tiger, Tiger! Come! Evita's asking questions that I can't answer. Please!"

"I just promised Lucy I'd stay with her and the boys today and I need sleep."

"She'll marry me if I can convince her my repentance is real. Come, Tiger!"

"Go." Lucy pushed me. "I release you from your promise—temporarily."

"Then come with me. We'll take the boys. Come, Tino."

"Take Davey, Papa. I'm busy making a Communion pitcher."

We found Evita weeping and Gadget whined, "I didn't do nothing!"

Evita dried her eyes. "Oh, Lucy, he's a new person! He treats me like a queen! But I can't share his devotion; I feel like a pagan, left out of his new life!"

Lucy took her hand. "Just receive Jesus and His forgiveness by faith, trusting Him as a child would. He said we'd enter His kingdom that way."

"It can't be so simple! How can I believe what I don't even understand?"

"I still don't understand it. We don't receive Jesus by grasping tenets of theology, but by trusting Him. Faith is God's gift to us by pure grace."

"Gadget talks about grace too, but it doesn't make sense to me."

"You do nice things for people, Evita, not because they always deserve it, but because you love them. That's grace. Tino told me you treated him kindly at school, even after he broke a window. The Bible says God's grace is boundless."

"I was taught to fear God—thunder and lightning on Mt. Sinai and the earth shaking—but you talk like Jesus is your friend, like someone at your side."

"He's at your side, too. *The fear of God is the beginning of wisdom.* It moves us to seek God's pardon; He assures us of that and our fear turns to love."

"I think of God and see Moses turning water to blood to curse Egypt."

I recalled, "That was Moses' first miracle, a curse that ushered in the old covenant with its fearful laws. Jesus' first miracle was turning water into wine, a blessing that signaled grace—a turning from terror to peace with God."

"But what do I have to do, Tiger? I've always attended Mass."

"We don't do anything to earn forgiveness; Jesus did all that's required. You know how He suffered. Just trust Him to forgive you now and forever. Can you thank Him for that and let Him change your heart? We all need that new life."

Evita's face showed a struggle and Lucy asked softly, "Do you feel the need of God's eternal forgiveness and the presence of His Holy Spirit in your life?"

"Yes, but . . . I don't know, Lucy!"

"We can pray together if you want and you can . . . "

"I've got to think about it."

Thus, both the wedding and Evita's soul remained on *hold*.

On the way home I asked Lucy, "Tino wanted to draw a *Communion pitcher*. What did he mean?"

"Well, we'll soon find out. Here he comes running with his tablet."

"Look! I drawed my pitcher! Pastor 'Turo's handing you Communion."

"*Picture*," Lucy corrected with a hug. "Tiger, God used your talk with Tino."

"It's because Tino wants to know God's truth. Some folks don't want to believe in a holy God that demands that we be holy too, and no amount of explaining will convince them; Jesus' words will always be an offense to rebel hearts."

"I wanted light to shine down from heaven, Papa, so I rubbed the white crayon hard, but it didn't come."

"Yes it did. Light from Jesus' face is shining on your heart. Eyes of flesh can't see it because it's a mystery like Communion, but in heaven we'll see it."

Lucy told me, "You stress Communion's *mystery*. Is that so important?"

"Those who reject it deny any real work of God, which doesn't help anyone."

"My Catholic catechist taught that the bread became Jesus' actual body."

"To transform lifeless bread doesn't help anyone, either. It's we the people that need transforming, Lu. God uses Communion to strengthen our spirits."

"People died because they didn't respect the body, it says in 1 Corinthians. But which body? The one on the cross? The bread? The congregation?"

"Scripture gives multiple meanings to key words. When Paul explained the Communion bread, the 'body' it signified was both Jesus' flesh and the church, in 1 Corinthians 10:16–17 and chapter 11."

"Didn't the first believers eat dinner together when they had Communion?"

"At first, but the Corinthians paid more attention to the roasted chicken and salsa than to the sacramental aspect so Paul told them to eat at home. We . . . "

Banging sounded at the door again. It was Gadget and Evita; she was bubbling. "I received Jesus! Like a child, Lucy, as you said! Nothing has been harder for me and at the same time, nothing has been easier! I'm so relieved!"

Lucy hugged her. "We'd hear rejoicing in heaven right now if we had angels' ears." Tino ran to a window and cupped a hand to his ear.

Gadget's grin widened. "Saturday we'll get married without no pomp."

Evita gave him a sidelong glance. "Without *any* pomp."

"See? She's acting like my wife already!"

Task 11–b.

GIVE BIBLICAL GUIDANCE TO COUPLES THAT HAVE A BUMPY RELATIONSHIP OR PLAN TO WED

There was one striking bit of pomp, Evita's elegant gown sewn by Martha. Close friends had gathered, and Arturo's preliminary words were a reminder that it prevents much misery to **give biblical guidance to couples that have a bumpy relationship or plan to wed.** Arturo faced Gadget and said in his sternest lawyer's voice, "You will not forget what we discussed. You do not force Evita to submit; you'll love her as Jesus loved the Church and died for it."

"I will, boss."

"Evita, God says to respect and submit to your husband as to the Lord."

Someone tapped my shoulder. Julio whispered, "A giant's out there asking for you. Be careful; he's scary looking! He has a hideous scar on his face."

I slipped out. Mincho held Popcorn, the white dog that attacked mine in Los Vientos. "You need him, Tiger; he's yours. Oh, a wedding! Go on in. I'll wait."

"He's grown into a powerfully muscled specimen! But he's yours; I can't . . . "

"Take him if you want to stay alive. You need him—trust me. He fears nothing . . . well, except snakes; one bit him as a pup."

"A thousand thanks!" I extended my hand to Mincho, but Popcorn growled. I reached my hand slowly toward the dog; he sniffed and licked it. I told him, "If you're going to keep me alive, then let's become friends, and soon. I promise to save the next bone for you, Pooch." His tail wagged and he rewarded me with a slobbery-tongued grin as I gave him a vigorous chin rub.

"He won't answer to 'Pooch'; he's '*Popcorn.*' Listen, you have to stay out of Los Vientos. Chuey vowed to kill you; he'll do it and say it was self-defense."

"Okay, I'll not go there, provided you come here to worship with us."

"Someday, Tiger. Now go back in. I'll hold Popcorn for you."

Arturo was concluding, "God joins you as *one flesh*. This isn't mere ceremonial jargon; you'll complete each other and sustain this bliss with patient forgiveness. Marriage mirrors the Church, the Bride of Christ; they both require sacrifice and God uses both to provide the two closest possible relationships, one with a partner in heaven, the other with a partner on earth. Satan will test this union; there'll be bumps, but you'll forgive and persevere with God's help."

After the nuptial kiss, Arturo said, "This man and wife have prepared a statement."

The groom blushed, clasped Evita's hand and they said in unison:

Before our God, our pledge we give

To heed His Word, serve those in need,

Whoe'er they are, where'er they live,

Those down we'll lift, the hungry feed.

On the way out, I hugged Lucy. "How much grief we'd have avoided had we known those spouses' duties when we wed!" She squeezed my hand.

The glowing newlyweds departed in a shower of rice, but Mincho and I had to repair a flat on the orange taxi before they sped off. The giant then handed me the dog's leash. "I heard their solemn promise before God to serve the needy. I liked that, Tiger; I see your church has practical love. I'll be back."

Things went smoothly then, until after our next worship.

Task 11–c.
RECOGNIZE LIMITATIONS OF DEMOCRATIC PROCESS IN CONGREGATIONAL MEETINGS

"Don't leave!" Simon ordered everyone sharply. "I'm calling a business session." Arturo objected, but Simon bawled, "Everyone sit!" A few kept standing and he aimed his hook at us. "I said sit!" We sat. I'd soon **recognize limitations of democratic process in congregational meetings.**

"Our bylaws give me this right, Arturo. Some of us reject your authoritarian leadership and since you lack ordination, it's illegal for you to officiate the Sacrament. We'll fix this now by democratic vote. Now, everyone raise your hand to replace Arturo so we can sell that worthless slope up there without further obstruction and get a real pastor who . . . "

"No!" protested Arturo. "We already settled the issue of that land, and . . . "

Simon waved a document in the air. "These statutes forbid Arturo to serve Communion. Our vote will stop him from serving it illegally, and then we can . . . "

"Wait! I'm in charge here and we'll do what our Lord Jesus commands, no matter what the bylaws say. As to voting, God's kingdom is not a democracy; it's a monarchy and Jesus is our King. He's the Head of this body, not you, Simon."

"Nor you, Arturo. Our statutes require the congregation to vote on legal matters such as selling property. You're a lawyer so you know this."

"I do. My father-in-law wrote that document. Legal transactions require the church's vote, and it also says I can't serve Communion, but I certainly will."

"Not if the majority votes to uphold our church's bylaws."

"Voting to disobey Jesus puts voters' authority above Almighty God!" Arturo snatched the statutes and held them over his Bible. "Do we put men's rules above God's? Have these rules more authority than the King of kings?"

He then held the Bible above the bylaws. "Or do Christ's commands have a higher place for us than the rules of men?"

"Enough riddles, I tell you! Who supports me? Raise your hands."

"Wait!" Colombo stood facing Simon. "No discussion? Why the urgency?"

"That's my business. Yours is to endorse the sale for the good of the church."

"You forbid Arturo to serve us Communion. We need it, Jesus commands it and Arturo meets the Scriptural requirements to serve as a shepherding elder. So if we must vote on something then let's vote to amend those obsolete bylaws!"

Pacho begged, "Let's discuss this. I've always said, 'Prudence pleads for . . .'"

"We've all heard your plea for patience!" Mouse interrupted. He grabbed the bylaws from Arturo and waved them. "Simon's right. Let's sell and build a sanctuary that'll hold thousands. Then I can . . . !"

"Let's vote," rasped Simon. "All who agree to sell raise your hands. Now!"

Only Simon, Wanda, Mouse, and a couple others voted to sell; Martha covered her face and most of the members just sat there. Arturo dismissed us and Mouse, his face flushed, tore a limb from a tree and pointed it at Arturo. "Aaron's staff gave him power from the Almighty and I have power too! O Most High, pour fire down on your enemies!" He marched down the street waving Aaron's staff. "Fire! Rain down, heaven's fury! Fire!" He passed a mule hitched to a cart and it broke out running wildly, scattering watermelons in the road.

"Mommy! Mommy!" cried a small boy running from Mouse. He tripped on a melon and fell in the mud. "Mommy! He's making it rain fire!"

"Come back, Mouse!" shouted Arturo. "I've something to tell you." Mouse stooped, scooped up a chunk of melon, stuffed it in his mouth and returned. Arturo told him, "You'll not pry a lock off the chapel again. Your group . . ."

"You can't stop me." He spit out seeds. "Your ban is illegal. You made it yourself without the members' vote. They'd support me."

"I doubt it. Even if they did, as long as I'm shepherding, I'll not yield to the will of an uninformed majority. That's not leading. A true leader does what's right; he doesn't follow opinions of people who don't even know the facts."

Hilda groaned. "No more business meetings for me! Too much bickering! Mouse's antics and Simon's bullying just keep getting worse."

Lucy whispered to me, "Arturo's adamant demeanor also makes me uneasy, even when I agree with his reasoning. Mulish men! They're like stubborn locomotives racing toward a sure collision! Oh, dear Lord, where will it all end?"

"I agree with Hilda," I said. "Rather than having bitter business meetings, our members, like Jerusalem's believers in Acts 15, could voice their views to our elders and let them decide important issues. Anyone can still blow off steam and help our elders discern God's will, but without voting formally on every issue."

Task 11–d.
PROCLAIM POSITIVE TRUTHS AND AVOID SCOLDING UNDULY

Evita invited my family to dinner, and warned us that it was her first attempt to cook for guests. Lucy glanced around. "How different things are, Evita! You've planted shrubs, and Gadget has straightened his sign, tidied up the shop and removed the ugly old wrecks. Oh! Look who's at the door! Father Camacho!" We'd presently see examples of why it's wise to **proclaim positive truths and avoid scolding unduly.**

The priest greeted us amicably, but his smile faded as he turned to Evita. "My daughter, you wed outside the church and I've missed you at Mass. I hear you've taken on another religion."

"I did not change my religion, *Señor* Camacho. I received Jesus in my heart."

"That's even more reason to stay with the church in which you were baptized. It is your family's church, the original church of our Lord Jesus Christ."

"Perhaps the fault was mine, Father, but during your Masses and festivals my devotion was given to saints of plaster, not to our Lord Jesus Christ."

"My daughter, with the authority of the Holy Apostolic Church, I prohibit you to wallow in the pestilent waters of Protestantism! Return to your spiritual mother, the only church authorized by God."

"With respect, sir, this is interesting. When I was getting drunk and committing all kinds of transgressions, you never went out of your way to correct me. But now that I follow Jesus and leave my sinful life, you come here scolding!" The priest raised an eyebrow, glared at Evita a moment and left.

That night Jaime Ordoñez showed up at my kiosk. "I'm not ranch foreman no more; Old Hookarm needs me more as his bodyguard. Got a cigarette?" I shook my head and he left. About 2:00 a.m., he returned, quite unsteady.

"You know that bearded bandit Chuey Ochoa?" He spoke indistinctly.

"Oh, yes, I know him, unfortunately."

"I just met him and I don't like Chuey. I don't like nobody in Bat Haven. I come to town, buy my bottle, and take it to my room. I'm an antisocial; I don't like nobody. I'm a hostile antisocial. A sorry, sad anti-everybody antisocial!"

"There's a remedy for that, Jaime. The Lord Jesus Christ will . . . "

"Don't want no remedy." He burped. "I like being a drunken, miserable antisocial. Listen to why I hate Chuey Ochoa. Me and him, we bet on who'd drink more. I won. Yeah. Easy. We argued who's killed more men and he won. He's bad, Tiger. Real bad! But not as bad as I am. I can beat him any day in badness. Yeah. You can bet on that, Tiger. Wanna bet how bad I am?"

"You boast about being a villain?"

"Haven't said yet why I hate Chuey. Listen good! He swore he'd eradicate you tonight. Liquidate you . . . " He jerked his fingers across his throat. "Exterminate you . . . Annihilate . . . "

"I think maybe I got your drift, Jaime. Thanks for sounding the red alert."

"He's out in that darkness. Keep your eyeballs peeled. All night. Keep moving. He won't hit no moving target; he's drunker 'n me." Jaime lurched away.

I kept moving, shining my light every direction, avoiding places where Chuey could approach in shadow, hoping he was too intoxicated to bother with me.

I needed new batteries in the morning and entered the store on the first floor of Simon's house. "How's your small group doing?" I asked him.

"I don't know, Wanda leads it. I hear you've befriended that crooked giant, Mincho Medina. He tries to organize my miners to extort more pay, to break me, I tell you." He pointed his hook at me and Popcorn snarled. Simon glanced at the dog, took a step back, and lowered his arm.

"I've been encouraging Mincho to attend our church, Simon, and . . . "

"Those parasites drain businessmen dry!" He kept ranting and the rabid intensity of his hatred annoyed me; I felt a bit angry too. "Mincho's corrupt ideology stirs workers to destroy our economic system."

"A few things about it need destroying."

"So you favor a revolution too, do you?"

"Only a revolution against greed and injustice. Your mine is a good place to start; let those who work well receive what they deserve and enjoy safe working conditions. Treat them with respect, Simon, and they'll work more efficiently. Everyone will profit from it and you'll see that . . . "

"So, now you're a professor of economics!"

"There's talk about radioactivity and miners are getting nervous, wondering how long it'll be before symptoms show up; prolonged exposure to . . . "

"Oh, you're a nuclear scientist now, are you? I know how to run my mine!"

He berated me and I left seething with fury so bitter that it led to a rash mistake. I hurried to Arturo's office and requested, "Let me preach a message against greed, Pastor." He looked surprised, but consented. I rushed home, but did not sleep; I was too busy finding Bible verses that condemned greed.

I preached against greed during our next worship and nobody listened; even Anna dozed. Starting home afterwards, I kicked a clod in the road. "Lucy, I'm not going to preach again—ever!"

"Patience! You'll learn. Inexperienced preachers *scold* and you were no exception! Next time, don't just attack greed; present the positive side, generosity."

We passed the square and Jaime greeted me. "I see you're still alive, Tiger!"

"Your warning saved my life."

"What?" Lucy turned sharply to face me. "A warning against *what*?"

I switched topics. "Jaime, I spotted wild horses near Buzzard's Banquet Hall. Want to go out with me and bring in a few?"

"With no brand? Duke Castillo's ancestor brought over well-bred stock from Spain, and some have escaped over the years. Let's go! I got tomorrow off."

The next day Jaime and I rode south beyond Lone Stone and trailed the horses' tracks to a secluded meadow. "Look!" I pointed at the big, swift gray that had led the herd when I came upon it after trekking through Buzzard's Banquet Hall! I admired how deftly Jaime drove the gray into a ravine and roped it. I lassoed another, just before the herd dashed into the woods and vanished.

"Call it for the gray stallion." Jaime tossed a coin.

"Tails."

It landed heads. Jaime kept eying his prize as we rode back to town. "Most wild horses are scrawny, but this specimen is magnificent! He's been invading the peasants' cornfields. He'll make me a pile of money when I break him. He's young and strong. Yeah! Money! Best thing there is. Without it, you can't even go on a good drunk or bet on a promising horse."

"Money's the greatest thing for you? That's sad! For me it's that Jesus Christ died and rose from the dead to forgive us, clean us up, and give us real life."

"I've done too many sins to share your hope in the Lord."

> **Task 11–e.**
>
> URGE THOSE WHO THINK THEIR SALVATION DEPENDS ON THEIR WORKS TO TRUST GOD'S GRACE

I prayed in my heart, "Lord, give me the ability to **urge those who think their salvation depends on their works to trust God's grace.**" I turned in the saddle to face Jaime. "No one's beyond God's forgiveness."

"You don't know the evil crimes I've committed, pal. There's not enough grace in the entire cosmos to pardon them."

"Yes, there is; God's grace is boundless. Trust Jesus to forgive you. He didn't come to seek good folks, but to save the lost—sinners like you and me."

He lit a cigarette and rode on in silence.

"Like to hear a story from the Bible?" I hoped to reach the hardened heart.

"Was there cowboys in the Bible?"

"The patriarchs had cattle. David was a brave shepherd; I'll tell you how he escaped from a jealous king." I recounted several of David's exploits and Jaime made an occasional grunt.

Back in town, he left me in the square and returned soon with a bottle. Men gathered to admire the gray; it jerked its tether, stomping, and Pacho backed away. "You have a strong-willed steed there! Seems a bit wild to me, Jaime."

"Yep. I'll bet I can break him before sunset, riding bareback. Any takers?"

Some bet ten to one on Jaime. I struggled to hold the gray as he mounted; it snorted, spun, reared, and threw him. He remounted and again hit the ground.

"Bucks like a kangaroo and spins like a tornado! I've had enough!" Jaime paid off the bets. "Know what? If I can't stay on him, nobody on earth can."

"I can," I blurted without thinking and several men jeered. "A skilled cowhand can ride any horse, using a bit of patience. Jaime, trade me horses."

"Not so fast! I can hobble this monster and break him. But I'll challenge you, Tiger. Ride him bareback around the square before the sun goes down and he's yours; there's not much time left. If you fail then both horses are mine. Deal?"

"Deal." Some bet high odds in favor of the horse and I led it to the Alvarez' pigpen, the only corral nearby. Using my lasso as a whip, I ran him in circles, facing him as a mare does a disobedient colt. After a few rounds, he chomped and lowered his head, a sign of submission. I looked away and he took a step toward me, and then another until he was right behind me. Speaking softly, I turned and caressed his neck, leaned lightly on him, and mounted. He exploded, leaping as he spun; my hat flew into the muck and I soon joined it. I pulled my face out of the reeking mire and laughter goaded me to try—and fail—six times as the sun neared the horizon. The gray then looked at me and nodded calmly; I got on, guided him to the square and circled it an instant before the sun went down.

"You got grit, man." Jaime's praise surprised me. "You have definitely earned a reward. Here." He handed me his half-full whiskey bottle.

"Thanks. I need it as liniment." I was teaching the gray his paces when Simon yelled, "Get off that animal; it's time to watch my house!" All night my clothes stunk from the pig's mire and I reeked of whiskey after rubbing Jaime's liniment on a dozen bruises. At dawn, I bathed the gray and myself in the river.

"To the beauty parlor you go!" I led it to the street. "You're famous now, so it's not becoming for you to go around town barefoot and uncombed."

The blacksmith used only superlatives to appraise the gray as he shod it; he laughed heartily when I recounted how I won it. I mounted and did maneuvers, showing off for the smith, "Brand it, Tiger, or some rascal will rob it before a week goes by! Brand it with an E—it's an Evangelical horse! It obeys devoutly!"

I told him I'd lost my branding iron in the flood and he replied, "I recall it: *L, lazy R,* for Los Robles; I'll improvise."

Los Robles Ranch Brand

Riding home, I goaded the gray's flanks with my heels and with a convulsive leap he broke into a gallop. I was holding my hat as I sped past Gadget's shop and he looked up. "What was that? It flew by faster 'n a high-powered bullet!"

Tino heard. "Bullet! Papa, let me ride with you! Mama! Davey! Come see! Papa's riding a bullet!" Thus, the gray got his name.

I told Lucy how I'd won *Bullet* and added, "I'll sell him to cancel our debts."

"Oh, no! God gave him to you. You need a good mount to evangelize the mountain villages. Oh, he's so beautiful!"

Task 11–f.

INCLUDE WORSHIP SONGS THAT ARE EASY TO RECALL AND SING DURING THE WEEK, AND RESPECT THE SENSITIVITIES OF YOUNG AND NEW BELIEVERS

Arturo came by to ask me to meet with Jethro and Pacho and I went with him. Julio shouted "Ahoy!" when we neared Arturo's office, and I wondered why Pacho had brought his son. The meeting would reveal why a wise worship leader will **include worship songs that are easy to recall and sing during the week, and respect the sensitivities of young and new believers.**

The session began and Arturo told the young man, "We want to know why so few young people attend our worship."

Julio squirmed in the leather chair and shrugged. Arturo urged, "Tell us frankly, son, even if it's a criticism of me."

"Well . . . Me and my friends don't like the old hymns translated from English; we like songs by Hispanics. The songs that *gringo* missionaries brought have too much 'I' and 'me.' We like our Latino hymns better; they say 'we' and 'us.' Also, we like to sing the songs during the week, but you keep introducing new ones that we don't know and many are hard to recall even if we did know them."

"Hear that, Arturo?" Jethro asked. "Some songs lead musicians to perform, others are easy for everyone to sing, and some worship leaders don't discern the difference. They could learn from commercial advertisers; they know how to select music that helps their message stick in one's mind."

Arturo hit a fist into his palm. "Okay! Three things. One, follow our own music style so all can sing easily. Two, select tunes that convey the message during the week so folks will sing them in their hearts as Paul said. Three, repeat a new song until folks learn it, before introducing a new one. What else, Julio?" The young man demurred and Arturo persisted, "Please. We're here to face the truth."

"Excuse me, sir . . . Um . . . Well . . . You preach at us dogmatically. You hardly ever let us discuss things with you. We want to ask questions and share our thoughts about what we're experiencing. It's okay to be dogmatic about important stuff like what Jesus commanded, but not about debatable details. That makes us young people distrust you; we fear abusive authority. We want to take part in worship and not just sit there being told what to think all the time."

"No, son!" Pacho was scowling. "Young people should appreciate the type of worship that their parents and grandparents have always had. True, Jethro?"

"Not always, brother. Older people should make any sacrifice necessary to keep their children and grandchildren in Christ's church. For example, I love the age-old hymns, but such nostalgia can be fatal to a congregation's future."

Pacho still scowled fiercely and Julio begged, "Aw, dad, flex a little! If we really love God then we won't inflict such ugly noise on His ears!"

Jethro laughed. "Son, what's ugly to you is beautiful to us old fogies, but I'm willing to endure what you prefer, out of love for you young people. You're the future of the church. Now finish. We'll restrain your dad if he assaults you!"

"Um . . . We don't mind singing some old hymns once in a while, provided we don't have to sing them with a lazy, funeral tempo."

Pacho sputtered, "New believers shouldn't dictate our policies, Jethro!"

"Some things they should. Older and newer ones need different things. Holding to ways of past generations cripples thousands of churches in the USA and Europe, but we'll avoid that. Educated young folks can't bear the arrogant dogmatism and archaic music style of us oldsters. Let's allow more lively music to avoid offending them and include more dialogue in our teaching as Paul advised. Let older folks sing the older songs too, even if it's in separate meetings."

I tried to soothe Pacho. "Julio wants lively music and he has good company—read the last two Psalms! He wants to exchange ideas freely and the New Testament requires this in *one another* commands. He wants to take part actively in worship and teaching, and 1 Corinthians 14 requires this also."

Jethro clasped Pacho's arm. "Paul told strong believers like you to receive the weak in faith without fussing over lesser matters. Debating trivia is the devil's bane; Romans 14 forbids the mature to let scruples of minor importance cause a weaker brother to stumble; many older believers are guilty of that. Pacho, if our petty preferences offend the weak, then we must yield. Paul demanded it."

Pacho slapped his knees. "Well, who am I to oppose Paul? If someone must suffer to endure others' preferences then let it be us oldsters." Julio hugged him.

After that, a variety of musical instruments showed up in our worship. Young folks came and not just to be entertained. They hated our old electric organ, but Wanda insisted on keeping it. Fortunately, a thief broke in one night and stole it.

Lucy grabbed my arm as I headed for bed the next morning. "Wait! We're going up the river for a picnic beneath those lofty cliffs. Hilda arranged it. Tino will be devastated if you don't go. Also, Jethro's coming; he'll cheer things up!"

"Oh, I'd forgotten! I told Hilda I'd go early and clear the area."

"Talk to Tino first. He won't wear his new glasses."

I told Tino firmly, "You'll wear those glasses or stand in the corner."

"I'll wear them, Papa. I promise."

I filed my machete and started out to clear the picnic site, but going through town, soldiers blocked my way. A corporal with beady eyes accused me, "You cooperated with subversives. This way. Now!" He walked behind me, pointing his rifle at me whenever I looked around. This annoyed me; I was not used to such treatment by the soldiers who augmented Gadget's one-man police force.

"Look everyone!" A little girl's shrill shouts drew attention. "They're taking a crook to jail!" Another girl remarked, "Yeah! He sure looks like a robber!"

"Robber! Robber!" joined in other children and I felt my face burning.

What would I tell interrogators? I had solemnly promised Mincho before God and his comrades not to reveal SRE operations; however, God forbids lying and resisting authorities. My mind was in turmoil; I slowed and the beady-eyed corporal jabbed me painfully in the ribs with the barrel of his rifle. "March!" Popcorn would have ripped out his throat if I had not held him.

At the shabby headquarters, a sergeant's nametag identified him as Perez. "Where do you meet to plan political action?"

"In our neighbors' houses. We all gripe about stupid things politicians do. It's no crime. Everyone does it." Beady-Eyes came and stood near me, arms folded.

"Where do the revolutionaries meet?" persisted Sergeant Perez.

"I suppose in Havana. Fidel Castro's accomplices . . . "

Whack! I tasted blood. Beady-Eyes had punched my mouth and I felt the painful cut with my tongue. "Enough, Corporal!" Sergeant Perez ordered. "Mr.

Garcia, in whose house have you discussed economic matters?"

"Well, at my boss's house, Simon Alvarez gripes about economic issues all the time. At home, my wife and I often discuss how family debts pile up."

Sergeant Perez left and the corporal sneered. "You'll talk to me!" His beady eyes disturbed me, like a hungry cobra eying its next meal! He tied my hands, hung me in the air, and beat me with a belt, but I told him nothing. Then he covered my face with a rubber inner tube, inserted a stick, and turned it to tighten the tube over my mouth and nose until I could not breathe; my heart pounded with panic.

"Nod when you decide to cooperate, you dim-witted jackass." I passed out.

When I came to, Beady-Eyes beat my back with the stick. He reminded me of the jailer who beat Paul and Silas and I recalled how they sang hymns to God. I had just learned the need to sing sacred songs during the week, but I didn't feel like it now. Nevertheless, I forced myself to sing, as Paul and Silas had done when flogged. Beady-Eyes slapped my mouth and again I tasted blood.

As it turned out, I had good reason to sing; Arturo had seen Popcorn waiting at the headquarters door and asked about me. The corporal untied me, growling, "You're lucky to have that lawyer for a friend. Get your sorry butt out of here!"

I told Arturo, "A soldier tortured me. Gadget's our police chief; shouldn't he correct that sadist?"

"His authority's limited to town affairs; the soldiers are federal and heed local authorities only if they want. Sergeant Perez is solid, but he can't control everything. Your family's up at the picnic, but you'd better go home and recover."

"I'm okay. Just rattled a wee bit and riled a big bit with a beady-eyed corporal. I'd rather lick my wounds up there with my family than at home alone."

We started up the path to join the picnickers below the towering cliffs.

CHAPTER 11: CONFIRM THE GRASP AND THE PRACTICE OF LEADERS' TASKS

11–a. Make it easy for believers to experience the divine mystery of the Communion bread and cup. The Apostle Paul did not call the Communion bread a *symbol*. Find the word he did use for it: *Is not the cup of blessing which we bless a sharing in the blood of Christ? Is not the bread which we break a sharing in the body of Christ?* 1 Cor 10:16

Note. The word "sharing" (*koinonia*) is also translated in other Bible versions as "fellowship," "communion," and "participation."

11–b. Give biblical guidance to couples that have a bumpy relationship or plan to wed. Note duties of spouses: *Wives, be subject to your husbands, as is fitting in the Lord. Husbands, love your wives and do not be embittered against them.* Col 3:18–19

11–c. Recognize limitations of democratic process in congregational meetings. Detect a common error. *You shall not follow the majority in doing evil, nor shall you testify in a dispute so as to turn aside after a crowd in order to pervert justice.* Ex 23:2

11–d. Proclaim positive truth and avoid scolding unduly. In his first attempt at public speaking, Tiger, like many inexperienced preachers, merely reprimanded. Choose the better way to encourage holiness:
[ ]   Rebuke people firmly and consistently for their faults.
[ ]   Help believers focus on Christian virtues.

ANSWER: Exhort in a positive way, 1 Cor 14:3.

11–e. Urge those who think their salvation depends on their works to trust God's grace. Jaime said he'd sinned too much. Find hope for such people: *(God) saved us, not on the basis of deeds which we have done in righteousness, but according to his mercy, by the washing of regeneration and renewing by the Holy Spirit.* Titus 3:5

Notice God's motive to send us His Son: *God shows His own love toward us, in that while we were yet sinners, Christ died for us.* Rom 5:8

See how much grace the Holy Spirit gives sinners: *The Law came in so that the transgression would increase; but where sin increased, grace abounded all the more.* Rom 5:20

Verify who intercedes for us on earth: *The Spirit also helps our weakness; for we do not know how to pray as we should, but the Spirit Himself intercedes for us with groanings too deep for words, and He who searches the hearts knows what the mind of the Spirit is, because He intercedes for the saints according to the will of God.* Rom 8:26–27

See if anything can separate us from Jesus: *Neither death, nor life, nor angels, nor principalities, nor things present, nor things to come, nor powers, nor height, nor depth, nor any other created thing, will be able to separate us from the love of God, which is in Christ Jesus our Lord.* Rom 8:38–39

Count how much a sinner must pay to be justified before God: *Being justified as a gift by his grace through the redemption which is in Christ Jesus.* Rom 3:24

Find whom among believers the Holy Spirit baptizes into Christ's body: *For by one Spirit we were all baptized into one body, whether Jews or Greeks, whether slaves or free, and we were all made to drink of one Spirit.* 1 Cor 12:13

Verify who ensures eternal life: *After listening to the . . . truth, the gospel of your salvation—having also believed, you were sealed in Him with the Holy Spirit of promise, who is given as a pledge of our inheritance, with a view to the redemption of God's own possession, to the praise of His glory.* Eph 1:13–14

11–f. Include worship songs that are easy to recall and sing during the week, and respect the sensitivities of young and new believers. Pacho disagreed with his son Julio about music, and some worship leaders perform and entertain rather than enable folks to take part as the Word requires. Note what leaders are to enable believers to do during the week: *Speak to one another in psalms and hymns and spiritual songs, singing and making melody with your heart to the Lord.* Eph 5:19

Note strong believers' duty with the weak: *Accept one who is weak in faith, but not for the purpose of passing judgment on his opinions. One person has faith that he may eat all things, but he who is weak eats vegetables only. The one who eats is not to regard with contempt the one who does not eat, and the one who does not eat is not to judge the one who eats . . . One person regards one day above another, another regards every day alike. Each person must be fully convinced in his own mind . . . Let us not judge one another anymore, but rather determine this—not to put an obstacle or a stumbling block in a brother's way . . . For the kingdom of God is not eating and drinking, but righteousness and peace and joy in the Holy Spirit . . . It is good not to eat meat or to drink wine, or to do anything by which your brother stumbles.* Rom 14:1–21

EVALUATE YOUR LEADERSHIP
1=Poor. 2=Planning to improve. 3=Doing well.

1-2-3   Experience the divine mystery of the bread and cup of Communion.

1-2-3   Give biblical guidance to couples that have a bumpy relationship or plan to wed.

1-2-3   Recognize limitations of the democratic process in business sessions.

1-2-3   Proclaim positive truths and avoid scolding unduly.

1-2-3   Urge those who think they're saved by their works to trust God's grace.

1-2-3   Include worship songs that are easy to recall and sing during the week, and respect the sensitivities of young and new believers.

Part II
THE SHEPHERD

12.
Tiger's Decisiveness Overcomes Panic and Spineless Conformity

"Do I have to wear my glasses here, Papa?" Tino whined when I joined my family at the picnic site at the foot of the towering cliffs.

"Get used to them, son, but put them in a safe spot when you go in the water."

"Mama, Papa, watch! I can swim. I'm gonna race crockerdiles!" He hastily set his glasses aside, dove clumsily from a ledge into the deep with an impressive splash, and dog paddled. Then, of course, other boys had to do it too. They eyed another higher ledge, but no boy dared try it—until girls came to watch.

Pointing up, I asked Jethro, "See this cliff's rim way up there above us? The path to Los Vientos borders its edge; I've seen this spot from up there."

"Sure is high! Oh! I got one!" The fishing line was tugging his pole; the fish darted into the blue-green midstream that flowed lazily through the channel, but he reeled it in. "Nothing like trout roasted over a campfire! Look, Grandma!"

"Eat that smelly thing later!" She gave us tamales steamed in banana leaves.

"That's odd!" Jethro looked up. "It's thundering, but no clouds. Oh, no, look! Stones bouncing down from those high crags—right above us! Look out!"

"Rocks falling!" I bellowed. "Get away! Everyone!"

Plummeting stones dislodged others, causing a slide, still far up.

<table>
<tr><td>

Task 12–a.

PRAYERFULLY EXERCISE
DECISIVE LEADERSHIP
WITHOUT BEING BOSSY

</td><td>

"Which way?" screamed Pacho. "Upstream or down?" God had another lesson for me— **prayerfully exercise decisive leadership without being bossy.**

Breathing a quick prayer I yelled, "Go up, those with Pacho! Downriver, the rest!"

</td></tr>
</table>

A girl Tino's age panicked, tripped, and fell into the current; I dove in, clothes and all, to pull her out and we scrambled, dripping, down the rocky path. A crash roared behind us; the ground shuddered and a forceful splash of water lashed my back, knocking me down. The din of plunging boulders ceased and I tried to call Lucy, but I'd inhaled a lungful of dust and only coughed. I heard her shouts and saw her downstream where frightened children cringed behind adults.

Cries came from upstream beyond the obliterated site; dust cloaked the area and when it settled, I saw Pacho holding two bawling tots. "We can't reach you!"

My lungs cleared enough to shout back, "Bring them through the water. Hold them with one arm and swim with the other."

"More stones might fall. Pebbles are still rolling."

"Now, Pacho! Whoever caused that avalanche can push more stones over the rim. Quick!" Pacho vacillated, so I told the girl I'd rescued to go to Lucy, and leaped into the river. I tried in vain to swim upstream against the muddy current; the Rio Furioso flowed swiftly where the slide blocked half of the channel.

"Help us!" Pacho pointed up. "Another big rock's tottering at the edge!"

Adrenaline reinforced my strokes and I overcame the current. I grabbed one child and Pacho the other, and we let the river sweep us downstream just before more stones crashed behind us. My chest was heaving as we climbed ashore and started down the path toward the others. Something caught my eye in the water. "Wait! There's Jethro's Skunk-skin hat!" It floated by and disappeared in rapids.

A moan sounded behind us and I spotted our elderly advisor lying near the rubble. "I tripped in my haste to get away," he gasped, "and a bouncing rock hit my hip. Help me up." I supported him as he limped, teeth clenched, toward the waiting group, and Pacho toted his black-and-white backpack.

"Tiger, where's Tino?" Lucy cried. "Wasn't he with you? Tino!"

"Oh no!" I raced back to the mass of fallen rocks and others followed. "Tino! Tino!" I yelled until I was hoarse. I heard coughing and spied my son camouflaged by dust, cringing on a ledge on the far side. I swam over and climbed up; he was unhurt and I embraced him, weeping and breathing a prayer of gratitude.

"Son, why didn't you escape down the path with the others?"

"I came back for my glasses. You told me to keep them in a safe place."

"I was so afraid the rocks had crushed you!"

"If they'd smashed me, would God make me wear my glasses in heaven?"

"Everyone's here," Pacho told the group when we joined it, "thanks to Tiger. He acted with decision, like David when he fought the original Palestinians."

"Why'd you say someone started the slide, Tiger?" Pacho asked. "Surely nobody would wantonly kill women and children!"

"Yes they would!" Jethro grimaced with pain. "History abounds with power-hungry fiends who've done so. Satan incites insatiable ambition and they'll do anything to get their way. Anything!"

Lucy was hugging Tino. "But who'd gain by burying these children alive?"

"It's to break our resolve," Pacho told her, "so we'll . . . "

"Discuss it later." I was scanning the high rim. "Let's get clear away from this cliff!" We hurried back down the river.

On the way, Pacho told Arturo, "That scare clarified my thinking. Tiger has the decisiveness that a leader of leaders needs. He should be group coordinator."

"We named you because you've had no vices. There's only one perfect leader, and you know who He is. I'm glad you'll overlook Tiger's faults. Demanding perfection stifles God's work; no one dares step out. David had faults, but he confessed them, God forgave him, and he led others to brave victories."

Pacho halted the group to plead, "While we're together, I have a proposal. Tiger should be group coordinator. He's resolute and can correct other leaders."

"You agree?" Arturo asked the assembly and everyone cheered.

My first act as coordinator was to give Gadget a job. "Hey, neighbor, will you host a *seekers' cell* for your pals?" A beaming grin signaled eager compliance.

I confessed to Jethro, "I feel inadequate to lead group leaders. What are the basic essentials of leadership that I must keep in mind?" In his typical way, Jethro pulled paper from his backpack and drew a chain with links labeled "*clear objective—measurable steps—delegating responsibilities—training made available to all—disciplined perseverance—sacrificial love.*"

"I see no link labeled 'prayer,' Jethro."

"Prayer's part of each link; only God holds it in place and makes it work."

I started for work that night and Lucy pointed at the mountain. "Black clouds are piling up. I'll get your poncho."

While circling the big house I heard a fuss and ran around front. Mouse was leaping with an agility rarely seen in a person of his bulk, slapping his legs. "A magic dance, Mouse? Are you trying to induce the gods to send rain?"

"Scorpions! They're stinging me!"

"Fire ants. You're stomping on their nest."

"Vile scorpions from hell, sent to afflict God's apostle!"

"Tiny messengers from heaven, sent to humble the haughty!"

"Why the fuss?" Simon was standing in the doorway scowling. "I was eating."

"I resign my offices, sir," Mouse thrust a large manila envelope into Simon's hand. "You've been the church's second elder; now you're first, and you're also treasurer." He left, slapping his legs.

Simon gaped at the envelope, turned and rasped, "Wanda! Guess what . . ." Thunder muffled his words and the churning clouds carried out their threat. Rain pelted me, driven by a sudden gust. I reached the guard's shack soaked; the downpour had caught me without my poncho.

"Mouse's rain dance worked, Popcorn! Heaven's weeping copious tears over this wretched town!" The dog wagged consent and shook. "Hey stop! You're spattering water on my Bible! Show more reverence!"

The rain ceased as abruptly as it had begun. It was a weekend and men roamed the streets wasting their week's pay. Two cursed each other in the square; they had pistols and fired at one another. Fortunately, they were drunk; nevertheless, a stray bullet penetrated the wall of my kiosk, leaving me jumpy. I was still edgy when I got home and it took quite a while to fall asleep. Slumber did not last long; an explosion jarred me awake. I ran and took my pistol from the wall. "Down, Lu, they're firing!"

"Calm down, love! Gadget's cab had a blowout; that's all. Its tires are bare."

Gadget changed the tire and came in tracking mud. "I invented an alarm, Tiger. Arturo tugs a wire by his office and a lever in a tall pine hits an iron rail from the old mine, to assemble us leaders for crises. You'll hear it from here."

"Clever, Einstein. For this nonsense you woke me up?"

"I need advice *pronto*. Should I accept a scholarship to study Christian leadership in the capital for four months? Wanda will pay all expenses, but she has to know by noon. She says I can't lead no group without a theology certificate."

"Why do Wanda's bidding? Has it occurred to you that perhaps she's trying to get you out of town? If so, why? And what would happen to your new group?"

"You think she's trying to sabotage our groups?"

"She and Simon don't care a rat's whisker about the groups. Maybe they want to stop your investigations. I'm worried. Prolonged exposure to radioactive ore in time becomes toxic and we need to make sure that doesn't happen. Even if the radioactivity is weak, without proper safeguards it's only a matter of time before miners get cancer or other ailments, which makes me more anxious every day."

"Me too, Tiger. Anyway, Wanda's right in saying I need training as a leader."

"Don't we all! Okay, let's go ask Arturo to give a course on leadership so no one has to leave the flock God has given him to tend to go away for training." We went and told this to Arturo; he agreed and said we'd be hearing from him.

Clang! Clang! We were hearing from him the next day; Gadget's gong called the leaders to his office and he said, "We need training to lead. I've taught all I know, and Jethro's still too bruised to travel from Arenas. Any suggestions?"

Pacho proposed, "The Reverend Doctor Amos Nuñez is a popular speaker. He pastors my cousin's church in the capital." Thus, we invited the Reverend Doctor Amos Nuñez.

> ## Task 12–b.
> ### SISTER CHURCHES AND CELLS HELP EACH OTHER DO VITAL MINISTRIES

"Wait," I begged as the leaders rose to go. "While we're here, let's help each others' groups do the tasks in our *Vital Ministries Checklist*." Colombo groaned and I pled, "Let me do my job as group coordinator. God's flocks flourish when **sister churches and cells help each other do vital ministries.**"

I handed each leader a copy of the *checklist* and Colombo protested, "My group can't do all these tasks, Tiger. Some require spiritual gifts that no one has."

"My point exactly! Other cells will help yours and gifted folks in yours will help them. This mutual support is biblical and works at three levels: *persons* serve each other, *small groups* serve each other, and *churches* serve each other. Neglect any level and a body contracts spiritual arthritis. Jethro's flock helps ours and we'll help new flocks. Now, let's arrange for our cells to serve each other."

Pacho worried, "Won't it be confusing if our groups mix it up that way?"

"Let's find out. Lead us off, Pacho. How can your cell help others'?"

"With kids. We can help other cells teach them to do things during meetings."

"Our kids cause pure bedlam," complained Colombo. "Help us, Pacho!"

"Okay, we'll prepare children's workers in your cell. Can you loan us a musician or two, to help us sing better and teach Roger to play the guitar on key for a change? Our music's worse than in new village churches; it hurts some folks' ears, especially young people who are hearing good musicians on the radio."

Colombo agreed and Pacho grinned broadly. "Well now, this really works!"

Heels clicked outside the office, heralding the advent of Wanda Alvarez. She bustled in without any greeting, handed Arturo a paper, and clicked her way out. He read it and groaned. "Simon's thrown down the gauntlet. Cattlemen and church members that haven't attended for years signed it, demanding the church to oust me because I've 'aided Tiger Garcia in abetting treasonous criminals.'"

"Crazy!" Colombo clenched a fist. "What'll we do, Pastor?"

HoUsE of DiVjne Revelation
Independent
DEMoNstrAtioNs *of* PoWer
PaStor: Prophet EzEkiel Maldonado

"Nothing." He wadded it up. "It's just to intimidate me."

Arturo was wrong; we'd find before long that it boded more than intimidation.

On our way in the rain to the first leadership lecture by Dr. Amos Nuñez, Lucy exclaimed, "What's Mouse doing up on that ladder in this downpour?" We stopped and watched my cousin nail a sloppily-lettered, misspelled sign on a house a short way down the street from the chapel: *House of Divine Revalation, Independant. Demonstrations of POWER. Minister, Prophet Moses Maldonado.*

"Hallelujah!" Mouse was dripping and the ladder flexed under his bulk. "Arturo can't stop me now. I'm renting this so the town can see my celestial power!"

Wanda's car drove up; she stepped out and announced grandly, "I'm honored to present our distinguished speaker." She opened a rear door with a flourish. "The Reverend Doctor Amos Nuñez honors us with his presence." The renowned orator emerged, waving like a politician saluting a vast crowd.

"Oooo!" squealed a small girl who was watching. "Such fancy white shoes!"

"Careful! You're splashing mud on them!" Nuñez then made a toothy grin. "Greetings, beloved brothers. My name is Dr. Amos Fernando Nuñez and Castillo, here to serve you. Now God will start working in Bat Haven!"

Popcorn growled and I held him. Nuñez shook hands and greeted the ladies with courtly politeness; he took Lucy's hand between his and the toothy grin widened. "Ah, don't tell me! The beauty queen of Bat Haven! Ha, ha!"

"We're ready to start, Doctor," I told him, "but not out here in this rain."

"In this tiny chapel?" He looked around as we entered, scowling. "It lacks room for all who'll want to hear me speak."

"It'll do. The course is just for our group leaders and their spouses."

"Oh? Ah . . . You don't say!" Rev. Nuñez spoke with Arturo and announced, "I've come through a misunderstanding. I'll return home tomorrow. And . . . Ah . . . Pastor, may I assume that your good church will reimburse my travel?"

"Briefest lecture I ever heard!" Lucy giggled after Nuñez left with Wanda.

"Wait, Tiger!" Arturo hurried over to us. "We still need a course on leading. Your groups have blossomed here and in Los Vientos. You should teach it."

"I can't, I don't have fancy white oxfords!"

"Tiger!" Lucy slapped my arm. "This is serious!"

"I'm not capable, sir. My experience would fit in a thimble."

"I disagree. You let your group members know exactly what to do and you make it easy and fun for them to do it."

"I'm not an 'up front' teacher, Arturo. You've seen that."

The helicopter lit nearby in dawn's first light the next morning and I held on to my hat. Abdul, Sebastian, and Panther emerged from it, and Simon hurried out from his house followed by the reverend Dr. Amos Nuñez. I walked home wondering why Panther was back and why Nuñez had gotten involved. I went to bed and a couple hours later laughter woke me. Dr. Nuñez! The great conference speaker in my home? I dressed and entered the living room.

"Mr. Garcia, I repented!" The toothy grin again. "Ha, ha. I'll teach the course, but not just to group leaders. I knew you'd both like to know."

I searched for words insulting enough to match his arrogance, but he left first. Tino crawled out from behind the sofa, followed by Davey. "Papa, that man with funny white shoes scares us!" Tino opened his mouth wide and snapped his teeth. "When he laughs, he looks like he's gonna bite us! He's a crockerdile."

On the way home after Dr. Nuñez' first lecture, I griped to Lucy, "Unbearable windbag! He said nothing but, oh, he said it with great conviction!"

"Give him time. We lack the education to appreciate his type of eloquence."

Time, however, only solidified my opinion. After his final lecture, I whispered to Lucy, "Cute jokes all week, but nothing of value about leading!"

"You're just sore because I got better marks on the exam than you! Now hush. He's starting a graduation ceremony."

Dr. Nuñez handed Evita her certificate. "This brilliant lady got highest marks." When Lucy stepped forward for hers, he took her hand. "I've fallen in love with Bat Haven! Ha, ha. I plan to stay on for a worthy project, folks. I have the greatest news: the gentleman who . . . "

"Are you going to give me my certificate, Doctor?"

"Oh! Ha, ha! Here, my dear. Now the sublime news. The gentleman who came in the helicopter, Mr. Panther Jones, will build a first-class theological seminary in Bat Haven! It will hold to the highest standards of excellence to train the most qualified pastors. Mr. Jones will pay faculty wages and I'll serve as President. Ha ha. I'll hire all who need work and pay liberal salaries, to construct classrooms, dormitories, library, and dining hall, and to do maintenance."

"What a blessing!" acclaimed Wanda. "Especially for ministerial students."

Arturo shook his head. "What ministerial students? Seminaries require prerequisite education. No one here qualifies except Roger and me, Reverend."

"We'll work out such minor details. Ha ha. Panther—ah, Mr. Jones—asks only that you sell him the worthless terrain that belongs to the church. He'll build you a huge, beautiful chapel in the center of town."

The next day brought another surprise. Arturo, Pacho, and Anna came and the ladies slipped into our kitchen. Pacho told me, "I like how you engage new leaders. I thought you went too fast, but now I see it's better to activate new workers and mentor them than to keep piling more work on those who already have jobs."

"You give apprentices real responsibility," Arturo added. "As a result your group is starting healthy new cells. All our leaders are going to do the same."

"I appreciate your approval, but I doubt that you came here to pat my back. Is it about Panther's offer to buy the church property?"

"No, that's still hanging over our heads." Arturo hit a fist into his palm. "Dr. Nuñez failed to teach the kind of leadership that expands God's work, so we've come to request you to teach it."

"You don't give up! You know that as a public speaker, I'm a burro."

"I like burros!" Pacho replied. "I keep two for pets."

"Bray like a burro if you like," Arturo advised, "But help us lead like you do. Please don't speechify like Nuñez did! Be yourself. Your passion to do God's work is contagious! I'm a teacher, but not action-oriented. You're both. Tell us, what would you teach as key duties of a dynamic group leader?"

I pondered a minute. "Five come to mind: *one*, verify what God wants your cell group to do and help it do it; *two*, stir up helpful dialogue; *three*, tactfully correct errors and useless chatter; *four*, make plans for tasks to do during the week; *and five*, mentor apprentice leaders to keep groups multiplying."

"Perfect!" Arturo clasped my hand firmly.

Pacho called the ladies back from the kitchen and Anna beckoned me aside. "Let's talk, cowboy. Pardon my meddling in family stuff, but I'm crowned with white hair and old enough to be your mom! Lucy thinks you give God's work all your attention and neglect your family. How do you plan to fix this?"

"Help Lucy share my view of the work and my desire to do it, Grandma."

"Oh, you hopeless male! Poor thing! Don't force Lucy to think as you do. God gave her other gifts and tasks." Her eyes locked on mine. "You tell the small group folks to speak with love to one another to build each other up. Well, your own family's the small group that you're to care for *first*, cowboy. Say 'Amen.'"

"Amen." Anna's words stuck with me after they left. I asked God to help me care for my family and told Lucy, "I'm going to spend more time with you and the boys from now on. To show you I mean it, I'll stay home all day today."

"Good! You can repair the front gate that Gadget smashed eons ago."

"Oh! Will you grant permission for me to go uptown to buy the boards?"

I went and toted the lumber back, but found no nails. Feeling too weary to walk back to the store, I took a nap.

Our group leaders gathered in Gadget's house, waiting for me to begin the course. A pleasant man with curly hair, about forty, had come and was discussing books with Roger. Another scholar? Roger introduced me to him, and he asked, "May I sit in on your leadership course?"

"Of course, sir. How'd you hear about it?"

"Our good barber. I'm Stephen Reyes, an agronomist doing forest conservation. I'm the mean old agent that keeps poor peasants from burning off hillsides to plant corn, so the fires won't cause erosion, floods, and destruction of wildlife."

"Welcome, Stephen. I hope you'll attend one of our small groups."

"I already lead one, sir. Father Camacho urged me to see if I could glean some useful guidelines from you. I'm to coordinate our groups."

Recovering from my surprise, I told the leaders, "I've compared what cells do in different cultures, especially those that multiply by winning folks to Christ. What they have in common you may find harsh. Do I have your permission to make this course tough enough to get the same results?" They nodded hesitantly.

Task 12–c.
HELP BELIEVERS TEACH EACH OTHER IN SMALL GROUPS

"Let's do things the way your cell's members will do them. Aim for a family atmosphere in which folks feel free to ask questions and discuss matters; effective leaders **help believers teach each other in small groups.** We'll begin with concerns that each of you has with your cell. Who's first?"

"Why'd you put the chairs in a circle?" Colombo asked in his baritone voice.

"Folks take part more actively when facing each other. We need to engage new believers and visitors, help everyone to feel at ease, and let anyone take part who wants to, like I'm doing now."

"I'm not used to this," Colombo told me, "but I'll try."

"It's not new. Paul told the Colossians to teach each other."

"But someone might bring in error if everyone teaches, Tiger."

"Yes, and let them speak their mind. Let folks bring up weird stuff so you can get it under the light and deal with it. Don't let devilish errors fester in the dark."

"But what if an opinion is dangerously wrong?"

"Use the opportunity to teach a truth, Colombo, like Jesus and Paul did."

"Tiger's right," Pacho said. "The most valuable stuff I've learned has come from Tiger and Arturo correcting my errors and fussy objections!"

I cautioned, "But correct innocent errors without shaming the speaker."

Colombo replied, "Errors aren't innocent if someone has a bad attitude,"

"True. Correct a bad attitude privately. If you must do it publicly, then smile. When someone says something really false, ask for opinions; when group members correct an error casually in open discussion, it seldom offends."

"I tried once to get my group to discuss freely," Colombo recalled, "but one guy talked too much and the rest clammed up."

Gadget poked the tall trucker. "I hope you weren't that guy!"

"I had a talker too," Roger recalled, "so after asking something, I'd say, 'Someone who's not spoken yet, please reply.' The guy still monopolized the dialogue, so I told him plainly that he was discouraging others from participating."

"Did he return to the next meeting after your reproof?" asked Stephen Reyes.

"Yes, and now he lets others talk—when he remembers."

"Correct such a guy," I advised. "He'll bounce back if he's God's man."

"Another way to rein in gabby folks," Roger suggested, "is to ask them ahead of time to come up with questions about the Bible text that you're studying. They can still talk, but do so in a way that invites others to join in."

Colombo told Roger, "You and Tiger are smart and can discuss freely, but I'm too dumb; my mind's too linear. Let me off the hook."

"You're discussing freely right now, Colombo," I pointed out. "To help folks take part, do two things in advance: write discussion questions and give others easy things to do to help you teach. Also, if folks in a group like to act, especially young people, then find an illustrative Bible story to have them tell or act out."

Pacho nodded. "Let's not be like those leaders that are too lazy to prepare others beforehand, and too self-absorbed to share the teaching time with others."

Evita asked me, "How can I teach teachers to teach? My colleagues overuse monologue lecture; they allow very little discussion and pupils become passive."

| **Task 12–d.** |
| TRAIN NEW |
| LEADERS LIKE JESUS |
| AND PAUL DID |

"I don't know about schoolteachers, but we'll **train new leaders like Jesus and Paul did.** Mentor apprentices, plan fieldwork, face current issues, and kindle lively dialogue. I learned it from Arturo; he got it from Jethro. Not everyone calls it *mentoring*; God uses any relational training to multiply leaders and flocks, provided a trainer invests himself in his trainees like Jesus and Paul did. That's crucial. Let's demonstrate it now. Who'd like us to focus on your group?"

"My cell's called 'David's Harp,'" Colombo told me in his melodic voice. "We sing to glorify Jesus. My question is how to mentor apprentices as you said."

"Let's do it now. What'll you tackle next on this *Vital Ministries Checklist*?"

He scanned it. "Hmm. We haven't started new flocks. I'd like to do it in Lone Stone; Hilda has kin there. Can you go with us to help us get started?"

"I'd love to! I made friends there after my ordeal in Buzzard's Banquet Hall. But I won't do your work for you; you'll make disciples and train their leaders."

"But I'm not a teacher. I'm a truck driver."

"You don't need to lecture. None of us do. Simply do as I've done with you the last few weeks: model pastoral work for trainees, assign studies from this *Vital Ministries Checklist* that fit their plans, and let them start at once to shepherd their families. Then, let them train other, newer leaders the same way and churches will multiply. This is easy if you pass on a *light baton*—use only equipment that trainees have and model skills in a way they can easily imitate." I helped Colombo make plans for Lone Stone, recorded them, and selected related reading from the *Checklist*. We then arranged for his group members to help other cell groups develop their music and prayed for the work he had planned.

"You watched me mentor Colombo," I told the group. "Now who can tell us what mentors do that mere lecturers do not do?"

Gadget responded, "They listen like you done, to know what a trainee's cell should do next and help him plan it."

"Exactly. We'll mentor each other now. Everyone select from the *Checklist* a ministry that you plan to develop and we'll help you make it easy. Who's next?"

"Yo!" Gadget replied. "My 'Good Samaritans' cell cares for folks in Leave-If-You-Can. We took aid to a starving family and others need help. But I see on this *Checklist* that we oughta baptize the new believers too, and organize 'em."

"Okay, let's help Gadget plan his next 'Good Samaritans' trip to Leave-If-You-Can." We discussed plans, prayed, and chose related reading from the *Checklist* for Gadget to study and discuss with his cell. I then asked, "Anyone else ready?"

"Aye aye, sir!" Julio jumped up and saluted sharply. "My crew calls itself 'King's Voyagers,' but we're a bit adrift." We helped him plan to teach Jesus' basic commands so his "crew" could get on course to be a genuine satellite church.

Pacho then asked, "Must we always *mentor* leaders? Can't we just train them in workshops like this one? Mentoring them one-on-one will take all our time!"

"Forget one-on-one, Pacho! Jesus rarely mentored only one, and Paul traveled with a small band. Don't worry about taking up time; mentoring saves time, as it multiplies workers. Luther, Wesley, Saint Francis, and other godly leaders did great work by assigning tasks to apprentices. Besides, every new leader needs some kind of mentoring; like a newborn child, he and his flock have urgent needs that an older leader must deal with. We'll still hold workshops like this one, but we can't rely on them alone; some trainees' work schedules will conflict."

"So true!" sighed Arturo. "Educators in fields like ours often give training just during working hours and only the unemployed attend, most of whom are single and young. These youngsters are then called 'elders' or 'pastors' and need support; the result is the work can never extend beyond the reach of available funds from the immature who lead it. Let's not hobble our work that way."

"This is all so new to me!" Colombo exclaimed. "Is mentoring really so crucial? Just a few can meet with a mentor, so only a few will receive training."

"Look down the road," Arturo replied. "If you mentor others and let them train still others in a chain as in 2 Timothy 2, then you'll soon reach many."

Stephen ran fingers through his curly hair. "Oh, so much to remember, yet too valuable to forget! Can we recap what a mentor does with new leaders?"

"He has two duties, *modeling* and *meeting*." I explained. "He models pastoral skills and meets with trainees in homes, buses, on horseback, by phone, or mail.

"To model skills, demonstrate them to trainees as you deal with folks, and always take apprentices with you as you do pastoral work. Remember what Paul told the Corinthians, "Imitate me as I imitate Christ."

"During meetings, deal with two pairs of tasks: *listen* and *plan* to deal with both *fieldwork* and *studies*." I showed a diagram of the two pairs of tasks.

	LISTEN	PLAN
FIELDWORK	LISTEN as trainee reports work done and needs of his flock.	PLAN together what trainee, his coworkers, and flock will do next.
STUDIES	LISTEN as trainee reviews studies done to recap their gist.	PLAN reading and written work that fits trainee's plans.

"The first pair of tasks deals with fieldwork. *Listen* and *plan*. Listen as each trainee reports what he and his flock have done. Then plan their new fieldwork; plans flow from a trainee's report and from using the *Vital Ministries Checklist* to detect neglected ministries. Record plans that you agree on. Pray as you plan; pray any time, especially whenever a problem crops up.

"The second pair of tasks deals with studies. Again, *listen* and *plan*. Listen as each trainee recaps reading previously assigned from the *Vital Ministries Checklist*, the Bible, or other sources. If he falters, assign it again. Then plan what he'll read next; assign what fits his flock's current needs or fieldwork. You might also assign reading for enrichment that has nothing to do with current plans. Record all assignments to review at the next meeting."

Colombo confessed, "One side of me balks at these procedures; so different from the churches' practices that I've known!" Others voiced the same concern.

"Okay, let's decide whose way we'll go," I replied. "Our two options are the *majority* whose familiar practices fail to multiply churches in the New Testament way, and the *minority* whose tougher ways yield a movement for Jesus."

Colombo laughed. "You remind me of an army drill sergeant I had! You keep us leaping over new hurdles—the total antithesis to Dr. Nuñez' teaching!"

"Welcome to reality's ruthless realm! I'm certain that you and every leader in this room will take on any hurdle and make any sacrifice, to keep extending Jesus' kingdom. Right?" They all cheered without hesitation.

"Taco time and *piña colada!*" Evita toted in a tray of food and games. "No sense in learning without some fun!"

She sketched a devil on a dartboard, and Anna hit it right between the horns every time. Evita kept missing and Pacho suggested, "Use a picture of Gadget!"

Laughter and tacos abated and I asked, "Anyone else's group need attention?"

"Um . . . My group . . . " Julio turned red. "Can we deal with a guy thing?"

"To the galley, girls!" Evita barked in her teacher's voice, "Forward march!"

The ladies went into the kitchen and Pacho followed them; I think he knew what was afoot and wanted to make it easy for his son. Julio squirmed in his chair. "Guys in my group struggle with lust. We're hooked on porn, fantasize, and go too far with girls. Can you fellows help us?"

<table>
<tr><td>

Task 12–e.

RESIST
TEMPTATIONS BY
DECISIVELY SLAYING
LUSTFUL DESIRES

</td></tr>
</table>

No one spoke for a while, and I said, "Okay I see we have to deal frankly with the need to **resist temptations by decisively slaying lustful desires.** We understand, Julio. Let's all be transparent. I'm tempted that way too, but God helps us live purely. Let the Holy Spirit slay your lust, as Galatians 5 says. When it strikes, ask Jesus to erase it at once. Now, promise three things: *one,* avoid traveling alone to do God's work; *two,* bounce your eyes or your mind off any enticing image; *and three,* let me hold you accountable, Julio; you'll tell me each week how things have gone and I'll tell you how it's gone with me."

Julio clasped my hand firmly. "Agreed. I'll do the same with my group."

"Good. The four letters in 'lust' give initials to four warnings that both men and women can recall when it lures: it is a **L**ying, **U**ngodly, **S**ubhuman **T**rap.

"*Lying.* Lust promises bliss, but delivers shame and pain.

"*Ungodly.* Lust corrupts morals and blocks one's fellowship with God.

"*Subhuman.* Lust behaves like a dog; it perverts one's normal, God-given sexual drive to destroy marriages, self-respect, and reputation.

"*Trap.* Lust chains one to irrational, immoral habits—overt or in the mind."

Julio whined, "But you can't do anything about it if hormones build up!"

"That's a myth. You know how quickly shame counteracts those hormones when your mom or someone you respect catches you doing a sinful act. Well, God is watching, 'catching' us, whenever lust strikes. Galatians 5 says to let the Holy Spirit put to death those passions of the flesh. When lust hits, pray, sing, recall the Word, or talk with moral folks. God helps us discipline ourselves."

Meanwhile, Nuñez had come to our house and told Lucy he was looking for me. Unhappy at seeing him still in town, she pointed to the house up the street. "Tiger's at Gadget's with our group leaders, Doctor."

"Oh, yes. Ha ha. I remember now; they had planned to meet there. I'll wait. I need to rest anyway; this hot sun has roasted me."

"Come in. Tino, run to Aunt Martha's and bring ice. Ask Martha to come over and talk with Dr. Nuñez too." Tino scampered off and soon returned with ice and Cousin Andy instead of Aunt Martha. The boys then tore outside to play.

"This poor *barrio* has no electricity," Lucy explained and started for the kitchen. "Martha across the street has a refrigerator that runs on kerosene."

"Sister, you're a beautiful lady," Nuñez purred, following her. "Ah, spiritually, of course. Well, in other ways too. Come. Forget the water. You are a . . . "

"I am a married woman." Lucy put the ice in a glass.

"Of course. Ha ha." He came close, his wide grin spreading across his face.

"Please, Dr. Nuñez. Have a seat in the living room. I'll bring this in a jiffy."

"I'm a man who is frank. When I see you, I feel a wave of passion."

Lucy turned her back on him, fighting the urge to voice her disgust in the most biting way possible. "You talk a lot."

"But how can a virile man contain such passion?" A hand caressed her side.

"Enough flirtatious foolishness! Sir, leave before I cool your school-boy passion with this!" She raised the ice water, eyes flashing, and he exited hastily.

> ## Task 12–f.
> ### Limit the size of new believers' cells and continually mentor their new leaders as the cells multiply

The ladies joined us again in Gadget's house, and Colombo asked how to help his cell multiply. I told the group, "**Limit the size of new believers' cells and continually mentor their new leaders as the cells multiply.** A cell's too big when only a small part of its members can take part actively; form new groups before that happens. A dozen or so adults are usually enough."

"Limit the size?" the curly-haired Catholic agronomist, Stephen Reyes, looked puzzled. "What if a cell just keeps growing? We can't just kick some folks out!"

"Foresee the growth, prepare apprentice leaders as Paul did, and let a few members go with them to form new groups. Usually the ladies more than the men will fear severing relationships, so let the parent cell keep strong ties with the new cells that it births by meeting together occasionally with them, mentoring their new leaders, and discipling members of the new cell."

Colombo asked, "Won't a group so tiny become ingrown and commit error?"

I was glad Mouse and Simon were absent so I could talk about independent leaders without a war. "Yes. Error is already at work when a leader isolates his cell and is not teachable. We've seen that, and our battle isn't over; but from now on our new leaders will have a mentor, cooperate with other cells, and meet regularly with the other leaders to coordinate activities."

"How refreshing to see a leader of leaders in action!" Stephen remarked.

I laughed. "You don't know the goofs I've made as a mentor! The worst was trying to gather all our elders for interactive training. Let's be careful to gather trainees of similar experience and education, or shy ones won't participate well. If affluent trainees easily intimidate poor ones, then mentor them separately."

"Again!" the curly haired agronomist exclaimed. "You keep awakening insights that have crossed my mind, but never fully surfaced! I see now how good leadership produces more leaders and makes their work easy by letting them help each other. Thank you for not teaching how to lead simply by lecturing at us!"

"Yea!" Gadget responded. "Satan blinds preachers to what real leadership is. It's their fault; all they do is teach. They don't organize for no action."

"Now wait!" Arturo begged. "Don't hit us preachers so hard! The remedy isn't to gag us, but for us to work closely with action-oriented shepherds. That's why I had Tiger teach this course. I'm a teacher, but not action-oriented. Tiger is both. Good teaching is *factual, forceful,* and *fruitful.*"

"Amos Nuñez' lectures were only factual," Evita said firmly, "about how biblical kings led. He shouted a lot, but his teaching was not *forceful*; the only thing he motivated me to do was to get a good grade on his exam."

"And it wasn't *fruitful,*" added Gadget. "He didn't help me lead no better."

"This is all so valuable!" Evita exclaimed. "I see there's an entirely different way of leading besides the way many priests and preachers do it."

Task 12–g.

MOBILIZE ALL FIVE KINDS OF GOD-GIVEN LEADERS

"Yes," I replied. "We'll **mobilize all five kinds of God-given leaders.** Some try to lead only by teaching, but that overlooks the other four kinds. God also gives: *apostles, prophets, evangelists, pastors,* and *teachers.*"

Colombo asked, "Don't they all mainly teach, but from a different angle?"

"Oh no! Their roles are very different. We'll demonstrate a common trap of Satan so that none of us falls into it. Gadget, you'll play the part of the devil."

"Appropriate casting!" giggled Julio. Gadget hissed at him, holding fingers up on each side of his head like horns.

"Perfect!" I said. "Now, how do you all suppose the Ephesians reacted to Paul's letter that lists five kinds of God-given leaders? I need five volunteers to be 'fools' for Christ. I'll read the list and when I say 'apostles,' the first one of you will shout, 'I'll be an apostle!' The next will want to be a prophet, and so on, for all five. 'Satan' will whisper something to each of you when you've shouted what you want to be, and you'll simply repeat the gist of what he says."

I told Gadget quietly how Satan would lure each leader, and then announced, "I'm Timothy reading Paul's letter. You 'Ephesians' listen well because Paul lists five types of leaders that God gives to your churches. First are those whom God sends to neglected people: *apostles.*"

"I want to be an apostle!" shouted the first "Ephesian."

Gadget sneaked up behind him, fingers forming horns. "You'll control all believers in vast areas, fly around in airplanes, and make huge sums of money!"

The "apostle" gleefully shouted what he'd do, repeating Satan's words. I clarified, "Some apostles are missionaries that travel far and get support, but for every full-time professional, God raises up hundreds of unpaid apostles who simply go to neglected people, taking volunteers with them. The word *apostle* means *sent one.* God gives them itchy feet, and most of them go nearby to start daughter churches or cells. An apostle is apt to initiate work with neglected peoples, as Romans 15 reveals, seizing opportunities. Some of you have this gift."

We did the same for the other four leaders. I'd mentioned one and the next "Ephesian" shouted that he'd be it. "Satan" then hissed in his ear an exaggerated form of professionalism, and I'd clarify that for every full-time, high-profile professional leader, God wants hundreds of volunteer leaders with the same gifting.

Satan promised the prophet that he'd exercise vast power over multitudes that would fear and cower before him as he predicted disasters and death. I then explained, "A New Testament prophet leads the faithful to act on God's truths, exhorting in love, as 1 Corinthians 13 and 14 reveal. He casts vision for the future, exposes gaps in a congregation's ministries, and encourages folks to deal with them. Some of you have the prophetic gift."

Satan told the evangelist he'd gain vast fame and riches preaching to admiring fans in huge stadiums and dining with dignitaries! I then explained, "An evangelist leads folks to Jesus. He's done his job when they're added to a church by baptism, as in Acts 2:41. Most evangelists simply witness for Christ quietly to friends. Some professionals hold big meetings that bring many to faith and disciple them. Others only count hands; they cannot evaluate their effectiveness and their agencies spend thousands on meetings that yield little lasting fruit."

Satan promised the pastor that he'd enjoy vast fame as people leave their churches to join his because of his unequaled charisma. I clarified, "A pastor oversees a flock. He can shepherd a very large flock if he's a 'pastor of pastors,' as Moses' father-in-law Jethro advised, to provide healthy shepherding in many small groups. Every one of you group leaders is a pastor."

Satan tempted the teacher saying he'd gain admiration and fortune as scholars from all over the world come sat at his feet to tap his vast wisdom. I countered, "A teacher, according to Ephesians 4, equips believers to build up the body of Christ and develop godly character; he does not simply talk about God's truth."

We discussed what kind of leaders we were, and I told them, "You'll rally all five kinds by helping believers try their gifts. Most believers can do at least one of these five leader's roles at home, on the job or with your group. Overly professional leaders keep many from using their God-given gifts, but we'll help all believers do their job. One cell rarely has all five, so you'll cooperate with other cells. Our new churches will cooperate with each other too, as they did in Acts; godly unity doesn't come by merely sending delegates to a convention."

"I see it now!" Colombo jumped up. "I'll mentor leaders in the Lone Stone area like you told me, Tiger, and churches will multiply. Hallelujah!" Others praised the Lord too, and it got a little noisy, even without Mouse.

Colombo reported to me a month later, "I arranged to widen the path to Lone Stone for vehicles. Mayor Campos sent a bulldozer, I donated diesel, villagers provided labor, and they're all happy now. Three churches are in embryo. Can you go with me to visit them? You can bring Lucy and the boys."

"We'll go! When a movement buds, drop all else and throw fuel on the fire!"

Simon grudgingly granted me two weeks off and Colombo loaded Hilda and my family into The Caribbean. It twisted its way around boulders and depressions down to where the climate was warmer and pine gave way to stately mahogany. Monkeys scolded from the branches, protesting the bright orange truck's invasion of their domain and parrots flew above us, adding to the cacophony. We loved the villagers, they loved us, and the Word spread.

When we arrived back home, Arturo came to confess, "I made a huge mistake, Tiger. I found these *4B* Bible studies, beautifully written by popular pastors, and made copies for all our groups. *4B* stands for '*Bible-Based Body Builders.*' They have edifying discussion questions, but later I noticed that they ignore mentoring leaders of seekers' cells and fail to ground new disciples on Jesus' commands."

"Okay, we'll deal with *4B* studies at our next group leaders' meeting."

Waiting was my mistake. By the time our leaders met in Arturo's office, a bomb had hit and paralyzed God's work! *4B* had invaded our cells and mesmerized them. Pacho's group had quit having children participate and train younger ones, and Gadget's cell was neglecting its outreach and mercy work. Groups now devoted themselves almost solely to the excellent *4B* Bible exposition. Heartsick, I told the leaders, "You agreed to make any sacrifice to follow biblical rules to deal with seekers and new believers. Remember? Stop a moment and think about those rules. Who recalls why older churches often fail to keep cells multiplying?"

After an uneasy silence, Roger slapped his forehead. "We fell into the trap! Jethro warned how older Bible study groups swallow up seekers and new believers before they've done their job. Wow! How'd Satan ever blindside us so quickly?"

"Ample practice—he's led thousands of churches into the same trap. Gadget, recap God's guidelines for dealing with three kinds of cells."

"I'll try. A seekers' cell gathers reprobates who need Jesus; it can be a party in their homes. These cells don't last; folks either receive Jesus or reject Him and drop out. Tiger had me host seekers while I was still a seeker; when we was baptized, we became a new believers' group and witnessed to our pals in new seekers' cells. Them *4B* studies were for mature believers who run out of friends that responded, so they just sit around feeding on all that deeper Bible stuff."

"Wait!" I laughed. "They don't all just sit around! They deal with current needs and train new leaders in new believers' groups."

Roger held up a *4B* study. "Do we still use these for older Bible study groups?"

"Yes, but not exclusively; God requires mature believers to do other activities besides learning the Bible. Let's renew our pact to follow biblical patterns to keep new believers' groups growing in Christ and multiplying."

After praying, Pacho asked, "Why do so few churches multiply cells the biblical way, Tiger? Is it because they simply try to divide old groups in two?"

"Yes, and that's not the biblical way. We deal differently with seekers, converts and the mature. In a movement, the same group might deal with all three types, but older churches push everyone into advanced Bible studies way too soon."

The cell leaders met a month later to report progress, and Stephen Reyes exulted, "Victory! We've formed four New Life groups with folks who met Jesus. I shared what I've learned about leading with Father Camacho; he's more effective in his leadership now, especially since receiving the baptism of the Holy Spirit."

"He spoke in tongues?" asked Colombo.

"I don't know. Some have. Others have received the baptism of the Spirit with other demonstrations of His gifting." This ignited a dispute; some said that all must speak in tongues and others said no.

"Do you speak in tongues?" a group leader asked me in a defiant tone.

"Hey, listen all of you! We won't let Satan impose his barrier between those who have the gift of tongues and others who don't. If you have it then heed Paul's warning not to give it greater importance than other gifts. If you don't have it, remember that Paul also said, *Do not prohibit tongues.* Now, Stephen, what does Father Camacho say about your small groups? Is he supportive?"

"Very! He now enjoys letting others lead. We acted out the devil's lies about the five kinds of leaders; folks had a good laugh and Father Camacho admitted that Satan had duped him into neglecting lay leadership. Some still give more devotion to the Virgin Mary and Saint Muñoz than to Jesus and avoid our groups."

We praised God for Stephen's report and he told us, "Father Camacho said competition from Evangelicals is good; it goads us into making useful reforms."

"This applies to all churches," I replied. "I've read their history; when any denomination has a monopoly in an area, its churches become sloppy."

Gadget sprang to his feet and embraced Stephen, and we all did the same.

CHAPTER 12: CONFIRM THE GRASP AND THE PRACTICE OF LEADERS' TASKS

12–a. Prayerfully exercise decisive leadership without being bossy. Note how God urged Joshua to lead firmly: *Arise, cross this Jordan, you and all this people, I will be with you; I will not . . . forsake you. Be strong and courageous, for you shall give this people possession of the land which I swore to their fathers to give them.* Josh 1:1–6

Gadget learned to lead by accompanying Tiger. Find how Jesus enabled men to lead: *He went up on the mountain and . . . appointed twelve, so that they would be with Him and that He could send them out to preach.* Mark 1:13–14

Verify. They watched Jesus do the work and He then sent them out to do it.

Choose Bible leaders' traits that you plan to emulate more conscientiously:

[ ]   **David** had passionate love for God and courageous decisiveness in crises.

[ ]   **Abraham** had a vision through faith of what God would do in the future.

[ ]   **Ezra** knew God's Word and had the skill to help others discuss and obey it.

[ ]   **Barnabas** had active compassion for others.

[ ]   **Joshua** persevered with courageous resolution.

[ ]   **Paul** prepared other leaders by setting the example of hard work.

12–b. Churches and cells help each other do ministries. Identify two things that Paul told Titus to do in Crete: *For this reason I left you in Crete, that you would set in order what remains and appoint elders in every city as I directed you.* Titus 1:5

Apostolic churches often sent workers to serve other churches, such as when Paul left Titus in Crete to name elders there. See the effect on Paul of Titus' arrival in Macedonia: *When we came into Macedonia our flesh had no rest . . . we were afflicted on every side . . . But God . . . comforted us by the coming of Titus.* 2 Cor 7:5–6

Tiger wanted Lucy to serve God just as he did and Anna corrected him. Note who metes out different spiritual gifts: *One and the same Spirit works all these things, distributing to each one individually just as He wills.* 1 Cor 12:11

12–c. Help believers teach each other in small groups. Verify what God tells "all" to do: *One who prophesies speaks to men for edification, exhortation, and consolation . . . If all prophesy, and an unbeliever or an ungifted man enters, he is convicted by all, he is called to account by all; the secrets of his heart are disclosed, and so he will fall on his face and worship God, declaring that God is certainly among you.* 1 Cor 14:3,24–25

Choose activities that your congregation or small group should develop more diligently to facilitate participation by everybody in meetings:

[ ]   Keep cells small and sit facing each other, so all can talk and edify others.

[ ]   Use God's gifts to serve one another; avoid being *hearers only* (Jas 1:22).

[ ]   Before a meeting starts, assign things to do to adults and children.

[ ]   Let older children lead younger children and disciple them.

[ ]   Adults and children act out Bible stories together. Everyone can join in some way; no audience is needed, as the aim is not to entertain or perform.

[ ]   Avoid dogmatism. Immature preachers easily fall into pride's trap (1 Tim 3:6). Some scold to make folks feel guilty, manipulating their consciences.

[ ]   Ask questions as Jesus did and let believers discuss freely (Mark 3:23,33).

[ ]   Encourage dialogue with a well-defined aim. The apostles often discussed things with other disciples, unbelievers, seekers, and groups.

[ ]   Let new believers host seekers' cells for friends and relatives where they can talk freely about Jesus and give others encouragement.

[ ]   Let the Holy Spirit display Christ's power and convince seekers, as they witness transformation, answered prayer, and believers' compassion.

12–d. Train new leaders like Jesus and Paul did. Find what Jesus did first after His disciples returned visiting towns: *And He said to them, "I was watching Satan fall from heaven like lightning. Behold, I have given you authority to tread on serpents and scorpions . . . and nothing will injure you. Nevertheless do not rejoice in this, that the spirits are subject to you, but rejoice that your names are recorded in heaven." The seventy returned with joy, saying, "Lord, even the demons are subject to us in Your name."* Luke 10:17–20

Answer: Jesus listened to His trainees' reports and responded at once.

Jesus told His disciples to tell the good news and heal the sick. They knew how because they had *watched* Him. Whom can you train on the job in this way?

Choose guidelines that you will heed more carefully to train new pastors:

[ ]   Serve as a model that less-educated trainees can imitate easily.

[ ]   Mentor an apprentice until his church or cell is practicing all the ministries that God requires of a group of believers.

[ ]   Listen to each trainee and ask questions to find out which vital ministries need further development by his church or cell.

[ ]   Help each trainee plan what his church or cell will do the next week or so.

[ ]   Provide studies for each trainee that deal with his flock's current need.

12–e. Resist temptations by decisively slaying lustful desires. Verify what godly believers do with fleshly appetites: *Set your mind on the things above, not on the things that are on earth. For you have died and your life is hidden with Christ in God. When Christ, who is our life, is revealed, then you also will be revealed with Him in glory. Therefore consider the members of your earthly body as dead to immorality, impurity, passion, evil desire, and greed, which amounts to idolatry.* Col 3:2–6

If you or your trainees struggle with lust, then arrange to be accountable to a caring person; if more help is needed, then meet regularly with a capable caregiver.

Commit to memory the four words beginning with the letters in the word "LUST" and repeat them whenever lust lures: it is a **L**ying, **U**ngodly, **S**ubhuman **T**rap.

12–f. Limit the size of new believers' cells and continually mentor their new leaders as cells multiply. Find the size of the groups that Moses formed: *Select . . . able men who fear God, men of truth, those who hate dishonest gain . . . as leaders of thousands, of hundreds, of fifties, and of tens.* Ex 18:21

Note the word Paul used to denote a group that met in a home, Philemon 1 and 2: *Paul . . . to Philemon our beloved brother and fellow worker . . . and to the church in your house.*

Choose any among the five types of God-given leaders that your trainees should give more attention to: *And He gave some as apostles, and some as prophets, and some as evangelists, and some as pastors and teachers, for the equipping of the saints for the work of service, to the building up of the body of Christ.* Eph 4:11–12

Find what kind of people a host normally invites to an exclusive seekers' gathering: *"Now Cornelius was waiting for them and had called together his relatives and close friends."* Acts 10:24

12–g. Mobilize all five kinds of God-given leaders. Ephesians 4 reveals that God gives churches gifted persons to lead His people in five ministries. Note any that your flock should mobilize more effectively:

[ ]   *Apostles* are those who are sent, mainly to neglected places. Some are "tentmakers" who support themselves as Aquila and the Apostle Paul did.

[ ]   *Prophets* edify, exhort, and console others, 1 Cor 14:3.

[ ]   *Evangelists* lead people to Jesus. Their duty with new believers is fulfilled when they are added to a congregation by baptism, Acts 2:41.

[ ]   *Pastors*, working together with the other types of leaders, mobilize members to serve in their respective ministries, Eph 4:11–16.

[ ]   *Teachers* apply God's Word in a way that equips disciples for the work of the ministry to build up the body of Christ, Eph 4:12.

EVALUATE YOUR LEADERSHIP

1=Poor. 2=Planning to improve. 3=Doing well.

1-2-3   Prayerfully exercise decisive leadership without being bossy.

1-2-3   Churches and cell groups help each other do vital ministries.

1-2-3   Have believers teach each other in small groups.

1-2-3   Train new leaders the way Jesus and Paul did.

1-2-3   Resist temptations by decisively slaying lustful desires.

1-2-3   Limit the size of new believers' cells and keep mentoring their new leaders to keep the cells multiplying.

1-2-3   Mobilize all five kinds of God-given leaders.

13.
Violence Erupts during Sham Worship

"Terrific news!" Colombo rushed into Arturo's legal office while he was mentoring Roger and me. "Three Lone Stone ranchers that signed Simon's protest are now leading cells. I train them as we planned and they're now paying their cowhands enough to raise families and live normally." We congratulated him and he added, "But it's caused a backlash. Simon's meeting now with cattlemen in our chapel. I eavesdropped; they're furious because those three ranchers raised their hands' wages. Simon told them to bring all the other cattlemen to another meeting Friday, to make sure no one weakens. He also told them, 'I give enough to the church to entitle me to run it as I please and I'll stop their meddling.'"

<table>
<tr><td>

Task 13–a.

PRACTICE

Christian

STEWARDSHIP

FOR THE RIGHT

MOTIVE

</td><td>

"They're in our chapel?" Arturo hit his desk with his fist. "I'll see that we all **practice Christian stewardship for the right motive!**" He grabbed his briefcase. "Come all of you. Well set Simon straight right now!"

On the way, Roger remarked to me, "Simon associates Christianity with capitalism and Mincho associates it with socialism, but Jesus avoided such

</td></tr>
</table>

"isms." He told Governor Pilate, 'My kingdom is not of this world.'"

Arturo waited for the cattlemen to leave, and told Simon without preamble, "Your group is too political; you'll give us your key to the chapel and you'll also relinquish the treasury because . . . "

"Stop harassing me, Arturo, or I'll tell the media how you cooperate with subversives." He waved his hook in the pastor's face. "Next thing, you'll be giving church funds to those filthy Socialists!" He started out the door.

"Wait please," begged Colombo. "We've been friends, Simon, and I want to keep it that way. At least stop holding political meetings here in our chapel."

"Gentlemen, I'm not your employee! I donate more to the church than anyone else, I tell you, and that gives me the right to use these facilities." He left quickly.

Arturo clenched a fist. "Tiger, attend that cattlemen's meeting Friday. You're a cattleman—or were. See what they're up to." I told him I'd attend.

I came, I saw, but did not conquer. Duke Reyes-Castillo, the dandy that slugged me when I kept him from mauling Evita, came into the chapel with other ranchers.

To my disgust, the Reverend Doctor Nuñez came with them. Jaime, now Simon's bodyguard, followed him in and sat in back smoking. I told him quietly, "We worship in here, Pal. Show respect!" He sneered, spit on the cigarette, and stuffed it into a shirt pocket. Fumes warned me that he was well lubricated.

Nuñez began sermonizing on tithing, orating as if to a crowd, and Duke stood. "Enough! To business, gentlemen!" Dressed like a matador, he clicked his shiny boot heels. "Just one item: we must stick together. Not one more rancher can give in and pay higher wages or it'll spread. That rotten union organizer from the SRE is telling our hands to hold out for . . . " He stopped, gaping toward the rear.

Task 13–b.

STRIVE TO RECONCILE ENEMIES

Mincho stood in the doorway, stooping to avoid bumping his head, and Simon barked, "Benjamin Medina, what're you doing here?" The big man said nothing; he sat near the back and bowed his head. I'd soon see why it's so crucial to **strive to reconcile enemies.**

"I asked you why you've come here!"

"To seek God's forgiveness. As the gentleman just said, I'm 'rotten.'"

Simon caught Jaime's eye and tilted his head slightly toward Mincho; the gunman moved stealthily to sit behind the giant. Duke folded his arms and looked Mincho up and down. "So you're Mincho the Monster! I see why they call you that. You're a big one and as ugly as they say; the over-stuffed union goon that stirs up our hands!" He stepped toward Mincho, his chin raised. "Well, sir, your size and battle scar do not intimidate me; I'm Duke Reyes-Castillo and what I pay my hands is not your (*bleep*) business. Now you listen, you meddler, I've a right to pay what I want to anyone who lives on my ranch. It's my land!"

Mincho stood and fixed his adversary in the eye. "I listened to you, sir, and you're a gentleman so you'll listen to me. You assume the right as a landowner to pay pathetically low wages and deny your hands any rights because they own no land. You claim the right to dictate all terms because Spain's royal monarch gave your ancestor a land grant three centuries ago. Well, la-de-dah!"

Duke reached for a knife in his belt. "You'll leave and let our workers alone or else I'll finish the job Picasso started on your face."

He stepped forward, but another cattleman grabbed his arm. "Let him talk, Duke. A rule of warfare is to know the enemy's mind."

Mincho had not moved. "You base your claim on that bit of history and I base mine on another. Spain never shared in the Protestant Reformation and the social reforms that grew out of it in later centuries, so the Spaniards who colonized my ancestors with muskets brought with them a medieval worldview and economic system. Your family, its beliefs, and your ranch administration are all an antiquated fossil left over from medieval times. You still cling to the feudal system, treating your hands and sharecroppers as serfs, little better than slaves."

Curses and obscenities spewed from Duke's lips and Simon pointed his hook at Mincho. "You hire thugs to kill landowners! They almost shot me, I tell you."

"And they'd surely have slain you by now, Simon Alvarez, if I hadn't organized them. But I didn't come here to debate ideology! I came in search of faith."

"Faith! I'll tell you what my faith is, you butcher! God gave me what I own and no union will take it from me. You don't belong here."

"Then excuse me, gentlemen." The big man walked forward, laid bills on the altar and turned to leave.

"We don't want your phony alms," growled Simon. "Take them with you."

"Are they counterfeit? I appreciate what the church is doing for needy people in Los Vientos and other hard-up villages and I want to help a little."

Simon threw the money to the floor and spat on it. He nodded toward Jaime, who rose quietly behind Mincho and struck his head viciously with his pistol butt. The giant collapsed with a thud that made me shudder; I feared he was dead. Jaime kicked him in the face and I rose to stop him, but Mincho shook his head, winced in pain, in a flash grabbed Jaime's leg, and twisted it. The gunman screamed and fell hard. Mincho seized the pistol and rose slowly, blood oozing from the back of his head; he emptied the bullets from the chamber and tossed the pistol back to its owner, who was lying on the floor holding his leg, groaning. Mincho turned and walked over to Simon who backed away; I'd never seen a man cringe and tremble so. His face reflected unmitigated terror.

"Relax, Simon! I won't touch you; I've not sunk so low as to do violence in God's presence. I'll make an offer and we'll let these gentlemen witness it. You own the mine and head the cattle association, and I have influence with the workers. Between the two of us, we can end the bloodshed. Here before God, let's agree on a fair accord that benefits both sides." He held out a massive hand.

Simon backed away, his face white, beads of sweat on his forehead. "You're crazy! I'll die before I negotiate with such a bloodthirsty rattlesnake, I tell you!"

"Do it for your workers, not for me. They earn too little to care for their families. Give them fair pay and no one will make trouble for you; you'll benefit as much as they will. Miners are saying you need to provide safeguards against radiation, that it's a race against time before they get cancer. Let's work together to do what's right, we'll end the violence and needless friction on both sides."

"You tell me to stop violence? Look at this arm, I tell you!" Simon unbuckled his hook and waved his stump at Mincho. "Look at it! Did you forget how I lost it? Get out of here, before I . . . before I . . . "

Mincho knelt and whispered, "Lord, forgive me! I failed!" He rose, placed the bills on the altar again, and stared at Simon who backed farther away. Mincho then turned to me. "Give this to your church's 'Good Samaritan' group. They aided the family of an injured miner and I'm grateful. Now, gentlemen, you witnessed my offer of a peaceful solution. I'm ready to parley whenever you are." He gave Duke a polite nod and left.

No one spoke for a while and Dr. Nuñez started to orate again, until Duke ordered him, "Shut your outsized mouth!" He faced the cattlemen. "We'll remain firm—agreed?" They voiced hearty consent and Duke strutted from the chapel, followed by the others, paying no attention to Nuñez' flowery benediction.

Jaime rose from the floor, eying the money. Simon roared, "Stop gaping like a fool and wipe up that blood! Tiger, get that stinking money out of here! Do what you want with it. Feed it to your horse!"

I knew I had to do something decisive about what I'd just witnessed, but what? I'd find out the next morning.

A stranger wore his pistol low when he came with Jaime at first light, and Simon's angry gestures told me what I needed to know. The two gunmen mounted and trotted toward Los Vientos. I ran as fast as I could to get Bullet, mounted bareback, gripped his mane, and kicked his flanks. "Go, go, go!" Racing up the mountain road, I thanked God for such a powerful horse. Popcorn ran ahead and stopped at a curve, bristling. Dismounting, I crept up in bushes and smelled tobacco smoke. Jaime and his partner had stopped their horses and were passing a flask back and forth. I crept back, mounted Bullet, and galloped whooping straight at the two gunmen whose startled horses shied to one side.

Reining in at Mincho's house, I shouted for him; he opened the door, his head bandaged. "Caramba, Tiger! You promised not to return here."

"Jaime and another hired gun are on their way up. You're their target."

"Am I now? Well, I'll be ready." Mincho took a rifle from the wall and loaded it. "Hide, Tiger. Don't let them see you. They'd kill you too."

"You'll need my help." I checked the cartridges in my pistol.

"Mincho!" Jaime yelled outside. "Good morning! Listen. Some fool accused you of rustling a steer. The police chief sent us to take you in to clear it up. Don't resist; they'll proceed judicially. I'm sure it's a mistake. Nothing to fear . . . "

"Lies!" I warned. We waited and I sensed that familiar, dry, adrenalin taste.

"I'm counting to three, then we come in firing. Last chance. One . . . Two . . . "

A window shattered and Mincho fired back. After another exchange of shots, Jaime yelled, "Hold your fire. No steer's worth gettin' shot for. We're leaving."

"Eyes open, Mincho!" I warned. "I see only Jaime riding off, too slowly."

"Woof!" Popcorn scurried toward a back door. Jaime's partner had sneaked in; his pistol rose, pointing at Mincho's back. The dog distracted him and the shot missed. Popcorn's teeth clamped onto the shooter's wrist and Mincho moved fast. He kicked the weapon from the intruder's hand and the gunman started to run out the door. Mincho tackled him and beat him with his fists until he stopped struggling. The giant lifted the limp body high and hurled it onto the stone-covered ground; I heard a crack when it hit. The assailant lay still and I held Popcorn to keep him from finishing the killer off.

"My leg's busted," the man moaned, and then screamed. "Jaime! Help me!"

Jaime galloped to where he could see the injured man from a distance, reined his horse around, jabbed his spurs brutally into its flanks, and raced toward town. His partner crawled and tried to mount his horse, but could not. Mincho lifted him onto it, slapped its rump, and it ambled slowly away.

"Jaime will be back," I warned. "Maybe tonight in the dark. You're not safe here, Mincho. Come stay at our house. Our neighbor Gadget is police chief and we'll see that you're protected until this is settled."

Task 13–c.
SERVE AS A MODEL OF A DILIGENT SHEPHERD THAT APPRENTICES CAN EASILY IMITATE

"A Giant!" Tino yelled when he saw Mincho the Monster come riding behind me down our lane, his head bandaged. "Davey, look! A giant!" What happened next underscored why a Christian leader **serves as a model of a diligent shepherd that apprentices can easily imitate.**

Gadget crawled out from under his taxi and gaped. "What's up?"

"Gunmen said you sent them to arrest me," Mincho said. "That's what's up!"

Gadget hurried after us. "Hey wait! I gotta hear this!"

Tino also followed us into the house and stared at Mincho. "You have a great big scar. What happened?"

I shoved him back out the door. "Never mind, son. Go play."

Lucy saw Mincho and shuddered. She brought coffee and I recounted the fight; Gadget listened without speaking, which was rare for him. I asked Mincho, "Would you have been ready to face God, if Jaime had shot you?"

"I don't know. I help the needy and love my neighbor. Well, *some* neighbors."

"I know you do, but no matter how much good we do, Scripture says we still fall short. Only Christ's sacrifice on our behalf covers our sins and He's our only door to heaven. Do you trust His promise to forgive us?"

"My catechist taught that He's the Savior of the world."

"Yes, but do you trust Him for your own salvation, Mincho?"

He sighed. "I'm a violent man, and it'll take violence to organize the miners and ranch hands that men like Simon mistreat. At times, bloodshed is unavoidable. I can't desert them."

"Our Heavenly Father loves you in spite of your violent vocation, and you certainly do not have to abandon the miners in order to follow Christ. I'm just as eager to help them as you are. So is Roger. Let's join forces."

Lucy brought scrambled eggs and corn tortillas, which soon vanished. Gadget glanced back and forth at Mincho and me as I asked the giant about his faith and answered his queries. I avoided arguing as we discussed what Jesus had done for us in our lives and historically and asked God to protect Mincho. The big man leaned back in his chair and held up a hand to stop Lucy from piling more food on his plate. "Oh, I appreciate you folks! You show genuine concern and let me share your home. I feel safe here; I sense God's presence. Now, may I lie down? My battered head is aching." Lucy told him to use our bed and he left the table.

Gadget told me, "I just seen how to present Jesus without no preachy arguing. You're a good model."

"Being a model is your job too. Demonstrate for your group's members how to do their duties, show your apprentices how to shepherd, and they'll all imitate you. Now, pray for me; I have an extremely distasteful confrontation to make."

Gadget offered to help me, but I said, "No. This I have to do alone tonight."

When I arrived at the big house, I immediately told Simon, "This is my last watch, sir. I don't work for anyone who hires assassins."

He stared at me for a tense moment. "I was hasty; anger blinded me. I'll not bother Mincho again. Please keep watching my house; you're the only one I trust not to sleep on the job. I'm begging. My life depends on it. My life, I tell you!"

"Well . . . If you'll give me your word not to sponsor any more violence, sir, in any way. Do we have an agreement?"

"Of course!" He laid his hand on his heart, smiling. "You have my word."

"And I'll hold you to it." I began my circuit around the big house.

Task 13–d. UNMASK FALSE FRIENDSHIP AND INSINCERE DIPLOMACY	"No, you fool!" I heard Simon rasp as I passed a window. "Don't mention the land; they see it as a war against the devil or something. Emphasize the benefits that'll accrue to them from the seminary." This reminded me that a cautious leader will **unmask false friendship and insincere diplomacy.**

"I'll get the vote," Nuñez' voice replied. "I'm befriending the stupider members, so they'll support us. Ah . . . I need a bit more reimbursement, now that . . . "

"You'll stick to our deal, I tell you. You'll earn plenty as seminary president."

CLANG! Gadget's alarm sounded late that night. An emergency? Why was Arturo calling the leaders to his office so late? I could not stop watching the house, so in the morning I rushed to see him. "What was the urgency last night?"

"A big owl landed on the wire and activated the alarm. There's no crisis."

"Yes there is—a ruse to get greedy church members to sell the land. I overheard

Nuñez admit faking friendship to get votes in a meeting, and Simon said to make the seminary the issue. How'll we keep folks from swallowing their bait?"

"Am I not a lawyer?" Arturo hit his desk. "I'll prepare a defense, you'll see!"

<table>
<tr><td>

Task 13–e.

PROVIDE PASTORAL TRAINING AT ALL ECONOMIC AND EDUCATIONAL LEVELS

</td><td>

While waiting for the rigged business meeting to start a week later, Arturo took papers from his briefcase and told Lucy and me, "Dr. Nuñez wants to require high level academic training, which would kill our movement. I'll explain why we **provide pastoral training at all economic and educational levels.**"

</td></tr>
</table>

"Look how many are arriving!" Lucy said. "There's no room for all to sit!"

"Oh, no!" Arturo groaned. "Some haven't attended worship in years and they don't know the situation. It's my fault, Lucy. I should've dropped them from the church rolls long ago; now it's too late to stop them from voting to sell the land."

"I wonder why we don't sell it, Pastor. I hope you explain it."

"We probably should sell it, but not to those liars. That won't be the issue. Nuñez will tout the proposed seminary and these folks are oblivious to the ruse."

"Will they listen to you? Nuñez will offer lucrative employment. Oh look! Jethro! He's limping; he never recovered fully from that landslide."

We had to endure Dr. Nuñez' crocodile grin as he presented his case and concluded, "So it's obvious that academic theological training is the only way to prepare God's ministers. An accredited seminary is the one recognized, time-honored method to prepare authentic pastors. We'll vote now for excellence in theological training for Bat Haven and this entire region. All who . . . "

"Not yet!" Arturo faced the assembly. "The Reverend Doctor Nuñez ably described benefits of a seminary and I agree. It can prepare leaders well for large, institutional churches. But in Bat Haven and its villages? Here we need to train leaders on the job by extension, which means no classrooms and . . . "

"And no scholarly instruction!" mocked Wanda. "Stop stalling the vote."

Arturo looked at his notes. "2 Timothy 2:2 shows how . . . "

"Enough!" interrupted Simon. "This is no Bible study, I tell you! We already know all that you have to say about this, Arturo. We'll vote now to . . . "

"You won't hear me? Okay. Reverend Jethro Mendez, come explain how you prepare pastors who don't fulfill a seminary's matriculation requirements."

"With all respect," objected Wanda shrilly, "Pastor Jethro is not a member of our church. He has no right to take part in our business meeting, Arturo."

"The Lord used brother Jethro to help us initiate our movement for Christ. He has certainly earned the right to advise us."

Jethro embraced Nuñez. "Thank you, Doctor, for reviewing the benefits of academic training. I learned valuable truths in seminary, although my motivation then was mainly to get good grades. Girls in the Christian education- department were attractive too; I met my wife there." I heard titters and my tension eased. "The professors loved Jesus and taught well the subjects that we wanted. My only complaint is that they didn't offer enough practical mentoring."

"Brother Jethro," Dr. Nuñez extended his arms toward him with his widest grin. "Oh, yes, yes! How the dear students will appreciate a kindhearted mentor! My good brother, I'll grant you the *Chair of Theological Mentoring* in our new seminary! With a top-level salary, of course. Ha."

Jethro made a mock bow and continued, "Institutional training—if true to the Word and faithful to Christ—has its place. But is that place Bat Haven? Most seminary alumni work in urban churches, not in villages."

"We'll offer certificates at a lower level," sputtered Nuñez.

"You overlook a vital fact, Doctor. Good theological academies locate where there are many churches so students can serve in them, practicing what they learn. Crowding them in one small-town congregation would be like corralling a hundred cows to graze in a tiny backyard!" Jethro limped back to his seat.

Nuñez rose, but Arturo said firmly, "Wait, sir! Another whom God has been using in Bat Haven's villages is Pastor Jacob Morán of Los Robles. His congregation has risen up daughter and granddaughter churches. Come, brother."

I hadn't noticed Jacob in the crowd; he shook hands with folks as he walked to the front. "Your brothers in Los Robles send greetings in the Lord. May I say a prayer, Pastor?" Arturo nodded and Jacob spoke in his peasant patois, "Good afternoon, beloved Father. Bless these good folks and please help your servant answer Mr. Arturo's questions. In Jesus' most holy and exalted name, Amen."

"Brother Jacob, could you enroll in the proposed seminary?"

"They'd laugh at me, sir. I barely squirmed through two years of schooling. I got a family to care for too. Our blessed Lord gave me a congregation to tend so I daren't leave it to go away to no theology seminary. I got a cow and corn too."

"And the other village pastors?"

"We'd all be mighty out of place in a hall of higher education, sir."

"Brother Jacob, how have you received training to serve as a pastor?"

"Brother Roger Diaz brings extension studies." He took a small booklet from his shirt pocket and held it up. "We plan our work every two weeks with him."

"Without this extension training, what would the village pastors do?"

"Well, sir, we'd be unbroken colts, running around ignorant and useless. Sheep with careless shepherds get hungry and wander off."

"Has God given you the pastoral gift, Brother Jacob?"

"Let me think on that. I lead my flock to green pastures and they feed on God's

Holy Word. A lamb strays and I leave the ninety-nine to bring 'em back. I mentor our daughter churches' leaders. So I guess so, sir; the Holy Spirit gave me a shepherd's heart by the grace of God or I couldn't do these chores."

"Brother Jacob, tell us how you start so many churches."

"Well, sir, I haven't read any big books on theology, much as I'd like to, but I know beans and corn. Our precious Lord Jesus taught that His kingdom grows like grain. I plant the Lord's seed and our blessed Creator makes it sprout. I water it with His Word and the Lord makes it grow. I weed it and keep the critters out, and God makes it multiply." Clapping broke out as Jacob sat again in back.

Arturo stood in front of Simon and looked him directly in the eye. "I'm well aware that Panther Jones is behind this seminary project and some of us wonder why. Maybe you'll explain, sir, or are you ready for the vote now?"

"Wait!" Simon rose and swung his hook in an arc, pointing at all the people. "Don't forget how much you'll earn working for the seminary. I tell you . . . "

"Pathetic!" exclaimed Colombo in his deep voice. "Brother Simon, you and Dr. Nuñez are buying our votes! Only God knows why. Well, I'm not for sale. I'd considered voting to sell the land, but not now. I'm not your hireling."

Those whom Nuñez had lured falsely to the meeting hung their heads when we voted. The sale lost and Arturo dismissed us. Nuñez stomped toward the door in his shiny white shoes, but Lucy stepped in his way smiling playfully.

"We'll miss you, Dr. Amos Fernando Nuñez and Castillo. When are you leaving? Your wife must miss you terribly! Oh, but the bus leaves at four a.m.!"

He glared at her, mouth working, face contorted with rage. "I will stay until I fulfill my mission, Mrs. Lucille Garcia, and you . . . you . . . " He gritted his teeth, pointed at her, and snarled hoarsely, "You will learn to keep out of my way."

CHAPTER 13: CONFIRM THE GRASP AND THE PRACTICE OF LEADERS' TASKS

13–a. Practice Christian stewardship for the right motive. Simon gave generously to the church in order to control things. Find a better motive to give: *Store up for yourselves treasures in heaven.* Matt 6:19–21

13–b. Strive to reconcile enemies. Note how to treat foes: *If your enemy is hungry, feed him, and if he is thirsty, give him a drink; for in so doing you will heap burning coals on his head. Do not be overcome by evil, but overcome evil with good.* Rom 12:20–21

Find how to deal with a leader that persists in sin: *Do not receive an accusation against an elder except on the basis of two or three witnesses. Those who continue in sin, rebuke in the presence of all, so that the rest also will be fearful of sinning.* 1 Tim 5:19–20

13–c. Serve as a model of a diligent shepherd that apprentices can easily imitate. Ego pushes one to do things in a way that others can only admire, but Tiger led in an imitable way. See what Paul told Corinthian believers to do: *Be imitators of me, just as I also am of Christ.* 1 Cor 11:1

13–d. Unmask false friendship and insincere diplomacy. Amos Nuñez befriended voters with the motive of greed. Consider God's view of false friend: *Faithful are the wounds of a friend, but deceitful are the kisses of an enemy.* Prov 27:6

13–e. Provide pastoral training at all economic and educational levels. Note what the Lord thinks of those who consider themselves wise: *He does not regard any who are wise of heart.* Job 37:24

Nuñez wanted a seminary where it didn't fit. Some seminaries base training on God's Word, others trust more in man's wisdom. Find a peril in this: *I will destroy the wisdom of the wise . . . Where is the wise man? Where is the scribe? Where is the debater of this age? Has not God made foolish the wisdom of the world? For since in the wisdom of God the world through its wisdom did not come to know God, God was well-pleased through the foolishness of the message preached to save those who believe.* 1 Cor 1:19–23

EVALUATE YOUR LEADERSHIP
1=Poor. 2=Planning to improve. 3=Doing well.

1-2-3   Practice Christian stewardship for the right motive.

1-2-3   Strive to reconcile enemies.

1-2-3   Serve as a model that apprentices easily imitate, of a diligent shepherd.

1-2-3   Unmask false friendship and deceptive diplomacy.

1-2-3   Provide pastoral training at all economic and educational levels.

14.
Despair Lures Tiger to Stumble

Task 14–a.

LET BELIEVERS USE THEIR SPIRITUAL GIFTS IN A WAY THAT FITS THEIR NATURAL PERSONALITY TYPES

Jethro had invited Roger and me to Arenas to tell his congregation what God was doing where we trained leaders, and I told them, "You've shared your pastor with us and God has used him to pry us out of a deep rut." Roger and I then learned from them how alert leaders **let believers use their spiritual gifts in a way that fits their natural personality types**.

A boy introduced Communion, reciting, "I'm Eleazar, a Hebrew boy. We lived in Egypt, but left in a hurry today. Yesterday Dad told me to get a lamb; I held it, Dad cut its throat, and blood splattered on me." A man and boy acted out cutting the lamb's throat, without speaking.

"They cut its guts out; it stunk and flies came. Then Dad daubed its blood on our doorposts. Moses had warned that a death angel would fly over Egypt and kill the oldest son in any house without that blood." The father pretended to paint blood on a door.

"We ate the lamb with herbs that were bitter. That night I couldn't sleep; I was scared because I'm the oldest son; I lay trembling in the dark silence. I waited and then heard terrified screams. Far off the wailing began. It got closer. Closer! I begged, 'Dear God, let the angel see the blood!' I heard shrieking nearby; I pressed my hands over my ears and shut my eyes as tightly as I could." A child flapped his arms, "flew" to the door, looked at it, and passed by.

"Silence gradually returned. I was alive! I opened my eyes and saw Dad and Mom standing over me, weeping. Dad held me and gasped, 'He saw it! He surely saw it! The angel of death saw the blood of the Lamb—and passed over!'"

I had damp eyes as we took Communion's Passover meal. Children then recited Bible verses and adults reported victories in cells and other ministries. Roger asked Jethro afterwards, "How do you get folks to do so many things?"

"I turn them loose to do whatever fits each one's gifts and personalities."

"Gifts I understand, but what do you mean by fitting one's personality?"

"Observe what kind of animal one is, Roger; which of the four classic personality types." Jethro drew four animals.

"'Brawny Bull' sees projects through. He's adept at directing and pushes obstacles aside, like Nehemiah. He abuses his authority and bruises folks if he fails to let the Holy Spirit restrain his brute force. Let him manage tough projects."

"'Playful Puppy' gets along with everyone, serving for the fun of being with folks, and spontaneous like Peter. He's easily swayed, as Peter was one sad night, if the Holy Spirit doesn't curb his bent. Let him evangelize and work with youth."

"'High-flying Eagle' is far-sighted and creative. He plans for the future like Jeremiah. However, he flies too high in the clouds and gets lost in a dream world if God is not guiding him. Let this visionary lay out a church's future course, develop strategies, and challenge folks in imaginative ways."

"'Steady Mule' perseveres patiently, content to follow a routine a step at a time. He's happy as long as he sees even small progress, is good with details or facts and can be a thorough Bible expositor like Ezra. However, he becomes obstinate and resists needed change if God doesn't remove rust from his mind. Let this constant servant do jobs that require detailed accuracy."

He drew a circle around all four pictures and explained, "Some rare animals are a *blend*, flexible like David and Paul. They're superb leaders, provided God keeps them focused, serving humbly with love in the Holy Spirit's power."

"Do these animals' traits correspond to spiritual gifts?" Roger asked.

"No, son. God gives spiritual gifts only to a believer, but every person inherits one or more of these natural traits. However, they affect how a spiritual gift is used. For example, a mule gifted to exhort will shepherd others behind the scenes, urging quietly, but a puppy will use the same gift publicly."

"Wow!" Roger exclaimed. "Animals, dramatic readings, timely testimonies, so many taking part! You're a great teacher, sir. I hope to teach as effectively."

"Be warned! Good teachers' gift can draw too much attention; the sun revolves around it, eclipsing other gift-based ministries, deforming Christ's body."

"What a chiropractor you are for church bodies!" Roger hugged the old man.

Back in Bat Haven, Evita sketched the animals as Roger described the four personality types to our cell leaders and their spouses. "We'll help folks use their spiritual gifts better if we know their natural bent. Which animal are you, Lucy?"

"I fear I have a sharp beak and talons! My eagle eye sees what others miss and my soaring imagination makes trouble if I don't follow God's leading."

"Screech! Screech!" chirped Evita, flapping her arms. "I'm an eagle too; I'll escape any cage folks try to put me in! I see future trends and their long-range results. And yes, my imagination often flies away with me to my regret!"

"Woof, woof!" barked Gadget. "I'm a wiggily waggily! Let me be with folks! My desire to get along spontaneously with everybody makes a mess of things if God doesn't jerk my leash. Which of them animals are you, Pacho?"

"Do I have to tell you? I'm the inflexible old mule, content to serve steadfastly and deal with details that bore the rest of you. I'll persevere, plodding along a step at a time. I gladly let others initiate and direct our projects."

Roger prodded, "What risk does a mule face if God is not leading it, Pacho?"

"Braying instead of praying! I gripe and resist change mulishly. And you?"

"Hmmm. I guess I'm a hybrid—half mule and half eagle."

"A flying *mulagle!*" Gadget laughed. "And you, Arturo?"

"I admit it; I'm the bull in our bunch. I'll see a project through and push aside anything or anybody that gets in the way. I have to be careful not to abuse my authority and gore others. What kind of animal are you, Tiger?"

"Ah . . . Problem is, I fit the dubious side of all four!"

"He's a tangled mix!" Lucy exclaimed. "An eagle's long-range vision, a puppy's lively empathy, a mule's stubborn steadiness, and a bull's drive! This confused creature needs a stout leash or he runs in all four directions at once!"

Roger told Lucy and me a month later after worship, "It took folks a while to realize their cage door had been left open, but now they're using their gifts in ways that fit their personalities, serving during worship, and during the week."

Lucy replied, "They're not only more active, but more joyful." Then, as if to stress the contrast, jarring cries sounded from the *House of Divine Revalation* down the street, and she sighed, "Poor Mouse! He failed to draw his crowds, so he preaches angrier than ever at any curious spectator who drops in."

Task 14–b.
CARE FOR SPOUSE AND CHILDREN BEFORE PURSUING EVERY PRESSING PROJECT

"Keep those rowdy kids quiet!" I shouted at Lucy the next morning. "They've awakened me twice! I need sleep if I'm going to coordinate our groups." I'd soon find that a leader with proper priorities will **care for spouse and children before pursuing every pressing project.**

"It's such a strain on the boys to keep silent every morning!"

Things had piled up on my to-do list and left me fretting so much over the unresolved problems that my tension rose to the point of detonation. My frustration finally boiled over in a bitter quarrel with Lucy over who should dictate our boys' behavior. Then, the aftermath—Lucy quit talking to me. She frowned as I sorted my studies as Arturo did, using dividers labeled with ministry titles.

"Look Lu." I pinned my *Vital Ministries Checklist* above my makeshift filing cabinet, a cardboard box. "Now I can find a study for any need."

More silence—the lull preceding a storm. The next morning my *Vital Ministries Checklist* was missing from the wall. "Why'd you take down my list of ministries?" I shouted at Lucy.

"King Hezekiah removed idols from the high places."

"What's King Hezekiah got to do with my . . . ?"

"Your church position has become a high place for you; you're more devoted to it than to God Himself and you give it more attention than your family."

"Now wait! What brought all this on, Lu?"

"I didn't trash your list. Here." She had scotch-taped another section to it.

"You're meddling in my ministry!"

She resumed silent mode and I read what she'd added to my list of vital ministries: "Family Duties." I recalled with a pang how Wanda the Wasp had decreed that nobody could lead who has family problems. I lost heart and neglected my leader's duties, moping, and wallowing in self-reproach, of no use to God or man.

I passed Gadget's shop three weeks later, and he asked, "What's up? You haven't been meeting with your trainees."

"I don't know. I don't feel fit."

Gadget began neglecting his group too, imitating his mentor. Noticing this, I forced myself to resume training cell leaders, but my heart was not in it. My despair peaked one day; I walked to the square and sat, trying to escape my gloom. Jaime sauntered over from the Alvarez' house and sat beside me. "You look as miserable as I feel, Tiger. A shot of rye will fix that. Got a cigarette?"

"You know I don't smoke."

"I'm sick of doing Simon's dirty work. That hypocrite won't soil his hands."

"His hook." I turned the other way hoping the uncouth rogue would go away.

"Makes me do all his unlawful and (*bleep*) dangerous stuff."

"I thought you enjoyed violence, Jaime."

"Only when my belly's full of my favorite anesthetic. Let's go get . . . "

"Greetings, gentlemen!" Torivio Ochoa, Chuey's brother, ambled toward us, holding a bottle high. "Ah! My favorite and most esteemed enemies!" He bowed.

I started to leave, but Torivio shouted, "Please let me join you, Mr. Garcia!"

I sat, hoping our friendly little chat would soon end. Torivio let everyone around hear his invitation, "Let's drink to a hearty enmity! Nothing more fulfilling in life than having worthy enemies!" He wedged himself between Jaime and me on the bench and put his arms around our shoulders. "Now that we're comrades in enmity, let's toast our fond feud!" He offered me his bottle and I shook my head. "So! Too holy to drink with an ex-con?" He rose, growling like a bear.

"No, man, it's not that at all. I used to drink too much so I promised God . . . "

"Nobody refuses to drink with Torivio Ochoa! Prepare yourself."

"I don't want to fight. The fact is, I've . . . "

"The fact is you're a self-righteous snob, as well as a sniveling coward!"

"I don't let anyone call me a coward." I stood.

He yelled obscene curses at me so belligerently that people came running to watch. An inner voice warned me to step away, but my fog of despair blinded me to the peril of irrational fury. Pacho had hurried over from the barber's shop and cried, "Back off, Tiger! Don't make a spectacle! You'll ruin your testimony."

Too heated to hear, I faced Torivio. "You're not only a liar, but an uncivilized beast. Your leftist pals pulled you down from a tree, lopped off your tail, and taught you to chatter that snotty filth that spews from your slimy lips!"

He caught me off guard, whirling and using martial arts with commendable skill that he had acquired in prison. I picked myself up and waded back in while Jaime shouted, "Come, everyone! Watch the Evangelical 'peacemaker' combat evil! I'll bet ten to one in favor of Torivio. Any takers?"

Torivio whacked me with feet and hands that came from nowhere. I got in a few blows, but could not evade karate chops that hammered my neck and face. Twice I tumbled to jeering laughter. Roger came running and pulled the wild man away from me, but Torivio threw him over his shoulder and he fell with a thud that left him dazed. Torivio attacked with fresh fury and I went down a third time. I started to rise, but collapsed from a final, wrenching kick to my left ear. Torivio wandered off laughing coarsely and waving his bottle like a drum major's baton, while Jaime collected a bet from some fool, and Roger stumbled around looking for his glasses. Pacho helped me up and I staggered toward home.

"Your eye's swollen shut!" Lucy cried.

"I got in a stupid fight. I don't want to discuss it." I fell on the bed and slept.

"Your husband started it, Lucy!" The Wasp's voice jarred me awake; she'd lost no time to come relate her version of the brawl. "He provoked that drunken ruffian. I watched it all from my upstairs window."

Shame kept me awake after Wanda left, intensified by guilt for neglecting Lucy and the boys. I began to doze, but Arturo's motorcycle woke me. Oh, no! The last one I cared to see! I opened a window to escape through it, but he entered toting that bulging black briefcase, which for some reason angered me. He prayed for me and nothing he said registered in my muddled mind. When he said Amen, I blurted, "I know, I know! I've neglected my family."

"I've a Bible study for that." He opened the black briefcase.

"Yeah, you would! Your fat old bag holds a study for everything! I had a frumpy old aunt who lugged around an all-purpose purse just like it; no matter what you needed, she pulled out of it. Well, I don't feel like studying, sir. Pull a sleeping pill out of your magic bag and leave me alone!"

"Stop jabbering nonsense!" Lucy cried. She took the one-page study from Arturo and pressed it into my hand. I read the title: "Family Duties."

Lucy turned to Arturo. "Have you been ill, Pastor? You look all worn out."

"It's a brutal headache. I've been working nights preparing to refute a devilish proposal that Panther's lawyer, Sebastian, made to the town council to force our congregation to sell its land, 'for the benefit of the community.'"

"Why fight it?" I grumbled. "It might benefit this retarded town. All Bat Haven does is run full-speed backwards and . . . "

Lucy clasped her hand over my mouth. "Go home and rest, Pastor."

He left and I sighed in relief. Lucy, however, stood, hands on hips, waiting as I read every word of the study. She then asked, "So what are your family duties?"

I knew there'd be no peace until I told her what she wanted. I counted "Family Duties" off on my five fingers, as the study had illustrated them:

"Thumb: *A husband loves his wife as himself.*

Pointer: *A wife respects and submits to him as to the Lord.*

Middle: *Parents raise kids in God's discipline without causing anger.*

Ring: *Kids obey their parents.*

Pinky: *Servants obey their masters sincerely as they would Christ.* Ha! I have to serve crabby old Simon with respect! What fun!"

"So sour! Are you going to take these duties seriously, Tiger?"

"Of course. The pointer finger is for wives." I aimed it at her. "You got to . . . "

"Whoa!" She pushed my finger around to point at me. "Did you skip one?"

"You heard me tell Arturo I haven't done my duty. Are you doing yours?"

"It'll be easier to submit to you when you treat me as Jesus does his bride—the Church. God tells you to do that. Do your part and I can do mine. You . . . " She bit her lip. "No . . . Wait. Grandma would scold me for making that command *conditional.* I'm to submit and respect you, whether you deserve it or not. You're also to do your duty whether I deserve it or not. I've failed. So have you."

I started to argue, but the Holy Spirit used Lucy's tearful plea to pry my eyes open to the truth; her words hit harder than Torivio's blows. The ensuing scuffle with my ego caused sharper pain than what the ex-convict had inflicted. "Forgive me, Lu. Thank you for prodding me." I also begged our Father in heaven to forgive me and to help me do my duty as a spouse and parent.

Lucy glanced at the study. "It says to raise children in the Lord's discipline and instruction. Was that command for parents or Sunday school teachers?"

"Okay, I got the point. I promise to spend good time with you and the boys."

I kept my word, but failed to cut other activities. No matter how frantically I tried, I could not work nights, care for my family, serve as cell leader, and do my coordinator's duties as I wanted, and tension mounted. I wasn't the only one; after worship, Lucy nudged me. "Arturo's thin and worn out! He has me worried."

"My idiotic brawl in the square only added to his headaches. He asked me to stay so the elders can deal with my offense. Go on home with the boys."

Task 14–c.

RESTORE THOSE WHO STRAY WITHOUT NEEDLESS DELAY

Arturo began the meeting, in which I'd find out why a non-judgmental leader will **restore those who stray without needless delay.** It bugged me to notice that Simon had stayed with the elders and Wanda the Wasp hovered nearby. She decreed, "Tiger needs a year of expulsion from our church!"

"Spare us!" snapped Arturo harshly. "Enough of your heartless invective! You're the one who needs the discipline! Go! Leave us alone!"

His anger shocked me; he normally did not lose his cool so readily. Wanda's voice rose an octave in response, "I'll go when you've heard what I have to say!"

Arturo breathed deeply and spoke quietly, "Then hear what Jesus and His apostles taught about corrective discipline such as disallowing Communion. It's not to punish; that's God's role. It's to *restore*. Also, it's not for a specified time; the apostles never decreed an arbitrary sentence of so many months; they restored offenders when they repented. To delay affirming God's pardon after one repents helps no one; it prolongs everyone's pain and cancels God's grace."

Colombo eyed my discolored face. "I think Tiger's had enough punishment."

Simon pointed his hook at him. "So uneducated truckers define church policy now!" and Wanda added, "Drunkards don't inherit the kingdom of God, sir!"

The trucker faced her. "Neither do slanderers, Mrs. Alvarez. You never mention the good things Tiger does, but he commits one error and you make a big ado!"

"So drunken brawlers get off free?"

"Tiger wasn't drunk," Arturo said in a tired voice. "But even if he was, our job is to restore him. Leave sentencing to the Lord; He's the only perfect Judge."

"So then, what does God do about a Christian's sins?" Pacho asked.

"Oh, this headache!" Arturo grimaced. "Tiger, you and I dealt with this earlier today. Tell these folks what sin's consequences are for a believer."

"I'll try. Three things occur. *First*, a believer's sin impairs fellowship with others and with God because it grieves the Holy Spirit as Ephesians 4:30 says."

Wanda cried, "Who are you of all people, to teach us? Elders, do your job; punish Tiger as he deserves!" She leered at me like a cobra eyeing its next meal.

Colombo intervened. "Please, Mrs. Alvarez. We elders need to hear this, in order to deal properly with Tiger."

"*Second*," I said, "a believer's sin brings God's punishment in this life; He disciplines His unruly sons because he loves us, according to Hebrews 12."

Arturo sighed. "God must love Tiger a lot, judging by the swollen eye and myriad bruises I saw when I visited him after his cute little escapade!"

"*Third*, a believer's sin subtracts from his reward in glory. We'll stand before Christ, who'll try our works by fire. Good works will stand the test and Jesus will reward us for them, but He'll burn our bad works and wipe away all tears forever. Imagine the blaze when He ignites my pile of worthless works. It'll be bi-i-g!"

Pacho asked, "What if a new believer dies before doing good works, Tiger?"

"1 Corinthians 3 says if his works are burned then he'll suffer loss, but his soul will be saved. This judgment by Jesus is for the saved, to test our works. It's not the judgment of unbelieving rebels before God's great white throne."

Arturo closed his briefcase. "Tiger repented; let's restore him and go home." The elders agreed and Arturo told me, "God forgives you, Tiger, and so do we."

"I'm grateful, but I have to resign my position as group coordinator."

Arturo looked at me with pained eyes. An elder who seldom spoke suggested, "Simon has the most experience as administrator. Let him be group coordinator if he'll promise to stop holding political meetings in the chapel. That'll solve two problems: it stops those meetings and provides an experienced administrator."

"I accept," responded Simon quickly.

"But you opposed the groups!" protested Colombo. "How can you . . . ?"

"We forgave Tiger," the elder insisted, "so we have to forgive Simon too."

I expected Arturo to bring up Simon's lack of repentance, but he and the other elders were already heading out the door.

Back home, I found Lucy washing dishes, and told her, "They pardoned me."

"I knew they would."

"Simon is group coordinator now."

"Simon!" A pan she was drying fell to the floor with a clank. "Madness! He's the last person on earth . . . The elders have gone out of their minds!"

Task 14–d.
PRAY WITH CONFIDENCE IN JESUS' NAME FOR HEALING

I no longer coordinated the groups, but I was mentoring more leaders in my Mudhole and Los Vientos groups. This and my other responsibilities left me exhausted and sleepless. I didn't realize I had become quite ill, and events would move me to **pray with confidence in Jesus' name for healing**. I had managed to doze when my son's screams woke me. "Papa, Papa!" "Andy fell in a pit! He didn't answer when I called!"

I grabbed a rope and galloped on Bullet with Tino to the slope above the chapel. "Andy!" I called. Someone had covered the pit with brush to hide it "Andy!"

No reply. I looped the rope around a boulder, lowered myself and tied the rope under the limp boy's arms. I climbed it and pulled him up.

Tino pointed, "Look, Papa! Another hole like this one!" My mind raced; we had to stop the idiot who was doing this, but how? Who was it?

The doctor examined Andy and took me to one side. "It's worse than a mere concussion; there's hemorrhaging. Please tell his family."

Anxious thoughts piled up after that: miners in danger, holes in the mountainside, neglecting my family, fighting like a rowdy schoolboy, and failing in my shepherding duties. I tried to sleep, but could not. I tried to read the Bible, but qualms distracted me; I could not stay focused on anything. Lucy sobbed and I felt befuddled; fatigue finally pushed me beyond the limit. My nerves collapsed.

I don't know how long I drifted in incoherent confusion; when the blur finally cleared, I was lying in the health center. Lucy was sitting by me, saw my eyes focus on her, and squeezed my hand. I asked, "How's Andy?"

"Still in a coma. Are you thinking straight now?" I nodded.

The doctor asked me questions and said, "You can get up and dress. Your physical exhaustion and lack of sleep triggered your mental distress. There's only one remedy, Mr. Garcia." He looked me in the eye. "Trim down your activities."

Lucy and I joined Martha who was watching Andy. Another patient, a wrinkled wisp of a lady, followed us and suggested in a reedy voice, "Take the lad to Tacualtuste. Our image of the Holy Virgin heals any ailment."

"So why are you here then?" grumbled Martha.

"I like it; they treat me good. Only some of the food's fit for cows—*leaves!*"

"Lettuce." Another lady quit sliding beads on her rosary and joined us. "Greens are good for you; didn't you know that? No wonder you're sick! Listen to me, Bones, take Andy to Lone Stone. An Indian there cured my aunt after a yellow viper bit her. He chanted over dried oak leaves and tied them on the bite."

Mouse arrived and prayed in a thunderous voice for God to wake up Andy. The doctor rushed to hush him and shooed us away from the bed. Mouse then prayed for other patients and Martha begged him, "Please lower your voice."

"I can heal!" cried Mouse. "I prayed for Hilda Estrada and many others and because of my prayers, they were healed. My prayers did it! I . . . "

"Quieter!" Lucy stood close, staring him down as she spoke softly. "You overlook others who prayed for Hilda and those whom God healed. He hears faithful believers who pray in Jesus' name; not just you, Mouse."

He sat sullenly for a while and bounced up again. Going from patient to patient, he shouted demands at heaven and I wondered why the doctor did not stop him. Martha tried and while Mouse was arguing with her, the doctor came to his side. "With profound sorrow I inform you, sir, your son has died."

"Andy! Mouse ran and embraced his son's body; Martha covered her pale face with emaciated hands, shaking with silent sobs. Mouse roared belligerently, "God, you didn't cure him when I prayed! You let him die! Why?" The doctor led Mouse into another room and shut the door.

Lucy embraced Martha. "Andy knew Jesus and the Lord is smiling at him right now, face to face. He's resting snugly in the Good Shepherd's arms."

"It's my fault. I let him go play on that devil's mountain. Oh, God sends so much suffering! Why, Lucy? *Why?*"

"We'll understand why one day, Martha. God promises that what we suffer here won't compare with the glory that'll soon be revealed to us."

Mouse returned subdued and silent, and I asked the doctor, "What did you do to him? Inject a triple dose of tranquilizer?"

"He's pondering something I told him. 'If God granted every plea for healing then heaven would be empty.'"

"And you'd be out of a job. The psalm writer said, 'Precious in the sight of the Lord is the home going of His godly ones.'"

Martha wrapped the small body in her coat; Mouse lifted it and they left.

Lucy and I prayed for patients, and when the doctor signed my release, he said, "Thanks for praying. I interned in Arenas where Jethro Mendez often came with his elders to pray for the sick. Two that I'd given up as terminal got well."

We went to tell Arturo I was well; he was informing Gadget and Jethro, "I persuaded the town council to reject Panther's petition to force us to sell. Finally my headache's gone—until Panther's bunch pulls off their next ploy."

I told him Andy had died, and he hit his desk. "What fool left that pit open?"

Gadget declared, "I'll investigate until I find out. Will you help me, Tiger?"

"Absolutely! No matter how much time it takes! For Andy."

"No you won't!" Jethro poked my chest with his cane. "You fell ill taking on too many tasks. You're won't do that all over again!" Lucy gave him thumbs up.

Task 14–e.

IDENTIFY THIEVES OF VALUABLE HOURS

Arturo told me, "We were in the same rat race; taking on too much caused my headaches. Listen. Jethro helped me **identify thieves of valuable hours.** Stewards of God-given time use it wisely. It's painful but, vital to cut pet activities from our agendas. Let Jethro help you do surgery on yours too, Tiger."

"You help him, Arturo," Jethro urged. "I showed you how to use the scalpel."

"Ready?" Arturo asked me. I agreed and he said, "Okay, the patient's on the table! Tell me, Tiger, which of your activities do not help anyone?"

I vacillated and he began questioning me as lawyers do, until my time-wasting activities became embarrassingly apparent. Lucy prodded me too, and I objected.

"Let her help," Arturo advised. "No one is objective with his own agenda. Let Lucy help you check it every few weeks or you'll kill yourself. Now list your time-wasters, things like going uptown repeatedly on errands when by planning ahead you could combine them on one trip." He handed me pen and paper.

I sighed, and with Arturo's goading listed my "*time thieves*":

Debating church policies too long with Pacho.

Failing to delegate visiting the sick and seekers to apprentices.

Failing to let Lucy help coordinate my schedule.

Discussing chronic economic issues too long with Roger.

Dealing constantly with the same old, lingering church ills.

Arguing too much about Bible interpretations and irrelevant dogma.

Daydreaming when I should be praying and planning.

Arriving late at meetings, wasting everyone's time.

Having my cell meet so often that it leaves folks no time to evangelize.

"You're a *doer*, Tiger." Arturo advised, "So you must discipline yourself harshly to follow your new agenda." I asked about some recreational activities and he cautioned, "Do them. A bit of play is healthy. Do you agree, Lucy?"

"Provided it's with his family. Tino feels insecure since Andy died; he follows Tiger and me around, keeping one of us in sight."

Task 14–f.	I thanked Arturo and started to the door, but
DISCERN AN ACTIVITY'S LEVEL OF AUTHORITY BEFORE SPECIFYING ITS PRIORITY	Jethro barred my way with his cane. "You're not done. Gentlemen, you prioritized your tasks; now do the same for your church. You must **discern an activity's level of authority before specifying its priority**. Lucy, please sketch a crown, footprints, and a key. We'll examine *three levels of authority* for church activities."

"The crown is *level one*. Give top priority to our King's commands. We obey without argument the King of kings and His apostles because we love Him."

I remarked, "You gave the apostles' orders the same authority as the Lord's."

"Yes. They commanded God's people with Jesus' authority and their commands help us apply what Jesus commanded. Jesus told followers to celebrate Communion, but the Corinthians abused this blessing and Paul gave additional commands about it. The apostles' commands are not foundational in the way that

Christ's are; their commands build on His, but are just as binding."

"The footprints are *level two*. Follow the apostles' steps, doing what they practiced, but didn't actually *command*. We don't prohibit these practices since the apostles did them and we don't enforce them as laws because God didn't do so. Paul taught, *Where the Spirit of the Lord is, there is liberty*. These practices include breaking bread the first day of the week and using one cup, holding property in common, fasting, worshipping in homes, and laying on hands when baptizing."

"The key is *level three*, Jesus' symbol of binding or releasing. Practices with no biblical basis can have limited authority, as God binds in heaven what two or three agree on gathered in Jesus' name. However, what one group binds does not obligate other groups; overlooking this causes friction nearly everywhere. Such customs can be good or bad, depending on conditions; they include having Communion the first Sunday of the month, using baptism as the graduation rite after a newcomer's class, wearing robes or ties to preach, and pulpits."

Arturo told Jethro, "Okay, we'll slash activities on the lower levels to give cell members more time for vital tasks and to care for their families."

"Do that. Many know the Bible well and enjoy spending time going over what they already know; but Hebrews 5:12 says, 'By this time you ought to be teachers.' They should be teaching about Jesus to friends in new cell groups. After discerning these three levels of authority, my flock spent less time teaching and more time doing practical service. Ironically, folks learned more Bible then because they applied what they'd studied. We stopped holding so many seminars on social action and started aiding families that were suffering injustices. We also started giving newcomers' teaching *after* baptism as the apostles did and found the new folks more eager to learn and apply it. Church arguments also melted away once our folks began to discern the levels of authority that applied."

I remarked, "A lot of arguments come from conflicting interpretations of Scripture, Jethro. People construe it in different ways to back their biases."

Task 14–g.
INTERPRET BIBLE TEXTS ACCORDING TO CONTEXT AND AVOID DOGMATISTS' NOVEL THEORIES

"So let's tackle this. Teach believers to **interpret Bible texts according to context and avoid dogmatists' novel theories.** How do you do this, Tiger?"

"I look up unclear words in a concordance and read about difficult verses in Arturo's commentaries. Do I need to learn Hebrew and Greek?"

"Knowing original languages helps, but isn't a cure-all or those who know them would stop disputing. Most important is to examine a text's three aspects of context: *textual, social,* and *historical*. Tell me what you think these three mean."

"*Textual* context includes what's written before and after a text. *Social* context refers to who wrote or spoke it, to whom and with what intent. *Historical* context is when a text arose, its occasion and era of sacred history. Can you give examples of these three aspects of context, Jethro?"

"I'll give you and Lucy a little test. You first. Moses had the elders execute a man who'd labored on the day of rest. Which aspect of context explains this?"

"*Historical*—its era of sacred history. God had just decreed that edict and it belonged to the old covenant of lethal law that no longer governs God's people."

"Your turn now, Lucy. Eve heard the words in Eden, 'You surely will not die.' Which aspect of context clarifies those words?"

"*Social*—who spoke it, to whom, and why. Satan said it to the first lady to lure her and Adam to disobey God and ruin our race. And I've got her genes!"

"What if a passage is still unclear," I asked, "after considering all this?"

"Leave it alone, Tiger. *Never* guess! Arrogant Bible expositors teach guesses as truth and that's a vile crime; the scaly old serpent uses such conjecture to inject his toxin into gullible dupes. Paul warned against *doctrines of demons*; lies that appear superficially to be true are more convincing and thus more damaging. Shun over-confident know-it-alls; they keep petty arguments festering, causing intelligent, but careless believers to waste time on trivia. I cringe to think how much time I wasted in my younger years, letting dogmatists fuel my interest in pet theories. I led many believers into destructively shifting winds before I learned to answer hard questions by simply saying, 'I don't know.'"

I asked, "Is that why James warned against many being teachers?"

CHAPTER 14: CONFIRM THE GRASP AND THE PRACTICE OF LEADERS' TASKS

14–a. Let believers use their spiritual gifts in ways that fit their natural personality types. What type (or types) influences how you use your gifts?

[ ] "I prefer to direct projects and carry them to completion. Without God's help I dominate too much and stifle folks' initiative."

[ ] "I behave spontaneously and enjoy being with people. Without God's help, others influence me too much."

[ ] "My imagination helps me consider deep things and the future. Without God's help, I get lost in the clouds, mixing dreams and reality."

[ ] "I tend details steadily and patiently, plodding a step at a time. Without God's help I stubbornly cling to obsolete traditions."

[ ]  "I'm a mix! I'll take on any job that's pressing. Without God's help, I try doing too much, fail and wear out!"

14–b. Care for spouse and children before pursuing every pressing project. Verify how God views family neglect: *If anyone does not provide for . . . his household, he has denied the faith and is worse than an unbeliever.* 1 Tim 5:8

Find in Ephesians 5:22–6:9 family duties that you and your flock should heed more:

WIVES, as the church is subject to Christ, you also ought to be to your husbands in all things.

HUSBANDS, love your wives, just as Christ also loved the church and gave Himself up for her . . . Husbands ought also to love their own wives as their own bodies. He who loves his own wife loves himself; for no one ever hated his own flesh, but nourishes and cherishes it, just as Christ also does the church, because we are members of his body. For this reason a man shall leave his father and mother and shall be joined to his wife, and the two shall become one flesh.

CHILDREN, obey your parents in the Lord, for this is right. Honor your father and mother (which is the first commandment with a promise), so that it may be well with you, and that you may live long on the earth.

FATHERS, do not provoke your children to anger, but bring them up in the discipline and instruction of the Lord.

SERVANTS (often slaves in Roman times) *be obedient to your masters according to the flesh, with fear and trembling, in the sincerity of your heart, as to Christ; not by way of eye service, as men-pleasers, but as slaves of Christ, doing the will of God from the heart.*

14–c. Restore those who stray without needless delay. Verify the aim of a church's corrective discipline: *If anyone is caught in any trespass, you who are spiritual, restore such a one in a spirit of gentleness; each one looking to yourself so that you too will not be tempted.* Gal 6:1

Note how Jesus will judge believers' works: *If any man builds on the foundation with gold, silver, precious stones, wood, hay, straw, each man's work will become evident . . . it is to be revealed with fire . . . the fire itself will test the quality of each man's work. If any man's work which he has built on it remains, he will receive a reward. If any man's work is burned up, he will suffer loss; but he himself will be saved, yet so as through fire.* 1 Cor 3:11–15

> ANSWER: Jesus lets no contraband enter heaven. His purifying fire will test our works, just as God had Moses order victorious Israelite soldiers to try booty by fire before bringing it into the sacred camp. Num 31:21–33

14–d. Pray with confidence in Jesus' name for healing. Notice what elders are to do when praying for the ill: *Is anyone among you sick? Then he must call for the elders of the church and they are to pray over him, anointing him with oil in the name of the Lord and the prayer offered in faith will restore the one who is sick and the Lord will raise him up and if he has committed sins, they will be forgiven him.* Jas 5:14–15

14–e. Identify thieves of valuable hours. Find how to assess our use of time: *Awake, sleeper and arise from the dead and Christ will shine on you . . . Be careful how you walk, not as unwise men but as wise, making the most of your time because the days are evil. So then do not be foolish, but understand what the will of the Lord is.* Eph 5:14–17

14–f. Discern an activity's authority level before specifying its priority for a church body. Recall levels from their symbols:

Confirm. 1: Command of Jesus or His apostles, 2: Apostolic practices not commanded, 3: Agreed on by those gathered in Jesus' name.

To which level of authority does baptism belong? Immediate baptism?

ANSWER: Baptize=level 1 (command). Baptize without delay=level 2.

Note what Jesus warned about some traditions, Matthew 15:9: *In vain do they worship Me, teaching as doctrines precepts of men.*

14–g. Interpret Bible texts according to context and avoid dogmatists' novel theories. Which of these questions probes the context of a Bible text?

[ ]   What goes before and after, that is related to it?

[ ]   Who wrote or spoke it?

[ ]   To whom was it written or spoken, and with what intention?

[ ]   In what historical occasion and setting was it written or spoken?

ANSWER: All these make up context.

EVALUATE YOUR LEADERSHIP

1=Poor. 2=Planning to improve. 3=Doing well.

1-2-3   Let believers use spiritual gifts in ways that fit their personality types.

1-2-3   Care for spouse and children before pursuing every pressing project.

1-2-3   Avoid needless delay in restoring those who stray.

1-2-3   Pray with confidence in Jesus' name for healing.

1-2-3   Identify thieves of valuable hours.

1-2-3   Discern levels of authority for what believers do to serve the Lord.

1-2-3   Interpret Bible texts in their context and avoid dogmatists' theories.

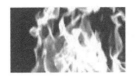

15.
Arson's Blaze Displays the World's Hatred for Jesus' Followers

The flaming red pantsuit caught Lucy's eye. "Oh, my!" Sashaying toward the chapel was a slim lady with long, artificial eyelashes, tattooed arms, short green hair, and a necklace strung with pecans hanging to her waist. I thought she was toting a fuzzy white purse until Popcorn sniffed it and the purse wiggled. The miniature poodle was so perfumed that Popcorn sneezed.

"Don't stare!" Lucy poked me with her elbow. "And stop snickering!"

"I'm Carmen Milano," the lady gushed. "Panther Jones—you surely know him—told us to vacation in this quaint town. It's, like, awesome! My husband Sebastian totally loves these trees; he's up on the slope visiting them now."

Lucy introduced us and asked, "You know Panther? Why's he called that?"

"My idea. His business dealing is so frightfully fierce! I called him a panther and it stuck. My husband Sebastian is his legal advisor; I call him Sebby. He's like in ecstasy up there meditating alone, accompanied by his friends the trees."

"All alone? What does Sebastian meditate on? Trees?"

"No, Lucy. Trees only inspire his transcendental journey; the pines point up, out of this world. He meditates on . . . well . . . nothing! He empties his mind of earthly affairs to become one with cosmic mind, joining his soul to mother Earth under these heavenward pointers. Isn't that like purely divine?"

"Goodness! But how can Sebastian meditate on *nothing*, off alone like a hermit? What's his purpose?"

> **Task 15–a.**
>
> AVOID INSIPID THEOLOGY AND ASSERT THE UNIVERSAL CONSEQUENCE OF ORIGINAL SIN

"Purpose?" Carmen flipped her hand as though tossing away a bit of trash. What ensued displayed the need to **avoid insipid theology and assert the universal consequence of original sin.** "Ah, lovely lady, you need enlightenment! *Purpose* causes all human misery. Sebby meditates without being driven, relaxing his mind in passive submission to pure spirit. Absence of concern links him to sheer abstraction, the divine light that transports the enlightened one's soul. I'm just a novice; I find it so tiresome to sit hours in the lotus position, legs crossed and palms of my feet facing up! Sebby channels his ecstatic vibrations to me after he's experienced his sublime encounters."

"Such mysticism! Isn't Sebastian concerned about anything when he meditates? Does he pray? Does he at least ask God to forgive his sins?"

"Dear girl, your 'sin' is mere delusion. Rise above it to transcendental existence! What you call 'evil' is only an effect of what you call 'good;' for every action there's an equal and opposite reaction, the inexorable cosmic process."

"Oh! I'm confused! Carmen, God's Word reveals that we've all done bad things. We've inherited original sin from Adam."

"Ah! Poor naive girl! 'Original sin' is such a stubborn myth! A child is born innocent, but unenlightened society corrupts the poor child, infusing into his mind the illusion of sin, so of course he fulfills the idea."

"Really! Nobody has to teach my boys to be selfish or tell lies; they do it by nature. But the virtues? Oh, yes! I have to work hard to teach them to my two rascals! Do you believe in Jesus Christ, Carmen?"

"Of course! Also in Buddha, Mohammed, Moses, all the ascended masters. Oh, what a quaint chapel! I'm so thrilled to have met you." Carmen glided inside.

Wanda sidled up to Lucy. "What did she tell you?"

"That no one ever sins. Isn't that perfectly lovely!"

"Look, Papa!" Tino tugged my sleeve, pointing at the papaya by the chapel door. "It's higher than the building now, really growing fast!"

"Like our congregation. So many receive Jesus in our seekers' cells that they no longer fit here all at once, so we hold three worship meetings now."

Lucy whispered to me, "Things are going too well; I wonder where the old serpent will strike next."

I'd find out that night. Icy wind made shadows dart at me as my light probed the daunting darkness; howling gusts blew my hat off twice, seeming to scream, "Death! Death!," and goading me to recall the morbid end of Davey's twin, Olga, and Andy. I put up a shield of prayer and dawn ended the night's torment.

I entered the big house for my week's pay; Abdul was there, his shirt bulging over the pistol strapped beneath. I wished him well and he nodded politely. "May Allah bless you too, Mr. Garcia."

"Have you found ore of commercial value in the mine or on that slope?" He shrugged, and I asked, "What's your view of how the mine's being developed?"

"I'd do it differently. You'll see changes."

Where are you from, Abdul?"

"Yemen."

"I take it you're a Muslim."

"Of course."

"What do you know about Jesus Christ?"

He cocked his head to one side. "*Isa* was a holy prophet, but not Allah's 'son' as some say, nor a savior. One finds favor with Allah only by submitting to him."

We discussed this, and I asked, "Does God lack power to enter His creation as a human to save us from our sins?"

"Of course not. The Almighty can do anything—if it's His will."

"Then, do you question His will to save sinners? Does He have enough compassion to take on our flesh that He created and suffer voluntarily in our place to take our punishment and save us?"

"No one can limit Allah or his mercy. He will do what he will do." He looked at his watch and took a small, square rug from a backpack. "Which way is east?"

Task 15–b.

AGREE WITH ONE'S SPOUSE ON PRUDENT MANAGEMENT OF FINANCES

I pocketed my paltry salary and started home, stopping to pay off an account I'd run up at a store, and canceling a loan from Gadget that he'd made when I was ill. Unfortunately, Lucy and I had not yet learned to **agree with one's spouse on prudent management of finances.** She stretched out her hand. "You promised me the money for a stove."

"Oh! Uh . . . There's not enough left. I canceled . . . "

"No, no, no!" She ran into the kitchen and I expected big trouble, but she did not badger me again for the stove money. Very good, I thought; that's settled.

But it wasn't. Mouse came to tell us a few weeks later that Martha hardly ate since Andy died, was losing weight, and sulked in the dark; he begged Lucy to help her. "I'll go see her," Lucy said. "Excuse me, tortillas need turning on our . . . " She faced me and finished acidly, "ancient, decrepit, earthen *stove*."

Mouse asked me, "Did you hide money in a fallen tree trunk at the end of our lane down by the river? I was picking berries and my dog sniffed a fallen cottonwood. It was hollow and I discovered a stash of coins."

"Only a fool would hide money in a rotten log!"

"No!" Lucy ran in from the kitchen. "I hid the money so Tiger wouldn't spend it. It's mine, Mouse, for a new stove! I . . . "

"Ha! You heard me tell Tiger and tried to take advantage. Pirates hid it and forgot the spot. Hallelujah! God has blessed his humble servant!" He hurried out.

Lucy sobbed, "I hid coins under the mattress, but you came in while I was lifting it and nearly saw them; so I stockpiled them in the log. I hate Mouse!"

Arturo had asked the elders to meet in his office, and I went early to ask for advice on my latest worry. "Tension's growing with Lucy over spending."

"Use the safety valve; discuss finances together. Spouses hold different views;

wives see needs that husbands miss or don't care about; husbands see needs that wives overlook. Jot down together monthly expenses, including something for unforeseen emergencies. Listen to Lucy; she'll appreciate it and will try to see your view, too. Try to agree without sparring over this common calamity."

"I wish I'd learned this before we married. Why'd you call this meeting?"

"Simon Alvarez does zero as group coordinator. He can't control all the cells so he'd just as soon let them die. I asked him to resign, but he said the elders had installed him, not I, so I'll let you elders remove him."

"Demote the town's most powerful man?" I felt a twinge of dread. "The elders won't all back you, sir. They fear Simon and won't cross him."

Task 15–c.
AVOID BOSSINESS WITH FAMILY, FRIENDS, AND FLOCK

I'd soon consider why godly leaders **avoid bossiness with family, friends, and flock.** When the elders and Alvarez arrived, Arturo got to the point. "Simon, you neglect your duties as group coordinator. We will name another."

Simon's face clouded and he looked at each of us. "Do you gentlemen agree?"

Colombo and I backed Arturo, but the others kept silent; Pacho kept his eyes turned away. Arturo hit his desk with a fist. "I can't lead a flock when its elders evade their duties!" He sighed and ran a hand through his hair. "It's not only about a group coordinator. How many of you've evangelized as I asked you to? He hit the desk again. "It means nothing to you that folks perish without Christ!"

Pacho whined, "This is your problem, Pastor. You make demands so severely! You force us to evangelize as if it were our only ministry and . . . "

"A pastor should resign if the elders don't back his agenda. I think I'll . . . "

"Wait!" I begged. "This isn't the time to decide such things. We need to . . . "

"This meeting's over!"

Simon was waiting for me outside. He aimed his hook at me and Popcorn bared his teeth. Glancing at the dog, he lowered it. "Arturo defied me and you joined him. Don't do it again, I warn you. I've proof that you abet subversives."

"I *what*? I only evangelize them, sir."

"Do as I say or I'll divulge my information to the authorities."

Another worry to fret about that night! Between rounds I read Jesus' words about leading by serving; I was trying to visualize it when I heard Wanda screech, "Don't bring that putrid weed into my house again!" A side door opened and Sebastian exited smoking as the door slammed shut with a bang behind him.

I went to him. "I met your wife Sunday. I hope you'll worship with us too."

He studied the stars. "My journey has taken me beyond that. Carmen said you still use the Bible and claim your religion is the only true one. That's bigotry."

"All who embrace a religion think theirs is true and have convictions. You have strong beliefs too, Sebastian. Do you want those who disagree with you to call you a bigot? Look wherever other religions have prevailed without restraints. Women lack rights, oppression is heavy, there is intense misery, and cruelty reigns. To deny this obvious truth is hardly bigotry; it's simply honesty."

"Your obsolete faith is irrelevant to our modern world."

"Really? Do you actually know what it is that you just condemned, Sebastian? Can you tell me what you think the Christian gospel really teaches?"

He blathered until he finished his joint, concluding, "All primitive religions say you merit higher rank in another life if you treat others kindly." The ridicule in his voice exasperated me.

"You haven't a clue as to what we believe, Sebastian! You condemn what you don't even know! Such willful blindness is spiritual suicide and the most snobbish form of intolerance. I've read what the old dragon's cruelest deception is; He tells a society it can be good without God. It tries, but never succeeds."

He looked the moonlit trees up and down for a minute and slipped back inside; that wasn't my most pleasant night vigil. It didn't improve with dawn; the helicopter lit nearby in its early light, and Simon hurried out to it with Sebastian at his heels. Curious, I sauntered over to where I could hear.

Panther's *gringo* accent and obscenities pained my ears. "No (*bleep*) excuses! I pay you to get those (*bleep*) church people off that (*bleep*) land."

Simon bleated, "You make me sell my soul! I tried, I tell you. Now they're whining about radioactivity. Miners who worked for the original mine by the river claimed there's no more silver ore, so I fired them and that caused an uproar. Things are about to explode, I tell you. SRE goons are planning to pounce; and their head, Chuey Ochoa, will incite major violence if they find out that . . . "

"So hire the (*bleep*) thug! Reward your violent friend for joining you secretly. Let him do the things you disdain for the sake of your immaculate dignity."

I hurried to tell Arturo what I'd heard and he sent word to the elders to gather in the town square. He begged them, "Be firm this time and stand with me."

We followed him to the big house and Simon invited us in. "What we came to do, we can do here," Arturo stated. "Simon you've neglected the groups and manipulated the church deviously. You must resign your offices. Give me your key to the chapel and the treasury, and we'll be gone."

Simon's eyes narrowed. "What do you others say about it?" Nobody spoke. "See, Arturo? I tell you they don't agree with you."

"What do you think about it, Tiger?" Arturo asked me. Simon threw me a threatening look and I hesitated. Arturo repeated, "Tiger?"

"I'll accept what the others say, sir."

"I asked for your opinion, not the others'."

"Go ahead, Tiger," Simon smiled confidently. "Tell us your opinion."

I recalled his threat; he had proof that I'd dealt with revolutionaries and would inform the government. To exacerbate my trepidation Wanda's parrot inside shrieked, "Shut up you fool!"

"Protect me, oh Lord!" I prayed silently. I stepped to where I could look Simon in the eye. "Boss, you control us with threats and that's not how to oversee God's work. Please, give up your offices and let us serve Christ in peace."

He glared at me and his hook shook. "Wait." He went inside, returned with a large envelop and threw it at Arturo's feet. "There's your miserable treasury. It's in order, I tell you." He also threw down the chapel key. "You have my resignation as group coordinator and church elder. Good day, gentlemen."

We turned to go, but Simon's hook caught the collar of my shirt and jerked me back. "Your *final* pay," he snarled between clenched teeth and counted it out.

Task 15–d.
HELP BELIEVERS KNOW AND USE THEIR GOD-GIVEN GIFTS FREELY, NOT JUST DOING WHAT PLEASES THE LEADER

I joined the elders in the square where I'd learn how hard it is for a strong leader to **help believers know and use their God-given gifts freely, not just doing what pleases the leader.** Arturo

was griping, "That bully has no gift to lead; he just lowers his head and charges!" I almost reminded Arturo that he led with sharp horns at times too, but said instead, "Your charging bull just ended my career as night watchman."

"Really? Well, we want your services if he doesn't. We've just agreed, you're group coordinator again; you're the one God gave us who can do it. Don't argue." Arturo watched the others leave and grumbled, "Those elders are not only weak, but fail to serve as shepherds; they just sit in sessions and make rules!"

"They're just obeying our bylaws, sir. Those rules don't recognize leaders according to their gifts. They stipulate electing six elders for three years to hold monthly sessions, but God requires elders to *shepherd the flock*, as you said. God has also given the pastoral gift to more than six and it lasts longer than three years! How can a Spirit-filled body sustain a dynamic movement when it follows restrictive statutes that contradict what God says about gifts?"

"We'll change that." Arturo looked hard at me. "What are your gifts, Tiger?"

"Ah . . . I like to evangelize, but I don't know if I have the gift."

"See those men gambling and drinking? Test your gift now; preach to them."

"Well . . . Okay. Lend me your Bible." I climbed a bench and scolded the men for their vices. They jeered and one threw an orange that hit my ear.

I returned to Arturo and he remarked, "Perhaps you have another gift."

"A lad raised his hand to receive Jesus."

"So his hand will go to heaven! He laughed at you along with the rest."

I turned to go, but Arturo grasped my arm, "You have an Evangelist's gift, but I pushed you to use it in a way that's unnatural for you. I'm sorry; I didn't think."

I felt wretched on the way home. How could I tell Lucy I'd lost my job? A shadow crept over me—Satan's hand! "You're a failure! A useless failure!"

Lucy surprised me; when I told her I'd been fired, she clapped and hugged me! Her elation was brief; Wanda's car pulled up and the Wasp wasted no time to gloat. "Well, Mrs. Lucy Garcia, we no longer employ your insubordinate husband. Tiger doesn't consider his family. How'll you feed your children now? Perhaps your son Tino's teacher will help; she's such a close friend of Tiger."

"I've developed immunity against your venom, ma'am, so you can cease injecting it."

"Well, don't forget its Tiger's fault when you fall on hard times. Good day."

On her way out, Wanda passed by the table where Lucy's hairbrush lay, quickly pulled a few hairs from it and stuffed them in her pocket. Very odd!

I watched her car pull away and said, "Look! Traffic's heavy today! A second car!" It halted at our house and the driver, wearing a suit, presented himself.

"Mr. Tiger Garcia? Alex Cabrero with *National Times*. Does the dog bite?" I held Popcorn's collar as the man opened a notebook. "A few questions, sir. What do you discuss with Benjamin Medina's gang in Los Vientos?"

"The gospel of Jesus Christ."

"And what else?"

"That's all I'll tell you, Mr. Cabrero."

"What occasioned your, ah, misunderstanding with Mr. Simon Alvarez?"

"With respect, sir, you're not to publish my private affairs."

"Refusing to oblige the press will make things worse for you, sir."

"Is that a threat, Mr. Cabrero?"

"People of culture cooperate with the media, Mr. Garcia."

"Then I lack culture. On *three*, I'll release my killer dog. *One!*"

"Wait. I only . . . "

"*Two!*" The journalist leaped into his car and sped off.

Soon a third car stopped in our lane! Gadget had brought Mouse's mother from the bus; she had come from Arenas to care for Martha. She stepped from the taxi and the source of Mouse's exceptional features became evident. In mass, she matched him kilo for kilo, in voice decibel for decibel. We heard her across the street as she started in on her daughter-in-law. "Martha, why'd you ever let Andy go play on that wretched mountain?"

Mouse shouted, "Mom, you're just making things worse!"

Lucy sighed and told me, "I try to follow Anna's caregiver guidelines to help Martha, but she blames herself for everything. I beg her to eat and visit friends, but she just shakes her head. Martha's so bitter! She's just wasting away!"

We heard Mouse's mother continue to berate her daughter-in-law. "Why don't you support my son's role as a great prophet, instead of moping around all day?"

"Mother, you're not helping!" cried Mouse. "Please, go back home!"

She took the next bus, but too late; she'd pushed Martha over the edge. Mouse came begging, "Lucy, Martha's blocked the bedroom door with a chair and won't come out! Come talk to her, please."

I went with them; Lucy spoke through the door, but Martha gave no reply.

"Stand back!" Mouse ran at the door, shattering it with his shoulder.

"Go 'way," Martha begged in a tired voice from her bed. She closed her eyes.

Lucy picked up an empty bottle. "Tranquilizers. The label says '*Overdose can be fatal.*' Oh dear God, help! What can we do? Help us, please!"

Gadget rushed the sleeper to the doctor. We watched her, waiting and praying. I told Mouse, "While you're here, ask the doctor to test your blood for radioactive poisoning." Mouse did so, and the doctor told him he was clean.

"My head's fuzzy," Martha murmured; we sighed in relief and took her home. For days, Lucy saw that Martha ate and followed the guidelines for caregivers, but she whimpered, "It's no use, Lucy. I've been a failure since childhood."

"Stop blaming yourself for everything! It's not logical. Stop and think."

"You can't understand what I'm going through."

"Yes I do! I tried to take my life too, but by God's grace I got care in time; Anna helped me undo faulty thinking and I'll help you the same way. Let's meet daily until you feel complete assurance that Jesus has freed you from Satan's lies. Whenever you feel suicidal or under attack, call me. Promise?" Martha agreed.

Lucy became an adept caregiver, using her gifts of exhortation and discernment. She asked Martha questions gently to help her see herself, and after several meetings, the troubled woman yielded to God. She asked Jesus to forgive her and confessed, "Yes, Lucy, I've blamed myself for nearly everything bad that happened, storing up bitterness against God and everyone else."

"Serving others will help you keep your mind off yourself. So use the talents that God has given you. What can you do well?"

"Nothing."

"Not true! You sew and embroider beautifully."

"I guess I can embroider samplers for folks to use as dishcloths."

Lucy clapped. "Folks will hang them on the wall to make their homes cheery. You're on the verge of a breakthrough!"

I went with Gadget to a cell leaders' planning meeting; nearing the chapel, he cried, "Flames! It's on fire!"

"Oh, no! It's still small; we can put it out." I raced to a house nearby for a pail of water, stripped off my shirt, soaked it, and slapped burning boards by a window, smothering the flames.

We rested, and Gadget wiped grime off his hands onto my soaked shirt. "I smell gasoline, Tiger; some fiend pried that window open, threw it in, and lit it."

The other leaders arrived. Soot covered the benches and the smell of wet, charred wood was pungent, so we met outside using a kerosene lamp. It attracted bugs and Arturo slapped them as he asserted, "You'll tell—and I mean *order*—your cell members to evangelize." The arson had intensified his stern demeanor.

"Please don't force everyone that way to evangelize," I begged. "We can't push folks into it. You've told us God gives gifts for different ministries and . . . "

"I promised Olga to devote myself and the church to evangelize, and I'll fulfill my vow. No one will deter me! Not even you, Tiger. You will all do as I say."

A sullen silence followed, broken by occasional slaps, as mosquitoes sought their evening meal. The quiet became more fluent than speech; Arturo looked at each of us, saw only stony faces, and picked up his briefcase. "Take over, Tiger."

His abrupt exit shook me; when I could think straight, I urged, "Let's develop ministries that use the spiritual gifts that God has given your cells' members."

"How do we know what gifts folks have?" Julio asked.

"Let folks help with different ministries to try their gifts. Don't paralyze a body by giving only one person the exclusive right to do a certain ministry."

"There are *gift inventories*—written assessments," Roger added, "but I've found it easier to help folks recognize their gifting by seeing how they relate to a Bible character that used a certain gift. It's fun, Tiger."

"Can you do that at our next worship if Arturo agrees?" Roger nodded and we left before the mosquitoes finished dining at our expense.

Back home, I expected Lucy to decry my sooty shirt, but she laughed, "What a clown! Your face is black as coal!" She quit laughing when I mentioned the fire.

At our next worship, Roger helped us discern our spiritual gifts. A poster listed scriptural, gift-based tasks. Roger pointed to them as we mentioned a Bible person who did them and whose work we liked.

Pacho (*Serve*): "Nehemiah let willing workers repair Jerusalem's walls."

Lucy (*Give*): "Abigail gave food to David's hungry soldiers."

Anna (*Encourage*): "Paul tearfully encouraged Ephesian elders."

Gadget (*Mercy*): "I admire the Samaritan who aided a wounded man."

Evita (*Prophesy*): "Jeremiah called folks to God with stirring passion."

Arturo (*Teach*): "Ezra explained details of God's *Torah*."

Tiger (*Lead*): "I want to be like Joshua who boldly led God's troops."

Anna (*Wisdom*): "Jethro reminds me of Solomon who advised wisely."

Roger (*Knowledge*): "The Bereans diligently examined God's Word."

Colombo (*Helps*): "Priscilla and Aquila aided Paul and Apollos."

Gadget (*Apostle*): "Jonah let God send him, after his deep sea training."

Martha (*Healing*): "Peter healed a lame beggar in Jesus' name."

Tiger (*Administrate*): "Nehemiah organized an entire city to serve."

Lucy (*Miracles*): "Elijah prayed for rain and God brought it."

Hilda (*Tongues*): "Cornelius received Jesus and spoke in tongues."

Colombo (*Interpret tongues*): "Peter saw that Gentiles received the Holy Spirit when they spoke in tongues in Cornelius' home."

Pacho (*Faith*): "Abraham believed and obeyed God."

Julio (*Evangelism*): "Philip evangelized an Ethiopian official."

Roger (*Leadership*): "James led God's flock in Jerusalem during controversy."

Arturo (*Discernment*): "Paul scolded Peter when he avoided Gentiles."

Evita added, "Moses also had a discerning love of justice. I think God gave both Lucy and Tiger the gift of discernment; they have a passion for truth and a nose for even a trace of anything phony."

<table>
<tr><td>

Task 15–e.

ASSURE THE
DYING, CONSOLE
MOURNERS, AND
HELP EVERYONE
CONSIDER ETERNITY

</td><td>

Following the meeting Julio told me, "Grandpa Gerardo's been failing and wants to see you, Tiger." In the Diaz' house I'd learn how to **assure the dying, console mourners, and help everyone consider eternity.** Jethro arrived too, walking slowly and stopping often to rest. The children of Pacho's group gathered around Gerardo's bed;

</td></tr>
</table>

each child in turn stood close as the dying man placed a trembling hand on the child's bowed head to bless him or her. The children then sang Colombo's song:

Come quickly dawn! God's glory fills the skies!

Hail the new beginning when with Christ we rise.

Oh joyful hope! God's trumpet gives us wing!

Gaze on Jesus' face and with archangels sing.

Gerardo beckoned to me; I knelt by him, head bowed as the children had done. With his hand on me, he spoke short phrases, pausing to breathe. "You'll lead the movement . . . like Moses . . . lead the town . . . out of darkness . . . it'll no longer be . . . a haven just for bats."

"Your words encourage me," I replied and read 1 Peter 5:10: *After suffering a little while, God will call you into His eternal glory, made perfect in Christ.*

"In Christ!" the gasping man gripped my hand. "My comfort! *In Christ!*"

Julio asked Jethro, "How can an abstraction like 'in Christ' comfort him so?"

"It's not abstract to one facing death. Peter compared being in Jesus to Noah's family being in the ark; we're raised to glory along with Him, in His body."

"But how can we be 'in Christ,' Pastor Jethro?"

"It's an important mystery, Julio, because those two words appear nearly a hundred times in Scripture. It says by your baptism you not only died and were buried with Christ to sin, but also . . . "

"I remember! I rose with Him! Rising with Him is essential to our salvation."

"Exactly. 1 Corinthians 15 states that we enter into eternal life only by participating in Jesus' resurrection, rising *in* Him."

"But Grandpa's resurrection won't be until the far future when Jesus returns."

"Not far future for God, son, and not for your grandfather; his resurrection has already happened as God sees it, as Ephesians 2 and Colossians 3 affirm."

"How can that be, Pastor Jethro?"

"God has neither past nor future; Jesus taught in John 5 that our resurrection *now is.* Time cannot govern the Eternal One; He created it—a thousand years is as a day to Him. Jesus declared, *before Abraham existed, I AM.* Gerardo's about to look upon Jesus' glorious face in the resurrection because in God's sight, your grandfather has already been raised in Christ."

"Amen!" affirmed the trembling voice. "Yes! Yes! Amen!"

Roger recalled, "I've read that the dead enter a long intermediate state in a temporary body in which they either suffer or are in bliss until the resurrection."

"A popular belief, son, but those rewards and punishments are a purpose of the resurrection and *follow* it, as Daniel 12 and Luke 14 show. 1 John reveals that we'll see Jesus as He is *at His coming* when he raises the dead."

"Then why do some theologians say that the dead have a 'temporary body' and put rewards and punishment *before* they are raised by Christ?" asked Roger.

"For centuries some have tried to account for the time that the dead endure until Jesus returns to raise them, and try to find it in Paul's phrase, *absent from the body . . . at home with the Lord.* However, Paul mentioned no temporary body. The dead in Christ are in God's hands and time rules neither God nor those in His hands. Can you grasp that? God created time for us on the fourth day of creation. That clock ticking on the wall there cannot limit God's experience to a moment at a time as it does for us; thus it cannot affect the dead in His hands."

We listened. *Tick . . . Tick . . . Tick . . .* Was the clock's face smiling or mocking?

"To respect some time-honored creeds," Jethro added, "I'll allow that God could provide a temporary body; it's not worth arguing over. What we can be sure of are two clear scriptural truths. *One,* our risen life comes only through Jesus' resurrection and our participation in it. *Two,* judgment, punishment, rewards, and seeing Jesus face to face are part of the resurrection. Shifting them to a time frame not even mentioned in Scripture is shaky speculation."

"That's heavy theology," whined Pacho. "My father won't understand it."

"I do, son," gasped Gerardo. "I'm on . . . its threshold."

"The time factor is what I don't grasp," Roger admitted.

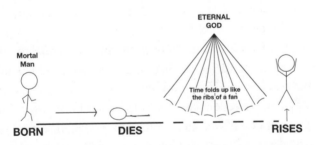

"God is *everywhen* as well as *everywhere*," explained the elderly mentor. "He reigns over time; this comforts us when facing death." He drew a line. "This is a believer's life. He's born here, dies here, and rises here. Between dying and rising, he *sleeps in Christ* as Paul said; his life is *hidden in Christ*. Between dying and rising, time folds up for him like the ribs of a paper fan." He drew it. "A believer dies and the next thing is eternal dawn, seeing Jesus face to face in a glorified body; Jesus said that hour *is coming and already is*, in John 5."

"Come quickly dawn!" Gerardo gasped, and pressed the sketch to his breast. *Tick . . . Tick . . . Tick . . . Tick . . .*

"Jesus . . . see You soon . . . not in limbo . . . blessed hope . . . blessed hope!"

"Don't talk, Papa," Anna begged. "Rest."

Tick . . . Tick . . . Tick . . .

Roger asked Jethro, "What about those who die without Jesus?"

"He said in John 5 that He'll raise them to a *resurrection of judgment.*

"Christ told Martha when her brother Lazarus died, *I am the resurrection and the life.* I see! Life, like forgiveness, comes through Jesus. Die with Him to receive pardon and rise with him to receive life. Why do theologians fog it up so?"

"Not all do, just those who stop at Jesus' death when telling the gospel, as do many gospel tracts. Every time the apostles testified for Jesus, they gave His resurrection prime importance, essential to His saving work. Your church will send workers where other worldviews prevail; it's crucial that they teach the apostles' view of Jesus' life-giving resurrection and not a moldy Western view. Entire people groups lie trapped under the evil one's blanket of darkness and need to see the risen Christ not only fulfilling heaven's legal requirements to save them, but also being their one escape route from death; He's the *life-giving Spirit* as the resurrection chapter says in 1 Corinthians 15."

We became silent as the clock ticked; it seemed to be running faster and louder. Time—heaven's fleeting gift to mortal man! Jethro gripped the old man's hand and leaned close. "I'll join you soon, pal. Say Hi to Jesus."

Tick . . . Tick . . . The dying man nodded, smiled, and closed his eyes. *TICK!*

"'Bye, Grandpa." Julio murmured and Anna sobbed. Julio turned and clung to his mother. "The end of a noble life!"

"Not the end," Roger said softly. "The *beginning* of a greater life in glory!"

We consoled the family, and Jethro told me, "Yesterday I was a child. Now I'm near the door God opened for Gerardo. You can't tie the clock's hands."

"You said that departed believers are in Christ and therefore outside of earth's created time, but that's hard for my mind to grasp."

"Paul said our resurrection's already happened and that our bodies of flesh aren't what's raised, we'll have vibrant, glorified bodies. Leave the time issue to the Eternal One; He rules time, it cannot rule Him. Sadly, some theologians still cling to the pagan Greek view of *absolute* time."

"To avoid that assumption, I guess one needs to be well educated, Jethro."

"No. The educated can struggle even more with it. You saw how Gerardo grasped it; his rural society hadn't been bombarded by a Socratic worldview in which time rules God, or 'gods' as the ancient Greeks put it. Also, the fact that God is outside of time eases the dilemma of His foreknowledge making us into robots destined to live out an inescapable fate."

"The resurrection chapter glorifies Jesus as *life-giver*, Jethro. I've noticed that false doctrine never glorifies Him; it diverts attention from His complete work."

> **Task 15–f.**
> ENCOURAGE THE
> FAITHFUL TO GIVE
> CHEERFULLY

Back home later that day, Martha brought us an embroidered sampler. "Stunning!" Lucy exclaimed. "It's Mount Silverado, but not scowling!" I was learning why wise leaders **encourage the faithful to give cheerfully.**

Martha explained, "Folks feel bad thinking the mountain is frowning at them, so I fixed that; I plan to do a sampler for every home in town."

At our next cell leaders' meeting in Arturo's office, he told us, "I have a confession. I feared your cells would neglect evangelism, so I rudely ordered you all to demand it. Now, under Tiger's leadership, your cells are doing it voluntarily and combining it with other ministries; the cells are healthier now and more active. Gadget's cell cares for the needy and leads many to Jesus at the same time."

Outside after the meeting, a new leader looked down as he handed me a note:

"*Group coordinator Tiger Garcia, Since you stipulate jobs of cell group leaders and order them to labor the same as in a work contract, the undersigned leaders request a salary commensurate to time required by assigned tasks.*"

"You go on strike to get pay from God? Will you accept what I get?"

"Yeah! How much?"

"I don't serve Jesus for silver. Neither does Pastor Arturo; he serves out of love without pay, in spite of his poverty."

"Poverty! He's a lousy lawyer. They're all rich!"

"Not Arturo. He doesn't accept a salary for the same reason the Apostle Paul refused it in Thessalonica, to serve as an example. There's also another reason why Arturo's poor; ranchers are boycotting his legal practice because he wants them to pay fair wages. What do you say about that?"

"I'm poor, Tiger. The church has money and the Bible tells Christians to share with the poor. I need a motorcycle and my . . . "

"Envy has soured you! Someone else will lead your group until you recover."

I went back into Arturo's office and begged, "Let us pay you *some*, sir. It's embarrassing that our pastor suffers poverty. God forbids His stewards to *muzzle the ox that treads the grain*. Paul told Timothy to let elders that shepherd well share in the believers' material resources. Don't deny us this privilege, Pastor."

Arturo stood and faced Olga's photo on the wall as I waited. "Agreed! But no more than 10 percent of an average member's income."

"Our members are poor, Pastor. 10 percent is inadequate to . . . "

"God wants me to set an example for self-supported pastors; I must keep it up. 10 percent is max, Tiger; it'll fulfill the Scriptural mandate for an ox like me."

A shockwave awaited me back home. Gadget waved a newspaper in my face; the top headline shouted, *"Evangelical Leader Heads Conspiracy."* The journalist Alex Cabrero had carried out his threat. Gadget read: *"Evangelical leader, Tiger Garcia, joined with Bat Haven's SRE (Social Reconstruction Engineers) in advocating violence to overthrow the government."* My head spun. Gadget warned, "It's grim, Tiger. They'll arrest you. The article's full of half-truths that'll stir up hotheads in our military government. Go while you can get away; hide in a far-off village until we clear it up. Don't waste a second. Pack supplies while I'll get Bullet. Hurry! Your life depends on it!"

Gadget left running, and Lucy wept as she threw tortillas and canned sardines into a sack. We were praying for my safety when we heard banging on the door. From a window, I saw soldiers surrounding the house. "Too late, Lu."

At headquarters, I told Sergeant Perez that I'd only evangelized the SRE and he studied my face a moment. "I'll go to Los Vientos and check out your story."

Perez left and Beady-Eyes pushed me into a filthy cell with a revolting odor; I had no food for two days, and reflected on the issue of *giving*. I felt sorry for that greedy cell leader that demanded pay; Paul told us to give cheerfully, but his greed robbed him of all cheer. Jesus taught us to give in order to lay up treasures in heaven; Arturo was giving so much time pro bono that his celestial bank account would be huge! Paul also said not to give out of obligation. Hmm. Interesting that the New Testament texts that urge giving don't mention *tithes*.

Perez returned, told Beady-Eyes to mop the cell and brought me a burrito. He said, "My uniform made folks in Los Vientos wary and they avoided me. So I went again in civilian clothes and verified your statement. I've wired my colonel to confirm your innocence; he's a fair man."

The next day Perez freed me. "Don't meet with those communists again for any reason. I won't help you if you do; no one will be able to. Go with God."

Back home Lucy told me, "The chapel's still a mess. Let's go make it usable." I borrowed tools from Gadget, and Lucy and I started out on Bullet to repair the chapel. Wanda's car cruised by and she eyed us imperiously. Lucy squirmed under the Wasp's stare and grumbled quietly, "Gossipmonger! Oh, I'd love to scratch that snobbish smirk off her face!"

I was prying burnt planks loose with a bar when I noticed movement above. A huge snake coiled on a low beam had the sickeningly wide head of a poison-ous *barba amarilla*. Its mouth opened wide and its fangs came right at my eyes! I dodged in time. Lucy saw it, screamed, and ran outside. I bashed the ugly, flat reptilian head with the bar and then spotted another under a bench. I killed it and dragged them both outside. Bullet saw them and jumped straight up, breaking his tether. It took me five minutes to calm him, and longer to calm Lucy.

Wanda arrived in her car and walked right past the lifeless serpents without a word. She held out a hand toward Lucy. "Look, girl. Simon gave me an anniversary diamond. See how big! Guess what. Today they take measurements for the foundation of my new house. It'll be twice as large with gothic arches, a pool, and shiny tiles with intricate designs. It'll have three floors and an elevator."

"I'm sure those things will gratify you, ma'am."

Back home, Lucy wailed, "Someone's determined to get us out of that miserable shack! I'll never enter it again. A fire, then those horrible snakes! Nothing's worse than a snake! Nothing!"

Tino heard. "The devil's a snake, isn't he Papa?"

"Well, kind of. He took the form of a serpent to tempt Eve. He lied and God cursed him. The Bible calls him *the old serpent* and a *dragon*. God removed its legs after it deceived Eve, to make it crawl on its belly."

"Papa, Pastor Arturo had tears when we took him cookies and jelly-jam. I don't get tears when you give me gifts!"

"Cookies and jelly?" I looked at Lucy.

"I decided to fatten up Arturo. We have a garden and chickens, but he has so little! Tino and Hilda's kids picked berries and she, Evita, Martha, and I made jellies and cookies. We had so much fun doing it!"

"Cheerful givers! That's what God loves! I'm proud of you, Tino and Lucy!"

A bicycle bell tinkled out on the street and I went to fetch a letter.

"Your daughter's beautiful, sir," remarked the post office boy, eying Lucy in the doorway. She heard and burst out laughing.

Back inside, I read the letter. "Listen to this, Lu. Jethro told his flock in Arenas that I needed work and a member has invited me to partner with him in a woodworking shop." I stepped to a window and looked out, wondering about it.

"When'll we go?" Lucy asked. "I can't bear more arsonists and vipers."

"Wave the white flag? Oh, so many temptations to desert God's work!"

I started to argue with Lucy, but we heard Arturo's motorcycle sputtering unhealthily and hurried outside. He thanked Lucy and Tino profusely for the gifts, and when he tried to start the bike, it balked. I helped push it to Gadget's shop; he tried to start it and shook his head. "I don't do these two-legged vehicles. Aldo Rosas calls himself a motorcycle mechanic; take it to his shop."

<table>
<tr><td>

Task 15–g.

INSTRUCT BELIEVERS
TO DO BUSINESS
DILIGENTLY AND
HONESTLY

</td></tr>
</table>

Arturo and I arrived out of breath after pushing the bike uptown to Aldo's shop located in the front room of his tiny house. This touched off events showing why to **instruct believers to do business diligently and honestly.** Aldo dismantled the motor, scattering parts all over the dirt floor while he griped, "We'd escape our poverty and the abuses of big business and landowners if our stupid politicians followed Cuba's example."

"I heard Fidel Castro on the radio," I replied. "He blamed all Cuba's woes on the United States. He ranted about the drought that dried up their cane, claiming it was because Americans had tested atom bombs."

"He's my son," said Aldo's aged mother from a corner; I hadn't noticed her.

"No, ma'am. We mean Fidel Castro, Cuba's dictator."

"He's my son. I cooked for Doña Argentina when Don Angel worked for the banana company in La Ceiba. He liked me and, well, I gave birth to my Oscar."

"But his name is Fidel, ma'am."

"Now it is. Doña Argentina changed it when they sailed back to Cuba."

"Well . . . Ah . . . Have you communicated with him? Perhaps he'd help you . . . "

"They say he's a communist. They scare me."

The next day we heard the motorcycle again, clanking and sounding even worse than before. Lucy and I went out to greet Arturo, but it was Gadget. He told us, "I bought Arturo's bike. He sold it cheap because he couldn't afford the repairs it lacks. Man, look at the bargain! I paid only a tenth of its worth!"

"You're cruel!" Lucy stood face to face with Gadget. "You took advantage of Arturo's poverty. He shepherds us nearly full time and receives almost nothing from the congregation. Shame!" She turned and clomped her way inside.

"The bike began clattering," Gadget told me, "so I examined it and guess what, that crooked mechanic, Aldo, replaced its almost new crankshaft with a worn-out one. Ha! He's Fidel Castro's half brother all right!"

"Can't you get the crankshaft back from Aldo?"

"I tried, but I can't prove that he stole it. Come with me to Arenas. We'll haul the bike on a trailer to a shop there."

We went to Arenas and a mechanic fixed the bike. Leaving his shop, we saw men racing on horseback. "Go, Jaime!" one shouted. "I bet a bundle on you!"

"That's Simon's bodyguard!" I exclaimed. "He's leading the race."

Jaime won and counted his winnings. Seeing us, he challenged Gadget, "Let's bet on a fifty meter race, my horse against that antique motorcycle."

Gadget and I went down the street to mark the finish line while Jaime and the cowhands examined the motorcycle at the starting line and bet against Gadget. The race began; the bike wobbled crazily and Jaime's horse won. Gadget protested, "You guys let the air out of my tires!" The men roared with laughter; they had raised the deflated tires up on rocks so that the flats were not noticeable.

On our return trip, Gadget spoke little—a rarity—until we arrived at his shop. "Loan me your horse tomorrow for a special task."

He rode to Arenas, and two days later, we heard honking and were amazed to see Bullet in a trailer behind a fairly new pickup. "I won it! I tied Bullet to an old cart, rubbed mud on him, and tied his head hanging down to make him look old and tired, up the street where them cowboys couldn't see him well. I acted drunk and ridiculed Jaime's horse, calling it ugly, stupid, and slow. He got mad and . . ."

Lucy interrupted, "Why all the fabrications, Gadget?"

"Wait! I bet with them cowboys on a race against my old carthorse. They marked a two-kilometer course and gave me great odds. We raced and Bullet won easily. I emptied their billfolds and bought this cool pickup."

"You cheated them! And you being our police chief!"

"It was perfectly legal, Lucy."

"But ethical?"

"Oh, stop molesting my conscience! It was pure fun!"

The next day, Gadget and I towed his old taxi to Arenas and a mechanic bought it for almost nothing. After visiting Jethro, we started home, but Jaime flagged us down as we were leaving town. The mechanic was with him and Jaime challenged, "Another race, friend? But this time, your former taxi against this pickup that you own now along the same course the horses ran."

The mechanic bragged, "I tuned up your old car and since I'm a better driver and mechanic, I'll win! Bet if you're not spineless. You'll own both cars if you win. I get my pickup back if I win and you can keep your useless old taxi." Gadget accepted gleefully, and the race began. I rode with Gadget and we soon left the taxi behind. In a marshy area, the truck bounced and mired down, and I pushed it. They had covered deep ruts with sticks, paper, and dust on top to hide the traps. The taxi cruised by to one side and the mechanic waved merrily.

Back home, Gadget whined to Lucy about how he lost the pickup. Her eyes flashed and she used his real name: "Timothy Caballeros, I don't feel a bit sorry for you! You got what you deserved, taking advantage of Arturo's poverty and cheating to win the race. Be glad God let you keep your ugly old orange taxi!"

Gadget looked so guilty that Lucy laughed. Staring at his feet, he argued, "Arturo hasn't no reason to be poor; he's a lawyer."

"Not every lawyer's rich. Stop making excuses. Arturo dedicates nearly all his time to the Lord's work with only tiny remuneration."

"It's his own stubbornness that he refuses a regular salary."

"Yes, because he's not materialistic like you." Lucy shot back.

"Whoa, you two!" I intervened. "Gadget, Arturo sets the pace for self-supported leaders of small churches and it's giving results; they're multiplying like rabbits in our area now. 'Elephant churches' with full-time staff and buildings can't multiply beyond the reach of available funds. It's that simple."

"Elephant churches? Are you saying big churches with buildings are bad?"

"Of course not, but their buildings can become idols; churches that spend way too much on boards and bricks are pathetic stewards of God's resources. Congregations that focus obsessively on buildings fail to raise up daughter churches. Some leaders strive only for their own flock to grow big—a selfish ambition."

Mouse had come riding home on his mule, heard my reply, and rebutted, "Gadget, what Tiger and Lucy haven't told you is that the elephants and rabbits will only compete with each other and weaken the work of the Almighty."

"They can strengthen each other," I replied, "provided the elephant doesn't trample the rabbits and they don't bite its toes. It's our job to see they don't."

Lucy remarked, "By God's grace, our congregation is a healthy hybrid, Mouse, both an elephant and a warren of rabbits, reaping the benefits of both."

"A rabbiphant!" Gadget quipped. His taxi refused to start and I began pushing it toward his shop.

"Wait, Tiger!" Mouse leaned back in the saddle and spread out his arms. "I have a grand announcement! Worry no more about losing your job; I'll employ you as manager of my child nutrition project. I solicited funds to fight malnutrition from Samaritans in Action, a humanitarian agency."

I stopped pushing and turned to face him. "Really! I'm glad you're concerned for the kids, but I'll not touch your project if your divisive group sponsors it."

"Make him think it over, Lucy. I offer you glorious liberation from your poverty. Hallelujah!"

Gadget slapped the mule's rump and it ran. "Resist the devil and he'll flee from you!" he called after Mouse. "On an old grey mule! I read that in James!"

"In an old orange taxi," Mouse yelled back. "You read it wrong."

CHAPTER 15: CONFIRM THE GRASP AND THE PRACTICE OF LEADERS' TASKS

15–a. Avoid insipid theology and assert the universal consequence of original sin. Romans 5 says all died in the first man, Adam. Find what 1 Corinthians 15:45 calls Jesus: *The first man, Adam, became a living soul. The last Adam became a life-giving spirit.*

15–b. Agree with one's spouse on prudent management of family finances. Lucy and Tiger clashed over how to spend their money. See how to settle knotty family issues: *Submit to one another in the fear of Christ.* Eph 5:21

Discern what believers are to be content with: *I have learned to be content in whatever circumstances I am, rich or poor, should be content with by God's grace.* Phil 4:11

15–c. Avoid bossiness with family, friends, and flock. Identify three things leaders are not to do with their authority and what they should do with it: *Shepherd the flock of God among you, exercising oversight not under compulsion, but voluntarily, according to the will of God, and not for sordid gain, but with eagerness; nor yet as lording it over those allotted to your charge, but proving to be examples to the flock. And when the Chief Shepherd appears, you will receive the unfading crown of glory.* 1 Pet 5:2–4

15–d. Help believers know and use their God-given gifts freely, not just doing what pleases a leader. Pushy leaders often hobble gifted persons. To discern gifting, see how believers identify with Bible characters' gifts (*15-d in the story*).

15–e. Assure the dying, console mourners, and help everyone to consider eternity. Gerardo rejoiced that Jesus' resurrection assured his. Verify the source of eternal life: *I am the resurrection and the life; he who believes in Me will live even if he dies, and everyone who lives and believes in Me will never die.* John 11:25–26

Note when believers receive rewards: *You will be blessed, since they do not have the means to repay you; for you will be repaid at the resurrection of the righteous.* Luke 14:14

Discover what the hope to see Jesus stirs one to do: *Beloved, now we are children of God, and it has not appeared as yet what we will be. We know that when He appears, we will be like Him, as we will see Him just as He is. And everyone who has this hope fixed on Him purifies himself, just as He is pure.* 1 John 3:2–3

1 Timothy 6:16 says only God possesses immortality. Verify how believers come to share in it: *We will all be changed, in a moment, in the twinkling of an eye, at the last trumpet; for the trumpet will sound, and the dead will be raised imperishable, and we will be changed. For this perishable must put on the imperishable, and this mortal must put on immortality . . . O death, where is your victory? O death, where is your sting? . . . Thanks be to God, who gives us the victory through our Lord Jesus Christ.* 1 Cor 15:51–53

Let children sing or recite Colombo's poem about heaven:

Come quickly dawn! God's glory fills the skies!

Hail the new beginning when with Christ we rise.

Oh joyful hope! God's trumpet gives us wing!

Gaze on Jesus' face and with archangels sing.

15–f. Encourage the faithful to give cheerfully. Identify four truths about giving: *He who sows sparingly will also reap sparingly, and he who sows bountifully will also reap bountifully. Each one must do just as he has purposed in his heart, not grudgingly or under compulsion, for God loves a cheerful giver.* 2 Cor 9:6–7

15–g. Instruct believers to do business diligently and honestly. Find how the old Law avoided fraud: *You shall have just balances and just weight.* Lev 19:36

EVALUATE YOUR LEADERSHIP

1=Poor. 2=Planning to improve. 3=Doing well.

1-2-3   Avoid insipid theology and assert the universal result of original sin.

1-2-3   Agree with one's spouse on prudent management of family finances.

1-2-3   Avoid bossiness with family, friends, and flock.

1-2-3   Use God-given gifts freely, not just doing what pleases ambitious leaders.

1-2-3   Assure the dying, console mourners, and help all to think about eternity.

1-2-3   Encourage the faithful to give cheerfully.

1-2-3   Instruct believers to do business diligently and honestly.

16.
A Hurricane's Fury Awakens Compassion in God's People

Wind bent the trees as I walked to an elders' meeting in Arturo's office, and a gust whisked my hat down the street; Pacho was coming and retrieved it. He pointed up. "Look. The sky's weird. It's a dirty gray color and the air's heavy. I don't like it."

"I haven't seen any birds. They're either hiding or flew off. Oh! Simon just went into Arturo's office. Why's he at the meeting? He's no longer an elder."

"I invited him. I hope we can make amends to him and keep a good relationship; he needs the church. Arturo removed him from his offices rather harshly."

A wiry-looking man with classical Mayan features also came and Arturo introduced him. "Dario Mendoza heads *Samaritans in Action*, a charitable agency."

Dario told us, "I checked out the child nutrition project that Mouse Maldonado has been administrating. We don't just feed children, we also teach parents to grow vegetables and raise poultry or rabbits to provide vitamins and proteins. Mouse failed to do this and to give proper accounting. I hope your church will provide the project administrator."

<table>
<tr><td>

Task 16–a.

HELP THE POOR EARN MORE AND NOT DEPEND ON OUTSIDE AID

</td><td>

I asked what the duties would entail and Dario explained them; he added, "We aim to **help the poor earn more and not depend on outside aid**, so the administrator should be one who's not tempted by money from abroad. It can stir up greed, especially if one is needy himself."

</td></tr>
</table>

Pacho replied, "Simon's the only one who's not on the edge of poverty."

"I'll be pleased to do it," Simon answered quickly and Mendoza nodded.

We'd had such grief from Simon that I advised, "Let's discuss this. We don't want another . . . "

"*Attention! Attention! Hurricane warning!*" An excited voice interrupted music from a radio next door. "Advisory for municipalities of Arenas and Saint Muñoz, also known as Bat Haven; winds surpassing 150 kilometers per hour and torrential rains are imminent. The governor orders everyone in low-lying areas to evacuate at once. Do not delay. Even small streams will soon flood. *Attention!*"

We stepped out of Arturo's office and Gadget remarked, "It's growing dark early and look how fast them clouds are scudding! My parents live by the river in the Leave-If-You-Can quarter without no radio!" He hurried to his taxi.

Simon shouted over the wind, "I'd better get the miners off the mountain before trees fall and slides block the road." He hurried toward his truck.

Dario Mendoza started toward his Jeep. "I'm getting home while I still can."

I told Pacho, "The People's Warehouse is down next to the river. I'll go help them move their grain." I ran and the howling wind buffeted me; warm rain pummeled my face and almost blinded me. I passed a field where cows had taken shelter from the rain under a lone tree; lightning hit it and the cows panicked. They ran crazily, broke through a fence beside the road, and I had to make a dash to avoid being trampled. Nearing the warehouse, I collided with Mincho who had come out running with a sack of corn under each arm. I then met Chuey at the door and he barred my way. "Not this again!" I groaned.

"We don't need your help, watchman." He cursed me obscenely.

"It'll soon flood." I pushed my way in. After we had taken most of the grain to a shed on higher ground, I asked Chuey, "What are those bales over there?"

He pointed at the door. "Out you go before I degut you!"

"I won't let your associates lose their harvest. Don't be such a crank!"

He pulled his cigar in two, extracted his stiletto, and started toward me. Popcorn leaped, but Chuey was ready. He stabbed the dog and it fell whimpering. "Pray to your God, Tiger. No longer will you endure!"

Stepping back, I fell over a sack. Chuey darted forward, thrusting the blade toward my belly. I lifted my left forearm; the blade slashed it and blood flowed.

"Unfair advantage!" Mincho had returned and pulled Chuey away. "Let me even the odds." He grabbed Chuey's wrist and forced him to drop the knife.

The swollen river was flowing into the warehouse, and I was lying in muddy water. I started to rise, but Chuey kicked my ribs; searing pain made it impossible to breathe. I fell back down and he kicked again. I seized his foot, but my injured arm lacked strength; I was losing blood rapidly. He reached for my throat.

"My last moment on earth!" The thought brought a rush of adrenalin; I yanked his shirt and he fell on me. We struggled in the rising water; he dug his thumbs into my esophagus and I was unable to loosen his grip. Again, I couldn't breathe; my fear turned to fury and I hit his nose with my right fist. He rose out of range and I kicked his groin. He doubled up as I staggered to my feet, feeling feeble; I was losing blood. Chuey backed away, grabbed a hook used to move bales, and swung its point at my head. I ducked and in desperation drove my shoulder into his stomach; we fell against a stack of bales that toppled on us. I broke free and pounded the bearded chin with my right until my knuckles bled and Chuey lay still. I raised the hook to finish him off, but pity made me hesitate.

"Get it over with!" Chuey gasped, blood running from his mouth.

I tossed the hook aside and Mincho told me, "He wouldn't have spared you!"

I reached down to help Chuey up. "I forgive you, just as Jesus Christ has forgiven me. Now I hope this settles things between us. No more war. Agreed?"

"You've convinced me, Tiger." His voice was weak. "Now I believe. Yes, I will accompany you in your merciful faith."

Mincho pointed at the blood dripping from my arm. "Get to the doctor."

Pressing on the gash to staunch the bleeding, I waded outside. The river roared and I saw debris rushing downstream. I felt dizzy, stumbled, and fell into the water. I heard a whine; Popcorn was limping toward me moving sideways. Leaving a wake of red, I tried to crawl to higher ground, but a wave of weakness and vertigo left me disoriented. I lost my way and found myself back by the warehouse. Mincho lifted me in his massive arms and carried me toward the health center.

My head cleared and I had to shout above the sound of the wind. It was no longer howling; it was shrieking. "Chuey embraced the faith, Mincho. You should trust Christ too. Let Him save you."

"Chuey lied so you'd not kill him." Mincho ducked abruptly as a sheet of tin roofing whipped by. "That almost decapitated me! Such rain! I can barely see!"

In the health center, the doctor gave me a serum intravenously, stitched me up, and bandaged Popcorn's gash. "You lost a lot of blood, Tiger. Stay lying down."

Mincho had stayed to see that I was all right and I told him, "The storm's worse. I've got to get to Lucy and the boys." I stood and the room spun; my wound was greater than my will. Mincho steadied me and I regained my balance. We left, leaning against the wind in the dark; Mincho carried Popcorn and supported me. Lightning hit nearby, all lights went out, and I heard trees fall.

Passing the Church of Saint Muñoz, the top of one of its high, ancient towers crashed to the street. The ground trembled and a huge iron bell rolled, clattering, to within inches of my feet. People fled screaming though the wide doors and a lady stumbled over a stone, fell, and wailed, "Saint Muñoz! Protect us! Mercy!"

Twice we detoured flooded lanes; Mincho left me at our house and returned to the warehouse. Stepped in out of the tempest I cried, "Lucy, are you all okay?"

"Get those muddy shoes off!"

I heard a groan. Mouse was sitting to one side, holding his head in his hands. "I sinned! The wrath of the Almighty is upon me! I'm shamed! Shamed!"

Lucy explained, "Mouse's group heard that he'd misused the child nutrition funds, and they left him. Even Martha's disgusted with him."

"I only used it for the Lord's work! Church expenses."

I shed my shoes, prayed briefly for Mouse, and headed for the bedroom.

"Don't throw those wet clothes on the bed!" Lucy cried. "Oh! Your arm!"

"I cut myself. I'm okay now." Uh oh—I'd lied to my wife again to shield her from unpleasantness. Not good. I started to say the truth, but wind shrieked and the roof vibrated, drowning me out. I fell on the bed and drops fell on me. A gust came in through cracks that I never knew existed, blowing papers from a shelf. Davey and Tino crawled in with me, hiding under the damp blanket.

Banging at the front door woke me. "Maybe looters," I warned. "I'll go, Lu."

I opened the door; wind blew in, showering the room with lukewarm water, and extinguishing our kerosene lamp. Shadowy figures entered in the dark. Lucy turned on a flashlight. "Soldiers!"

"We come peaceful, ma'am," Sergeant Perez assured her. "We need help urgently. Debris piled up against the north bridge forming a dam; it broke and a wave swept a swath downstream. It carried off the People's Warehouse with

Mincho inside. It's lodged in a curve of the river down beyond the end of your lane and is breaking up; only the roof's intact. Mincho's on it and he'll drown if we can't throw a rope to him. I'm no good with a rope."

I grabbed a lasso and we hurried down the lane. My arm throbbed; dizziness hit me and I vomited. Sergeant Perez steadied me as we waded through muck. The river was deafening; waves leaped, tossing spray and debris into the air. Perez aimed his light on the roof; the giant was clinging to it, staring eye to eye with a huge viper also seeking refuge. I tried futilely to throw the lasso against the wind. The roof shuddered and jerked downstream a short distance.

I heard a yelp; Popcorn had followed. I tied the rope to his collar and took him upstream. "Okay, you're hurt and I hate to do this; but it's our only hope." I threw him into the current and he vanished in the foaming maelstrom. Soon he emerged, paddling in circles. "Mincho! Call Popcorn!"

The din muted my voice, but the flow carried the whining dog past Mincho, who threw himself into the churning water. A log hit the roof with a shattering crunch and an explosion of spray hid all from sight. When chaos subsided, the roof had disintegrated and we saw nothing, but the racing current. "Pull!" I cried. The soldiers reeled in the dog; Mincho was hanging on to it, coughing.

Going back, we climbed over trees that had fallen since we'd come; Perez steadied me and another soldier packed Popcorn. I fainted then and Mincho carried me to my bed.

"Come, Tiger!" Gadget was shaking me. "I got my parents out; they'd climbed a tree. Others drowned and some are injured. Soldiers are bringing them, but they need help with the horses; so much noise is frightening them."

I stood, but Lucy pushed me back down. "He has a fever, Gadget. Leave him. Bring the injured; Evita and I'll help them until they can get to the health center."

The night had calmed when voices woke me. I dressed and left the bedroom; folks were sitting on every square inch of our living room floor. I asked a man, "Are you a survivor from the Leave-If-You-Can quarter?"

"No. We're waiting for the soldiers to bring the survivors. My brother and his family live there. It's taking a long time; the road's awash."

Hooves sounded outside and Sergeant Perez entered. "We brought the last of them, folks." He recorded the survivors' names, and relatives embraced them. Others still waited. The man I'd spoken to begged Perez, "Please keep searching, Sergeant! Please!" Perez said he would and hurried out.

They waited and all was silent. Dawn glowed faintly in the east and Perez returned. He faced the group, shook his head slowly, and left. They still waited. No more came and the sun rose over a grieving procession weeping its way up the street, mud reaching above their ankles.

Bat Haven was isolated for weeks; landslides blocked all roads and hundreds of families had lost homes and farms. In the market, vegetable stands stood empty; Lucy boiled green bananas and yucca that grew locally. Confusion would reign during the ensuing months of relief work. As soon as the mud-filled streets drained, Colombo hauled gravel with *The Caribbean* to make them passable. Soon after, Tino came rushing into our house. "Gadget crashed!"

Lucy and I ran and found Evita dabbing purple salve all over Gadget. He forced a smile. "Just bruises. The gravel was loose and I skidded."

"Blame the gravel!" chided Evita. "You were racing another crazy biker."

He got up with a groan, limped out the door, and showed us the bike, bent and scraped. "You can buy it cheap, Tiger, real low monthly payments. I'll repair the dents and paint it free. Evita won't let me ride it no more."

"How much?" I asked.

"Oh no!" Lucy cried. "Not even if it's free! You'd ride it just as you ride Bullet and kill yourself on these rutted roads! Speed turns you as crazy as Gadget!"

I found Gadget painting the bike the next day when I went to see how he was mending. Evita pointed at the mountainside. "Look at how many trees fell from wind and slides! Thousands! They'll provide cheap lumber for years."

"No," Gadget corrected her. "Beetles will ruin them logs and they'll rot quickly. Millions of good lumber wasted!"

Braying sounded from the road to the south; Dario Mendoza and a helper were leading a long string of burros. "Relief from the outside!" Lucy cried. "Finally!" We cheered and rushed to embrace the director of Samaritans in Action.

He pointed at his cargo. "Water purification pills, medicine, food, and fuel. We had to come in over Buzzard's Banquet Hall; that desert's not too dry now."

Many believers volunteered to do relief work. Mincho and Roger formed a co-operative for those who lost houses near the Rio Furioso to the south, laid out a refugee camp, and helped them build simple dwellings with resources provided by our church. Believers gave generously, even poor ones, and grateful families received Jesus because of the compassionate testimony. Mouse took supplies on his mule to mountain villages, and Colombo cooperated with Father Camacho and his Catholic volunteers to clear roads and transport provisions to needy towns. Our chapel became a distribution center and a cramped emergency home for six families.

> ## Task 16–b.
> ### RELY ON THE AUTHORITY OF JESUS' NAME TO DISCERN AND EXPEL EVIL SPIRITS

Evita was managing the distribution when Lorenzo Guzman came wearing his neon blue shirt, and we'd soon consider why we **rely on the authority of Jesus' name to discern and expel evil spirits.** "I came for our share," Lorenzo announced. "I'm pastor of a new church and we need help."

"What new church? Your *anti*-group disbanded months ago."

"I started it again today. Since we're of the same faith, I came to get . . . "

"These supplies aren't for Christians, but for the destitute, whoever they are."

"I have serious need, teacher. I'm poor. You people obey the Bible, so you got to distribute these provisions to whoever's needy."

"Lorenzo, if you're a sincere Christian, you'll give something to those who've lost everything. Put it in that donation box by the door on your way out."

"Give? Me? Everybody knows that a foreign organization sent you provisions. I only ask for my fair portion."

Evita took a deep breath to restrain her fury. "Emergencies reveal Christians' character. Some have given a double tithe to help those who lost everything; others only covet the supplies. Which are you, Lorenzo? Giver or greedy?" Lorenzo argued and the dispute became loud and bitter.

Mouse exorcized him: "Leave this covetous man at once, Satan!" Lorenzo reciprocated; he shouted an angry exorcism at Mouse and left. Evita's fists were clenched and Mouse told her, "It's okay now; I cast the demon out."

"Not far enough," Gadget advised. "I seen him swipe two boxes of canned tuna on his way out! Lorenzo exorcised a lady yesterday in the town square; she had a stomachache and he kept screaming at her to get rid of the devil until she vomited. He said that was the demon. He's a genuine phony. I don't understand what them demons are. Have you cast any out, Tiger?"

"Yes. Like the apostles, I deal with them only when they afflict a victim; it's unpleasant to face sheer evil. Jesus' disciples celebrated after expelling demons in His name, and he said to rejoice rather, that their names were written in heaven. He said they'd trample serpents and scorpions; these signify demons that were once angels in glory, but rebelled, and God cast them out. Jesus saw Satan fall."

Anna shoved a crate of supplies into my hands. "Back to work. Let's all watch out for greedy liars like Lorenzo who exaggerate their needs. Helping the poor unwisely makes their poverty worse; handouts rob their initiative and self-respect. Some have come to rely on our aid, and it's our fault."

"Such dependency is not limited to the poor," advised Arturo. "Depending on others' gifts corrupts believers with money too. The 'demon of sophisticated dependency' is an invisible member of many Christian advisory boards."

"Demon of sophisticated dependency?" I asked. "I never heard of him."

> ## Task 16–c.
> DETECT AND AVOID WHATEVER HINDERS MOBILIZING MANY VOLUNTEER WORKERS

"He keeps hidden to conceal his ruse, to keep us from **detecting and avoiding whatever hinders mobilizing many volunteer workers.** He lures leaders with money to rely too much on budgets. Opulence over obedience."

Pacho scowled. "You lost me. It's biblical to support some workers, Arturo."

"Of course—*some*. This demon overdoes support. Income's always short; thus, a material lack often becomes a spiritual barrier. Many churches could appoint more self-supported or partially supported volunteers, as in the New Testament. We'll un-shackle Christ's body from restrictive budgets!"

Dario looked doubtful. "You say a *demon* makes a person dependent, Arturo?"

"Well, some kind of evil spirit must cause the irrational paralysis of an otherwise intelligent body of believers. Jethro Mendez warned me about this when I first asked him to mentor me; he told me, 'Your eyes glazed over with indifference when I mentioned *non-budgeted* projects. My mentoring won't help if you can't visualize the Holy Spirit moving volunteers to serve spontaneously in a widespread movement. Come back when you're free from this blind dependency on material resources.' Well that shook me up! It changed everything for me."

Roger remarked, "I've read that some seminaries cut back mission training due to lack of funds, but they had enough to finance other programs. I guess that demon had whispered in their ears. They'd reach thousands more for Christ if they'd use all that brain power to mobilize an auxiliary army of volunteers."

I recalled my reading too. "When political upheaval has cut the flow of dollars from the West, it has freed churches from dependency and they multiplied way beyond what the missionaries had hoped. Mao in China forced churches to break lucrative ties with the West, so believers met in homes with unpaid lay pastors, and as a result, millions more are coming to Christ."

Pacho added, "Good stewards wait on a project until it's financially viable so we don't have to mortgage our souls, taking on excessive debt. It's a sad testimony when believers default on promises or abort highly touted projects."

Dario Mendoza pretended to duck. "Ouch! Painful truths are landing too close! I fear I've created dependency and let lack of funds curb our work needlessly. I could have recruited more local volunteers and avoided several project failures."

I urged, "So let's all agree right now in Jesus' name, to detect and bypass blockages imposed by the 'demon of sophisticated dependency.'"

Task 16–d.
IN DISASTER'S WAKE, DEAL WITH BOTH SPIRITUAL AND PHYSICAL NEEDS

Intense relief work would soon impart a crucial lesson: **in disaster's wake, deal with both spiritual and physical needs.** Gadget's father and others from Leave-If-You-Can came while we were preparing relief packages; he told us, "We're grateful. You helped us recover and gave us hope." He shook our hands and told Gadget, "Son, the flood left marijuana bales near our house. Guess you ought to know, being police chief."

"I'll get soldiers and arrest the SRE leaders. Every one of 'em, right now!"

"Wait!" Roger begged Gadget. "Let me speak with Mincho first."

"Go quick then because I'm going to halt that illegal traffic once and for all."

"I hope so," declared Mendoza. "Americans buy that stuff and Latino thugs use the billions for guns and bribes. Bad guys get rich and good guys stay poor!"

"We're rich in Christ, anyway," Evita remarked. "Dario, what do you think destroys more people, wars or illicit drugs?"

"Over the last twenty years, illegal drugs have destroyed far more, both physically and spiritually. Drug abuse and demonic attacks often go together; demons easily invade minds adrift from reality. Almost everyone I know has a relative whose personality has deteriorated because of drugs or has died young."

"Tiger, come with me," Roger begged. "Let's talk to Mincho, before Gadget arrests him. He's at the SRE's new warehouse."

Mincho was untying a bale by the river and hurled it in. He saw us then and begged, "Guys, help me dump this poison before Chuey returns. Let the poor fish go *loco*! I'm discarding a fortune, but what a relief!" We threw all the bales in the water and sat to rest. Mincho sighed, "Almost drowning made me reevaluate

my vocation, fellows. I never dealt with drugs, but stood by while others did. I'm going to follow Christ now, whatever it costs me."

I cheered. "Let's celebrate this, guys! Come to my house."

We met Dario Mendoza on the way; he joined us and remarked, "Your churches do relief work better than my agency does. I want to discuss this."

Mincho told Dario, "I've seen how effective they are too. Their churches bring more justice to the oppressed than our SRE. Roger, what's your secret?"

> ## Task 16–e.
>
> ### INTEGRATE BENEVOLENT WORK THOROUGHLY WITH PASTORAL MINISTRIES

Roger pointed up. "See that bird soaring? Its wings stand for Jesus' two *Great* commands, the *Great Commission*, to make disciples, and the *Great Commandment*, to love God and neighbor. Like that bird, we **integrate benevolent work thoroughly with pastoral ministries;** one reinforces the other."

Mincho watched the soaring eagle for a moment. "Excellent, Roger! I attended a 'lame bird' church long ago. It had a big beak and chirped a lot about social justice, but did little about it. Both wings were lame!"

Dario confessed, "It's hard for me to do both ministries at the same time, Roger; I'm trained to specialize in development. I can't combine both."

"Of course—so don't! Here's what to do. Dario, your left arm is the mercy wing and the feathers on you're right have been clipped; let it hang limp. Tiger, your right arm's the gospel wing and your left wing is clipped. Mincho, you're a hungry unbeliever and need both of these birds; go stand over there and be needy. Now, birds, fly to him!" Dario and I flew in circles, using only one wing. Roger asked, "So what's the cure? How'll you reach that starving pagan?"

"Join arms!" exclaimed Dario. We linked our weak "wings" and flew straight.

"That's the key—work closely together," Roger stated. "Another 'must' is to let local villagers coordinate mercy work; they know their people and local conditions. Our Leave-If-You-Can quarter needs better sanitation, relocation of homes to higher ground, and cash crops. Gadget's dad is a born leader, so Gadget and I are training him to lead the project. We're started a church at the same time; the believers have the right motive to do the relief and development work."

Dario sighed. "I wish all believers had pure motives. We've provided Lorenzo Guzman funds to care for orphans and today I investigated his project. We allotted funds for eleven orphans, but he had only two and didn't let folks adopt them. I sent them to kinfolk who wanted them and terminated the project. It's hard to help the poor without them coming to depend on us or ripping us off."

Roger replied, "Giving goods or money inevitably corrupts, except in life-and-death emergencies such as the Good Samaritan faced. We help the poor develop vocations, small businesses, and cooperatives so farmers can grow more and sell it. Our new churches help the poor take responsibility for their development."

Dario patted Roger's back. "Samaritans in Action is going to flap both wings! If there's no church where we do development, then we'll plant one and have locals oversee the work. Our workers with the gift of compassion will join arms— wings—with those with other gifts. I'll need your help to orient them, Roger."

Mincho told Roger, "We both do development; let's work together. How do you train so many new development workers and pastors?"

Roger explained our extension training and remarked as we entered our lane, "The flood over the long run has actually made our work easier; folks face reality. Many are turning to God and churches are multiplying, so I travel a lot to train the new leaders. Most villages lack roads and I'm allergic to horses; I rode one to Los Vientos and got a rash, so I hike on my two hind hooves now, packing books, Bibles, and studies."

Mincho replied, "I noticed the heels of your shoes were worn down." We passed Gadget's shop, and his bike had a sign: *FOR SALE, CHEAP*. Mincho told Roger, "Our joint venture begins now. That motorcycle's yours."

"You're kidding, Mincho!"

"Hey, Gadget! Attach saddlebags to this bike, to hold this scholar's books."

CHAPTER 16: CONFIRM THE GRASP AND THE PRACTICE OF LEADERS' TASKS

16–a. Help the poor earn more and not depend on outside aid. Note how vital it was to Jesus to care for the needy: *The righteous will answer Him, "Lord, when did we see You hungry, and feed You, or thirsty, and give You something to drink? And when did we see You a stranger, and invite You in, or naked, and clothe You? When did we see You sick, or in prison, and come to You?" The King will answer . . . "To the extent that you did it to one of these brothers of Mine, even the least of them, you did it to Me."* Matt 25:37–40

Find Jesus' view of hoarding for one's self: *Do not store up . . . treasures on earth, where moth and rust destroy, and where thieves break in and steal. But store up for yourselves treasures in heaven, where neither moth nor rust destroys, and where thieves do not break in or steal; for where your treasure is, there your heart will be also.* Matt 6:19–21

16–b. Rely on the authority of Jesus' name to discern and expel evil spirits. Identify our worst foe: *Put on the full armor of God, so that you will be able to stand firm against the schemes of the devil. For our struggle is not against flesh and blood, but against the rulers, against the powers, against the world forces of this darkness, against the spiritual forces of wickedness in the heavenly places.* Eph 6:10–12

Verify what Jesus did to demons: *When He had disarmed the rulers and authorities, He made a public display of them, having triumphed over them through Him.* Col 2:15

Detect a veiled root of deceptive ideology and dogma: *In later times some will fall away from the faith, paying attention to deceitful spirits and doctrines of demons.* 1 Tim 4:1

16–c. Detect and avoid whatever hinders mobilizing many volunteer workers. Find what Paul advised Ephesian elders about support: *These hands ministered to my own needs and to the men who were with me. In everything I showed you that by working hard in this manner you must help the weak and remember the words of the Lord Jesus, that He Himself said, "It is more blessed to give than to receive."* Acts 20:34–35

Notice what Paul exemplified for leaders: *We did not . . . eat anyone's bread without paying for it, but with labor and hardship we kept working night and day so that we would not be a burden to any of you; not because we do not have the right to this, but in order to offer ourselves as a model for you, so that you would follow our example. For . . . we (gave) you this order: if anyone is not willing to work, then he is not to eat, either.* 2 Thess 3:7–10

16–d. In disaster's wake, deal with both spiritual and physical needs. Calamities move many to think about God and repent. Identify another benefit of suffering: *Consider it all joy, my brethren, when you encounter various trials, knowing that the testing of your faith produces endurance. And let endurance have its perfect result, so that you may be perfect and complete, lacking in nothing.* Jas 1:2–4

16–e. Integrate benevolent work with pastoral ministries. See why workers should not specialize always in one ministry: *The body is not one member, but many. If the foot says, "Because I am not a hand, I am not a part of the body," it is not for this reason any the less a part of the body . . . God has placed the members, each one of them, in the body, just as He desired. If they were all one member, where would the body be? But now there are many members, but one body. And the eye cannot say to the hand, "I have no need of you"; or again the head to the feet, "I have no need of you."* 1 Cor 12:14–21

EVALUATE YOUR LEADERSHIP

1=Poor. 2=Planning to improve. 3=Doing well.

1-2-3   Help the poor earn more and not depend on outside aid.

1-2-3   Rely on the authority of Jesus' name to expel evil spirits.

1-2-3   Detect and avoid whatever hinders mobilizing volunteer workers.

1-2-3   In disaster's wake, deal with both spiritual and physical needs.

1-2-3   Integrate relief and development work thoroughly with pastoral ministries.

17.
A Deal Made in Darkness Imperils the Faithful

Two fifty-nine a.m., Chuey's watch read. He switched his light off and listened in the starlight. Hooves sounded on the stony riverbank path near the old mine—right on time. The rider led another pack-horse and kept his face and arms hidden under a cape. The SRE chief growled, "Identify yourself."

A note fell; Chuey turned his light on it and chuckled. "And my first half?"

Bills fell at his feet. He counted, whistled softly, and unloaded the packhorse: dynamite, a large roll of insulated wire, and detonation equipment. All this I learned later. Had I known what Chuey was capable of at that time, I'd have avoided putting my family in mortal danger.

"Oh no!" I groaned on our way home after worship. "I forgot to lock the door, Lu." We hurried back; Popcorn chased a cat behind the chapel and then began barking in a warning tone.

Task 17–a.
STRIVE FOR SOCIAL
JUSTICE IN A PEACEFUL,
POSITIVE WAY
WITHOUT RANCOR

Mincho was leaving too, and heard the dog. "That's not his cat bark, Tiger. Let's go see. Lucy, you'd better wait inside with the boys." We hurried after Popcorn as he sniffed his way up the rocky slope. Ensuing events would show the need to **strive for social justice in a peaceful, positive way without rancor.**

"Look, Mincho, a wire! What's it doing here? Oh, it leads to the chapel. I'm thinking it may lead to explosives! Someone up there's going to blow up the . . . "

"Lucy! Lucy! Get out of the building!" We both bellowed with all our might, but were far up the slope where a strong wind muffled the sound.

"We've got to cut it, Tiger!" But we had no knife. We tried to jerk it loose, pulling it both ways, but it stayed attached. Mincho wound it around his arm and lunged down the slope, but the wire held, gouging his arm. "Hold it over a stone," he cried and raised a rock over his head that I could not have lifted to my knees. He crashed it against the wire and kept pounding until it parted.

"It's heavier than the detonation wire used in the mine, Mincho."

"That's to reel it out a long distance, so they could get away before investigators like us spotted them. Wish I was armed; I'd . . . Let's go down."

"It's a single wire; it takes two to complete a circuit, like in extension cords."

"Not if the detonation cap's attached to a ground, Tiger."

We followed it down to the chapel and my heart skipped a beat. "Sure enough, Mincho! Enough explosive to flatten a fort!"

"Guns are the only answer!" the big man declared while Lucy bandaged his bleeding arm when we got home. "You can't deny that now, Tiger. Admit it. You nearly lost your family!" He clenched a massive fist. "We'll never see justice without violence; businessmen and ranchers are all ruthless crooks! All of them!"

He continued to revile ranchers with ardent fury and Lucy covered her ears, grimacing. When Mincho wound down, she told him, "We were ranchers. Do you loathe us too? It's something in your past, isn't it?"

He sighed and lowered his voice. "You don't want to know, Lucy."

"I do. It had to be something terrible to inflame such vitriolic hatred."

Mincho hid his face in his hands for a minute. When he removed them, Lucy cried, "Oh Mincho! Your pain is deep. You can't hide it, I see it in your eyes."

"I knew Simon Alvarez when he had nothing. He branded my cattle with his iron, but I couldn't prove it. Well, he didn't steal only animals from me." He unfastened a medallion that hung from his neck, opened it, and handed it to Lucy.

"She's beautiful! Who . . . ?"

"Send the children away."

"Go play outside, boys," Lucy ordered.

Tino dallied. "Now!" I said firmly, and he whined his way out.

Mincho buried his face in his arms on the table and we waited. He raised his head, shook it, and sighed. "We were engaged. Simon abducted her, took her to his shack, and raped her. She was ashamed and afraid to return, so she stayed."

He shook his head again, as though trying to dislodge images from his mind, and Lucy clasped his huge hand. "I'm so sorry!"

"I went to find her, and she told me everything. I was lifting her up onto my horse when Simon attacked me with a machete." He pointed at the livid scar on his cheek, moist now from tears. "I knocked the blade away. I could not control myself; I grabbed his arm, and broke it against my knee. Then I tore it off."

"Oh, no, no!" Lucy screamed and covered her face.

"In spite of losing blood, Simon got a rifle and shot her. He was insane; we both were. He tried to kill me too, but couldn't steady the rifle with one arm."

We were quiet; my mind reeled with horror and disgust. I recovered and took his hand. "You, Mincho, no one else, will break this satanic chain of acrimony and revenge; God will help you forgive, as Jesus forgave you. His transformation is the only way; violence only provokes more violence. Justice comes when God changes hearts. Jesus said to be peacemakers, to turn the other cheek."

"Had I turned my other cheek to Simon, I'd have twin scars and be symmetrical—an improvement, right, Lucy?" He had a teasing twinkle in his eye.

"Oh, Mincho! I don't know whether to laugh or cry!" She did the latter.

The giant sighed deeply. "Give me time to think this through, Tiger."

He stayed overnight and told me the next day, "I can't organize the miners without violence; even if I hold off, they won't. But at least I'll stop seeking revenge."

"That's a start. I share your concern for the miners. They haven't shown symptoms of radioactivity yet, but I'm afraid it's coming. It's their right to organize to protect themselves from injustices, but without bloodshed. You don't need to use criminal methods if it's God's will."

"Listen, Tiger. I've heard whispers. SRE extremists aim to liquidate your church's leaders. They don't realize you're their best allies; Chuey's got them bamboozled. I don't know if they're who tried to blow up the chapel, but they'll try something like that; most of them are too cowardly to do anything face to face." Lucy clutched my arm, and fear stabbed me. For an instant, I shared Mincho's craving for violence.

The warning moved me to gather our cell leaders with Jethro in Arturo's office to alert them to the SRE's threat, and I told them about the explosives. We asked the Lord what we should do to protect our families and our lives. Colombo advised, "Let's not meet again in that God-forsaken house of death!" All agreed.

I urged, "But let's not sell its land to Panther, either."

Jethro told us, "You can manage without the chapel. By God's grace, you have healthy, reproductive cell groups and leaders prepared to shepherd them in homes. Also, your groups can still all meet together occasionally in the open air."

"Another painful matter . . . " Colombo waited until we were paying attention. "We have to deal with it. Pastor Arturo, please excuse me, but you preach only about salvation. New believers need that, but it doesn't edify the rest of us."

Arturo did not reply, and Pacho added, "It's true, Pastor. Clients complain that salvation is your obsession; one said your guitar has, but one string. There's only one way to preach and meet everyone's needs—go through Bible books."

"So do you all want me to resign?"

"Of course not," I answered. "We only want you to . . . "

"Nobody should dictate what a pastor preaches. Never!"

"Sometimes yes, brother Arturo," Jethro replied gently. "To keep exhorting believers who already know Jesus to receive Him can cause them to doubt."

"As long as some haven't received Christ and fail to follow Him, I will not change the topic. I made this pledge to Olga, Jethro, and nothing will deter me."

> ## Task 17–b.
> TEACH WHAT LEARNERS CURRENTLY NEED, NOT SIMPLY WHAT FITS A PREFERRED HOMILETIC STYLE OR CURRENT INTEREST

"Nothing? Not even Jesus' example? How'd He and His apostles select topics? **Teach what learners currently need, not simply what fits a preferred homiletic style or current interest.** If folks need a topic, teach it! Use common sense. Also do Bible exposition; you never know all the needs and book studies will eventually deal with them; just avoid doing books verse by verse so exclusively that you overlook urgent needs. Do both to edify new and old, weak and strong. Teach new ones Jesus' commands before doing Habakkuk verse-by-verse and teach books to the mature who have fewer urgent spiritual needs."

Colombo asked, "Shouldn't we also review basic doctrines regularly?"

"Let there be light!" Jethro said and took a sketch from his skunk skin pack.

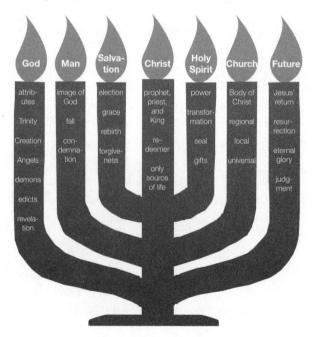

Christian Doctrines and Hebrew Lampstand

"The ancient Hebrew lampstand's flames show classic areas of theology and related doctrines on its arms. Review these some way periodically, but not simply by reading verses to support an abstract truth. Relate what happened historically to reveal it, how Jesus worked it out in the flesh, and ways we can obey it."

I asked, "What events revealed *election*? It's on the arm under *salvation*."

"Election? Hmm. Well, God chose oppressed Israelites from among pagan Egyptians and He used Queen Esther to preserve a chosen remnant after He exiled the idolatrous nation. God also chose Jacob over his firstborn twin Esau, before either had been born or done any good works or bad. Does that help?"

"Yes, but what about obeying as you said? What does election lead us to *do*?"

"Help me someone!" Jethro begged.

Roger suggested, "It helps us trust God's grace and praise Him for transforming His chosen ones. We also witness for Jesus with confidence, knowing that seekers' faith is God's gift. It makes evangelism easier; we don't have to push folks toward Jesus. The Holy Spirit does that; we can let Him do the convincing."

"Superb!" I replied. "What else can we tackle while Jethro's helping us?"

> ### Task 17–c.
> #### BUILD LOVING RELATIONSHIPS BETWEEN "LAMBS" AND "RAMS"

"A wicked wall!" blurted Gadget. "It runs right through this room, separating new members from old. I want to be friends with you, Pacho, but you stiff-arm me. You harp on my immaturity and others follow your lead. I feel awkward with you guys; you make me feel dumb because you know the Bible better. Can't we **build loving relationships between 'lambs' and 'rams'?"**

Tense silence ensued and Pacho stood. "If there's nothing more of importance to discuss then excuse me. I'm sure clients are waiting for my shop to open."

That ended the session and I took Gadget to the barbershop. Pacho clipped a client in silence, throwing suspicious glances at Gadget. The client left and Pacho remarked, "I have no problem with you, Gadget. I admire how you've grown."

"You've a weird way of showing it."

I told Pacho, "Older members follow you and resist whatever the new ones who follow Gadget want. You don't listen to each other. Let's change this."

"Why listen to them? A father doesn't let a two-year-old tell him what to do."

"He does when something's hurting the child. Jesus mentioned vineyard workers who came late, but got the same pay as those who'd worked all day; God uses the same measure to give grace to new disciples as He does for older ones who've suffered for Christ. He does not want us to disparage new believers."

"I don't disparage them, but I'll be frank when they need advice." Pacho climbed into his barber's chair, pulled his moustache, and sighed. "Gadget, some of your ideas are okay, but to do what all you new ones want would bring chaos."

"You gripe whenever I mention an opinion, no matter what. You don't weigh new suggestions. You keep your mind shut and bolted, Pacho. I'm young in the faith, but I'm not completely crazy. Maybe half. But you treat me as if I'm a total fool. You're a closed-minded, outdated, stubborn old mule!"

Pacho stood and started sweeping, humming. Our chat was over. On the way to Mudhole, I told Gadget, "That settled nothing! Don't leave it this way. Apologize to Pacho for scolding him so rudely and forgive him as Jesus said to do."

"Sure! I'll forgive Pacho if he changes his way."

"No, Gadget! Don't put conditions on your forgiveness."

"Okay, okay! I forgive Pacho for being a stubborn old stick-in-the-mud!"

"Ask him to forgive you too, and apologize for not respecting him. It does not matter how much fault he has; Paul told us to accept being defrauded instead of fighting with a Christian brother. Listen to Pacho's concerns and he'll listen to you. I know he will, Gadget, because Pacho's a godly man. You'll see, if you'll stop rubbing him the wrong way. Please go see him again."

Back home I complained to Lucy, "The devil's built a broad barrier between our older and newer believers, as daunting as the stone wall around Jericho."

"And just as vulnerable. Let's ask the Lord to knock the wall down."

After praying I said, "Jethro told Arturo to preach things besides salvation."

"About time! When Arturo preaches, the argumentative lawyer emerges, intent on repairing the harm done by Olga's killer, seeking to avenge her."

"He never got over her death. I think I'll try to talk with Pacho again, Lu. There'll be no peace while that wall stands between 'lambs' and 'rams.'"

At the barber's shop, I asked Pacho, "Remember how Jesus related in Luke 15 that a greedy son demanded his inheritance before his dad died?"

"So what's the point?"

"The son repented and his dad forgave him, but the older, obedient son resented such grace. It's easy for us older brothers to resent new believers' receiving God's grace so freely, especially if we've suffered for Jesus as you have."

"I'll think about it, Tiger."

Gadget thought it over too, and came to tell Pacho, "I apologize."

"So what trickery are you setting me up for now?"

"I didn't show you the respect I owe to an older brother in Christ. Sorry."

The moustache got its usual twist. "I forgive you, brother. Of course!"

At the next meeting of group leaders, Pacho announced, "Tiger helped Gadget and me communicate and guess what . . . Gadget mended his ways!" A bit one-sided, but it was a crack in the wall and it grew, like the papaya.

A few weeks later, I told Lucy, "Gadget and Pacho are great friends now. A miracle! Gadget helps Pacho see the bright side of things, Pacho helps Gadget consider ventures before leaping. Both lambs and rams follow their example."

"Jericho's wall has fallen!" Lucy clapped.

Task 17–d.
PRACTICE HONEST PASTORAL ETHICS

A knock sounded at the door. Two ladies had come and I assumed they were seeking pastoral care, so I invited them in. Events were about to focus on **practicing honest pastoral ethics**. The older, stern-faced lady tried to sell me a book with a bright green cover offering a Bible course.

"What church are you with?" Lucy asked Stern Face.

"No church. We're witnesses of the one true God."

Uh oh! Since I'd let them in, I struggled to be polite. "Jehovah's Witnesses?"

"This course has proofs that all churches are false and that the kingdom of the one and only, all-powerful God is given only to His true witnesses."

"You think God receives only those of your sect?" I told myself to keep cool.

"Yes, because you believe in three gods. The Trinity is false."

"Three gods!" Lucy exclaimed. "Nobody believes that! There's only One."

"One cent, plus one cent, plus one cent comes to three cents, no matter what."

The younger lady appeared to be willing to listen, so I pursued the polemic. "The divine Persons are not coins, ma'am. The Father eternally 'generates' the Son, so *multiply* if you must use arithmetic. One times one, times one is . . ."

"Still one!" exclaimed the younger one; Stern Face cast her a disdainful look.

I added, "The Father told the Lamb slain before the founding of the world in Psalm 2, *You are my Son; this day I have begotten You*—multiplication!"

"You interpret it that way because Satan has blinded the world," sputtered Stern Face. "Emperor Constantine invented the Trinity fiction."

"I've studied that; Constantine believed as you do when he imprisoned Bishop Athanasius for affirming the Trinity, but he came to affirm it. He surely didn't invent it. Someone, or some spirit, is keeping you from glorifying Christ."

"We glorify only the one all-powerful God, sir."

"In His final words in Matthew, Jesus claimed all power and His disciples worshipped him, but some doubted. Are you with those who worship Him or those who doubt?" Stern Face looked even sterner, and I suggested, "Philippians says every knee will bow before Jesus, so let's kneel and glorify Him!"

The younger lady started to kneel, but Stern Face jerked her back up.

"Ceasefire!" Lucy begged. "I'm bringing coffee and cookies." While the ladies ate, Lucy beckoned me into the kitchen. "Tiger, why duel with her? Let me befriend them. Last night I asked God to pardon me for being a nag; I asked Him to give me humble and cheerful words from now on. Let me practice on them!"

"John said not to receive any who teach falsely about Christ."

"Yes, but the younger one appears open." We joined them and when Stern Face had her mouth full Lucy said, "When I first trusted in Jesus, He gave me joy and peace. I appreciate the pain that He suffered to forgive our sins. His resurrection gives us hope too; He promised to raise us also. I've suffered from despairing moods, and without Jesus' promise of new life and forgiveness I . . . well, I probably wouldn't be alive now. I really need Him in my life. Do you?"

Stern Face muttered something about Jesus being merely a "ransom."

I stated, "The entire Bible testifies of Jesus, and every page in the New Testament glorifies Him. We love Him and try to glorify Him."

"Our teachers never taught us this!" the younger lady replied. "They only . . . "

"We'll go now," interrupted Stern Face. "Thank you for the refreshments."

Victor Calderon's small son was playing with Tino, and I heard him say, "I'll let you in on a secret. That big-mouthed man with funny white shoes is holding a secret meeting at our house at six." Something sneaky was afoot!

I took Arturo with me to crash the party, and Victor invited us in genially. Dr. Nuñez was telling some believers, "And he commands like a colonel! He only preaches salvation, and . . . Ah, welcome, brothers. Ah . . . Have a seat. Ha ha. I'm glad you joined us!" The others hung their heads as Nuñez said, "We're studying . . . ah . . . Daniel 1!"

Victor told the group, "I had no idea Dr. Nuñez intended an anti-meeting. He'd said it was to give testimonies and pray. Well, that's all we're going to do."

Back home, Lucy was bubbling. "The JW girl came back alone. We read Peter's testimony at Pentecost and that of other *true* witnesses for Jesus, and guess what, she asked Jesus to save her. Old Stern Face and her ilk will reject her now, so I offered to introduce her to other believers her age, and she was thrilled."

The young lady came to our next united worship and blessed us with a joyful testimony. We met in the soccer field and curious cows stood on the other side of a fence watching with an occasional moo. A shock followed the final prayer; Arturo announced, "I've prayerfully decided to resign as pastor, effective now."

A silence was broken only by moos until Pacho cried, "Oh no! Why?"

"The body lacks balance with me leading. I'm not sore at anyone, and there's no big sin forcing me to resign. I'm just doing what I know God wants."

"But what'll you do? You can't just stop teaching God's Word!"

"I won't. I'll mentor pastors, especially where God's work is new, folks are coming to Jesus and I can fulfill my promise to Olga. God bless you all." Picking up the black briefcase, he left abruptly as Anna, Lucy, and others wept.

<table>
<tr><td>

Task 17–e.

NAME SHEPHERDS
CAREFULLY, ACCORDING
TO CHARACTER
QUALITIES THAT GOD
REQUIRES

</td></tr>
</table>

Jethro had come to worship with us and advised, "I've discussed this with Arturo; he'll be pastoring even more strategically now by doing extension training." This and similar concerns would spur us to **name shepherds carefully, according to character qualities that God requires**.

The elders gathered to decide what to do about replacing Arturo, and Pacho asked Jethro, "How did New Testament congregations call a pastor?"

"They didn't. The New Testament uses the word 'pastor' only once for human leaders, in Ephesians. Elders shepherded the flocks and that's an option for you."

"I can't see that working here." Pacho twisted his moustache. "Let's ask the National Alliance to suggest a candidate. We can afford to pay an interim pastor meanwhile." He paused and added, "We need a good *preacher*, right, Jethro?"

"It's better to be a good *shepherd* and a true pastor knows the difference."

"Let's not bring one from outside," I cautioned, "unless he shares our vision to multiply flocks and to train new leaders the way Jesus and Paul did."

"Meanwhile," Jethro exhorted, "you must all help with the pastoral work."

Simon had been listening to the elders, and urged, "Ask Dr. Nuñez to serve as pastor. He's the only good preacher in town, and gets along well with people."

"No, Simon!" Pacho answered so harshly that it surprised me. "Peter prohibits an elder to be a lover of money and Dr. Nuñez is greedy."

Roger spoke quietly to me, "I've been thinking about resigning too."

"Oh no!" I took him off to one side where we could talk. "Why, Roger?"

"Promise not to tell dad."

"True Christian leaders do not divulge what people tell them in confidence."

"Some of the churches whose leaders I train are inert. They do nothing unless I'm there; no one baptizes anybody and few men attend."

"Never make a crucial decision while you feel dejected, Roger. I'll visit those churches with you and we'll discover the root of their paralysis."

While visiting a troubled church, one of Roger's "preacher boys" kept grinning at a cute *señorita* in the front row as he lectured. Two men watched from the doorway for a while, and then turned away, snickering. "It's my fault," Roger admitted afterwards. "I named single young men as pastors; they were better educated, used good grammar, and were eager to lead."

"But they don't meet biblical requirements for elders; they're immature. Most people don't respect the leadership of a young, single man unless he shows extraordinary maturity, and has a record of effective service. A serious family man resents being led by a youngster who lacks pastoral experience."

"Not only that. The young men don't prepare well to teach, in spite of my urging; they just parrot what they've read and neglect other pastoral duties."

"We'll fix that. Let's apply biblical norms for elders, naming only proven, godly men who are already shepherding their families. Let's not name pastors just because they have a more formal education unless they also meet biblical requirements. Let's help those immature young men do other ministries."

Roger did as planned and a few weeks later told me, "The village churches are doing well with mature elders. One church authorized a younger man to teach, but since folks knew an older man was in charge they accepted the arrangement."

"Great! I feared the work in town would lag with no regular pastor and not meeting in the chapel, but it's thriving. Where dictators ban institutional churches, believers form cells like in the New Testament and find it wholesome. With the experience we're gaining, we could send qualified workers to such fields."

"At least someone's using the chapel; Nuñez gathers a group in it. He says they're the legitimate church and we're separatists! Should we stop him, Tiger?"

"No. He'd just spread his poison in homes as he tried to do in Victor's."

CHAPTER 17: CONFIRM THE GRASP AND THE PRACTICE OF LEADERS' TASKS

17–a. Strive for social justice in a peaceful, positive way without rancor. Find Jesus' promise to earnest seekers of justice: *Blessed are those who hunger and thirst for righteousness, for they shall be satisfied.* Matt 5:6

17–b. Teach what learners currently need, not simply what fits a preferred homiletic style or current interest. Jethro urged both Bible book study and dealing with needs. Which is normally more edifying?

[ ]   Go through a Bible book or passage and teach what it says.

[ ]   Deal with current topics of interest to the people.

[ ]   Do both in the same message or give both types of messages.

ANSWER: Do both for balance; respond to issues and explain Bible texts.

17–c. Build loving relationships between "lambs" and "rams". Do you need to improve communication between older and newer members of your flock?

Note what Jesus said to do with a brother in Christ whom one has resented: *Everyone who is angry with his brother shall be guilty before the court . . . Therefore if you are presenting your offering at the altar, and there remember that your brother has something against you, leave your offering there before the altar and go; first be reconciled to your brother, and then come and present your offering.* Matt 5:22–24

17–d. Practice honest pastoral ethics. Nuñez did not respect other pastors. Note how to treat one who causes division: *Brethren, keep your eye on those who cause dissensions and hindrances contrary to the teaching which you learned, and turn away from them. For such men are slaves, not of our Lord Christ but of their own appetites, and by their smooth and flattering speech they deceive the hearts of the unsuspecting.* Rom 16:17–18
Choose ethical biblical principles that your flock should follow more carefully:

[ ]   Keep confidential information to yourself and avoid gossip, Jas 3:5–12.

[ ]   Respect other shepherd's flocks and shun any person who causes division, Rom 15:20–21; Titus 3:10–11.

[ ]   Do not meet alone with a person of the opposite sex, 1 Thess 5:22.

[ ]   Do not control believers by lording it over them, 1 Pet 5:1–4.

[ ]   Form new flocks rather than only growing your own forever larger.

Note Jesus' wolf warning: *Beware of the false prophets, who come to you in sheep's clothing, but inwardly are ravenous wolves. You will know them by their fruits.* Matt 7:15–16

17–e. Name shepherds carefully, according to character qualities that God requires. Which among these criteria to choose a shepherd is a biblical guideline?

[ ]   A Bible school or seminary diploma.

[ ]   A majority of members vote in favor of a new pastor.

[ ]   Spiritually maturity.

[ ]   Willing to work for a wage on a par with an average member.

ANSWER: Spiritual maturity is the only biblical requisite in the list.

EVALUATE YOUR LEADERSHIP

1=Poor. 2=Planning to improve. 3=Doing well.

1-2-3   Strive for social justice in a peaceful, positive way without rancor.

1-2-3   Teach what learners currently need, not merely what fits a teaching style.

1-2-3   Build loving relationships between "lambs" and "rams."

1-2-3   Practice honest pastoral ethics.

1-2-3   Name shepherds according to character traits that God requires.

18.
Tiger Shuns Popular Trends that Lure Churches into Mediocrity

Task 18–a.

SEND WORKERS WHO KNOW HOW TO MULTIPLY FLOCKS TO NEGLECTED PEOPLES

I wrote Roy and Daisy Watts to tell about our work and mentioned that parts of our country still lacked churches. Their surprising reply sparked events that would awaken us to the need to **send workers who know how to multiply flocks to neglected peoples:** "*Daisy and I have a heart for your type of field; we're saving up to look over the area with another missionary, Fred McNary.*"

Grateful for their paying my airfare during our crisis two years before and helping me know Jesus, an idea hit me. I rode to Lone Stone to find the wild horses. Only two remained, and I saw why they'd evaded capture; they were almost as swift as Bullet. After a wild ride, I roped them, took them home, broke them, and sold them for enough to buy airline tickets. Roy, Daisy, and Fred flew into our capital city, and the next day we went to Bat Haven's square to meet their bus; they filed off with huge smiles.

"Look! *Gringos!*" cried a small girl. "Tall!" Children came yelling, pointing at the aliens, and reaching up to feel Daisy's long blond hair. Then came a moment of confusion—Fred was missing. "Where's the other missionary?" I asked Roy.

"Fred got travel-weary and is resting in the capital. He'll charter a small plane to fly to Arenas tomorrow, the nearest airfield."

Gadget drove Roy and me to Arenas in the orange taxi the next day. We shooed cows from the dirt airstrip and an ancient Cessna touched down. The tail-dragger was hard to steer on uneven ground, and my heart beat faster to watch it bounce, swerve, and make a ground loop, coming to a stop in bushes beside the runway. Fred emerged white-faced, which accentuated his freckles and red hair; he took photos of the Cessna and scenery before greeting us. What sort of fellow was this who'd give so little attention to meeting his host?

On the way back, heavy rain fell; we forded a swift river and halfway across, the motor died. Gadget moaned, "Shoulda took off the fan belt. Spray wet them spark plugs." We pushed the car, but it mired in loose sand. The muddy water had risen to my waist when a neighbor came with an ox team and pulled the taxi out.

Gadget checked the oil and whined, "Water's in the oil; if I start the car it'll emulsify and ruin the engine." We returned on foot to Arenas to buy oil and Fred looked like he was ready to cut and run back to the States. Such woes were routine for Gadget and me, and Roy enjoyed the adventure, but I pitied Fred; he was sweating in spite of the cool air, clearly unused to physical exertion.

Back at the car, the oxen's owner came to say, "You gentlemen are soaked and shivering. Stay in our house tonight. You can't cross the river yet, anyway."

Ernesto's two-room house had mud walls whitewashed with lime, a roof of palm fronds, and glassless windows with rustic wooden shutters. His wife roasted coffee mixed with corn and raw cane sugar on an outside, earthen stove until the mixture was almost ash; the process was too smoky to do inside. The potent brew penetrated to our bones and we stopped shivering. I was grateful, but Fred spit the black stimulant back into the cup. "Bitter!"

"Add sugar, man!" Ernesto laughed. "No one can take that stuff plain!" He shaved sugar from a brown block into Fred's cup.

"You call that sugar? It smells like molasses."

"The best!" Ernesto pointed at an apparatus outside. "We squeeze cane with that *ñongoté*, and then boil it down in a round mold."

"*Ñongoté?*" queried Roy. "How does it work?"

"I'll show you; the rain's quit." Ernesto sat bouncing on the end of a pole while his ten-year-old daughter Rina inserted cane stalks under the pliers-like lever, squeezing out the sweet juice, and we all drank the raw beverage. To warm us, Ernesto built a small fire on the mud floor in the middle of the room. We tried to sleep on the floor, but even with our exhaustion, we couldn't ignore the floor's unforgiving hardness, the smoke that stung our eyes, and odorous emanations from an obese sow that accompanied us. Fred griped, "You'd think they'd at least get some decent furniture."

"They have what they can afford," I replied. "Poverty's extreme in these villages, and yet they share with us what they have. Be grateful, sir."

Roy affirmed, "I'm grateful; such hospitality to strangers warms my heart."

The next morning Rina petted the pig and boasted, "She's mine!"

"I'll buy her from you," Gadget teased. "She'll make tasty bacon."

"No!"

"I'll pay to you ten times the value of a big pig, *Señorita*."

"No!"

"Let's swap, then, Rina. My luxury car out there for your fat sow."

"No!"

Ernesto's wife brought beans and tortillas. There were too few chairs for all of us, so we took turns eating. Rina watched for a while, fascinated by Fred's red hair and freckles. "You're awfully pale. You been sick? Your skin's ugly."

"Rina!" her mother scolded, "Don't be rude! That's the natural color of the *gringos*. Their skin lacks normal pigment and they can't help it."

"Maybe if they'd eat chocolate or licorice . . . "

"That's enough Rina. Finish your tortillas."

I told Ernesto, "We follow Jesus Christ, and it's our practice to pray in His name for folks' needs. Is there something you'd like us to pray for?"

"Oh, yes! Our corn. Animals got into it and ruined half of it; tapirs, maybe. And my aunt who lives in the next village up the river is down with malaria."

We prayed for these, and asked God to bless each family member; Ernesto thanked us heartily. Fred muttered to Roy, "I'm surprised how they welcomed your prayer so readily; it didn't seem at all unusual to them. Most of the Americans I've been around would've been uncomfortable."

"Not here, Fred, and not in most of the world's major societies. They've escaped Western rationalism; Hindus, Buddhists, Muslims, and even many Communists respond readily to an offer to pray for them or their families."

I asked Ernesto, "Do you pray with your family?"

"No. We're rather out of touch with God. Haven't been to a church for years; it's a bit far to town. Your prayers are different from what I've heard in Mass. You pray like you're talking right to God, like to a friend you know."

"I used to find prayer hard; my sins made it unpleasant to talk to God. But Roy here and his family led me into the presence of Christ and I discovered His forgiveness. He died on the cross for us, as you know, rose from the dead, and promised followers forgiveness and new life. He called it being 'born again.'"

"I've heard that, but never understood it."

"He gives us a new, loving heart, a desire to obey Him joyfully and eternal life as part of His heavenly family. He'll give you and your family the same assurance. We don't earn this blessing by doing good works; it's all by His grace."

To illustrate grace, Roy related the parable of the prodigal son and other Bible stories. The entire family listened, their eyes reflecting intense interest. Fred started to expound the doctrine of salvation in an abstract way; those eyes lost their luster, and Rina followed her mother away to do chores.

The next morning Ernesto was all smiles when I offered to return another day to talk again, pray together, and have worship with his family and friends.

"We'd appreciate that very much, Tiger. Most of our neighbors too."

On our way again to Bat Haven, Fred remarked, "You were rushing things, Tiger, to offer to have *worship* with them on your next trip."

"They'll be ready for it, and we might baptize them." Fred looked shocked at this, and I explained, "When the Holy Spirit brings families and social networks to Christ, things can move lightning fast compared to a traditional church like ours once was, which demands a slower speed. Don't doubt the work of God in those folks' hearts. If you do, such doubts become contagious and discouraging."

"Wonderful!" exclaimed Roy. "I feel like I've stepped into heaven!"

"You're blind then," Fred growled. "I feel like I've fallen into hell!"

This dampened conversation until Fred remarked, "Few Americans are that receptive to the gospel and I wonder why not."

"Some are," Roy replied, "especially among the poor. Fred, in America you've been trying to push 'camels' from the middle class through the needle's eye, as Jesus put it. Rationalists say religion is for the poor and uneducated, and in a sense, they're right. God wants to save everybody, but the poor respond quicker; Jesus said it would be that way. Poverty helps people face reality and trust in God; wealth lures people to trust in themselves."

I asked Roy, "Is that why God allows so much poverty?"

"Widespread movements have always begun with the poorer working class, Tiger. It trickles up; poor believers' children become the next middle class."

"Did you notice how much easier it was to talk with Ernesto and his family about the Lord after we'd eaten in his home? Some Christians try to theologize too soon, before the Holy Spirit has awakened seekers' thirst for God, and they act superior because they know Christ and theology; this deters seekers. The apostles never witnessed in a theological way; they simply related the good news—the historical facts—and let the Holy Spirit convict and convince."

"You dealt with the entire family as a unit," Roy said. "Most Americans tend to view salvation as an individual affair and aim for one to make a decision on his own, to receive Jesus as his personal Savior."

"You said 'decision' and 'personal'—two enemies of evangelism; Scripture uses neither word in connection with it. Mere decisions rarely include repentance; most folks who merely make decisions fall away. Faith is personal only in that one's heart consciously embraces it, and not simply because one is a member of a social group; the word is fatal for a movement if we add the Western spin to mean 'private.' God doesn't see a person as an isolated individual, but part of a network. The apostles dealt with the networks of the jailer, Cornelius, Lydia, and Crispus. People repent more readily along with their friends and kin."

"Very true," Roy replied, "now that I think about it. I came here to learn."

"Well, I didn't come as a pupil," Fred grumbled. "I came to start churches."

I told him, "If you're looking for neglected fields, then you'll have to travel a ways from Bat Haven. We already have churches in the villages nearby."

"So you've got the area all sewed up, have you?" Fred sneered.

Folks smiled and waved as we drove slowly through a mountain village, and

Roy waved back. "This culture fascinates me. It's delightful, except the poverty."

"It doesn't impress me," growled Fred. "I'm going to change things." The stark contrast between the two Americans stirred anxiety in my mind.

"Wow!" Roy exclaimed. "The sun goes down fast in these high mountains!"

"The brief twilight is not due to the altitude," I explained. "It's because we're near the equator where the sun does not cross over the horizon at a slow slant as you're used to in the north; it swoops almost straight down. The morning's the same; dawn, once it makes up its stubborn mind to emerge, leaps up boldly!"

Back in Bat Haven, I took Fred and Roy to meet Arturo and showed them our hand-drawn map depicting village churches, names of leaders, and of their mentors from "mother" churches. Fred was writing something avidly, and I wondered what. Roy asked Arturo, "How do pastors in all these villages receive training?"

"By extension. I used to shepherd the congregation here in town, but I found that my spiritual gifts serve better to mentor new pastors."

Roy traced a mentoring chain on the map with a finger, with names of mentors and trainees. "Explain this."

"Trainees tell a mentor how their new churches are going; the mentor helps them make plans and assign related reading. They in turn do the same for newer leaders of their daughter churches. Thus, the chain."

Roy had many questions, but I noticed Fred's face turning redder and he exploded. "Degrading! Your extension training denigrates true theological education; those village leaders lack solid academic discipline."

"Oh, no!" Roy faced his colleague. "God is using their training, Fred. I admire how their churches multiply. They don't need our help; let's go where . . . "

"You go, but I'll stay. They have no real churches here, Roy; they lack pastors from a proper institution."

"I'm sorry, brother. You want things to be like what you're used to, but . . . "

Fred turned without a goodbye, and slammed the door behind him.

Mission Frontiers

1st coastal cities
2nd interior of dark continents
3rd all tribes and language groups
4th (current) where authorities outlaw evangelism

I asked Roy to explain missions to our cell and he unfolded a large world map. "Jesus' final command was to *make disciples of all nations,* meaning cultural groups, not political states. Evangelical missions have had four frontiers. The first frontier was *coastal cities.* Before 1800, most missionaries from Europe went with sailors, soldiers, and merchants as chaplains to pastor their countrymen, and churches arose along the coasts."

Daisy pointed to coasts of Africa, Asia, and the Americas.

"The second frontier was the *continents' interior,*" Roy said. "Missionaries penetrated deeply into them before the year 1900, as the Moravians did in this country, going inland from the Caribbean."

Daisy pointed to inland areas of Brazil, China, and Africa.

"The third frontier in the 1900's was *all ethnic groups,*" Roy continued. "Missionaries reached beyond the dominant culture to other tribes and people groups."

I noticed Gadget and Evita taking notes on every detail.

"The fourth and current frontier is where authorities outlaw missionary work—a third of the world's people, mainly *Muslims, Buddhists, Hindus,* and *Communists.*" Daisy pointed to Northern Africa, Indonesia, and across southern Asia, and Roy explained, "According to their laws, only a criminal can plant churches; unfortunately, most missionaries lack criminal experience!"

"So, let's learn to be sneaky!" laughed Gadget. "Can you teach us, Roy?"

"I prefer calling it 'sensitivity to culture.' Missionaries deal with vastly diverse worldviews; some folks in the southern hemisphere prefer maps to show the earth from a viewpoint upside-down to us." He showed a world map that made no sense until he turned it over to show the continents with our northern perspective.

WORLD MAP
Kiwi Cartographers

Daisy recounted abuses suffered by Hindu and Muslim women and it touched Evita. Weeping, she cried, "That's terrible! Utterly satanic!"

Gadget took her hand. "Maybe someday God will let us go free them."

Roy commented, "Daisy and I prayed last night about where we should work. India has thousands of neglected people groups; we might go there."

"What do you mean by a 'people group'?" Roger asked.

"It's a group in which the gospel can flow easily without a barrier stopping it—barriers such as culture, mountains, borders, race, or language, whatever stops the flow. Economic disparity often poses a worse wall than race. With God's help, trained workers cross these barriers, come to enjoy a different culture, and love the people, as Ruth did with the Moabites, and the Apostle Paul."

"I read that it's better to start in big cities," Roger said, "and go from there."

"That's a popular strategy, but don't make it law. We can't limit the Holy Spirit; He's not a 'direct current' flowing just one way. It's often easier to reach folks in villages and let them take Jesus to the city, going with the general flow. Also, some city workers have a haughty attitude toward their poorer country cousins. In most fields where churches are multiplying underground, it began in villages."

"That's happening in our country too, for the most part," I remarked.

Roy and Daisy were staying with us and he told me, "We learn so much by observing God's work here!" I told him we'd learned a lot from them too, about other cultures; we were discussing this when knocking at the door interrupted.

| **Task 18–b.** |
| RESPECT CHRISTIAN LEADERS REGARDLESS OF THEIR EDUCATION OR ECONOMIC LEVEL |

"Oh oh! Crisis is written all over your face!" I told the new pastor who had arrived at our house. Toño lived in the refugee camp that Roger and Mincho had helped build after the hurricane. His plight would show us why we must **respect Christian leaders regardless of their education or economic level.**

"Wolves, Tiger! Fred McNary and Freckles are forming churches with foreign customs by taking people from ours without doing any evangelism."

Roy groaned and I asked, "Who's Freckles, Toño?"

"Fred McNary's freckled son; he has cinnamon hair like his dad. They lure weak believers to follow them and love to control. Fred offered two pastors a tiny salary to join him. These pastors are poor and just handed their flocks over to the wolves. Those two *gringos* cause deep resentment everywhere they go, Tiger."

"Fred's a parasite, Toño. Surely those men see that!"

"Oh, they do! One of them told me, '*I hate the cow, but love the milk!*'"

"Fred can't buy loyalty, he can only rent it. They'll come back."

Roy, Roger, Mincho, and I accompanied Toño to the refugee camp to help him combat the wolves, and two churches gathered for united worship; Toño's was Latino, the other tribal, and new pastors from other villages arrived. Some sang songs they had composed, and leaders gave progress reports, prayed for the sick, and commissioned a pastor of a new church by laying hands on him.

"This ceremony's very important to us buffoons," Toño told Roy. "We're new and ignorant and need a double dose of the Holy Spirit's anointing!"

Toño asked Roy to preach and he told them he'd come to learn, not to teach. I was glad he recognized that they'd simply asked out of courtesy. Toño then asked me to preach—more courtesy—and I told him, "We want folks to see we respect the new leaders and prepare them to teach their own people." I remarked to Roy, "They mature rapidly when we trust them and let them lead."

Mincho met with some farmers to make plans to improve their agriculture and Roger began a training workshop for new pastors. Roy asked me, "Why don't you teach the workshop? Aren't you more experienced?"

"We delegate responsibilities to new leaders as soon as we can. Roger's grown rapidly by shouldering responsibility for pastoral training in this area. His trainees are training newer leaders now, to keep the work expanding."

"Don't so many new trainers and trainees commit a lot of errors?"

"Oh yes! Almost as many as I did when I started! We use their errors as occasions to teach them theology and pastoral work, just as Jesus and Paul did."

> ## Task 18–c.
> ### FOCUS ON POSITIVE ACTION WITHOUT SQUANDERING TIME ON INSOLUBLE PROBLEMS

We listened to Roger encourage the leaders to **focus on positive action without squandering time on insoluble problems.** Roy told him later, "You wasted no time on the old, chronic problems that some complained about."

"Why dance with the devil? I used to run around putting out fires that he'd started and it took all my time. Now when we visit a village we don't leave until we've done something positive such as lead seekers to Jesus, enroll pastoral students, organize a daughter church, or initiate ministries. Chase after Satan and he'll keep you too busy to serve Christ. Don't let deceivers dictate your moves."

Deceivers would soon test our resolve. Toño was serving Communion in the shade of a tree when an army truck came raising clouds of dust. It halted; soldiers leaped down and surrounded us, rifles at the ready. Women screamed, and we waited to see what they'd do. To my astonishment, Mouse and the Reverend Doctor Nuñez stepped down from the cab. Mouse hurried to my side and whispered. "Get away. Don't get involved." I stayed; however, my heart racing.

"Attention!" Nuñez strutted over to the group. "The Cattlemen's Association authorized me to investigate seditious activities here, with military aid. I need names of all who've met with a Mr. Benjamin Medina."

"That's me," Mincho stood. "The Cattlemen's Association has no right to butt in here; we're worshipping. You can join us, but you're not going to stop us."

The rifles aimed at Mincho, and Nuñez asked, "So you're in charge here?"

Toño answered, "I am." He walked over to Nuñez. "I answer for what our Latin church does here." The rifle barrels swung toward him.

"And I answer for what our tribal church does here." A swarthy man stood beside Toño facing Nuñez, and the rifles turned his way.

Eying their patched clothes, Nuñez sneered. "Who authorized you to lead?"

"Our trainer, Roger Diaz, together with members of our congregations."

"They had no authority! I pastor the church that meets in Bat Haven's chapel now, so I supervise things here too. Brothers, these men cannot serve as pastors until I authorize it. Meanwhile, Mouse Maldonado will preach here."

"Hallelujah!" Mouse started to orate, but Dr. Nuñez stopped him. "Wait. I'm not through." He asked the tribal pastor, "Do your people speak Spanish?"

"Yes, sir. But it's not our heart language and our women speak little."

"Then why have two churches in this tiny hamlet? You divide Christ's body."

"We have unity, sir," Toño answered. "We work together. My flock respects the customs of our tribal brothers and they respect ours. We have different ways and if we love people, then we'll respect their culture. Only a cruel bully would separate people from their culture; the Apostle Paul made that clear."

"To have unity requires having the same church practices."

"Not so, Dr. Nuñez," I intervened. "You impose *political* unity, compulsory conformity. We already have unity in Jesus through the Holy Spirit, and it requires neither physical proximity nor conformity of practice. You don't create unity in Christ by corralling two races under one roof. Failing to allow culturally relevant churches is a devastating obstacle to bringing tribal people to Christ."

"But we must strive to create amicable understanding between races."

"Of course, but without forcing false unity and making one culture extinct, as has happened a thousand times in Latin America. It pains folks to have to worship in another culture's style. It takes education to appreciate other cultures and it should not be forced onto new believers."

Mouse resumed orating, the crowd melted away, and the soldiers looked puzzled. One questioned Toño, then ordered Mouse and Nuñez back to the truck and they sped off. The believers returned to finish receiving Communion and afterwards Roger told Toño, "Those guys will deceive these villagers if they return."

"Oh no they won't! We're not as dumb as they think we are."

The tribal pastor added, "They won't deceive us either. We've a history of abuses from haughty snobs and landowners, and know how to avoid them."

Task 18–d.

EVALUATE PASTORAL TRAINEES' FIELDWORK FREQUENTLY AND FRANKLY

Roy, Roger, Toño, and I started out to visit churches started by believers in the refugee camp and Roy would learn two things. His first lesson to ride; he fell off his horse twice before mastering that curriculum. His second was to **evaluate pastoral trainees' fieldwork frequently and frankly.**

Crossing a creek where banana trees thrived in the wet soil, we startled a green lizard that ran erect on its hind legs. "Hey! It ran right over the stream!" exclaimed Roy, pointing and laughing. "It looks like an iguana, but churns its legs so fast that it stays on top of the water! Amazing! What is it, Toño?"

"A *jamo*, the only animal that walks on water like Jesus did." Toño's dog quickly showed he also enjoyed the quick little lizard, but not for its aquatic feat.

We came to a mountain ridge and Roger pointed at a picturesque hamlet at least a kilometer below. "Las Flores, our next stop, Roy."

"Beautiful! It nestles so snuggly among the trees by that stream! So serene!"

"Serene only from a safe distance," Roger replied as we wound our way down. He found the church leader and asked, "How's the work going, Ricardo?"

"I won't lie. I didn't do what we planned. Also, the 'wolf' has been back."

"We'll deal with the wolf later. First, why didn't you do as you planned?" Ricardo had no answer and Roger told him, "Twice now you haven't carried out your plans. Is it time to assign you another job that fits your gifting better?"

After a gentle, but pointed discussion to tease out the root of Ricardo's failure, he admitted, "Yes, I'd like a different ministry. I'd rather help needy people, the sick and suffering. My uncle René should be our leader. He's wise and reliable."

René was a jovial man with tribal features and the believers approved him as an elder, but a *provisional* one, as he was new in the faith. They also named Ricardo as a deacon to care for the needy. Roy remarked to me, "I see these new village churches are moldable when you show them in Scripture what to do."

"I'm glad you noticed that. Older churches often stick in their ways, resisting needed changes. Some are too conservative."

"Too conservative? Hmm. So are your churches *conservative* or *liberal*?"

"Conservative, the way *gringos* use the word—biblical. But here 'conservative' implies control of body and soul by Spanish landowners and Jesuit priests."

Task 18–e.

EXPOSE AND SHUN FALSE PASTORS WITHOUT COMPROMISE OR DELAY

They'd been right to approve René; he acted at once to stop the wolves. He told us, "Fred McNary and Freckles buy the souls of the poor by handing out old clothes as bait; they go even to remote hamlets to take over our churches, exploiting our lack of experience. They'll destroy God's work unless we act. We're determined to **expose and shun false pastors without compromise or delay,** but we don't know how to proceed. Tell us, guys. We're ready to act."

I replied, "Jesus said wolves would cross sea and land to make a proselyte, René, and here they come! You can form a 'wolf repellent squad.' Let your area elders write an agreement based on Romans 15:20–21 not to deal with members of others leaders' flocks without their invitation, and sign it in Fred's presence."

"We'll do that, but what if Fred refuses to sign? He's wily."

"Then he admits he's a wolf; he'll shame himself, and few will follow him."

René sent word to nearby churches. The next day their elders formed the "wolf squad" and wrote the pact to respect other flocks. We all went together and found Fred with his son Freckles who was a replica of his dad, with the same cross demeanor. They refused to add their signatures to the agreement.

Roy begged, "Fred, surely you agree to respect other pastors' flocks!"

"How can I respect pastors who don't even have a theological education?"

I struggled with anger. "They have it—extension education, on the job."

Freckles puffed his chest. "My seminary profs taught about theological education and never mentioned 'extension training.' So it's not biblical, Tiger."

"Mentoring like Jesus and Paul did isn't biblical? King Jehosaphat sent extension teachers to Judah's towns, and Paul, like Moses, trained elders in extension chains. Thousands of churches in fields like ours owe their birth to extension training. To miss this is blindness that educators can't afford, Freckles. In most of the neglected fields of the world, institutional education is impractical. Many churches must multiply underground and trainers mentor as Jesus and Paul did."

Freckles looked as though I'd lashed him. Then his demeanor began to reek of such superiority that I felt like really swatting them.

> **Task 18–f.**
>
> PROVIDE THE KIND OF PASTORAL TRAINING THAT FITS TRAINEES' CIRCUMSTANCES

Roger explained. "I've investigated extension training; it's common and there are different kinds. Good extension trainers **provide the kind of pastoral training that fits trainees' circumstances.** Movements falter where missionaries allow only the kind of education they're familiar with; it's like trying to tighten every bolt on a car with a wrench of one size."

Roy said, "I need to learn those different kinds of extension training, Roger."

"Okay. We can examine how six features of extension training can apply to different fields. Do you want to know these features, gentlemen?"

Fred and Freckles firmly said no; Toño and René firmly said yes. Roger said, "Here's a list of *Extension Training Features*. A conscientious educator applies those that will keep churches and cells multiplying in his field."

1. *Church involvement*: Pastors and laymen train students who serve locally; an experienced person or organization trains the trainers and provides materials.
2. *Menu*: Participants select topics that fit current needs and opportunities.
3. *Autodidactic studies*: Self-teaching texts let one learn without a tutor present, at home, or during breaks at work. Studies describe a truth and verify learning it.
3. *Responsibility for trainees' effective ministry*: A trainer mentors a trainee until his flock is doing all the tasks that God requires of it.
4. *Multiplication*: Trainees mentor newer trainees in a chain such as in 2 Timothy 2:2, to keep churches and cells multiplying.
5. *Availability to all who need training*: Extension training has no restrictive fees and prerequisites are only those of Scripture.

Fred griped, "These peons can't grasp such complex educational philosophy."

René bristled. "We do too, sir! It may come as a surprise to you, but we're not idiots just because we farm God's good earth and dwell in tiny villages."

Roy recalled, "We had a decentralized extension program with no church involvement. I lived far from a seminary, but a professor came once a month."

"It met a need for you," I said, "and we've benefitted from it through you."

Toño affirmed, "My wife became a health promoter that way. An extension agent gave classes on common illnesses and injuries."

Fred made a display of looking away, disdaining the discussion, but his son paid attention, although scowling. Toño took a small booklet from his shirt pocket. "We need these autodidactic studies. I can afford them and read them out in my cornfield while I'm resting. Our church ministries depend on such materials."

Freckles grabbed it, flipped through its pages, and pronounced judgment. "I thought so! Too simplistic for real theological study! It fits these guys."

"So we lack brains?" Toño grabbed the booklet back. "We lack your formal education, but we learn a lot from these studies; we mine the gold in God's Word rather than having a fat book hand-feed us. Inductive Bible studies don't explain everything; they tell us what to look for, and we find the truths ourselves."

Roger held up a handful of small training booklets, "Reading liberates us backward villagers. I grew up in these hills and books freed me from the ignorance that confines a villager to his tiny corner of the world. These men learn just as Jesus' trainees did, and Paul's. That's why their flocks are multiplying."

"Such multiplying is reckless!" cried Fred. "Heresy will infest the churches."

"Only if proselytizers like you bring it," I replied, irked. "I read church history, and widespread heresies have not come from movements like ours; it brews in old, sterile, ingrown churches that disobey Christ and apostate seminaries. What should disturb you isn't church multiplication, but its absence."

Fred grumbled, "You'll lose control if churches multiply as you say, Tiger."

"Not while our extension mentors coordinate the work like the apostles did. I prefer to say 'coordinate' rather than 'control.' They coach local leaders, sir."

"I understand your desire to multiply churches," remarked Freckles. "What worries me is that so many new churches will entail huge expenses, Tiger."

"Then stop worrying. People meet Jesus in new congregations and give enough to sustain the work, as long as most of the leaders are self-supported."

René handed the pact to respect others' flocks to Freckles. "Now that you know we receive training and direction, I'm sure you'll join us in signing this."

Freckles took a pen from his pocket, but Fred slapped his hand sharply, knocking the pen to the floor. "Well!" our host exclaimed. "That clarified things! Roger, I didn't know Fred had separated from you. I'll be loyal to my own church."

On the way home Roy remarked, "I'm amazed how your flocks multiply in villages and cells in town! I've learned so much, Tiger! Daisy and I will fly back to the States tomorrow, and someday we'll adapt your methods to India."

"They're not *our* methods; the apostles modeled them to be used anywhere."

Task 18–g.

ORGANIZE DIFFERENT TYPES OF GROUPS ACCORDING TO CHANGING NEEDS AND OPPORTUNITIES

Although we no longer used the "house of death," Anna kept tending the chapel's plants; the papaya grew and things were calm until Mincho came to face me with a challenge to **organize different types of groups according to changing needs and opportunities.** "I've watched your small groups reconcile rivals and know what I have to do—resolve things with Simon Alvarez in a group of three: you, Simon, and me." I agreed and off we went.

On the way, Mincho told me, "Names of your groups confuse me: cell, house church, flock, regional church. Enlighten me."

"A 'cell' is any small group of believers, often a satellite of a larger church. A seekers' cell can be a church in embryo, like the group in Cornelius' house.

"A 'house church' is a small flock meeting anywhere convenient; it's a real church if it obeys all of Jesus' commands, baptizing and having Communion.

"A 'flock' is any believers' assembly, church, or cell led by one or more leaders.

"A 'regional church' means flocks that network. The Jerusalem church was a cluster of house churches. Some projects need several flocks' cooperation."

"Most folks I know use the word church to mean a building."

"Scripture uses the word church in only three ways: a gathering of believers, the universal church throughout the ages, and all the flocks of a city or region."

"Our Los Vientos group is a house church then; we're obeying Jesus. Chorcho's leading it, we're having Communion, and doing all the rest. It's a joy!"

"Ah-ee!" Wanda was straining at a high note when we arrived. Simon opened the door and gasped. "Mincho! You attack me in my own house?"

"I come to ask your forgiveness. I now follow Jesus Christ."

"Hah! You've committed so many atrocities that you cannot bear the pain of your own conscience anymore." Sheer hatred in his eyes repulsed me.

"I ask your forgiveness," repeated Mincho. "Because God has washed away the hatred I had for you." I marveled at the new Mincho's gentleness.

"I'll consider it when you stop meddling with my miners."

"Shut up, you fool!" Wanda's parrot screamed inside.

"The mine's another matter. I apologize for my cruelties; it's up to you to ask God's forgiveness for yours. A tunnel caved in on Nando Diaz due to inadequate shoring, miners work amid radioactive dust without proper protection, one fell down a shaft lacking safeguards and you didn't help his widow. But I didn't come to complain about this; I came to make peace." Mincho offered his hand.

Simon backed away. "You have your way of life, I tell you, and I have mine."

Screeching had resumed and it wasn't the parrot. Mincho winced and said loudly, "I'm sorry, Simon, what did you say? I couldn't hear you."

Simon shouted, "God favors my way of life—it's obvious! Look at what I own: a mine, a ranch, and this house. Look at it, I tell you!"

"Oh, Simon, you're the poorest man in town!"

"What do you mean?" The hook shook.

"You've lost everything of real value in life and don't even know it! You're left only with . . . Oh, I see no point in continuing this parley."

We left and I mused, "Simon makes riches his god. Paul said greed is idolatry. Power, drugs, sex, fame, revenge, and learning can all become idols."

"My grandmother once told me there are no singles before God. One is wed either to Him or to an idol that Satan puts in God's place."

"Your grandmother was wise, Mincho. God likened idolatry to prostitution. Hosea said God yearned to be His people's husband rather than their master."

"Tiger, a miner told me today he has symptoms of radiation poisoning. It's starting. The toxic effect will only get worse and the miners are out for blood."

"Oh, no! Just when I thought things couldn't get worse! What can I do?"

"Let me handle it; you'll just get hurt . . . but pray."

CHAPTER 18: CONFIRM THE GRASP AND THE PRACTICE OF LEADERS' TASKS

18–a. Send workers who know how to multiply flocks to neglected peoples. Verify where they'd normally go: *I aspired to preach the gospel, not where Christ was already named, so that I would not build on another man's foundation.* Rom 15:20–21.

18–b. Respect Christian leaders regardless of their education or economic level. Identify four things that believers owe their God-given leaders: *Remember those who led you, who spoke the word of God to you, and considering the result of their conduct, imitate their faith . . . Obey your leaders and submit to them, for they keep watch over your souls as those who will give an account. Let them do this with joy.* Heb 13:7,17

18–c. Focus on positive action without squandering time on insoluble problems. Roger helped leaders plan for future progress. Verify what should occupy our minds: *Whatever is true, whatever is honorable, whatever is right, whatever is pure, whatever is lovely, whatever is of good repute, if there is any excellence and if anything worthy of praise, dwell on these things. The things you have learned and received and heard and seen in me, practice these things, and the God of peace will be with you.* Phil 4:8–9

18–d. Evaluate pastoral trainees' fieldwork frequently and frankly. Choose guidelines that you will heed more attentively to train leaders:
- [ ] To escape old ruts caused by chronic problems, focus on what edifies when dealing with a new flock; always add something positive.
- [ ] Let area churches gather to plan, celebrate, and report progress or problems.
- [ ] Let maps show plans for new flocks and names of workers who go to them.
- [ ] Have area elders meet with wolves to ask them to respect others' churches.
- [ ] Name provisional elders to lead where experienced shepherds are lacking.
- [ ] Demonstrate to apprentices how to do pastoral work.
- [ ] Arrange for apprentice leaders to train other newer leaders without delay.
- [ ] Deal with a new flock through its local leaders without controlling them.
- [ ] Give an apprentice leader another task if he fails to carry out his own plans.

18–e. Expose and shun false pastors without compromise or delay.
See what to do if a leader keeps sinning after private reproof: *Do not receive an accusation against an elder except on the basis of two or three witnesses. Those who continue in sin, rebuke in the presence of all, so that the rest also will be fearful of sinning.* 1 Tim 5:19–20

18–f. Provide the kind of pastoral training that fits trainees' circumstances. Note extension training features that you need to develop more:

[ ]   Church involvement

[ ]   A menu that lets participants select studies that fit current needs

[ ]   Autodidactic studies that let readers find answers and evaluate recall

[ ]   Responsibility for trainees' effective ministry shared by trainers

[ ]   Training geared to church or cell multiplication

[ ]   Training available to all who need it

Verify why wise teachers link doctrine and duty: *But prove yourselves doers of the word, and not merely hearers who delude themselves.* Jas 1:22

Notice how Jesus urged teachers to offer variety to fulfill immediate needs: *Every scribe who has become a disciple of the kingdom of heaven is like a head of a household, who brings out of his treasure things new and old.* Matt 13:52

The following pastoral training materials are written for menu-driven training:

- Paul-Timothy Pastoral studies (for both pastoral trainees and children's leaders). Download freely at: http://www.Paul-Timothy.net
- Shepherd's Storybook (basic level). Download freely at: http://www.paul-timothy.net/html/storybook.html
- Train and Multiply (fee for reproduction rights). Download at: https://trainandmultiply.com

18–g. Organize different types of groups according to changing needs and opportunities. Mincho learned meanings of the word "church" in the New Testament. It means "a local congregation," "the universal body of Christ," and . . .

[ ]   churches of a city or region that cooperate as a body.

[ ]   a building in which the followers of Jesus Christ meet.

ANSWER: Congregations in an area that serve each other.

Do you need to form cells that focus on *seekers*?

EVALUATE YOUR LEADERSHIP

1=Poor. 2=Planning to improve. 3=Doing well.

1-2-3 Send workers who know how to multiply flocks to neglected peoples.

1-2-3 Respect Christian leaders regardless of their education or economic level.

1-2-3 Focus on positive action without squandering time on insoluble problems.

1-2-3 Evaluate pastoral trainees' fieldwork frequently and frankly.

1-2-3 Expose and shun false pastors without compromise or delay.

1-2-3 Use the type of pastoral training that fits your field's circumstances.

1-2-3 Organize different types of groups according to needs and opportunities.

Part III
THE LEADER OF LEADERS

19.
The Path to Becoming a Godly Leader
Holds Unwanted Surprises

<table>
<tr><td>

Task 19–a.

DETECT AND
PREVENT A CLIQUE
FROM USURPING
CONTROL OF A
CHURCH

</td><td>

"Big campaign!" Dr. Nuñez' booming voice interrupted Mincho and me as we chatted in our lane; Wanda's car came cruising with a bulky loudspeaker mounted on top. What ensued would show the need to **detect and prevent a clique from usurping control of a church**. "Seven days' dynamic preaching by the renowned Reverend Doctor Amos Nuñez! Come! Seven

</td></tr>
</table>

p.m. in the town square. Sponsored by all Evangelical churches of Bat Haven."

I flagged them down. "Our church doesn't sponsor your campaign, Doc."

"But it does. Everyone in your church wants it."

"'Everyone?' I don't believe that at all. You mean Wanda's little clique."

Wanda rolled a window down to look at Mincho's deformed face, gasped, and turned away. She then turned to look directly at me. "I knew our church folks would want it. I'm rehearsing an aria from *Aida*. Bring your friends."

"An aria from what?"

"Verdi's opera *Aida*; Italian, of course. Educated people would know that."

"Really! I'll wear a tux next time the troupe comes here from Rome! But why a secular song, ma'am? The campaign was your idea, both of you, wasn't it?"

"A public campaign is always the best way to evangelize," declared Nuñez.

"Not *always*. Big meetings bring folks to Jesus, but when we overdo them believers stop witnessing for Jesus, leaving it up to professionals. Most believers I know received Christ because relatives and friends witnessed to them, and the few who received Him in big meetings were influenced by praying friends."

They drove on, and Mincho exclaimed, "Wow! Who's she? Queen of Sheba?"

"Queen of Bat Haven—she thinks. Her clique has controlled our church until lately. She's Wanda, Simon Alvarez' wife." At this Mincho flinched, looked pained, and grasped a medallion around his neck. I wondered why.

A fair crowd attended the campaign. Wanda sang, Nuñez preached in his fancy shoes, and Mouse added boisterous "Amens." Suddenly without warning, a gust swept the square surprising us with rain that drenched the loudspeaker with its makeshift wiring. Pop! Sparks flew, and then with a flash it, became reticent.

"Wait!" cried Nuñez as folks ran for shelter. "A few droplets won't hurt you!"

All fled except Nuñez, a drunk, and Mouse who was shivering. A sore throat kept him home the next day, but Wanda sang, Nuñez denounced the town's debauchery, and the same drunk "accepted Jesus" just as he had done the night before. They called off the remaining meetings.

I didn't see Nuñez again until all our cells gathered a few weeks later to worship in the soccer field by the cow pasture. He arrived with a few followers and announced grandly, "We shall return to this church; I won't continue the division that your leaders have caused." He stepped to my side and muttered, "They didn't respond to my campaign because you and Arturo have ruined them with your simplistic teaching. Bat Haven's people now have hard hearts."

"They're not hard, sir. You scolded and manipulated their consciences to make them feel guilty. We should let the Holy Spirit convince folks of sin as Jesus taught. They receive Him when we tell what He did for them and show love."

Nuñez went around greeting everyone with his toothy smile and when the meeting ended, Gadget warned me, "I smell a plot." Gadget's sense of smell had not misled him; Nuñez began visiting our members, campaigning like a politician, and at our next united worship people arrived that we'd not seen for years. Arturo groaned, "Oh no! They're up to something, Tiger. I thought the battle was over and never did remove those inactive members' names from the role!"

Nuñez faced the assembly, held up a letter, and announced with his broadest grin, "Wonderful, thrilling news! Panther Jones responded to a request I sent on our behalf. Ha ha! It requires our immediate vote." He read, "*Esteemed friends of Bat Haven Evangelical Church. Considering the beauty of your property, I triple my offer and will pay top wages to any who need work, to build offices, do secretarial work, and develop the mine. There is a condition: you must name Dr. Amos Nuñez as pastor, to prevent further obstructions. I will finalize the sale in a ceremony during the festivities on Saint Muñoz' day. I need a most immediate reply.*"

The most immediate reply came from a cow that mooed loudly in the next field, after which Pacho leaped to his feet. "That letter came from hell!"

Lucy gasped at his vehemence, and whispered to me, "Good for Pacho!"

Nuñez rejoined, "Please be reverent, brother Diaz. All in favor of building the most spacious, beautiful, and illustrious church in the republic raise your hand!" It happened so quickly! The majority favored the sale, and we got the Reverend Doctor Nuñez in the bargain as our pastor.

"Illegal!" Pacho screamed, "The vote was illegal! Arturo! Tell them, Arturo!"

"It was legal. Totally mistaken, but legal." Pacho sat with his head in his hands while Arturo and witnesses signed a paper that Sebastian had prepared.

"Oh, this wonderful, precious agreement!" Dr. Nuñez held it up high, bouncing up and down on his tiptoes. "It binds the church to transfer its property to Mr. Jones upon receiving his most generous payment in full during the public ceremony on Saint Muñoz' festival day. Oh, glorious day!"

Pacho came to our home the next day holding a letter, his face grim. "It's from my cousin, in reply to an inquiry I made. Listen to this. *'Amos Nuñez' doctorate is from a phony diploma mill in Miami. Also, he's no reverend; the synod refused to ordain him, and we removed him as pastor due to inappropriate behavior.'*"

Task 19–b.
TAKE THE STEPS JESUS ORDERED TO DEAL WITH OFFENDERS

"Okay, Pacho, we'll **take the steps Jesus ordered to deal with offenders**. The first one is for you to go alone to face him with his deception."

"I already did; he laughed at me, the devious imposter! He's totally confident since those greedy voters backed him. His arrogance almost made me vomit."

"Well then, we'll face him with witnesses, the second step." Pacho and I took Colombo with us and showed Nuñez the letter.

"Lies!" he stormed. "I resigned from that church on my own. The truth is your cousin resents me; he wrote that out of envy, Pacho Diaz. Pure envy!"

"Search your conscience, sir," I replied. "You deceived us. Resign as pastor, or we'll take the final step that Jesus ordered to deal with such offences."

"You can't stop me now! The church installed me legally and won't reject Panther's big-hearted offer." The hated crocodile grin widened. "Ha ha ha!"

The showdown followed our next united worship. I announced, "We must deal with an unpleasant, but unavoidable issue. Dr. Amos Nuñez has deceived us on an important issue, and we're taking the steps required by Matthew 18. Pacho Diaz spoke to him privately and he paid no heed. Witnesses spoke with him and he rejected them. Since Jesus requires it, we must bring his case before this assembly. Pacho, please read the letter from your cousin."

"Wait!" Nuñez interrupted. "No need to go into details. I resign on my own account. I'll not argue and take part in this farce, stooping to Tiger's level."

"A shame!" Wanda whined. "At least the sale is for sure, Amos." She turned to Arturo. "You can use the chapel until the festival; then we'll tear it down."

"What?" Lucy cried. "Enter that wretched shack after all that's happened? A spirit of darkness saturates even the air we inhale inside its walls!" Others agreed.

Nuñez took advantage of the empty chapel again and gathered a few followers in an anti-church. I felt no desire to stop him; no one respected him except a few who coveted the salaries he promised. What more mischief could he do beyond what he'd done? I continued to coordinate the cells calmly, determined not to let rivals vex me, assuming things could not get worse. But they did.

Julio and Roger arrived out of breath at our house and Julio exclaimed, "The wolf's robbing sheep again! Right here in Bat Haven!" Roger added, "Fred's luring our new believers into a divisive anti-church. He's in Victor Calderon's house right now. What'll we do?"

"Well, what did Jesus do when faced with seditious hypocrites, Roger?"

"Oho! He shot with both barrels! We're going wolf-hunting!"

We hurried to Victor's house and I challenged Fred, "You do not respect other shepherds' flocks."

"How can I, when your phony church's women paint themselves like Evita does, and . . . Oh, give up, Tiger, your ministry's a disaster! You lack education and can't even preach a sermon with proper homiletic form!"

"Do I hear discord?" Victor turned to Fred. "Sir, in my home we deal with Christian brothers respectfully. One cannot do God's will by going around acting in a spiteful way, looking for things to criticize. You lied to me; you said when you entered that you only wanted to pray with me, but you had another plan."

Fred mumbled threats as he left, and I congratulated Victor. "You know how to discern God's will; Jesus said we'd know false prophets by their fruits."

<table>
<tr><td>

Task 19–c.

DISCERN GOD'S
WILL WITH
CERTAINTY

</td><td>

When we left, Julio told me, "Me and Roger also need to know how to **discern God's will with certainty.** Our uncle that hired Nando will employ us on his fishing boat with a super salary. He said Nando was his best sailor and wants us if we're as conscientious."

</td></tr>
</table>

"We could evangelize sailors," added Roger. "Don't tell dad; we haven't talked to him yet. What do you think, Tiger?"

My heart sank, and my first impulse was to grab them by the neck and shake them. "Don't make me your conscience; you'll discern God's will for yourselves. You tell me how one goes about knowing His will, Roger."

"Well, we ask God for wisdom, and when we do what Jesus and His apostles commanded, we know we're doing His stated will. However, His commands don't define every step we take, so we let God's Spirit show us the way."

"Right. Also, examine similar cases in Scripture and consult wise believers."

"You're wise, Tiger," Roger replied. "So just tell us what to do."

"No! But I'll ask another question. You're bringing many to Christ by starting village churches; will you have such a fruitful ministry aboard a boat?"

"We can't guess the future," Julio answered. "We're not clairvoyants!"

Roger poked his brother. "See? I told you he'd say that!"

Julio left the next day, but Roger kept training new church leaders. Some of them were having a constant battle against the wolves, but otherwise things went smoothly for a few months. Elders preached by rotation during the united worship in the soccer field, and when it came to my turn, I was in for a larger-than-average surprise. Jethro arrived limping, leaning heavily on his cane, and I asked him to teach in my place, but he only gave a greeting. Afterwards, Arturo asked everyone to stay and announced, "We've examined pastoral candidates and none had a vision of multiplying flocks as we have. It's our decision, confirmed by prayer, to ask Tiger Garcia to serve as our main pastor."

I was stunned! Apparently, others were too; I heard murmurs: "Packed a gun . . . talks to his dog . . . hangs out with ruffians . . . scrapped in the square . . . lacks higher education . . . can't preach normal sermons . . . has a peasant's accent . . . doesn't even use a pulpit."

My shortcomings flooded my mind and I took a deep breath to voice my reluctance, but Jethro stood. A cow mooed, Jethro mooed back at it; everyone laughed and relaxed. "Tiger doesn't use a pulpit? Horrors! Hang him at sundown! Folks, many pastors, myself included, have stopped using a pulpit to have more direct contact with our people. I once thought a monologue sermon was all there was, but we learn some things better with dialogue. The New Testament's 'one-another' commands require interaction. Wise pastors use the teaching method that fits the occasion. Tiger, like Moses, is a shepherd that gets results. Also, like Moses, he's not an eloquent orator. But tell me folks . . . Did you learn the Word of God to good avail today from his teaching? Think before answering."

After a pause, one of those who had voiced objections replied, "Well, now that you make us think on it, I did learn a lot from Tiger." Another added, "I did too. I guess we were simply expecting the usual three-point monologue, Jethro."

"Then let me give a monologue on monologues. I once was a lazy orator, trusting in my eloquence. I prepared no one to join in my teaching, no children acted out Bible stories to illustrate my text, I asked no discussion questions, and no one testified of victories won after doing what a prior message had advocated. However, in my old age God woke me up. Through wider participation and keeping discussions moving toward a definite aim, believers in Arenas are growing in Christ more than ever. So now most of my monologues are short, like this one." He sat.

> ## Task 19–d.
> SHARE IMPORTANT PASTORAL DUTIES AMONG ELDERS, AVOIDING A ONE-MAN SHOW

Roger faced the assembly. "More is at stake than our church. Our entire movement needs a *pastor of pastors*. Tiger mobilizes new leaders and that's what we need; this overrides concerns over his petty faults. He knows how to **share important pastoral duties among elders, avoiding a one-man show.** He equips others to share leadership as the apostles did; he works with them behind the scenes, drawing no attention to himself, and helps them serve without competing, and without asking always for pay. Come, Tiger; let the elders confirm this."

I hesitated, but Lucy pushed me, whispering, "Let God do His will." The elders laid hands on me and I received power to shepherd the flock and the movement.

Arturo asked me if I was going to make an acceptance speech, and I laughed. "Sure, in one sentence—let's let Gadget be group coordinator in my place."

Gadget looked shocked. "Better let the congregation vote on that, to see if . . . "

"Nope! If I'm leading, I'll call no congregational meetings until the body has healed. You've seen what folks do: discuss issues with acrimony, vote without caring what the Bible says about a concern, enact rules counter to Jesus' commands, and name persons to a post who have neither gift nor will to fill it."

"Viva!" cried Hilda, clapping. "Now God has given us a real leader!"

"Members will have no voice at all?" Pacho's moustache got a hard twist.

"They will, but like in Acts 15. Members can tell our elders their opinions and then let them decide vital issues; to avoid having the uninformed debate over every detail."

A lot of appointing happened then; I'd given much thought to it and the time was right. We named Gadget to coordinate groups in Bat Haven and named regional directors for pastoral training: Roger for the refugee camp area, Mincho for the mountains to the north, Colombo for Lone Stone, and Arturo as a mentor for all the regional directors. The session ended and Jethro told me, "I need to fulfill my mission in Bat Haven. Let me accompany you and Lucy to your house."

His "mission?" What did he mean? It pained Jethro to walk, so Gadget drove us. After talking with Tino about horses, Jethro told me, "You're taking my place, Tiger. Arturo told me he wants to mentor other trainers under your supervision so you can coach him, help him mobilize them for action, and curb his pedantic bent. I also want you to mentor our regional directors in Arenas. I'm phasing out." He laid hands on me a second time that day. "Lord, empower Tiger to serve as a 'mentor of mentors.'" He also prayed for Lucy and the boys, and his eyes moistened as he told us, "This is my last trip to Bat Haven."

Task 19–e. DELEGATE A TASK TO A PASTORAL TRAINEE AFTER DOING IT TOGETHER TO MODEL IT	A month later the "mentor of mentors" was staring at beans on his plate and Lucy asked me what was wrong with them. I said, "Nothing. I've too much to do: letters, see sick folks, calm a row over the child nutrition project, give premarital advice, help new believers join a cell . . . " I'd discover how crucial

it is to **delegate a task to a pastoral trainee after doing it together to model it.**

"You're falling into the same old pitfall! Just rest today."

"Meet with new pastoral trainees, plan our next united worship, restore believers that Fred McNary discouraged, prepare a message . . . "

"Stop!" Lucy covered her ears.

"Okay. So what should I do first?"

"Eat your beans. They're getting cold."

Mincho arrived and did not dither when Lucy spooned beans onto another plate. She poked me. "At least one guy here is sane enough to take nourishment!"

The big man pushed back the empty plate and sighed. "I need crisis advice, Tiger. The SRE's desperate to get members, and Chuey went with Aaron to the refugees' camp to recruit malcontents. Toño, the camp's pastor, has asked me to defend those who oppose the SRE. There'll be violence if I go, but I have to finish organizing their cooperative. Roger's away so I'll have to go alone. I can rally loyal men and whip those rebels, but now that I'm following Christ I wonder if that's what I ought to do."

"You know my answer to that. Whatever you do, don't go alone. We shouldn't do God's work alone. Jesus usually worked with twelve and never sent a worker out by himself."

"Okay, Tiger, you can accompany me. Can you go today?"

"No, Mincho!" cried Lucy. "My overloaded husband needs rest. Take Roger."

I told him all the chores I had to do and he shook his head. "The answer's obvious: share more pastoral responsibilities with group leaders—a lot more!"

Mincho left, and I finally lifted a forkful of beans, but a bicycle bell rang and I fetched a letter from the post office boy. "It's from Dr. Nuñez," I told Lucy.

She snatched it. "You have enough on your mind." She read it and grumbled, "Crazy idiot! He accuses you of sabotaging his pastorate and lists your failings. The coward! He couldn't discuss it to your face? Greedy, ambitions Amos!"

I grabbed the letter, read it, and shoved my plate away. "My appetite's gone."

"It's all lies, love," Lucy shoved the plate back and pushed a fork into my fist.

"Some of the errors he listed are true, Lu. I've got to straighten things out." I got up, took my hat, and started up the street. "Popcorn," I griped, "your mixed-up master has lots to learn to be a pastor!"

"Stop talking to that mongrel!" Lucy shouted from the door. "Come back and talk to me!" I kept going, to see a family that Nuñez had lured into his clique. They were gone and a wave of discouragement hit me. I started back home feeling trapped in a dark pit and fell into a vinegary mood.

"I don't want to talk about it!" I snapped when Lucy met me at the door.

"Talk about what?"

"Whatever you were going to say!" I sat and took up my fork.

"Look, Papa!" Tino ran in yelling, waving a bow and arrow. "Gadget made it. Come! Let's go kill birds!" I laid the fork down.

"Not birds son." I drew a target, went outside, pinned it to a tree, and we shot arrows. Tino finally hit the bull's-eye and his interest waned.

"Come eat, O great archer," Lucy called, "before I drag you in by the ear!"

She refried the refried beans, I sat, and she stood by me holding a mop like a soldier in *present arms* position. "If you get up again without emptying that plate, I'll swat you!" I laughed, my appetite returned, and I enjoyed the legumes.

"Okay, Lu, I'll delegate more pastoral duties as Mincho said. Many more!"

"Good! Then you have time to take a nice relaxing nap. You need it—you're a grump!" She pulled me by the hand to the bedroom, shoved me in, and closed the door. "Come out after you've had a good rest!"

It was my first siesta in months; I woke refreshed and prayed, "Dear God, help me take Mincho's advice and delegate pastoral duties as Jesus and Paul did."

God helped. A few weeks later, I told Lucy, "I've gotten lazier than an overstuffed bear in winter! It's easy to delegate pastoral work to those I mentor! I show an apprentice once or twice what to do and then let him do it. Folks are more active than ever, and I don't do hardly nuttin'!"

"But you do, love! You give precious time to your family. Blessed be the Lord, who has returned my husband to me and the boys' father to them!"

Blessings sometimes come in bunches. A gracious appearing couple arrived along with Gadget and Evita. "I'm Thomas Rodríguez," the gentleman said, "and this is my wife Sarah. I pastor Holy Trinity Church in the capital." Sarah handed a pen to both our boys, saying, "There's a message on it for you."

"Read it! Read it, Tino!" Davey was having his first literary experience.

Jesus, the Way, the Truth, and the Life.

Thomas turned to me. "We come in quest of wisdom. We visited Sarah's parents in Los Robles and saw Pastor Jacob Morán's rustic map of extension centers, daughter churches, and plans for granddaughter churches. I asked how they extended the work so, and he sent us to you. I want to take the exact same steps."

"Not the exact steps!" Gadget laughed. "Some left scars, Pastor Thomas."

"Oh? Even so, I'll stay in Bat Haven until I discover your secret, Tiger."

"Then you'll stay a long time, because there's no secret—only hard work doing what the Apostle Paul did."

Sarah sank into a chair. "I hope the good apostle will forgive us if we deal with him later; I'm bushed. Please, Mister Cabdriver, take us to a decent hotel."

Evita grimaced. "On this mountain? There's only a shabby inn by the market, with microscopic rooms. It lacks accommodations, but has an adequate supply of bedbugs. I stayed there—once."

Sarah looked alarmed, and Lucy came to her rescue. "We'll be honored to host you. Humble lodgings, but a few less bugs."

> ## Task 19–f.
> ### BECOME A LEADER OF LEADERS BY MOBILIZING AND MENTORING THEM

For several days, I helped Thomas see how to **become a leader of leaders by mobilizing and mentoring them.** I'd gone to bed tired one night when knocking woke me; I pulled on trousers and went to the door. It was Fred!

"I beg a favor, Tiger. Freckles escorted a drunk from a meeting and the guy stabbed him. He bled and needs a transfusion. His blood type's rare, but according to the health center records, you have it."

On our way, we passed horses tied outside a noisy bar. Walking behind one, I jerked Fred in time to avoid lethal hooves as it backed up and kicked wildly. "That beast tried to kill me!" he cried. "It must have noticed I'm a foreigner!"

"No. Horses don't have racial prejudice like humans do, but some get nervous when anyone they're not familiar with comes close behind them."

I watched my blood fill a plastic bag while Fred exhorted me. "Freckles has the academic preparation that you lack; he graduates from seminary this year. For the good of the Lord's work, let him set up proper pastoral training for your village pastors, a small Bible institute. He's bright and a born leader."

"Lead our training? We raise nobody over other leaders that way, no matter how well educated. One becomes a leader of leaders in our movement by mobilizing new workers and serving them as a mentor, as the apostles did."

"That's how you developed your outreach and it's commendable. But face what you have now—a bunch of untrained men pretending to be pastors, lacking adequate preparation. Let Freckles lead the educational side of your movement."

"Our leaders don't climb over the backs of others up an organizational ladder; they extend new rungs below them, training apprentices who train others as they multiply. I'll help Freckles do this if he'll heed the biblical guidelines for . . . "

"Good night, Tiger. Thanks for your red corpuscles."

Coffee aroma woke me, and I found Arturo sipping with Thomas and Sarah. She asked about Arturo's family, and he recounted Olga's tragedy, stopping to wipe a tear. "Pardon my sogginess. I should be over it; it's going on two years."

"That long?" Lucy eyed him. "Pastor, how skinny you are! You need a wife!"

"I'll never remarry; I cannot forget Olga. I'll remain a widower, forever!"

"Oho!" Sarah winked at Lucy. "I've heard that before. We'll see about that!"

"I teach missions in our seminary," Thomas told Arturo. "Movements like yours are going on in many fields; we don't hear about some, as they work secretly. Hostile officials force churches out of their buildings and many have found this liberating; they've multiplied in small groups, bringing thousands to Christ. Some churches choose to keep their buildings and accept government control; this often causes friction between *registered* churches and illegal ones."

"Other factors forced us out of our chapel." Arturo replied. "We enjoy our home groups now; believers edify one another and many become more active."

"Our church is a bit traditional," Thomas said. "We formed Bible study groups, but folks brought into them the same passive laziness that has weakened our members for years. How can I get them to be more active, Tiger?"

<table>
<tr><td>

Task 19–g.

KEEP THE BODY
BALANCED AND
AVOID FOCUSING
TOO EXCLUSIVELY
ON ANY ONE PET
MINISTRY

</td><td>

"Don't merely form study groups; form *task* groups. They still study, but not as passive hearers; you engage them in ministries that fit their gifting. That's the key. We had to analyze our church's agenda to **keep the body balanced and avoid focusing too exclusively on any one pet ministry**."

"Help me analyze our church's agenda, Tiger. I know it needs balancing."

</td></tr>
</table>

"Well, which of your ministries do you consider to be most effective?"

"I'd like to think our greatest strength is Bible exposition. Why?"

"A church's strongest ministry can lure it to neglect other vital tasks."

"Hmmm. Oh, Lord, give me courage to face what may be the root of our ills!"

I told him, "We had to stop emphasizing our teaching ministry so exclusively and let the Holy Spirit harmonize all the vital ministries. Now our members can use the gifts that God had given them."

"Sarah, is it possible that we've taken biblical exposition to an excess?"

"Folks love your preaching; I wouldn't say it's in excess, Thomas."

"You can't take a good ministry to excess," I said, "but doing it well can lure you to neglect other tasks. The key isn't to curtail what you do well, but to develop the other tasks. Here, Thomas." I let him scan our *Vital Ministries Checklist*.

"Wow! This exposes our weak spots!" He showed the list to Sarah and remarked, "We have no daughter churches and seldom evangelize families in their homes. I want to model these tasks for my flock, but I lack experience, Tiger."

"Then come with me. I'm starting a new group in a very poor neighborhood."

<table>
<tr><td>

Task 19–h.

EVANGELIZE THE HEAD
OF A FAMILY FIRST OR AS
SOON AS POSSIBLE

</td><td>

Leave-If-You-Can held a valuable lesson for Thomas: **evangelize the head of a family first or as soon as possible.** A lady was patting corn dough into tortillas in an outdoor kitchen, and I asked, "Is your husband home?"

</td></tr>
</table>

"Berto took the burro to get firewood. He'll be back any minute. Come on in."

"Thank you. We'll return later." We walked on.

"You didn't evangelize her."

"We show respect to the male head of the family when we deal with him first. It usually divides a family if the woman comes to Jesus alone, first. The family normally follows if the man responds first. I've read that church planters fail to sustain a movement if they fail to recognize and work through the family head. Some assume that a society is matriarchal when it only appears that way, superficially. The actual family head isn't always the one who does most of the talking when you visit a home, but the one that brings the family along to follow Christ."

"Look. Berto's coming with the loaded burro. Let's go back."

We prayed for a sick child, and I told the family about the paralytic whose friends lowered him through a roof so Jesus could heal him. I asked Berto, "Can we return and teach the gospel to your friends too?" He agreed and I urged, "Meanwhile, tell your friends about the paralytic. Let's see if you can tell the story back to us now." He repeated it by memory and his family cheered.

"Good!" Thomas exclaimed and he offered Berto a pen with the inscription.

Berto admitted in a shamed voice, "I can't read, sir."

I told him, "I'll see that someone teaches you, if you want to learn."

"Tried once. I couldn't make out the letters; I'm too dumb."

"No you're not! You probably only need reading glasses."

Thomas handed his glasses to Berto, and he tried them, looking at the pen. "Hey! I can make out the differences in the letters now! Even tiny details!"

I told him, "Our church has collected discarded reading glasses for folks like you. Want me to bring some for you to try out?"

"Wonderful! Too good to be true!"

Making our way around mud holes on the way home, Thomas remarked, "I'm surprised that Berto, who does not yet know Christ, would teach the story of the paralytic. Do you think he'll tell it to his friends?"

"Yes. Illiterates enjoy learning worthwhile stuff and share it, and it's better when folks hear the gospel from friends. I'll go with Lucy and help Berto form a seekers' cell with friends and kin; soon it'll be a house church."

"Why didn't you invite Berto's family to a cell group meeting?"

"They'd feel uneasy. We do as Jesus did; let a seeker first assemble his friends, especially if he's head of family. We don't invite them to another cell or the united worship with other cells until they've settled in their 'home church'—the cell that meets in their house or that of a friend. For now, Berto and his family should meet with other illiterate folks."

"You're living in the book of Acts, Tiger! A modern-day apostle! Tell me, what would you do first to spread God's work throughout a city like we live in?"

"A city poses its own challenges. Jethro Mendez can help you better than I can.

He works in both urban and rural areas and is the one who helped us launch our movement. We can drive to Arenas tomorrow and see him."

<table>
<tr><td>

Task 19–i.

FORM CELLS THAT
MULTIPLY RAPIDLY
WITHIN A LARGER
URBAN CHURCH

</td><td>

Gadget drove Thomas, Roger, and me to Jethro's house in Arenas and we found a grieving crowd. A man was saying, "Over fifty years he pastored us. I asked once why he wanted house churches when we already had an active church and a chapel. He pointed out a window and said, 'See those homes? Most of those folks won't come to worship with

</td></tr>
</table>

us, so we take the church to them.' Jethro had us **form cells that multiply rapidly within a larger urban church**."

I started to console Jethro's widow, but she held up a hand to stop me and thrust his skunk-skin backpack into my arms. "He wanted you to have it. Hard use has rubbed off half the fur, so trash it if you want. It's just a symbolic gesture. Too bad the matching hat got lost." I took it and wept like a child.

On the way back to Bat Haven, we stopped to see Ernesto who had pulled the taxi from the river with his oxen on a prior trip, and we'd spent the night again with his daughter Rina's pet pig. Ernesto called in neighbors, and we worshipped. Thomas helped Rina memorize Bible verses and Ernesto bought a New Testament from Roger who always carried a supply of books and studies.

Ernesto's wife begged us to eat with them; she was preparing the food and he was doing chores, so I suggested to Roger, "You studied how Jethro developed urban cells. Can you explain it to Thomas while we're waiting?"

Roger replied, "The guidelines are similar to those we follow in villages, only more sophisticated." Thomas wrote while Roger drew icons and explained *Six Guidelines to Develop Urban Cells.*

"Family: *Work with entire families and within social networks.* Gather friends of new disciples in their homes as a house church or cell, before taking them to public worship. Discern urban networks by seeing how the gospel flows from family to family, and befriend new arrivals. Don't force folks of different backgrounds to worship together until they are ready."

"Crown: *Let cells' primary focus be to obey Jesus.* Make disciples by teaching them from the start to crown Him as King by obeying His commands in love. This creates an active cell, not simply another study group."

"Table: *Develop loving fellowship including Communion.* Sit in a circle so all can converse easily; let adults and children do activities together. Do what small groups can do better; don't imitate the worship of large assemblies. In a tiny group, folks get on each other's nerves in time as rough edges emerge; this is good, as the group can correct them with love."

"Passing a baton: *Develop mentoring in extension chains.* Pass on to new leaders a light baton with only the essentials—New Testament commands and vital truths. Develop separate mentoring chains for different social networks."

"Network: *Develop a cell network.* Let cells serve each other, plan together, and enjoy united worship regularly, in which members share victories and plan mutual projects. One can feel alone in a crowd and the same applies to cells."

"Bunny: *Let cells keep multiplying like rabbits.* Ask the Lord of the Harvest to send workers. Seeing cells multiply, leaders often fear loss of control; allay this fear by letting disciplined mentoring chains serve as the movement's backbone."

Back at our house, Thomas told Sarah, "A pearl has fallen from heaven! I discovered Bat Haven's secret, but not without sadness." We told them about Jethro, and Lucy wept as I had done when she saw the skunk-skin backpack. Thomas showed Sarah his notes. "My seminary students' education is incomplete without this. We're going to see cells multiply!"

Her eyebrows rose. "Sum up those scribbles for me it in one sentence."

"*Take the church to the people!* Jethro Mendez followed Jesus' steps; Tiger and Roger do too. Jesus didn't settle in a training center in Jerusalem; He traveled to its suburbs, other cities, and villages, as did His apostles. Decentralize!"

"An outward outlook!" Sarah took Thomas' hand. "We got *centralized!* Jesus warned not to put our light under a basket, but as soon as our church was born, we set up a fund and built the basket around it!"

Task 19–j.
ARRANGE FOR GODLY LEADERS WHO LACK DEGREES TO SERVE WHERE NEEDED AND WANTED

Thomas told Roger, "You're a scholar, but I notice that you **arrange for godly leaders who lack degrees to serve where needed and wanted.** Educated leaders work with the deprived without friction. That's rare!"

"We shun academics who condescend. I wrestled with that at first; apart from Arturo, I'm the only one in our movement with a degree."

"I know the danger, Roger. Some of my seminary students proudly assume they understand a truth when all they've done is pin a Latin or Greek name on it. I caution them not to turn God's dynamic verbs into abstract nouns."

"Those who only want degrees don't try to understand our way of training leaders. Our movement needs many new leaders, and biblical mentoring equips them not only to shepherd a flock, but to train newer leaders in the process."

"I agree, Roger," Thomas stated. "We surely need both types of training."

Task 19–k.

DETECT FRAUDS
AND LOOK INTO A
BENEVOLENT PROJECT
BEFORE CONTRIBUTING

A telegram arrived and Lucy read it silently. "Guess what!" she said with a playful smirk. "We're rich! It's from a widow in Nigeria who read about our work and wants to donate millions to it!" This and similar issues would clarify the need to **detect frauds and look into a benevolent project before contributing.** Lucy read it aloud, "*A year ago, I turned from Islam to Christianity. I have cancer and am dying, and desire to invest my fortune in the work of my dear Savior. Arrange with your bank for me to share the same account, and I will transfer the funds. Please send your account number right away; my time is short.*" Lucy crumpled it up. "Widow, indeed! It's a hoax. Anyway, we have no bank account; Bat Haven doesn't even have a bank yet."

Thomas said, "I've received those too. Crooks and terrorists empty the bank accounts of gullible fools. Greedy leaders of several churches and Christian organizations have let con men dupe them. Some swindlers are Christians who never got victory over their avarice." We'd soon witness an example of that.

Colombo took a good number of us to Los Robles in *The Caribbean* to celebrate with Jacob's flock; Evita and Lucy rode in front. On the way, Thomas grimaced as we bounced over rocks and I yelled "Slower!"

We stopped to pump up a tire and smelled diesel; Colombo raised the hood, closed it, and crawled underneath. He crawled back out and said, "A rock poked a small hole in the front edge of the tank." He ran the truck's front wheels up

a bank so the inclined tank would not empty completely, hurried to a house nearby,   returned with a sliver of soap, and plugged the hole.

While boarding *The Caribbean* again, two young men with shaggy hair came by and begged for a ride. While driving past a thatched house they cried, "Chao, father-in-law!" A man ran out waving a machete and two teenage girls followed, covering their mouths to muffle giggles, waving behind their father's back.

Colombo stopped on the crest of a steep hill and told us, "Go down on foot. The brakes are too worn to slow the truck with all your weight on it." The group walked down and climbed back on the truck. After fording a river, *The Caribbean* crept up another slope, passing women carrying water jugs on their heads.

In Los Robles, a swarm of small boys came running. "A ride! A ride!" They climbed over the truck like an army of ants, and Colombo granted their plea.

We chatted with Jacob, and I enjoyed listening to sounds that I had grown up with: a hen calling her chicks, the pitty-pat of ground corn being flattened into tortillas, and parrots conversing in the trees. My reverie did not last long. To my surprise, Nuñez pulled up in a van. An assistant set up a TV camera and generator and photographed sick folk by a deserted house. Nuñez' held a microphone, his voice cracking forlornly, "How wretchedly these starving hurricane victims live amid devastation! I know it breaks your heart! We'll feed them with your help. Send your donation now!" He finished and stashed his gear.

"Phony!" Jacob watched the van leave. "No one's starving, by God's grace; the river never reached us. He brought that camera before, but no aid. He's a liar."

I told him, "I'm glad you see through his tear-jerking pleas. Some don't."

"Can a phony like him really be a Christian?" Colombo asked me.

"Yes, we all have faults. He knows Christ, it's just that his flaw is more ambitious and revolting than most." Lucy frowned, started to reply, but said nothing.

We sang our way to the river to baptize new believers; two nephews of Sarah Rodríguez were among them. A trainee of Jacob, assisted by a deaconess, started to baptize a lady when stones came hurtling down from a bank. The lady fell and the water turned red. I rushed in, lifted the limp body, and carried her to the bank.

"My vision is cloudy," she gasped as blood dripped from an ugly contusion.

I waited tensely until she could see okay. Then, furious, I climbed the bank and spied the two shaggy-haired youths that had ridden with us, too far away to pursue. I went back down, and Jacob told me, "Help me carry her home."

"No! Baptize me!" she insisted in a weak voice. "Baptize me!" They did so.

Elders prayed for the sick and for new leaders, and at noon we sat on a log to eat. A bright-eyed girl in a neatly ironed blue dress brought Roger a plate piled high. She sat, purring, "I'm Lorena. I'm nineteen, but look younger. And you?"

"Roger. Ah . . . Roger Diaz, at your service, *Señorita*."

In the morning, Lorena asked Lucy, "Do you need a housemaid?"

"We can't afford help. I'm sorry."

"I can't bear living in this backward place any longer. Please, Mrs. Lucy, I'm nineteen, even though I look younger."

"I know how you feel, Lorena; I felt it too when I was nineteen and single. I almost married the wrong guy just to escape the poverty in our village."

Colombo pumped air again into *The Caribbean's* leaky tire, fidgeted with the coughing motor, and yelled, "All aboard! Time to go." Villagers joined us, some sat on sacks of corn, I squeezed between two pigs, and men clung on the outside.

Lorena was standing by and asked, "When will you return, brother Roger?"

Colombo stopped at the river, to wash his hands. I saw a snout approaching out of nowhere, followed by two bulging eyes. "Gator!" I cried. It left the water and ran amazingly fast after the trucker who leaped like an Olympian onto the truck. The green dragon halted, belching hollow grunts, its hungry eyes on Colombo. I told Lucy, "Glad we left Popcorn home or we'd have a lively scrap!"

Roger wanted to catch it, so I made a loop by tying my belt to a pole and slipped it over the ugly snout. It swatted me with its tail until Roger and I lifted its front legs off the ground so it couldn't thrash so wildly. "Lift it higher!" Roger pled, "It's still able to thrash us with its tail."

"It's hard to lift; without my belt I have to hold my pants up with one hand."

Colombo found rope under the truck seat and secured the monster to the pole. Lucy asked Roger, "What'll you do with that thing? Give your mom a pet?"

We started to load our prize onto the truck, but the ladies screamed so that we took it back to the river, let it go, and resumed our trip home. On the way, Lucy teased Roger, "Who was the adorable maiden in the blue dress?"

"Ah . . . several girls wore blue dresses. It's a favorite color in Los Robles."

"Oh really! You didn't notice the lass who bid you goodbye three times?" Roger turned crimson.

The soap plug held and back home Thomas leaped from the truck, dusted himself off, and ran to find Sarah. He told her how we did evangelism and added, "I was awed too, by how they healed the sick in Jesus' name."

"That's a mercy!" she replied. "There's no doctor in those villages."

"Your two nephews were baptized," he added and they embraced.

CHAPTER 19: CONFIRM THE GRASP AND THE PRACTICE OF LEADERS' TASKS

19–a. Detect and prevent a clique from usurping control of a church.
Find who resolved a debate that was troubling new churches: *It seemed good to the apostles and the elders, with the whole church, to choose men from among them to send to Antioch with Paul and Barnabas . . . and they sent a letter with them . . .* Acts 15:22

19–b. Take the steps that Jesus ordered to deal with offenders. Note them in Matthew 18:15–17: *If your brother sins, go and show him his fault in private . . . If he does not listen to you, take one or two more with you, so that by the mouth of two or three witnesses every fact may be confirmed. If he refuses to listen to them, tell it to the church, and if he refuses to listen even to the church, let him be to you as a Gentile and a tax collector.*

19–c. Discern God's will with certainty. Choose among these guidelines any that you or your trainees should follow more carefully:
[ ]   Ask God's Spirit to guide you, Eph 1:17–19, Jas 1:5.
[ ]   Obey first the things Jesus and His apostles commanded, Matt 28:18–20.
[ ]   Consult with wise believers, 1 Kgs 12; 1 Cor 6:5.
[ ]   Confess to God sins that hinder prayer and fellowship with Him, 1 John 1:9.
[ ]   Glorify Jesus Christ with every decision. 1 Cor 10:31.
[ ]   Do not censure one who errs innocently; instruct him patiently, John 7:24.

19–d. Share important pastoral duties among elders, avoiding a one-man show. Find ways in which Josiah got folks to cooperate in renewal: *The king went up to the house of the Lord and all the men of Judah and all the inhabitants of Jerusalem with him, and the priests and the prophets and all the people, both small and great, and he read in their hearing all the words of the book of the covenant which was found in the house of the Lord. (They) made a covenant before the Lord, to walk after the Lord, and to keep his commandments . . . with all his heart and all his soul, to carry out the words of this covenant that were written in this book. And all the people entered into the covenant.* 2 Kgs 23:1–3

19–e. Delegate a task to a pastoral trainee after doing it together to model it. Find what Moses' father-in-law Jethro told him when he was leading too many by himself: *You will surely wear out, both yourself and these people who are with you . . . Select out of all the people able men who fear God, men of truth, those who hate dishonest gain, and you shall place these over them as leaders of thousands, of hundreds, of fifties, and of tens. Let them judge the people . . . and let it be that every major dispute they will bring to you, but every minor dispute they themselves will judge . . . They will bear the burden with you.* Ex 18:18–22

Note how Jesus sent out workers: *The Lord appointed seventy others and sent them in pairs ahead of Him to every city and place where He Himself was going to come.* Luke 10:1

19–f. Become a leader of leaders by mobilizing and mentoring them. Find what Paul told Titus to do where believers had no leaders yet: *I left you in Crete . . . (to) set in order what remains and appoint elders in every city as I directed you.* Titus 1:5

Notice what the apostles did to become leaders of leaders, without climbing an organizational ladder: *When they had appointed elders for them in every church, having prayed with fasting, they commended them to the Lord . . .* Acts 14:23

19–g. Keep the body balanced and avoid focusing too exclusively on any one pet ministry. Please scan the complete *Vital Ministry Checklist* in Appendix A to see the whole scope of ministries required by Scripture. List any that your church should give more attention and plan with coworkers to develop them. This may be a huge project and take time, but it could revitalize your church.

19–h. Evangelize the head of a family first or as soon as possible. Find whom Cornelius had gathered to hear Peter tell about Jesus: *Cornelius was waiting for them and had called together his relatives and close friends.* Acts 10:24

19–i. Form cells that multiply rapidly within a larger urban church. Identify where congregations served Communion: . . . *Breaking bread from house to house, they were taking their meals together with gladness and sincerity of heart.* Acts 2:46

Roger told Thomas how urban churches can easily multiply cells. Select guidelines that you should demonstrate to trainees:

[ ]   Evangelize a family in its home and establish its cell as their main church before they get used to the mother church being the primary church home.

[ ]   To find folks ready to receive Christ, go to those who are in need, are suffering, or who are desperately seeking change in the life of their family.

[ ]   Adapt the style of worship to a small group in which all take part actively.

[ ]   Make disciples by teaching them to obey Jesus' commands above all.

[ ]   Prepare new leaders on the job the same way that the Apostle Paul did.

[ ]   Commission volunteer workers to start new congregations or cells.

19–j. Arrange for godly leaders who lack degrees to serve where needed and wanted. Note shepherd's qualities to look for in potential pastoral leaders: *An overseer must be above reproach, the husband of one wife, prudent, respectable, hospitable, able to teach, not addicted to wine, not belligerent, but gentle, peaceable, not greedy for money, managing his own household well, keeping his children under control with all dignity, not a new convert, have a good reputation with those outside the church.* 1 Tim 3:1–7

19–k. Detect frauds and look into a benevolent project before contributing. Liars exaggerate needs to wheedle charity from the unwary. Note what God told greedy Gehazi after he lied to General Naaman: *"The leprosy of Naaman shall cling to you . . ." So he went out from his presence a leper as white as snow.* 2 Kgs 5:27

EVALUATE YOUR LEADERSHIP

1=Poor. 2=Planning to improve. 3=Doing well.

1-2-3 Detect and prevent a clique usurping control of a congregation.

1-2-3 Follow the steps that Jesus ordered to deal with offenders.

1-2-3 Discern God's will with certainty.

1-2-3 Share vital pastoral duties among elders, avoiding a one-man show.

1-2-3 Delegate a task to a pastoral trainee after doing it together to model it.

1-2-3 Become a leader of leaders by mobilizing and mentoring them.

1-2-3 Avoid focusing too much on a pet ministry: keep the body balanced.

1-2-3 Evangelize a head of a family first or as soon as possible.

1-2-3 Form the kind of cells that multiply rapidly within larger urban churches.

1-2-3 Urge leaders who lack degrees to serve where needed and wanted.

1-2-3 Avoid frauds; verify a benevolent project before contributing to it.

20.
Concerned Leaders Balance Discipling with Mercy Work

Roger ran his motorcycle through our small yard right up to our door. "Tiger! Tiger! Julio's in prison in the capital, charged with drug dealing!"

Arturo, Pacho, and I went by bus to see Julio. A guard brought the sad-faced young man out and he told us, "A small cargo boat offered me more pay. I filled its hold with sacks of coconuts and we sailed for Florida. A naval patrol boat soon overtook us; officers searched the hold and found contraband in the bottom of the coconut sacks. I'm in big trouble! Are you angry with me, Dad?"

"Oh, son! Don't think such a thing." Pacho and Julio wept.

Thomas and Sarah arrived; she was carrying a bowl. "Chicken and rice for a hungry sailor!" The guard poked around in it with a knife and gave it to Julio.

"Sure better than prison fare!" He cast a peeved glance at the guard.

Arturo convinced the judge that Julio was unaware of the illegal cargo, we returned home. When we filed off the bus, Beady-Eyes greeted me, along with another soldier. "Tiger Garcia, we found a bale of marijuana behind your house."

"What? I don't know anything about that."

"Of course not," he sneered. "Come with us to headquarters."

"Someone put it there to frame me. Who told you to look there?" He pointed his rifle at me and I went with them. I was in the same fix as Julio!

Sergeant Perez was not as friendly as before. "Who buys your marijuana?"

"*My* marijuana? You know I don't . . ."

"Wanda Alvarez saw you carry it from the People's Warehouse."

"Yes, there were many bales there, and if she hadn't been so intent on stirring up trouble, she'd have told you that we dumped them into the river."

"You expect me to buy that? You'll stay here until you tell the truth."

"Did Wanda Alvarez also tell you to look behind our house for marijuana?"

"What if she did? Listen. I sent two soldiers up to Los Vientos yesterday to bring Chuey Ochoa in for questioning and someone shot them. It wasn't Chuey; he's hanging out in the hills to the east, hatching some new scheme. Perhaps you know something that'll help me find the killer."

"The SRE breeds killers; it could have been any number of them."

"The SRE's dwindling, Tiger. Chuey lets other radicals lead it now; its associates are mostly illiterate die-hards, desperate and dangerous as a wounded bear." Perez put me in a cell and let no one near me except to bring food.

On the third day, Beady-Eyes marched me to the courthouse. So much whitewashed had flaked off its walls that it looked uglier than ever. "It matches this whole miserable town," I thought to myself in my bitter mood. Arturo was there, and Mayor Campos informed me, "Tiger Garcia, Mrs. Wanda Alvarez declares that she saw you take bales of marijuana from the People's Warehouse."

"Yes, and I threw it in the river. Someone planted the bale behind our house."

Campos glanced at Arturo who nodded. The mayor then asked him, "Will you answer for Tiger if I free him in your custody?" Arturo nodded again.

I felt relieved as we left until Arturo warned, "Wanda and Simon fear you. And that means you'd better fear them! Who knows what they'll try next!"

"They needn't fear me. I'm not planning to make them trouble."

"You know their schemes—or they think you do. You'd better assure Simon."

"I will, sir. Jesus said to love one's neighbor and I guess that includes the rich; I've begged God to give me love for Simon." I went to the big house; Simon was out so I started to the child nutrition storehouse to look for him.

Drawing near I smelled tobacco smoke and saw Jaime loading sacks onto a wheelbarrow. He pushed it down a path beside the river and I followed quietly. "What ya hauling?" shouted a lady who was scrubbing clothes in the river.

> ## Task 20–a.
> ARRANGE FOR DEACONS TO LEAD OTHERS IN CARING FOR THE NEEDY AND OPPRESSED

"Cement." He stopped at the pigpen and opened a sack with the stub of a worn-out machete. This led to events that would show why compassionate leaders **arrange for deacons to lead others in caring for the needy and oppressed.**

"Feeding the hogs cement?" I asked, approaching. "It'll harden their arteries and folks will chip their teeth chewing pork chops!"

"What're you doing here, preacher? You don't work for Simon no more."

"I'm glad I don't. It turns one into a thief."

"I just carry out orders. I'll put a bullet in you if you tell anyone."

"Well, do it now, because I plan to inform the director of Samaritans in Action, The thought of what Simon has you do with the kid's milk sickens me!"

Like a fool, I had forgotten his gun, but soon I saw that he intended to use it. He raised it, and I pretended to stumble on a sack and fall. Scooping up powdered milk, I hurled it into his eyes; then raising the sack, I slammed it into his face, covering him with white powder, and pounded him with both fists until he fell. I kicked the gun from his hand, grabbed it, and in my rage pointed it at him.

"So you've become a murderer too!" he cried in a choked voice.

Disgusted with myself, I flung the gun into the stinking pigpen. Jaime rose, tore a board from the fence, and swung it. I ducked to avoid its rusty nails but they lacerated my shoulder. He reached for the machete stub, but I threw myself against his legs, knocking him against the fence. It broke and we fell together into the pestilent mire and wrestled in its filth. Fear and pain redoubled my fury, and I grabbed Jaime's hair and slammed his head against a post several times; he squealed just like the pigs. He stopped struggling, my anger subsided, and I backed away. He crawled from the sty groaning and limped away. I found his gun, hurled it into the river, and threw myself in too, to wash off the muck.

My torn shoulder throbbed and I was no longer in a mood to tell Simon how much I loved him, so I went home. The rusty nails had infected my shoulder and I awoke the next day with a fever. Lucy told me to stay in bed, but something drove me to face Simon with the revolting way he was stealing the children's milk. I forced myself to dress even though it hurt and I felt lightheaded. I went to ask Gadget to assemble the elders to deal with Simon, and as we approached the big house, I recounted my brawl with Jaime to them. Pacho groaned. "Will you never stop scrapping? You forget you're a pastor!"

"He pulled a gun on me!"

I saw Wanda watching us from a window, and Simon met us at the door. I accused him, "You had Jaime feed the children's milk to your hogs." He denied it and I said, "I plan to ask Samaritans in Action to end the child nutrition project. Those who eat there are mainly believers' children already well fed, anyway."

"So you've declared war on me, Tiger? You'll regret it, I tell you!"

"Milkman! Milkman!" Neighbor children had been eavesdropping and mocked. "Hook-arm milkman! Fatten your pigs with our milk!" As we left, my fever became worse and I felt weak; Gadget drove me home and I fell on the bed.

Gadget came with Evita to pray for my shoulder, and I told them, "That fiasco with the child nutrition project showed me that we must follow Acts 6 and name deacons to serve the needy, but only believers filled with the Holy Spirit. It can require as much spiritual power to avoid temptations that come from managing material things for the Lord, as to do pastoral work."

"Amen!" Evita agreed. "I think any task done in love is a spiritual task."

Gadget told me, "I'd like to teach poor villagers to grow vegetables. They don't eat right. Half the babies die in some villages—bad food and worse water."

"We'll name you as deacon and deaconess—the Holy Spirit's hands that serve the needy. Evita, you can train health promoters to teach parents nutrition, gardening, and childcare. Gadget, you can organize villagers to dig wells to get clean water and improve agriculture. Get Mincho to help you, and you can help him form co-ops. Work with Roger too; he trains pastors."

"Wonderful!" Evita's mind was already busy making plans to do even more. "We'll also teach young folks vocations and help illiterate adults learn to read."

The newly commissioned couple began training deacons in the new churches. After a few weeks, Gadget, Evita, and Roger came to give their progress report, and Evita was ecstatic. "Six villages have improved sanitation, got clean water, and no more children have died in infancy from diarrhea. At first we gave things to the poor, but saw them come to depend on it, losing their self-respect and initiative, so from now on we'll give money or goods only in emergencies such as *the Good Samaritan* faced. Oh, and Roger has an exciting report too."

He blushed. "Um . . . I'm getting married!"

"Wonderful!" Lucy clapped her hands. "Who's the lucky girl?"

"A believer in Los Robles. She helps me train the deaconesses and . . . "

"Lorena! The nineteen-year-old who looks younger! Right? I'm so happy for you, Roger! A thousand blessings! She's a gem! Cute too!"

After the exuberant workers left, two barefoot men—new church members—arrived at our door; one was Aaron, the bitter SRE associate. I had rejoiced when he told me he was going to follow Christ, but my joy ended when I realized why. He told me, "God says you're to give to the poor, and we're the poorest in town."

"Go talk with our deacons, Aaron. They deal with such needs."

"We talked with Gadget, but he hasn't got no compassion. You have the last word in the church. Recognize our need, or we'll take measures. You'll see."

"You don't move me with threats, Aaron. Enjoy taking your 'measures.'"

"The SRE will help us if you don't. At least they care about the poor."

Roger told Aaron's companion, "You've been avoiding work, friend, living off handouts from Christians. The Apostle Paul told the Thessalonians, *If anyone does not want to work, neither should he eat.*" They left and Roger asked me, "Many are truly needy and we can't help them all. Whom do we help first?"

"Paul told the Galatians to 'do good to all people, and especially to those who are of the household of the faith.'"

Tino came in laughing. "Papa, those two men who left with their barefeet, had their shoes hidden in bushes!"

Roger shook his head. "They have no conscience, Tiger!"

"They do, but it's twisted. Some who've been raised in poverty never recover from the scars it leaves in their souls, and it actually bothers their conscience if they don't steal from people better off when they have the chance."

Soon after that, Roger informed me, "Aaron joined Lorenzo's anti-church and is promoting the agenda of the SRE even more recklessly than Chuey did. Somehow he associates Jesus Christ with Karl Marx."

"Why not? They were both Jews, both had a cause, and both transformed society! I'm glad we got rid of those guys. Let Lorenzo have them!"

In the dead of night, Lucy shook me awake. "I've got a bad feeling."

"Something you ate?"

"That malicious mountain. I dreamt it blew up; it separated us and . . . Promise me you'll never leave me."

"I already did, Lu, when we married. Go back to sleep."

"Again. Promise me again." I promised again.

Lucy was washing breakfast dishes when Roger and Lorena came; it was a joy to see the cheery couple and hear their happy report. He told us, "We just came from Los Robles; Gadget and Evita are teaching agriculture and other vocations, and it's made a huge difference in folks' lives. We wish you could see it!"

Lorena added, "Now we villagers have hope of a better future and young people don't feel as desperately pessimistic." The couple looked at each other, he blushed and she smiled, saying, "We want you to help us plan our wedding."

"And tell us how to have a happy marriage like you two have," Roger added.

I replied, "Well, if you want to get any sleep, don't let Lorena dream about mountains!" Lucy gave me a teasing swat with the dishtowel. Roger and I suggested some wedding plans, but Lorena and Lucy laughed at our "typical male stupidity." So the stupid males stepped aside to let the ladies plan.

Task 20–b.
AVOID MAKING CHANGES MERELY TO PLEASE INSISTENT PEOPLE

When the ladies let us join them again, I glanced out the window. "Oh! This might be interesting. See those two guys? They've been coming by bus from Arenas to attend our church; they're quite involved in it and also a bit critical." What followed would show why a steady leader will **avoid making changes merely to please insistent people.**

"Why do people come so far?" asked Lorena.

"Some seek to serve the Lord more effectively, but others are religious 'frogs' that hop from church to church seeking a thrill. When the Lord's work flourishes, it attracts the curious. Quite a few people come from other towns now; some invade a congregation simply to get it to conform to their ideas; the first time those two frogs came they told me it was because they didn't agree with Jethro's church." I opened the door and said, "Hop in!"

Lorena giggled, and Lucy cast me a scolding glance. "Have a seat," I bid the pair, and the ladies retreated into the kitchen.

One, a round-faced fellow, cleared his throat loudly. Puffy cheeks accentuated a large mouth as he spoke in an officious tone. "Mr. Garcia, we have been praying for you in sister Wanda's house and have come to help you improve the way you perform your pastoral office." I told him I surely needed prayer and waited.

He glanced at Roger. "It might be easier if we talked privately."

"Say whatever you have to say before Roger. We work together."

"Well then . . . We have four proposals so your church can become normal." He unfolded a paper and glanced at it. "First, work on your rustic speech, Mr. Garcia. Pardon our frankness, but your mountaineer accent is crude. Meanwhile, let others preach so learned people can respect the teaching; a church cannot grow beyond the level of its leader. I'm ready to take the pulpit any time."

"I'm sure you are."

"Secondly, you must structure sermons properly. You ask too many questions and let anyone voice opinions. You even let new believers tell what's happened in their house groups; we who are mature learn little of value from them. You could learn from teachers with experience in mature churches."

"I'm sure I could. Go on."

My reformer cleared his throat again, and I heard Tino in the kitchen. "Mama, he croaks like a bullfrog!" Roger turned his head to hide his amusement.

"Thirdly, you baptize people before they fully demonstrate a holy life, and let them gather friends in their houses while they're still ignorant novices. Even children take part in the teaching when they should keep still and listen. Your cell groups divide a church body, impairing its unity." He waited for a response.

"And the fourth item?"

"You might balk at this since you have so many followers, but you really should take them back into the original church that Dr. Amos Nuñez leads. We've consulted with him and you could serve as co-pastor under his direction. His group maintains proper order and occupies the chapel that would give you a visible presence in the community so your church can prosper. With minor alterations you could improve the acoustics to enhance a worship team's music."

Frog number-two leaned forward, pulling his chair toward me. "Now, Mr. Garcia, we'd like to know if you'll comply."

"I appreciate your desire to help; however, except for speaking like a mountain moron, what you deplore about my work is New Testament practice. If you dislike it, you're free to hop back to churches that do things better. Good day."

"Well!" croaked the wide-mouthed frog. "So that's how it is! Please excuse us, sir. We'll make our departure—and I do mean *departure*!" They hurried out.

The ladies came back from the kitchen, and Tino began croaking loudly. Lucy told me, "They sure won't attend our church now! Weren't you a bit severe?"

"Better to confront a foe in open battle than to dodge a conflict only to let it evolve into a major, painful war later on."

Roger commented, "Paul was severe when he wrote Galatians. Legalistic 'frogs' from Jerusalem had imposed traditions that annulled God's grace. Those two that just left do the same—pity any flock they infiltrate!"

Roger and Lorena left, and I sighed. "I'm bushed, Lu. I'm taking a vacation, a week without pastoral work!" I flopped down on our sofa and closed my eyes.

"Superb! When you've rested, you can fix the gate. It's been more than . . . " I was snoring before she finished.

A wire arrived with five words and our vacation hopes, like the gate, were left shattered: *YOUR PRESENCE NEEDED URGENT JACOB.* Roger took me on his motorcycle to Los Robles; we found Jacob and he moaned, "I was abed with fever, when preachy visitors came from some church with a long list of things 'real Christians' don't do. Half of our flock's tried to be 'real Christians' and got confuddled. Then your constituents came and confuddled the other half."

Task 20–c.
KEEP BYLAWS GENERAL AND ALLOW FREEDOM TO ADAPT TO LOCAL CONDITIONS

More frogs! "What did you mean, 'constituents'?" I'd soon see why to **keep bylaws general and allow freedom to adapt to local conditions**.

Jacob handed us a copy of our church's outdated constitution and bylaws. "My son was in town; Wanda Alvarez gave him this and said we're to heed it. It says to name six trustees to watch over the physical plant and maintain the grounds, but we don't know what all that means. It also says to name six elders to serve three years, but we have more than that and they're unhappy now; they don't want to stop shepherding their small groups after three years are up."

I groaned. "It's foolish to use bylaws from a church in a different setting."

Roger added, "Those rules were written years ago for a rigid, traditional church. Since God has renewed it, we cannot follow them to the letter. Many of those rules are not from Scripture and are too inflexible for a church body that's filled with the Spirit and obeying Jesus' commands before men's."

"I know, but I was away teaching new village pastors when it happened. I'm not the leader no more; these constituents exclude me. Porfilio's our leader—that young fellow coming yonder combing his hair." I greeted Porfilio and asked how his work was going.

"I don't work now. I preach."

"What do you do for the flock besides preaching, brother Porfilio?"

"I am pastor of the church."

"But what do you do as pastor?"

"I preach and people have to do what I say. Right?"

"Jesus taught that to lead people in His kingdom we must be their servants."

"People don't obey unless someone commands with firm authority, Tiger."

"There's a right and wrong way to be firm. Gideon let soldiers who feared return home without shaming them and gave inspiration to those who stayed. And Jesus didn't decree petty rules and enforce them with the sword."

"Lunch!" Jacob's wife Susan called. "The corn ran out, but there's yucca."

We ate yucca for two days and advised Porfilio; he tore up the obsolete bylaws, asked Jacob to pastor again, and began serving happily as Jacob's assistant.

Fright shone from Lucy's eyes when I arrived home that night. She showed me a newspaper headline: "*Pistol Packing Pastor Incites Violence.*" "The media is blitzing again, Tiger, more ruthless than ever! Get away while it's dark. Soldiers came twice looking for you, and a federal agent questioned me."

I read, "*Terrorist Tiger Garcia leads rebels in a conspiracy against the homeland. Is it a coincidence that Garcia 'happened' to be in the same area at the time of Olga Gomez' murder and of several major crimes and homicides that federal detectives have failed to solve in that part of the country?*"

"I'll hide in a village and send word. Pack provisions and I'll get Bullet."

"I already got him; he's in back. This bag has tortillas. I wrapped matches to keep them dry, in case you camp out." I hugged Lucy and the boys.

I mounted Bullet in the dark and spurred him when a light blinded me and Bullet reared. Soldiers had formed a perimeter, rifles pointing at my heart. Beady-Eyes jerked me off and they pinned my arms. Popcorn attacked, diverting them, and I pulled loose, kicked the light away and fled in the shadows amid a volley of shots. I scrambled up a hill to the west, tripping in the dark. I stopped to rest, but saw lights coming; I'd left footprints in the wet soil! I ran, taking care not to leave tracks, until I was sure I'd left the soldier far behind; then I fell, exhausted.

The late night air chilled me as clouds covered the quarter moon and my nemesis, the darkness, swallowed me up as hungrily as the giant fish did Jonah. I tried to sleep, but shivered too much; the dog and I huddled to keep warm. When dawn rolled back the night's shroud, my heart sank; I had no idea which way to go! Gloomy gray clouds blanketed the sky, and I wandered around in the woods, but cliffs or thorn bushes blocked my way in every direction. Lost! I had never been in these hills, even though they were not far from home.

Two more cold nights, no food, and thrashing through tangled vines left me too weak to explore further. I found yellow berries, but they were bitter and burned in my stomach. Then the clouds cleared and Popcorn caught a rabbit. I lit a fire, but wet sticks sent up white smoke and I feared the soldiers would see it; so to Popcorn's delight we dined on raw rabbit. I felt better and told him, "Just think, Paris cafés probably serve raw hare, but make it tasty by giving it an exotic name!" Guided by the sun, I plodded northward, hoping to reach Los Vientos.

I came to a footpath along a ridge with recent hoof prints heading south and followed it north. From a ridge, I saw a thatched house in a clearing and hurried down. A scrawny dog heralded our arrival with vigor, but Popcorn replied with equal verve and it hid. A man stepped out with a rifle, and a woman in the doorway warned, "Look out! He's a savage—unkempt beard, clothes all ragged."

"He's bad all right; them soldiers warned me. He's the one they was hunting."

"I'm not a very dangerous savage, ma'am. And, sir, it's true I'm avoiding the soldiers, but it's because of false accusations. I'm an Evangelical pastor."

"Tiger Garcia! Yes! It's you! I've been to your meetings. Come in! Come in!"

His wife warmed beans, and I wolfed them down while Popcorn worked on a bone from a haunch of venison. He made a truce with the resident dog and they kept watch while I slept in a hammock. Hearing the dogs growl, the man hurried outside and soon rushed back in. "Two soldiers comin' down the path! Still a ways up, but they'll see you if you leave the house."

"Wear these!" His wife handed me a dress and bonnet. "Roll up your trouser legs. Leave the clothes behind that tall pine yonder."

Wearing the garb, I left taking short steps and plucked flowers. I stowed the garments by the pine and crept through thorn bushes that would deter the soldiers. I headed north for hours and a drizzle chilled me; I looked up and inky clouds frowned back at me. Feeling feverish, I sank to my knees. "Dear God, lead me to shelter or I'm finished!" I dozed, using Popcorn as a pillow; cold woke me, and the slender moon lit up a vague deer path descending to the east. I stumbled downward in a stupor, leaning on a stick. I spotted lights and a dim reflection from the remaining tower of the church of Saint Muñoz. It was risky to enter town, but sure death to stay in the cold with my fever; I staggered on.

A soldier was watching our house. I tried to awaken Gadget, but his dog barked and the soldier came running. I slipped into the bushes and whistled for Bullet; it took all my strength to climb up on a stump and mount him. He galloped up the street and the soldier shouted, firing twice. I raced through the empty town center and headed up to Los Vientos. The wind sweeping the mesa on that cruel night felt icy. I no longer had the strength to stay mounted riding bareback, and fell. I could not remount, so I shuffled on to Mincho's house leaning on Bullet, clutching his mane. I called, but Mincho did not answer. My voice sounded weird; I was shivering so much that it warbled. I pounded on the door with a stone, and a light came on; Mincho opened the door, blinking.

"Tiger? You're shaking!" I had fallen to my knees, and he lifted me, carried me inside, laid me on a cot, and lit a fire. "Oh, you're in for it, Tiger! The papers accuse you of vile crimes, even of murdering Olga Gomez!"

The warm fire put me to sleep. I awoke late the next day, and Lucy was there; Mincho had sent for her. "I left the boys with Evita," she told me. "When I first saw you here so pale and emaciated, I thought it was someone else!" Chicken broth simmered on the earthen stove and Lucy brought me bowl after bowl.

Task 20–d.

TAKE TIME OFF AS JESUS DID, LIVE CALMLY, AND LEAVE WORRIES TO GOD

When my strength returned I confessed to Lucy, "I've been too stupid to take a non-working vacation, but painful events are reminding me to **take time off as Jesus did, live calmly, and leave worries to God.**

"You call this ordeal a vacation?"

"At least it let me reflect. We'll take real vacations from now on, I promise."

"I'll make sure you keep that promise, love. Mincho, you're a witness."

Lucy and I slipped back into town in the dark, and again I spied a soldier watching our house. We waited in bushes until dawn and I told Lucy, "I'll stay in Gadget's house, but to cross the lane to it, I'd be in view of the soldier. Go distract him. Wait! First, go tell Gadget to hold his yappy dog's mouth closed."

After alerting Gadget, Lucy walked down the street, passed the soldier, and then turned to greet him. "Hi! Hey, I have a question. Will the army let me enlist? How do I do it? Do you let women shoot guns? I'd love to gun down wicked criminals like Tiger Garcia. Is this really his house?"

"Um . . . You'd better talk with Sergeant Perez, ma'am, up at headquarters."

Evita closed the shutters. "Listen, Tiger. Mouse brought ore samples, and I sent them to the university to analyze. Federal investigators came from the Ministry of Natural Resources and interrogated half the town. They wouldn't tell me the ore content. One yakked on a shortwave radio each time we said anything, but he'd step away so we couldn't hear. They tested all the miners' blood and found traces of radioactivity in some, not enough to be lethal. What do we do now?"

"Uranium is contaminating Bat Haven—not just its radioactivity, but the greed and violence it provokes. You do what you want; I've quit fretting about things I can't change. God gave me a harsh lesson about that. I'll lead His people more calmly now, without letting problems drive me so, and take more time off. I now know what Peter meant when he warned elders not to shepherd the Lord's people out of compulsion. I'm going to let others do a lot more of the pastoral work."

"Gadget's been pastoring, and even Pacho remarked how well he's done!"

The soldiers discontinued their surveillance. I ventured out and repaired the gate that Gadget's taxi had bashed nearly two years before. I also bought Lucy her stove that many years later she'd still call, "my *new* stove." She was ecstatic but not for long; I told her, "I can't keep hiding like a scared rabbit in a hole. I'm turning myself in. From now on, I'll live—or die—by faith."

"No!" Lucy cried. "No! No! Tino, run and bring Gadget!"

Gadget arrived out of breath and I told him, "You're our town's police officer, and I'm wanted by the authorities. So here I am—arrest me."

"Am I Judas Iscariot? Your fever warped your brain! You won't get no fair trial, Tiger. Simon will bribe the judge with Panther's money."

"So keep praying." I hugged everyone and headed up the lane toward Sergeant Perez' headquarters.

CHAPTER 20: CONFIRM THE GRASP AND THE PRACTICE OF LEADERS' TASKS

20–a. Arrange for deacons to lead others in caring for the needy and oppressed. Find what the Jerusalem church did when widows were neglected: *The twelve summoned the congregation of the disciples and said, "It is not desirable for us to neglect the word of God in order to serve tables. Therefore, brethren, select from among you seven men of good reputation, full of the Spirit and of wisdom, whom we may put in charge of this task. But we will devote ourselves to prayer and to the ministry of the Word."* Acts 6:1–34

20–b. Avoid making changes merely to please insistent people. See what legalistic Jews did to Galatians believers: *I do not nullify the grace of God, for if righteousness comes through the Law, then Christ died needlessly. You foolish Galatians, who has bewitched you, before whose eyes Jesus Christ was publicly portrayed as crucified?* Gal 2:21–3:1

20–c. Keep bylaws general and allow freedom to adapt to local conditions. The Los Robles flock foolishly heeded rules written for another congregation. Notice why church bylaws should avoid specifying minute details about God's work: *The Lord is the Spirit and where the Spirit of the Lord is, there is liberty.* 2 Cor 3:17

20–d. Take time off as Jesus did, live calmly, and leave worries to God. Note what Jesus told tired followers: *Come to Me, all who are weary and heavy-laden and I will give you rest. Take My yoke upon you and learn from Me, for I am gentle and humble in heart and you will find rest for your souls. For My yoke is easy and My burden is light.* Matt 11:28–30

As a man, Jesus needed rest. Find what He told tired followers after hearing their reports: *"Come away by yourselves to a secluded place and rest a while." For there were many people coming and going and they did not even have time to eat.* Mark 6:30–32

EVALUATE YOUR LEADERSHIP

1=Poor. 2=Planning to improve. 3=Doing well.

1-2-3 Train deacons to lead others in caring for the needy and oppressed.

1-2-3 Avoid making changes merely to please insistent people.

1-2-3 Keep bylaws general and allow freedom to adapt to local conditions.

1-2-3 Take time off as Jesus did, live calmly, and leave worries to God.

21.
False Religion and the Occult Open Hell's Broad Door

Sergeant Perez was writing when I arrived and I stood waiting. He glanced up, dropped his pen, and reached for his sidearm. "Garcia!" Over the next few days, I'd learn to **respond by faith to interrogation by hostile authorities.**

"At your service, Sarge." I forced a smile.

Leaning back, he slid the gun into its holster. "I've hunted for you all over."

"That's why I came. I've missed your congenial company."

"The feds accuse you of criminal treason! You're their *Most Wanted*."

"They're supposed to protect the innocent, not make phony charges."

"The papers call you a ruthless assassin, worse than the infamous Chorcho."

I laughed at that and for some reason could not stop laughing.

A bright light stayed on all night in my cell in federal prison in the capital, and it was hard to sleep; guards would not let me cover my head. Each morning they took me to interrogation, and on the fourth day, Arturo was there with a different interrogator—a grim, serious type. "How's my family, Arturo?" I asked.

"Fine, and the churches too. Simon and Wanda are too busy spending Panther's money on a new house next to their old one; it'll be a huge, showy palace."

The examiner motioned to a chair and asked the same questions as others had. I groaned and said, "This is tedious, sir. Do you enjoy comparing my answers?"

"Relax, Tiger," Arturo scolded. "Just tell the gentleman the truth."

"Explain your political ideology. This time don't leave out details."

"I've said a dozen times, sir, I'm not political. I don't trust politicians."

"Every thinking adult has some concept of politics. Answer my question."

"Yes, sir. As I've said, social justice will come only through Jesus Christ."

An hour passed this way and the official gathered his papers. "Mr. Garcia, you're a bit feisty, but I'll recommend your acquittal." He stood.

My heart leaped. "Well, thank you, sir, for opening my cage!"

He stopped at the door to face me. "On one condition. You'll join the SRE, act like you agree with them, and find the source of their arms." He turned to go.

My heart fell. "Wait! Sir, I'm no spy. I'm a pastor and serve Jesus without pretense. I can't deceive the SRE; I promised an SRE leader before God never to expose their activities so he'd let me evangelize them. I cannot violate my word."

"Which leader?"

"It was a sacred vow, sir, made it before the Most Holy God." I recalled Jesus' promise that the Holy Spirit would tell us when the time came what to say to hostile authorities. Well, the time had come, and I feared if I said what they wanted to hear, that they'd imprison Mincho unjustly. I prayed for faith and courage.

"Do as I say or remain prisoner; that's my condition. It's your choice."

My choice? His brutal coercion to get me to violate a promise to God reminded me of the thousands that choose prison every year rather than betray their Lord. I answered, "Very well. I choose to remain prisoner."

A federal court held a hearing to sentence me, and the room filled with lawyers, reporters, and officials. Then, to my astonishment, the last person on earth that I expected walked in—Mincho!

A white-haired judge entered exuding such officialdom that it panicked me, and Arturo gripped my arm. "Relax. And for heaven's sake, don't get feisty!"

An accusing prosecutor described my crimes in such *legalese* that I could only guess at the meaning. Mincho then asked permission to speak; the judge said, "You may. Start by giving your name."

"I am Benjamin Medina. I used to be a leader in the SRE. My job was to form unions, plan strikes, and, when necessary, apply a little muscle."

The room exploded with exclamations and the stony-faced judge rapped for silence. "Proceed, Mr. Medina."

"I now follow Jesus Christ because of the testimony of the accused. Tiger Garcia taught me by his example to fight social injustice with love. I have discovered that a follower of our Lord Jesus Christ achieves reform in a more permanent and thorough way than political revolutionaries do."

"Now the sermon!" someone muttered, followed by stifled chortles, and the glowering judge stared the offenders into silence.

An hour later, the prosecutor ran out of questions for Mincho. With no change of expression, the judge stated, "Mr. Medina, I admire your courage and integrity." He then told me to stand. "Mr. Garcia, I exonerate you. You are free to go."

Did I hear right? Outside, Arturo hugged Mincho and me. "I was amazed they didn't sentence you both! You impressed the old judge with your valor, Mincho."

"Well, I couldn't guess that by reading his face. He scowled at every word!"

Arturo said, "A government lawyer told me this morning that they plan to enact laws restricting what 'registered' churches can teach. I suspect Amos Nuñez will comply, but no leader with convictions will. The biblical role of government is to protect and maintain justice; beyond that, it becomes intrusive."

"Bad news from Bat Haven," Mincho told us. "The SRE is forcing coffee growers to sell to them at half the going rate. A violent clash is brewing and blood will flow. Dark, evil hatred is suffocating Bat Haven!"

> **Task 21–b.**
>
> AVERT DIVISION BY HELPING FEUDING BELIEVERS AFFIRM A PEACE ACCORD.

Riding back in an ancient, dusty bus, we discussed how to combat that hatred, and Mincho urged, "How about a *peace pact* that some on both sides will agree to? **Avert division by helping feuding believers affirm a peace accord.** Return good for evil in a 'war of love.' How does that sound, Arturo?"

"Fine. Point a gun and say, 'Agree to love me or I'll kill you!'"

"Not quite," Mincho said. "As *light of the world* we're to set the example; the accord could be to *forgive grievances, stop attacking,* and *seek our rivals' good.*"

Arturo thought a while, and answered, "A big pill to swallow, but I can't think of a better plan."

A few miles from Bat Haven, the bus braked abruptly. "Road block!" groaned Mincho. "Things are heating up."

Soldiers boarded and checked passengers' identification; one looked at my ID card and stared at me. "Here he is, Corporal!"

Beady-Eyes, who had almost killed me by tightening an inner tube over my face the day of the picnic by the river, jabbed his rifle barrel painfully into my ribs. "You're under arrest, Garcia, for the murder of Olga Gomez. Clasp your hands behind your head." He jabbed me again. "Get up."

"You enjoy making people suffer, don't you?"

"Congratulations on escaping from prison. Off the bus."

"He didn't escape," Arturo asserted, "and he didn't kill my wife; I was with him when that happened. Look. Here's his discharge signed by the judge."

Beady-Eyes pushed it away. "Show it to higher authorities. My orders are to detain this assassin; we heard he was on the loose again."

Arturo told Mincho, "I'll take this to Sergeant Perez; at least he knows how to read! Stay here with Tiger—no telling what these clowns intend to do with him."

The soldiers forced two tribal peasants off the bus who had no ID cards; Beady-Eyes took their money, let them back on, and the bus left. He had me kneel, hands clasped on my head, as he sat with his rifle aimed at my gut. At times, he raised it to point between my eyes. I dreaded to think what he'd have done had Mincho not stayed. At sunset, an army truck came and the driver told the soldiers, "That's it for today." He jerked a thumb toward me. "Let him go."

I begged them to let us ride in the truck, but they left without us, and it was well after dark when we trudged into town. Passing the square, I saw Beady-Eyes guarding Simon's house, and remarked to Mincho, "How kind of the army to relieve me of my night duty! I hope Corporal Beady-Eyes enjoys the bats."

Back home, after a long, tearful hug, Lucy exclaimed, "You're shaggier than a yak! Get to the barber shop early tomorrow before people see you!"

Pacho was clipping me when Colombo stopped *The Caribbean* outside, heavily loaded; Mincho and Gadget followed him in and he told me, "Chuey said he'll slit my throat if I don't take this coffee to the SRE warehouse, but they pay only half the market price. The growers are waiting with guns and machetes to unload it at the market, and SRE goons are waiting there to stop them. Do I give in and take it to the SRE, or risk taking it to the market?"

"Look across the street!" I said. "SRE men are watching to see what you do."

"Three, two, one, *open fire!*" Mincho started toward the market. "The war of love has begun! Let's go calm the growers and the SRE gang. Leave the truck."

"Wait, Tiger!" protested Pacho. "I haven't finished your hair!"

Mincho's grim expression reflected bitter anger, and I remarked, "You hardly seem in a mood for a war of *love*."

"I'm not; I'm ready to crush skulls. Someone burned my house down. When I got home last night, it was incinerated. Clothes, books, my parents' photos!"

"No! That's terrible! Who did it?"

"Who knows? I now have as many enemies on the left as on the right. This war of love is taking more effort than I'd expected, Tiger."

"Well, you can stay in our house as long as you need to."

"A curious thing," the giant remarked. "Chuey bought me a taco and soda, and told me he'd cooperate to stop the violence—not that I believe him."

The growers had gathered on a lane behind the market where trucks unloaded, and I told them, "Gentlemen, I'm angry too, but the town will think you're as lawless as the SRE if you fight this way." I waited for them to stop jeering. "Now listen. We'll ask soldiers to protect us while we unload the coffee. Wait here, keep calm, and I'll go talk with Sergeant Perez."

"We'll wait," replied a grower, "but this is just a temporary fix, Preacher. Those bandits will not stop their extortions. A showdown will come when there aren't no soldiers to stop it, and we'll wipe out them thugs!"

"Don't be so bloodthirsty!" scolded Gadget. "Let us proceed legally against the SRE. Give me time to expose their crimes with conclusive evidence."

"Time? Ha!" protested the grower. "Legal action takes too long. We got to sell our coffee—we need the cash now, Gadget."

"Okay then, we won't waste no time. We'll go to the People's Warehouse, and since Mincho's no longer curbing their crooked antics, I think we will find the evidence we need to arrest Chuey and his aides. We'll be back with soldiers." I noticed movement in bushes across the street and walked over; Aaron and other SRE thugs slipped out of sight into underbrush near the river.

Colombo, Mincho, and I went with Gadget to the People's Warehouse; we saw no one and Colombo advised, "They're here all right, waiting for my coffee. Come, there's a loading dock around back; keep out of sight in the bushes."

We went and I could not believe what I saw. "Look! The chief executioners of both extremes, right and left, are working in harmony!" Jaime Ordoñez and Chuey Ochoa were packing between them a heavy crate from a truck.

"Rifles!" growled Mincho. "I've handled those crates before." We watched a while. "Look! Now they're loading bales and covering them with sacks of grain. Swapping rifles for marijuana! Undeniable proof! Bring the soldiers, Gadget."

Soldiers came with Beady-Eyes who looked sleepy. He shouted at Jaime and Chuey, "Freeze! Raise your hands." The two men dashed for the trees and Beady-Eyes fired. Jaime fell, rose, and ran holding an arm. Both escaped.

We all climbed on the sides of *The Caribbean* and rode to the market. Seeing the soldiers, the SRE goons fled. We unloaded the truck and the soldiers left too. A buyer weighed the coffee, and the growers came out with the cash to face a larger SRE mob across the street—and no soldiers! The growers grabbed their weapons, and I heard rifle bolts slide into firing position. At least three rifles were trained on me; I tasted raw fear and the scene froze.

Mincho stepped into the street and stood between both sides, rifles pointing at him from both. "Comrades and coffee growers, you're going to ratify a peace pact, right now, before shedding blood in a battle that we'd all lose. We'll all promise before God to forgive past offences without further violence and be reconciled with those whom we've hated. Save your own lives and each others'."

"This won't work, Mincho." Gadget advised. "Too much resentment!"

Aaron and other SRE fighters hurled angry threats at the big man who pled, "Armed combat is futile and foolish, men. Think! Consider the peace accord."

After parleying with Mincho, a few on both sides agreed on the peace pact; he asked God's help to forgive, stop fighting, and treat former foes as friends. He then repeated each promise and they said "Amen" to affirm it before God.

Suddenly Mincho sat in the dusty street, breathing hard. "I'm weak, Tiger. Real weak!" Men on both sides who had not accepted the accord stood looking at each other, uncertain of what to do, and then started slipping away. Colombo rushed Mincho to the health center in *The Caribbean*; the nurse on duty found nothing wrong, so we took him to our house to rest.

When I got home, Lucy cried, "Your hair! One side is long, the other short! Was Pacho drunk? Go let him finish his job. Wear your hat!" She laughed until I told her why Pacho's job had been interrupted and that Mincho was ill.

I went back to Pacho's shop; when I returned with my head symmetrical, Mincho was sleeping and Martha was telling Lucy between sobs, "The mine quit blasting for a few weeks, and Mouse went to the hills with the mule to fast and be with God. I'm worried, it's been four days."

"Did he take canned food?" I asked. Martha nodded and I assured her, "He'll be back when it runs out."

Mincho still felt weak and ate nothing that evening. He read the Bible and told us, "Listen to Psalm 112:4: *Light arises in the darkness for the upright; he is gracious and compassionate and righteous.* Oh, I hope the Lord can say I've been righteous and compassionate to the poor when I stand before Him in glory!"

Task 21–c. DETECT AND RESIST DEMONIC FORCES OF DARKNESS	Only the full moon witnessed what happened later that night. It silhouetted a short, bent woman smoking a pipe and trudging barefoot downhill along a mountain ridge. A knotty hand clutched a cord, leading a cat; the other hand gripped a doll made of dirty rags, vulture feathers, snakeskin, and hair made of cord except for a few long, black strands of real hair.

Thus began an episode that would force us to **detect and resist demonic forces of darkness**.

Saint Muñoz' bell clanged twelve times in town and the hag stopped, gazed at the moon with cloudy eyes, and turned her bent back to it. She removed her pipe, lifted the doll toward the darkness, and repeated an incantation six times in a tribal tongue. She resumed her arduous journey and arrived in Mudhole in the dead of night. The witch found a gate with an X marked on it, knelt beside the house, and dug with a knife. Stretching out the cat's neck, she slit its throat, and bathed the black-haired doll in its blood. She buried the gory doll, rose, extended gnarled hands toward the darkness, and repeated in a hushed voice the incantation that she had uttered at midnight. She then hobbled to the town square and sat on a bench, lit her pipe with bloodstained hands, and faced Wanda Alvarez' house, waiting.

"Are you awake, brother Mincho?" Lucy called in the morning. "Feel better? Here's coffee. Mincho? Mincho? Tiger, come! Something's wrong! He's white!"

I shook Mincho, but there was no response. I felt for a pulse, but he was gone. I dropped to my knees beside the huge, cold body. "Oh Mincho! Mincho!"

The burial brought together an unusual blend of mourners: coffee growers, SRE, miners, villagers, and cowhands. They were surprised to see each other, and even more surprised to see some of the toughest, most calloused men weeping. "He was a big man," one eulogized, "and not only in body. I never knew nobody with more compassion, a poor man's friend."

"I had to pay my hands more because of Mincho," an elderly cattleman told us, "and I hated him for it. But then my crew started working conscientiously, quit stealing stuff, and we're all happier. Most of us trust in Jesus Christ now."

Jacob Morán had carried a bundle of yucca to town as a gift to our family and he praised the deceased: "Brother Mincho, by the grace of God, got our agriculture up to date and formed a co-op. We grow enough beans now to sell the extra and buy shoes for our little ones."

"I'd have bullet holes in my heart now," an SRE associate testified, "if Mincho hadn't got us to agree on a peace pact. We promised God to forgive past offences, stop attacking, and seek the good of our former foes."

I had inscribed Mincho's verse on the grave marker—a cross—and Mayor Campos read it. "*Light arises in the darkness for the upright; he is gracious and compassionate and righteous.* Listen, folks, this light will shine again in Bat Haven if we all swear Mincho's pledge to each other and to God. Say it, Tiger, and we'll repeat each of its promises together."

After this I asked, "Folks, are you ready to start living normal, peaceful lives? If you've had enough fear and violence and are willing to enjoy normal, peaceful lives, then right now is the moment to begin doing what you just promised. Don't leave here until you've talked with a former enemy, to forgive and ask forgiveness." Many stayed and started practicing what they were calling "*our pact.*"

After watching SRE associates and coffee growers embrace and ask forgiveness, Mayor Campos exclaimed. "Incredible! I'd never have believed it, Tiger!"

"It's a start, sir. Some thugs on both sides still deal in illegal drugs and arms."

"Simon Alvarez said Mincho had a heart attack. You agree?"

"Hmm. Mincho told me last night that Chuey Ochoa had given him a taco and soda. I wonder . . . Well, it's too late now to do anything."

Sergeant Perez had come and told me, "We station squads in larger towns to keep order, but sometimes they have untrained recruits and bullies who take bribes. I lack the rank to change things here, so I asked my colonel to come investigate. He's a man of integrity, a real soldier. Can you come and help me explain to him what's been going on? He might authorize the discipline we need." I told Lucy to go on home and wondered why she chose to walk alone, avoiding company. I went with Perez and told the colonel what Beady-Eyes had done;

he wrote on a pad, saying nothing.

Back home I found Lucy depressed; the boys sensed her gloom and shared it. I tried to cheer her, but she remained morose. Two weeks went by without relief, and I asked Lucy, "Can you go to the united worship today? The cells' monthly reports should cheer you up." She agreed.

At the soccer field we watched the final minutes of a game; Julio kicked a goal putting Bat Haven ahead of Arenas. Wanda arrived, the first time in weeks, and asked Lucy, "Have you seen my new house, girl? It's almost finished. I have a huge window so I can observe the town square. I also got a stereo sound system with speakers in six rooms, and I've collected recordings of the finest music."

"I'm sure you'll enjoy those things very much, Mrs. Alvarez."

The Wasp eyed Lucy like a hawk eying a lame chipmunk, and I felt uneasy. She griped, "Tiger, I didn't come to watch boys kick a ball around; I'll be back."

We began worship, and shouting distracted us. "Power of Almighty!" Mouse entered, bearded, and waving a pole with a rustically carved snake twined around it. "Behold the staff of Moses! Now you'll see who the real prophet is! Hallelujah! I've been in the Divine's presence, forty days of fasting!" His shouts stirred up a bull that bellowed angrily in the next field. He began swinging the staff of Moses in a wide orbit as people backed away. Hearing the commotion, Wanda rushed back in. Mouse did not see her; he whirled and inadvertently swatted her behind; she fell, roaring so angrily that the bull responded again.

"Clumsy hippo!" she shrilled. "You lie! It hasn't been forty days and you've come back fatter than ever!"

I helped Wanda up and told Mouse, "That's enough entertainment for the day; we're trying to worship. Please sit down and be quiet."

He had no intention to sit quietly. "With this staff I'll do wonders!" He pointed it at me. "You'll bow before it, Tiger!" With volume on max, he bawled, "To heal your church's division, everyone will fast as I've done. You'll all . . . "

"God already healed the division, and you're not to publicize fasting; Jesus condemned that. Any who choose to fast can do so without forcing them."

Wanda sneaked up behind Mouse, seized his staff, and hurled it away. She opened her little notebook and started shouting cases of Mouse's misconduct. I advised her to stop, but she only screeched louder and pointed an accusing finger at me. "You, Tiger, are the root of all this disgrace! You let boys play soccer on Sunday and your wife spreads lies about me so they don't ask me to sing solos anymore. I've seen her strut arrogantly in front of gawking men so they'll lust after her." The accusations were ridiculous, but made with such stinging venom that Lucy couldn't stop tears from forming in the corners of her eyes.

"Stop!" I raged. "Stop injecting your paranoid poison into my wife!" I'd had enough and a storm of fury hit me. I seized the notebook, picked up Mouse's staff, and held both items high, shouting condemnations. Lucy begged me to calm down, but I bellowed, "Wanda, this filthy notebook with its catalog of sins is diabolical! Mouse, this silly staff is simply evil, a disgusting idol! You hid out just to impress the town. You both have become servants of hell, bringing Satan's affliction on us. We'll burn this cursed staff and notebook right now!"

"Burn them!" cried the crowd. "Burn the staff! Burn the devil's notebook!"

Someone handed me matches and newspapers and I lit them, but Lucy grabbed the burning paper, stamped on it and shouted, "The pact! The pact!"

The peace pact! I'd forgotten what I had vowed and had urged everyone to do, the day before! Regaining control, I turned to Mouse and Wanda. "Forgive me for condemning you. Here." I returned the staff and notebook. "Mouse, please don't use that staff to frighten people again; Paul had believers do away with their own idols, and I beg you to do so too. Wanda, please discard that notebook by your own choice. Instead of using it as a weapon; let the Holy Spirit and your love move folks to leave their sins without threatening and shaming them."

Lucy grabbed my arm, looking pale and shaken, and I saw it was time to leave. Evita noticed her sagging in my arms, and had Gadget drive us home.

The next day Lucy felt weaker and sadder. The doctor prescribed pills, but to no avail. Gadget and Evita came to pray for her; afterwards they took me outside where Lucy couldn't hear and he asked me, "How could we get into Simon's house sometime when they're away, to examine his financial records and . . . "

"Forget it! You must stop investigating now, Gadget."

"Why? I can't quit until I find out who killed Olga."

"Do that and they'll kill you too. Let the federal agents continue their inquiring; this is no longer Bat Haven's exclusive concern. Oh, look at Popcorn!" The dog was sniffing around excitedly. "He's after something. Let's follow him." Popcorn stopped beside the house suddenly, crowded against my legs trembling, and then dug up the gory doll.

"How curious!" exclaimed Evita. "Did your boys bury it there?"

"They never had such an ugly doll. Maybe Andy had put it there." I took it across the road to Martha, and asked if she'd seen it before.

She stepped back and turned pale. "Burn it! For God's sake, burn the filthy obscenity! Burn it!"

"What is it, Martha?"

"The few real hairs, long and black, are Lucy's! Someone put a curse on her."

I recalled Wanda plucking hair from Lucy's brush and burned the doll. After throwing the ashes in the river, Gadget, Evita, and I prayed in Jesus' name to bind any spirit of darkness that remained and any demonic power linked to the fetish. Evita asked me, "Can demons possess a believer? The thought panics me."

"They can oppress us, but not separate us from Christ, as Romans 8 assures. Paul said that God let a messenger of Satan torment him. Lucy's mother exposed her to demonic powers and she's had troubled moments of doubt ever since." We discussed these things at length with Lucy and prayed for her recovery.

The next day Gadget and Evita came and she observed, "Laughter has returned to your home! Lucy, you're cheerful again! Tiger, I'm struggling to understand all of this. Do you think that fetish had power to torment her?"

"Not the fetish; Paul taught that idols are nothing; but we're to resist demonic powers. Demons enjoy the attention that idolaters give to the *forces of darkness* through a fetish. We're to repulse them in Jesus' name."

"But Lucy's no idolater. She knew nothing about that diabolical doll."

"The fiend who made it had invoked demons, and they have malignant power. God limits it as he did for Job, and we have authority in Jesus' name over them. Because of this, Lucy's been freed from any demons' evil tormenting."

"Tiger," Gadget asked, "Popcorn trembled in fear before he dug up that doll. Do you think he sensed a demonic presence?"

"I doubt it. He smelled the doll's dress of rattlesnake skin; Mincho told me that Popcorn feared nothing, but snakes, as one had bitten him as a pup. His God-given instinct to protect us overrode his fear, and he dug the doll up anyway."

Others in Bat Haven suffered torment similar to Lucy's; she went with Martha to pray for them and most were freed. Martha remarked to Lucy, "Strange! The residences we've visited had an X somewhere marking them."

Task 21–d.
LET A "MOTHER CHURCH" HOLD ACCOUNTABLE THE WORKERS IT SENDS TO FOREIGN FIELDS

Roy and Daisy arrived again from California; after a glad reunion, we discussed how to **let a "mother church" hold accountable the workers it sends to foreign fields**. Roy explained, "Institutional church planting in most of today's pioneer fields is ineffective; missionaries need experience with flocks that multiply by evangelizing, so we came to learn from you again." They stayed with Gadget and Evita who had many questions, and the four poured over maps.

During our next united worship, Gadget announced, "Me and Evita been praying for the millions of India's poor who don't know our Savior. We're going with Roy and Daisy to northern India, hopefully within a year, to where authorities don't let no missionaries reside; I'll develop a business that they'll approve."

Roy outlined their plans. "We'll have two vocations; doing God's work covertly and running a business overtly. Even if Gadget's business earns well, I hope you will still give them partial support. Churches that give a missionary no financial support also give them scant prayer support. Also, without some financial support, there's usually no accountability. Believers pray for missionaries whose work they invest in and hold accountable."

I asked the assembly, "What about it?" They cheered and I assured Gadget and Evita, "We'll support you, pray for you regularly, and hold you accountable."

Gadget replied, "And we promise to report our progress and problems, no matter what they are, so you can pray and advise us. We'll be accountable to you as well as to any mission agency involved."

Pacho fretted, "With a business, they'll have little time to make disciples."

"We'll work as a team," replied Roy, "so nobody has to spend all their time with the business, and we'll have a business that lets us make disciples while we're working. You can be sure the Apostle Paul taught while he sewed tents."

"Gadget's uneducated," Pacho worried. "Is he prepared for mission work?"

"He's well prepared," Roy replied. "He's started village churches and trained their leaders; he'll also work with villagers in India. He and Evita lack cross-cultural experience, but we'll help them with that. Gadget grew up in a large, poor family, the same as India's villagers, and will identify easily with them."

I asked Roy, "Will a mission agency let you multiply congregations the way we've done here? We've had friction with traditional leaders, and I don't want you to suffer such bullying in India. I've heard that the most common cause of missionaries burning out is that they can't get along with coworkers."

"Wrong! Most missionaries are genial and get along well with folks. The discord is rarely the *cause* of burnout; it's a *symptom* of a deeper cause—directors or coworkers don't let a worker serve in a way in which he can use his God-given gifts to pursue his vision. Sometimes experienced workers mistakenly take control over new workers and assign tasks for which they're not gifted. We'll work with an agency that lets your church hold Gadget and Evita accountable and agrees with your aim. Your church will inform their supervisor what you've commissioned them to do; this lets the experienced missionary know that the new missionaries aren't arrogantly telling him how to work. Gadget knows how to multiply churches, and you must protect him from your end from organization managers who merely think they do; they abound and cause no end of misery."

"Got it! Who they work with can decide results as much as what they do."

Roy clasped my hand. "We'll check out a field overseer before committing to serve under him, to avoid a micromanager who's more ambitious to develop his organization than to develop churches and see a widespread movement. I think we can find one with Samaritans in Action that you folks helped train, Tiger."

"I hope you'll be careful how you gather a team, and not just push workers together because they work in the same region; that just invites friction. Put together folks who focus on the same *project*, and don't worry about keeping the team together; there were no permanent apostolic teams in the New Testament."

"Right," Roy replied. "Remember Fred? Sustaining a team is not our aim; new churches are. If we try to have perfect relationships among team members, then we'll bond with our teammates instead of the people God has sent us to serve. We adapt to a culture well only when we love the people; that is why Ruth in the Bible bonded so well with Jewish culture; we'll live among the Asian Indians and be at home in their culture. It's the best way to learn a language too."

Task 21–e.

PREPARE WORKERS TO GO TO A NEGLECTED PEOPLE AND BOND WITH THEM AND THEIR CULTURE

Our next serious concern was to **prepare workers to go to a neglected people and bond with them and their culture.** Gadget's first lesson on culture came soon. Roger had asked Arturo and me to help him give a training workshop in Los Robles, and Lorena wanted to go along to visit her family. Gadget offered to squeeze us into his taxi and when Lorena left her house he exclaimed, "Uh oh! The liberated woman! Her glossy, jet-black dress will be a novelty in Los Robles; it's slinkier than anything ever worn in these hills! Brave girl!"

On the way, Gadget stopped on a hill and looked through binoculars. "See them fields? Could be marijuana. Let's investigate. A trail runs along the river we just crossed on that high bridge." We went back, drove down the trail a short distance, and Gadget said, "Can't go no farther by car. You'd better stay here, Lorena, it'll be rough going on foot. Roger can stay with you."

"Did you forget where I'm from? I can hike anywhere you can!" Lorena set the pace on the trail that at times led up away from the river. We passed coffee trees, in places lush foliage let only soft light penetrate while vividly colored birds squawked their protest at intruders. Lorena plucked a lavender orchid and put it in her hair. Bananas grew where the ground was moist and Roger picked some. "These are smaller than commercially grown ones, but tastier."

Faint thumps of thunder sounded from mountains to the north and I predicted rain soon. Lorena cried, "No! No! False prophet! It'd ruin my beautiful dress." We trudged on; the air had grown heavier, and a soft wind rustled the treetops.

We heard a whinny where another trail led away from the river; Gadget said, "Come, Tiger. Let's check it out. The rest of you wait here." We came to a clearing and heard galloping. Gadget said, "It's just beans and corn, but someone's in a hurry to get away. It sounds like two horses." We went back to the others.

Thunder sounded closer; wind bent the trees and we hurried. We took our shoes off to cross a stream, and lightning hit an *alamo* with a deafening blast right beside us. A large, dead piece of the cottonwood trunk fell burning; one end sticking in the mud. We raced away barefoot as large drops of water filtered through the leaves. "My dress!" wailed Lorena. We met a shirtless man leading a donkey loaded with bulging sacks; he stared at Lorena's dress, now shrunken tighter than before by the rain, and guffawed. Soon the rain and wind ceased, and mist rose lazily from the warm ground.

We came to another clearing and Gadget cried, "Here it is! This is the field I saw from the hilltop." He rushed in among the plants. "Wow! Enough to poison the minds of a thousand addicts!" A shot sounded, and a stem shattered inches from his head. Lorena screamed and we retreated into the trees. Gadget cried, "Go! Go! I'll come back later with soldiers."

When we reached Lorena's house in Los Robles, her mother saw her skin-tight dress and screamed, "My daughter!" She dragged Lorena into the house.

After visiting Jacob, we returned for Lorena and she came out gloomy, wearing an ankle-length, saggy gray dress of the traditional village type. Her mother followed her and came marching directly toward me, her eyes flashing. I rose to evade her, but she ordered, "Tiger Garcia, you stay right there! You people have alienated Lorena from Christian norms! How could you do this to my daughter?"

"Sister, what you call 'Christian norms' are fashions that differ in . . . "

"Roger, you let Lorena become corrupted! Come into the house."

He followed her inside like a lamb and Lorena's father chuckled, "Poor kid!"

Gadget commented, "What I just learned will save us from grief in India; we'll respect local customs. I see why Paul said to 'be all things to all men.'"

CHAPTER 21: CONFIRM THE GRASP AND THE PRACTICE OF LEADERS' TASKS

21–a. Respond by faith to interrogation by hostile authorities. Find how Jesus said to answer them: *Do not worry about how or what you are to speak in your defense, or what you are to say; for the Holy Spirit will teach you in that very hour what you ought to say.* Luke 12:11–12

21–b. Avert division by helping feuding believers affirm a peace accord. It could ask them to do such things as: *forgive, show love to rivals, stop griping about past offences, accept an offence rather than litigate or continue quarreling* (1 Cor 6:7,5), and *shun any who prolong the division* (Titus 3:10–11).

Verify the right attitude toward believers' offenses: *Does any one of you, when he has a case against his neighbor, dare to go to law before the unrighteous and not before the saints? . . . Is there not among you one wise man who will be able to decide between his brethren, but brother goes to law with brother, and that before unbelievers? . . . Why not rather be wronged? Why not rather be defrauded?* 1 Cor 6:1–7

21–c. Detect and resist demonic forces of darkness. Overt demonic activity is common in some fields. Identify the peril of offering things to idols: *What do I mean then? That a thing sacrificed to idols is anything, or that an idol is anything? No, but I say that the things which the Gentiles sacrifice, they sacrifice to demons and not to God, and I do not want you to become sharers in demons.* 1 Cor 10:19–20

Verify with what authority believers can repulse demons, according to Jesus: *In My name they will cast out demons . . .* Mark 16:17

A hag used a doll to put a curse on Lucy. Note what God told ancient Israel to do with witches. *You shall not allow a sorceress to live.* Ex 22:18

Witchcraft is prevalent, although many Western Christians are unaware. Consider God's view of trying to contact spirits of the dead: *As for the person who turns to mediums and to spiritists, to play the harlot after them, I will also set My face against that person and will cut him off from among his people.* Lev 20:6

21–d. Let a "mother church" hold accountable the workers it sends to foreign fields. Find what Paul and Barnabas did with their sending church after returning from a long trip. *From there they sailed to Antioch, from which they had been commended to the grace of God for the work that they had accomplished. When they had arrived and gathered the church* *together, they began to report all things that God had done with them and how He had opened a door of faith to the Gentiles.* Acts 14:26–27

21–e. Prepare workers to go to a neglected people and bond with them and their culture. Lorena, by her dress, failed to respect her village culture. Find what she should have done: *Though I am free from all men, I have made myself a slave to all, so that I may win more. To the Jews I became as a Jew, so that I might win Jews; to those who are under the Law, as under the Law though not being myself under the Law, so that I might win those who are under the Law; to those who are without law, as without law . . . so that I might win those who are without law. To the weak I became weak, that I might win the weak; I have become all things to all men, so that I may by all means save some.* 1 Cor 9:19–22

God's covenant with Abraham was the foundation for everything from then on in the Bible. Verify God's plan for all cultures: *The Lord said to Abram, "Go forth from your country, and from your relatives and from your father's house, to the land which I will show you, and I will make you a great nation and I will bless you and make your name great and so you shall be a blessing and I will bless those who bless you and the one who curses you I will curse. And in you all the families of the earth will be blessed." Gen 12:1–3*

For political reasons missionaries often serve as "tentmakers." These . . .

[ ]   have one vocation to earn a living and another to do Christian ministry.

[ ]   raise full-time support and then pretend that they are earning their living.

  Answer: Paul supported himself and coworkers. Wise "tentmakers" accept partial support from churches, to insure prayer support and accountability.

EVALUATE YOUR LEADERSHIP
1=Poor. 2=Planning to improve. 3=Doing well.

1-2-3 Respond by faith to interrogation by hostile authorities.

1-2-3 Avert division by helping feuding believers affirm a peace accord.

1-2-3 Detect and resist demonic forces of darkness (Eph 4:12).

1-2-3 Let a "mother church" hold accountable workers it sends to foreign fields.

1-2-3 Send workers to go to neglected people and bond with them and their culture.

22.
Peacemakers Raze Satan's Divisive Walls

Task 22–a.

BE PEACEMAKERS AND
FORGIVE THOSE WHO
HAVE CAUSED PAINFUL
INJURY

"A wounded stranger with a gun is hanging out in that abandoned shack yonder by them mangos," Jacob told Arturo, Gadget, and I while waiting for village elders to arrive for Roger's workshop. "He may be dead now; he wouldn't let me in to pray for 'im." An encounter in Los Robles was about to highlight the importance of **being peacemakers and forgiving those who have caused painful injury.**

"I'll go see." Arturo walked over to the derelict, mud-walled hut, the same one that Amos Nuñez had photographed to show deceptively how destitute the people were. It leaned, its thatching had rotted and holes gaped in the roof. Arturo rapped on the sagging door several times.

"Who?" came a weak, hoarse voice.

"I came to pray for you. I'm a pastor."

"I'm too far gone for prayers or pills, Father. Go 'way. Let me die in peace."

"To die in peace needs prayer. Please let me in."

The door opened a crack and Arturo saw a flushed face and bloodshot eyes appraising him. A shaky hand held a pistol and the other arm was bandaged. "Got a cigarette?"

"Something better—Jesus' forgiveness and healing in His name."

"God is punishing me, Father. There isn't no remedy for me now. Go away."

"God will forgive you. Just trust our Savior Jesus Christ."

The door shut, but then opened a crack again. "Do you Evangelical pastors heed the same ethic as Catholic Fathers, never to reveal what penitents confess?"

"I certainly do. Absolutely!"

"Not even to government investigators?"

"No one. It's our sacred duty. True pastors never reveal confessions."

The door opened and the man fell to his knees, begging. "Bless me Father, for I have sinned. I'm dying and guilt is crushing me. I tried to kill Mincho Medina in Los Vientos and failed. I killed others. My employers deceived me into killing innocent men. You've probably heard how wicked I am—I'm Jaime Ordoñez."

"I've heard things, but God promised: *If we confess our sins, he is faithful and just to forgive us our sins and to cleanse us from all unrighteousness.*"

"I've sinned too much!" Jaime sobbed. "Tiger Garcia told me how Jesus forgives, but it's way beyond me."

"No, friend. No one has sinned too much for . . . "

"My conscience didn't bother me none when I killed bad men; they deserved it. But that girl . . . They got me drunk. Told me she was a spy sending messages to KGB agents so they could blow up Bat Haven; I was God's instrument to save the town. I didn't ask her name; that would've made it harder to do. Later in a bar, I heard she was just the good wife of a decent lawyer."

Arturo's mind reeled! Olga's killer, kneeling at his feet! Silence followed.

"I'm dying now," gasped the fevered voice, "and I can't bear the pain of my guilt no longer. Can God forgive such a vile crime?" Another silence. "Didn't think so." Jaime rose slowly, unsteady on his feet.

"How can I forgive you?" gasped Arturo. "My God! I cannot!"

"I understand, Father. So God will not forgive me neither. Let me die in peace and go to hell where I belong." He held the door open. "Thanks for coming."

Arturo did not move. Agony tore him as conflicting urges battled in his spirit, whirling like debris in a tornado, a vortex of hatred vying with compassion, doubt with faith, a furious craving for revenge with longing for quiet closure. He clenched his teeth and a rasping moan rose from the depths of his tortured soul, "My God! Oh, my God! In the Name of our Lord Jesus Christ, Jaime Ordoñez, receive God's pardon for your horrible crimes. God forgives you. And I . . . I forgive you too. By God's grace alone I forgive you!"

"Really? Oh . . . thank you, Father! Oh, may God be blessed!" He knelt again and another silence followed. "Promise not to repeat what I told you. The husband of the girl I slew will surely kill me if he finds out—if I survive this fever."

Lightning struck nearby with deafening thunder, but neither man noticed. "I am the husband. You slew my wife Olga."

"You tricked me!" Jaime rose, stepped back, and aimed his gun at Arturo.

"I did not deceive you," Arturo groaned in a choked voice. "I forgive you! Yes, I forgive you, Jaime! Christ forgave us, and so I forgive you."

Arturo fell to his knees and covered his face with his hands, quaking with bitter sobs. "Olga! My Olga!" Jaime stood trembling, vacillating. Water trickled through a hole in the rotting roof soaking the two men, but neither moved to avoid it. Suddenly Jaime knelt too, and embraced Arturo. The pistol lay between them, baptized by the mingled tears of two mortal enemies drawn together by the scarred hands of Jesus Christ.

Arturo called from the shack and told me to bring a blanket. Supporting Jaime between us, we brought him to Jacob's house, and Susan assured him, "My blend of herbal tea will cure you." She poured the steaming brew into a hollowed-out gourd and Jaime sipped it while she boiled cloths to dress his wound. We prayed for him and by the time Roger began his workshop, the fever had ebbed a bit; the hard look on the gunman's face gradually gave way to one of calm contentment. He listened with interest as the elders arrived, gave reports, and made plans.

> ## Task 22–b.
> ### COOPERATE CLOSELY WITH OTHER CHURCHES IN THE AREA

What followed showed the need to **cooperate closely with other churches in the area.** A village elder said, "My aunt's teaching prophecies from the horoscope. What should I do? She's got gullible believers all mixed up."

"My wife and I will go help you unmix them," offered another trainee, and a third elder agreed to accompany them.

Gadget told me, "I see churches get along much better by working together closely with other churches. I'll develop this kind of networking in India, Tiger."

"Good. An isolated church never reaches its full potential. New Testament churches cooperated as the regional body of Christ. Communication between flocks is as crucial as between allied armies fighting side by side; our enemy is as real and our objective more vital, as peoples' eternal destiny is at stake."

Roger added, "We arrange for all our new churches to serve one another. The Arenas church has imparted to ours the impulse for our renewal, two churches in the refugee's camp support and protect each other, and our church in Bat Haven is providing extension training for many new village churches."

On our way back to Bat Haven the next morning, a sullen Lorena in her old dress said nothing, and Arturo remained silent too. I told him, "You've been thoughtful." But he gave no reply.

Passing the path to the marijuana field, Gadget asked Arturo, "Do you think they poisoned Mincho 'cause he knew where them crooks grow the weed?"

"Just let me forget the whole thing!" Arturo snapped.

"Not me. I plan to exhume Mincho's body and check for poison."

"No, Gadget!" cried Arturo. "Leave it! Don't stir up more violence."

Arturo never revealed the injured man's confession; Jaime told me years later.

Task 22–c.

ORGANIZE EXTENSION TRAINING TO KEEP FLOCKS MULTIPLYING IN THEIR NORMAL, BIBLICAL WAY

Thomas had invited Roger and me to go help his Holy Trinity Church **organize extension training to keep flocks multiplying in their normal, biblical way.** He met us at the bus stop and told us, "My seminary students enjoyed hearing about my trip and have questions for you."

"Roger's better equipped to speak to seminarians," I demurred.

"They'll respect your experience," Thomas assured me.

We found a redhead among the Hispanic students and I told Freckles, "I'm glad you've recovered from the stabbing." He thanked me without smiling.

Roger explained our work to the class, and a lanky student with long sideburns asked him, "Do you need a special spiritual gift to plant churches?"

"No. I have the gift of compassion, so I deal with social justice and community development while starting churches. Working with persons whose gifts complement mine, I train both deacons and pastors."

"But surely you need a special gift to plant churches like you guys do, Roger."

"Scripture mentions no such gift. When believers use their gifts together freely, flocks multiply. God uses believers with any gift if they do what Paul did; he and his apprentices gathered a few congregations in a region, installed their leaders, and let them plant the rest of the churches in the area."

Freckles griped, "Starting churches as fast as you guys do brings problems."

Roger hesitated, and I replied, "There are always problems, just as in the New Testament churches. To avoid problems, don't have new churches and don't have children! However, to plant churches the slow way brings even worse problems."

"Not many missionaries multiply churches as you guys say," snorted Freckles.

The lanky student countered, "And not many see churches multiply as they do. Please, Tiger, explain how you multiply them and bring so many to Jesus."

I asked his name and he replied, "Sylvester, here to serve you. Call me Cy."

"Help me, Cy. Please sketch an elephant, a rabbit, and a bunch of tiny rabbits."

Cy sketched them, and I held my arms out like a balance scales. "Hand me the rabbit. And now, the elephant in my other hand." My arm with the elephant dropped sharply as the rabbit arm rose. "An elephants weighs over 2,000 times more than a rabbit. Now, Cy, replace the bunny with the bunch of rabbits."

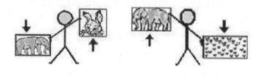

The rabbits dropped sharply as the elephant rose. "In three years there'll be three elephants, but millions of rabbits. Their large litters multiply fast; they'll weigh a thousand times more than the elephants. Some churches try to grow forever larger like an elephant and never multiply."

"So what's the point?" growled the redhead.

"It's obvious!" Cy told Freckles. "House churches can multiply rapidly like rabbits, unlimited by lack of funds and complex policies that large churches need. Folks receive Jesus more easily among friends and family, and a small group enables them to build friendships and serve one another with confidence."

"Do you condemn large churches, Roger?" Freckles asked.

"Oh, no! Our church is big now, but has 'rabbit' groups. It's grown through evangelism; we avoid the farce of growing a church by luring believers from small flocks in which they're active, to become 'hearers only' in the big one."

Freckles countered, "Large churches lose members to small ones too. Some folks prefer a smaller church and can be just as passive in it as in a large church."

"True," Roger agreed, "but when a church plants daughter churches, God blesses its obedience and enables it to reach far more people than if it remained sterile. With many new churches in an area, all find it easier to win sinners to Christ. We multiply both house churches and cell groups within large churches."

Cy asked, "But how do you start so many house churches and cells, Roger?"

"When a family receives Jesus we don't take it at once to an existing church; we help the father shepherd his family and have simple worship. Friends readily join this nucleus. The father serves as a provisional leader until we recognize him as a biblically qualified shepherding elder. Sometimes the father cannot lead, so we train others in the group to lead. Once the tiny flock is stabilized, we invite its members to our united, monthly worship with other cell churches." A flurry of questions ensued, but class was over and we agreed to return the next day.

That evening, Roger stumbled into paradise—the seminary library! Church history, commentaries, social issues! Each chapter of a tome I examined probed some "-ology." Roger would have stayed all night, but a librarian shooed us out.

The next morning Roger remarked to Thomas, "All these great resources of history and theology must be a powerful reinforcement of one's faith."

"Not always, son. Even professors who are devout believers sometimes come to rely on their keen intellect to affirm the authenticity of the faith. That's a step toward apostasy—man's intellect becomes the highest judge, not the Holy Spirit using Scripture. Our trustees recently refused a grant that would have given a questionable accreditation board the final word on policy and curriculum."

Cy arrived at class with a large box. "It's to illustrate what we're learning. Here—catch it!" He released a rabbit. After a wild chase, Freckles caught it, and with a rare smile told us he'd bring the elephant the next day.

Cy began a barrage of questions. "Tiger, when flocks multiply as you say, how can they have enough maturity to plant healthy daughter churches?"

"It doesn't require lengthy experience to instruct new leaders in the basics. When a church waits a long time to birth a daughter church, it becomes more difficult, as it grows accustomed to being disobedient and inactive. Besides, we cannot measure spiritual maturity with a calendar. Those who've known Jesus for just a few weeks sometimes show more maturity than many longtime believers."

Thomas asked the class if they thought churches multiplied in apostolic times the way we had described. Cy replied, "Sure. In 2 Timothy 2:2, Paul told Timothy to train faithful men who would train others and . . . "

"But that was pastoral training," Freckles remarked, "not church planting."

"It was both, combined," I clarified. "Many churches grew out of that mentoring chain. Let's reenact what God did." I had the students form four huddles and told the first, "You're Antioch. Name someone as Saul and another as Barnabas."

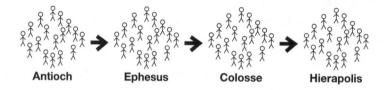

Antioch   **Ephesus**   **Colosse**   **Hierapolis**

The second huddle was Ephesus and named "Timothy" and an aide. The third huddle was Colosse and named "Epaphras" and a helper. The fourth huddle was Hierapolis and named a girl as "Nympha" who hosted a church in her house, as Colossians 4 says.

"As we reenact what happened historically, notice who the four links were. 'Saul and Barny,' please carry a Bible from Antioch to 'Timothy' in Ephesus." They did, and then Timothy and his assistant took it from Ephesus to Epaphras in Colosse. Epaphras and his helper then took it to Nympha in Hierapolis. I explained, "This chain didn't go only to four cities; it reached a huge area in Asia Minor, as Acts 19 says, as each church had several daughter churches."

"But times have changed, Tiger," Freckles argued, "In such a chain reaction, churches will grow weaker with every link, as in the game of *Telephone*."

"Did the Holy Spirit tire as He walked from Antioch to Ephesus? If the impulse always faded, there'd be no vital church left in the world today. God repeats the same miracle each time a church is born; the whole process starts over."

Freckles looked the other way, combing his cinnamon hair, but Cy applauded and asked, "Is it really that easy to multiply churches, Tiger?"

"Yes and no. Do what the apostles did and leave the growth to God—that's the easy part. The hard part is withstanding Satan's counterattacks. We help him when we make church planting expensive, high tech, sophisticated or too institutional. Also, some societies simply do not respond, especially wealthier ones. When this happens, some fail to do what Jesus said to do. Who recalls it?"

"Shake the dust," Cy replied. "Move on to find people who are receptive."

"Exactly!" Thomas advised, "Churches can also multiply this way secretly, and some of you will work where authorities ban church planting. You will need to sustain the movement by mentoring new leaders the same way Paul did."

"Liberating!" exclaimed Cy. "You guys have given me a fresh vision."

"Too fresh!" griped Freckles. "A true pastor needs theological education with the highest standards of excellence. These innovators with simplistic mentoring are introducing inferior training for pastors that'll eventually weaken them."

"No!" answered Cy. "It's obviously biblical and helps me correct errors in my thinking. I've dreamt about the church that I would pastor growing forever larger and becoming the largest in the city. Now I see this grew out of my prideful ego."

"Now wait!" replied Freckles. "A legitimate church has a building, an ample budget, and an ordained pastor who has graduated from a reputable theological seminary. Leaders will lose control, bad doctrine will infiltrate, and costs will soar, if churches multiply like these guys say."

Thomas intervened. "I feared all that too, Freckles, until I visited their work. They have less disorder, falsehood, and money worries than our institutional churches. History shows that leaders trained by godly mentors do well. They don't need degrees if they meet biblical qualifications of a shepherd. Men with little formal education can be the best pastors for those who also have little."

"But false doctrine will surely infiltrate those churches," Freckles contested.

"I see more false teaching in old, sterile churches," Thomas told him. "They violate Jesus' command to harvest ripe fields and forfeit His blessing."

Cy asked Roger, "Would you mentor me the way you do your workers?"

"I certainly will. I'll mentor any of you who contact me." He gave his address.

We discussed differences between classroom and mentored training, and Thomas remarked, "A hazard lurks in theological institutions like ours—*seeing truth only from a philosophical, analytical view.* Let's crawl out of our abstract box right now. Who here resembles Leonardo da Vinci's *Mona Lisa* painting?"

"Sandra!" Cy exclaimed. "Her dad's Italian."

Thomas asked the blushing student to stand. "Sandra, why do you suppose Mona had that enigmatic half-smile when Leonardo da Vinci painted her?"

"Hmm. Mona Lisa—Ramona Elizabeth—was probably thinking in her Italian way: 'Hurry up, Lenny! Keepa painting. Stopa staring anda finish this stupid portrait. I'ma getting tireda sitting still in the sun all day!'"

It took a while for Thomas to stop laughing. "Now I'm an art critic examining your portrait in Paris, to tell my friends back home about you. I use a tape to measure your dimensions." He pretended to measure her and jot in a notebook; he then pretended to peer through a magnifying glass to analyze the chemical composition of the paint's pigment and record it. "Eyes?" He looked and pretended to write. "Two!" He examined her again. "Hair?" He wrote again. "Yes!" He asked the students, "Now, will I be able to tell people about Mona Lisa?"

Cy exclaimed, "I see now! That's how some scholars try to present Jesus! Let's introduce people to the living, dynamic Christ who dwells in our midst and not simply repeat theological truths about Him."

"Your comparison breaks down, Professor," Freckles told Thomas. "Sandra's more alluring than the drab dame in that painting." Sandra blushed again.

Leaving the room, Roger commented to me, "That Freckles is bad, totally."

"I hope not totally; he has a bit of me inside him! I donated blood to him."

"Then it hasn't reached his heart yet!"

"Tiger, Roger, wait!" Freckles was running to catch us. "Forgive my arguing so much. What you taught assaults everything I've hoped for! It contradicts my entire background. I'm going to consider it, though. Just wanted you to know."

Thomas took us to a Christian bookstore that afternoon, and Roger told me, "I wish we had a store like this in Bat Haven. But, something bothers me; nearly all the books are on how to improve one's self. Few deal with how to serve others."

<table>
<tr><td>

Task 22–d.

RESPECT SINCERE

BELIEVERS,

REGARDLESS OF

MINOR DIFFERENCES

IN DOCTRINE OR

PRACTICE

</td><td>

Supper with Thomas and Sarah led us to **respect sincere believers, regardless of minor differences in doctrine or practice.** A couple brought a baby and the father said, "Reverend, our newborn needs to be done."

"Done?" Thomas looked puzzled.

"You know—baptized, like you did my cousin Armando's kid Sunday."

</td></tr>
</table>

"We don't simply 'do' babies. Parents must affirm their faith in Christ first." Thomas explained this, and the couple agreed to attend a class for new parents.

"You baptize babies?" Roger asked Thomas when they left.

"Yes, and we validate it when a child comes of age with Confirmation."

Roger threw me a questioning glance and I said, "Not all Evangelicals wait to baptize until a child receives Christ by his own faith. Arturo established believers' baptism in our church, but some members would prefer to baptize infants."

Roger told Thomas, "My grandmother was baptized as a baby and she repeats prayers to saints, not to Jesus. Do you think her faith is valid?"

"Only God knows. When I baptize a child, its believing parents enter into a covenant with God, promising to bring the child to faith and repentance. They claim God's promise in Acts 16:31 to save a believer's entire family. We believe that baptism is the sign of the New Covenant, corresponding to circumcision—the sign God gave to Abraham. I've seen God honor the parents' faith who complied. Most churches whose roots go back to the Reformation hold this covenant view."

I told Roger, "We embrace the same covenant, but differently; parents dedicate their newborn to God without baptizing them. What godly, Spirit-filled leaders avoid is saying to one another, 'I'm right, you're wrong. Go away!' Without compromising our convictions, we should recognize what the Holy Spirit has done by means of a practice different from ours. If it's done in sincere faith focused on Jesus then thank God for it; don't fight over it."

"Are there other differences between our churches?" Roger asked Thomas.

"A few minor ones—nothing vital. We say, 'In essentials unity, in non-essentials liberty, in all things charity.' For instance, we do parts of the ancient liturgy and are quieter during worship than you are. We repeat ancient prayers, identifying with believers of all ages. To lead the prayer of confession I turn and face the front altar together with the congregation, because I'm also a sinner. We keep more sacred holidays such as Pentecost and Ash Wednesday, and observe the sacred seasons of the Christian calendar, including Advent and Lent."

"Why emphasize those times of the year?" Roger asked.

"Nominal believers think about sacred things then, and we help them refocus and receive Jesus with true faith. Here, Roger, this book's a gift—*Sacred Liturgy*. It provides key Bible texts to use in worship, covering the Bible in a three-year cycle; it keeps pastors from focusing on only a few pet passages and doctrines."

Roger was reluctant to leave the city; he wanted to hang out longer in the seminary library, but I'd promised Gadget to go with him to burn the field of marijuana that we'd stumbled onto, and we returned to Bat Haven.

We followed an army truck the next morning in the orange taxi to the trail by the high bridge; Gadget, Arturo, and I then led the soldiers to the illegal plants. Walking through the woods, we heard horses galloping off to our left again, as we had on our prior trip, and I wondered who was avoiding us. At the field, the soldiers formed a skirmish line and told us to stay well behind as they advanced to the far side. They came upon three men lounging in the shade of a mud-walled house. "Get off your behinds!" ordered Sergeant Perez. "Burn this field. Now!"

They did not move. One lit a cigarette and took a slow drag. "It's too wet."

"I'm police chief in Bat Haven's area," Gadget stated. "Who owns this land?"

"The government. It's public land, but our employer has *dominio útil*, the right of use and to own improvements made on it."

"His *dominio útil* is legal," replied Arturo. "But these plants sure aren't!"

"Oh? Imagine that! He told us they were hemp, to make rope."

"I bet," snarled Sergeant Perez. "Who's your employer?"

"Don't recall his name, Sergeant."

"Describe him."

"Average height. Average build. Right fellows?"

"Oh, very average," replied another. "Outstandingly, uniquely average."

"I'll return," warned Perez, "and imprison you if these weeds aren't ashes."

The army truck returned to Bat Haven, but Gadget had to adjust the taxi's timing before we started back.

Everything exploded in front of us as we approached the high bridge over the river. Planks flew, dust blinded us, and Gadget swerved to avoid hurtling into the chasm. The car crashed downward through brush, bouncing crazily. It struck a log, overturned, landed on its wheels, and kept bounding. It finally stopped and I wondered where we were until I felt cold water pouring in rapidly. The river! I heard groans and helped the others climb out. The plunge had dented and scraped every surface on the car and on us too, but we were alive. Arturo had bumped his head and it took a while to clear his mind. He took a step and fell into the waist-deep water; the crash had twisted his ankle.

Ping!

Something hit the car roof and we heard the shot from up the river; another bullet spattered water on me. We could not wade fast, so we dropped into the water and let the current carry us downstream. Out of range of the shooter, we scrambled ashore, and Arturo used a stick as a cane to return to the road.

Chuey, as we learned later, waded to the taxi, seeking what he might pilfer. He found Arturo's briefcase and assumed we would return for it. He waded back to a packhorse, unloaded dynamite, and set a timer that Aaron had filched from the mine. He waded back and placed the bundle of death inside Arturo's briefcase. Back on shore, he led the horse out of sight and waited.

We arrived at the road near a dilapidated shack where a lady served cheap meals on dishes washed all day in the same water. A truck driver belched after drinking warm beer and grumbled, "Some idiot blew up the bridge. Looks like the three of you got tangled up in the tumult! I have to go back to Bat Haven and I'll take you guys if you need a lift."

Arturo limped toward the truck and suddenly halted. "My briefcase! That knock on my head left me too stunned to miss it. It has irreplaceable papers."

"I'll get it," I said. "You're lame. Whoever shot at us should be gone by now."

I approached the fallen bridge warily, but saw no one and waded to the wreck. The briefcase lay on the back seat above the water; I picked it up and it appeared dry and undamaged. As I turned to go, a familiar voice made my skin crawl.

"Good afternoon, Night Watchman!" Chuey stood on the bank with his rifle. "Nice day for an accident, isn't it? Enjoy it; it'll be your last." He was too close to miss a shot at me. He placed the long cigar in his mouth as the familiar, twisted smile formed on his bearded face.

I dropped the briefcase and quickly waded to the other side of the car, but he followed me, wading. We repeated this little dance and he laughed, "Oh, this is fun!" I saw the rifle rise suddenly and a bullet grazed the side of my head; I fell across the car's dented hood, wondering how much longer I'd be alive. He laughed harder, his face reflecting raw hatred as he aimed at my belly.

"Don't play with me, man," I begged.

"Why not? A little stomachache will be amusing." Savoring his moment of triumph, Chuey did not notice the briefcase floating toward him.

In the next instant, the cigar and bearded-head ceased to exist.

Task 22–e.

RESTRAIN SHAM SPIRITUAL POWER BEFORE IT CORRUPTS AND DESTROYS THOSE WHO SEEK IT

Back home, Lucy was bandaging my grazed temple when Martha arrived. "Come and calm Mouse down, Tiger! He goes wild in Lorenzo's meetings. They vie to see who has more power and each time it gets crazier. Come!" The crisis would show the need to **restrain sham spiritual power before it corrupts and destroys those who seek it.**

We found Mouse with his staff of Moses arguing with Lorenzo, who dared him, "If you have power to do signs and wonders, then throw yourself from the high bridge into the river." Neighbors were watching, and we started toward the bridge; such contests of power were common among uneducated religious fanatics in those days. Martha pulled on Mouse's arm, begging him not to go.

Lorenzo climbed the bridge railing and cried, "Now, a sign of real power!"

I went out on the bridge to exhort him, "Jesus taught that perverse people seek signs. If you want to show His power, then witness for Him or pray in His name for healing. You can start with me." I pointed to my bandaged head.

"Stop butting in, Tiger. I'm pastor of these people." Lorenzo closed his eyes, jumped, and hit the water with a huge splash. After a tense moment, he crawled out sputtering and coughing; when he could talk he gasped, "Your turn, Mouse."

I started toward Mouse to restrain him, but men held my arms; they craved the entertainment. Martha cried, "No, no! It's high! You're too heavy! It'll kill you!"

Mouse handed Lorenzo the staff of Moses, climbed the railing, and peered down. The look on his face revealed that it was higher than he had thought. The longer he waited, the paler he got. "Another day," he said and stepped down.

"Ha! See, folks?" Lorenzo exulted. "This proves who has greater power!"

Mouse shut his eyes, waited a moment, and cried, "Heaven says to show true power, not just show off. Strike me, Lorenzo! Beat me with the staff of Moses!"

Lorenzo raised the staff, but Martha wailed, "Stop this madness!"

He lowered it. "I see what you want to do, Mouse. You hit me first with it."

Mouse grabbed the staff and struck Lorenzo on the side of the head. He fell and lay still, bleeding from ears and mouth. When he came to, his speech was slurred and never became normal. He wouldn't let us take him to the doctor and we carried him to his house. On the way, I tried to convince Mouse. "All that power portrayal is sham; you saw what it did to Lorenzo, and if you don't stop, it'll be your undoing too. Heed Jesus' warnings!" He was too busy gloating to listen to reason and walked away.

Arriving home, I was startled to find Torivio Ochoa waiting, and asked, "Are you here to finish what your brother Chuey failed to do?" He was unarmed, but with his skill, he needed no weapon to finish me off, and I backed away.

"I came to ask you . . . " He gulped. "To hold a funeral for Chuey."

That was the hardest pastoral job I ever had; the entire SRE attended, listened to the gospel more closely than before, and to the peace pact. Torivio told me afterwards, "I'm the one who killed my younger brother; I taught him to enjoy hating and violence. My cruelty makes me sick when I'm sober. I've regretted it ever since I saw God change Mincho the Monster. He said Jesus could transform me too, but I was afraid the transformation would make me a freak like Mouse."

"Torivio, we wouldn't be conversing now if God hadn't already begun softening your heart." He left two hours later with Christ in his repentant heart.

CHAPTER 22: CONFIRM THE GRASP AND THE PRACTICE OF LEADERS' TASKS

22–a. Be peacemakers and forgive those who have caused painful injury. Arturo finally forgave his wife's slayer. Notice what Jesus begged on the cross: *Father, forgive them, for they do not know what they are doing.* Luke 23:34

Identify a believer's responsibility when at odds with others: *So far as it depends on you, be at peace with all men.* Rom 12:18

Verify what to do with enemies: *I say to you who hear, love your enemies, do good to those who hate you, bless those who curse you, pray for those who mistreat you. Whoever hits you on the cheek, offer him the other also, and whoever takes away your coat, do not withhold your shirt from him either.* Luke 6:27–29

22–b. Cooperate closely with other churches in the area. Tiger's church served other flocks. See to what degree poor Macedonians sacrificed to aid believers of other churches who suffered severer need: *In a great ordeal of affliction their abundance of joy and their deep poverty overflowed in the wealth of their liberality. For I testify that according to their ability and beyond their ability, they gave of their own accord, begging us with much urging for the favor of participation in the support of the saints.* 2 Cor 8:1–5

22–c. Organgize extensions training to keep flocks multiplying in their normal, biblical way. Find what moved Antioch believers to send workers far away: *While they were ministering to the Lord and fasting, the Holy Spirit said, "Set apart for Me Barnabas and Saul for the work to which I have called them." Then, when they had fasted and prayed and laid their hands on them, they sent them away.* Acts 13:1–3

22–d. Respect sincere believers, regardless of minor differences in doctrine or practice. Disputes over baptism sometimes stifle a movement. Understanding reasons for churches' diverse practices defuses hostility. Find how believers can have variety in unity: *Where the Spirit of the Lord is, there is liberty.* 2 Cor 3:17

22–e. Restrain sham spiritual power before it corrupts and destroys those who seek it. Contests of power are common in many societies. Note what Jesus will tell those who falsely claim divine power: *Beware of the false prophets, who come to you in sheep's clothing, but inwardly are ravenous wolves. . . . Not everyone who says to Me, "Lord, Lord," will enter the kingdom of heaven, but he who does the will of My Father who is in* *heaven . . . Many will say to Me . . . "Lord, Lord, did we not prophesy in Your name and in Your name cast out demons and in Your name perform many miracles?" And then I will declare to them, "I never knew you; depart from Me, you who practice lawlessness."* Matt 7:15–23

EVALUATE YOUR LEADERSHIP
1=Poor. 2=Planning to improve. 3=Doing well.

1-2-3   Be peacemakers and forgive those who have caused painful injury.

1-2-3   Cooperate with other congregations in your area.

1-2-3   Keep congregations and cells multiplying in their normal, biblical way.

1-2-3   Respect sincere believers in spite of minor differences in belief or practice.

1-2-3   Restrain sham spiritual power before it corrupts those who seek it.

23.
Rabbits and Elephants Love
and Serve Each Other

"Is it Devils' Day, Papa?" Tino had risen early and was shaking my arm.

"Tomorrow, son. But call it *Saint Muñoz' Day*."

"Is Mr. Muñoz a devil too?"

"He's the patron saint that's supposed to be watching over Bat Haven, but he's doing a lousy job. You'd think he was a drunken gambler the way the town honors him. The town celebrates the birthday of a godly man by boozing!"

"Boozing, Papa? We're going to celebrate by boozing? How do I do that?"

"It means getting drunk or being an alcoholic. Back to bed, son. I need sleep."

But the interrogation persisted. "Why do devils come on his birthday?"

"An old legend taught that they try to keep the saint from entering town on his birthday. Men tote his life-size image around town, and when the procession returns to the square, the saint drives off the devils and they take off running."

"Last year they ran around throwing mud. Is that because they're alcoholics?"

"Could be. Young men portray them clowning, running around doing mischief. Folks toss them coins so they won't throw mud at them or something worse. Some smear slimy grime on themselves and hug you if you don't give them a coin."

"Can I be a devil, Papa, and throw mud if I'm not an alcoholic?"

"No you can't be a devil! We don't enter into every aspect of the celebration. The holiday had a sacred origin, so we show respect and tell folks about Jesus."

Lucy reminded me, "There'll be another big event on Saint Muñoz' day, the formal ceremony to transfer the deed to the church's land to Panther."

Task 23–a.
DEAL MORE DECISIVELY WITH DESTRUCTIVE ADDICTIONS

Seeing I'd get no more sleep, I got up. "Lucy, I wish they didn't give all their attention to the silly devils and Saint Muñoz. He might as well be the patron saint of alcoholics since Bat Haven's plagued with so many of them! Our church should **deal more decisively with destructive addictions.**"

I was soon to do so; Jaime arrived, clean-shaven and wearing an ironed shirt. He told me, "For the first time, I'm going to spend a holiday sober; I plan to enjoy the festivities with my new friends. But I still got a snag, Tiger, and I need help; my vice wastes the money I'd need to support a family."

"But you're through with alcohol."

"Yeah. God used our small group to free me from it. What still shackles me is my compulsion to gamble. I can't stop betting. If anything's bettable, I bet."

"I once did too; it went beyond an occasional playful bet to become an obsession. But when I trusted Jesus, I quit; He assured us that our heavenly Father provides our needs without taking from others."

"*Taking* sounds like stealing. I haven't stole nothing since I received Christ."

"Not directly, Jaime, but the effect is the same. You win by making others lose. The result is always misery. Some losers have committed suicide."

"I've considered it. There'll be plenty of gambling tomorrow; help me avoid it."

"You must discipline yourself. To trust in the goddess of luck is idolatry, and those who win big become idle playboys. My grandfather had a saying about it:

Win and turn lazy, lose and turn poor;

Win or lose, either way, you'll rue fate's false lure."

Sighing, Jaime extracted a handful of lottery tickets from a pocket. "I admit I've sought my fortune through luck or as a hit man, not by honest, hard work."

"Read Proverbs 6:6." I opened my Bible to it and handed it to him.

"Go to the ant, O sluggard. Observe her ways and be wise." He slapped his chest. "I'm going to be an ant and quit betting. Can I be accountable to you?"

"Yes, provided you start right now, this very instant. Lucy, bring Jaime a match." She did and I pointed at the tickets.

"But . . . "

"Now, Jaime! Breaking with a bad habit must be *full* and *final*."

He groaned, gritted his teeth, and struck the match.

| **Task 23–b.** |
| COMMISSION NEW |
| LEADERS LIKE THE |
| APOSTLES DID |

As he left, Jaime said he felt relieved, and I started out to curry Bullet when a spiffy new Jeep pulled up. A straight-backed man emerged, brushed off his suit, adjusted his tie, and announced, "I'm the Reverend Doctor Alfonso Leon and Cortez, executive secretary of the National Alliance of Churches." Dr. Leon would test our resolve to **commission new leaders like the apostles did.**

"I've seen you somewhere, Dr. Leon."

"Not in these mountains! Perhaps on the back cover of my book, *Leon's Standardized Church Protocol*?"

"Yes! That's where! I read it."

"Really! Ah . . . I trust you agreed with my premises?"

"Some. Mainly, sir, I read it because of your challenge to our premises."

"Well . . . That points to why I came, Pastor Garcia. Some Alliance members have heard concerns about your village work and asked me to check it out."

"Okay, we've been under the microscope before. I'm visiting a church near Los Vientos this morning. Come with me; I'll get another horse." I noticed his stylish suit. "Maybe you should take the Jeep; you'd still have to walk part way."

Leon drove Gadget and me as far as his Jeep could go and we hiked on. He complained about the steep climb, grumbling more sulkily the higher we went. We stopped to let him rest; Gadget stepped away to pick berries and motioned to me to join him. He asked softly, "Why do wealthy folks and foreigners that visit us complain so much, but our villagers rarely gripe about their many hardships?"

"Life would be unbearable if they did; they have so many needs and knocks."

We arrived in the tiny hamlet near the mountaintop; its houses were too small to meet in and the believers gathered in a rustic shelter. Its floor was rocky ground, its roof neatly thatched, with its one stone wall facing windward. Hand-hewn benches without backs formed a circle, and a tiny, crudely made table in the center held a plate with tortillas and a cup made from a gourd. We sang, confessed our sins to God, and Chorcho held up a tortilla. "Take, eat, this is . . . "

"One moment!" Leon stood and spoke firmly. "Excuse me, brother, but what you're doing might not be proper order. Are you an ordained minister?"

"Ordained?" Chorcho lowered the bread and looked at me questioningly.

"Continue, *Pastor* Chorcho," I ordered in an equally stern voice.

"Take, eat, this is . . . "

"Stop! I'm sorry, but I cannot accept the Holy Sacrament from layman's hands. We authorize only ordained ministers to consecrate the Holy Eucharist. Let us maintain sound ecclesiastical polity, brothers. God blesses proper order."

"Reverend Leon," I replied sharply, "Our churches obey the commands of Jesus above any human rule. Please don't hinder us from obeying our Lord."

"This peasant is no pastor; he dishonors the sacrament. Sloppiness does not glorify our Lord Jesus Christ. What he does violates my conscience."

I took a deep breath and prayed silently, "Lord, help me love this man!" I said softly, "Sir, the apostles did not decree that only professionals shepherd God's people. Jesus claimed all authority in heaven and earth, so we obey him and break bread just as He commanded, with or without ordained clergy. Now, tell me frankly, which you prefer us to do—obey you or Jesus? We can't obey both."

He looked at me with a perplexed expression before answering. "Our Alliance statutes stipulate only ministers ordained by an official council will officiate the Eucharist and baptism. It's that simple. Do you agree with this, Pastor Garcia?"

"Pardon me. You evaded my question by switching the topic. This violates your own rule in your chapter on 'ethical debate.' I await your reply to my question."

"All right. We ordain only alumni of accredited theological seminaries."

"Excuse me," responded Gadget acidly. "I regret that you, the learned and *Reverendísimo* Alfonso Leon and Cortez, lack the brains to understand. We obey only Jesus the King of kings, and you, sir, do not wear his crown!"

"Calm yourself, Gadget," I urged. "Please pardon him, brother Leon. On this mountain there's no way we can observe policies of urban churches. Do you admit that the rule that you just quoted did not come from the New Testament?"

"I did not come to debate. Do you recognize the authority of the Alliance?"

"Let's not dispute in front of these folks." We stepped aside, and I told him, "We heed the Alliance's counsels that are consistent with obeying Jesus. I do not oppose formal ordination; churches have the right to agree on standards for their leaders. Let well-educated people ask for a high level of theological education; the rub comes when they impose their rules on churches where conditions differ. In these villages, lay pastors serve well; it's the only way. To deny our rural churches Communion and forbid their baptisms would brand their pastors as second-rate, make us disobedient, and cut the heart out of the body of Christ."

"Our Alliance has developed its protocols over generations and God has blessed them. To break its rules as you say would destroy its integrity. Discipline breaks down totally if each church does as it pleases."

"I'm not advocating chaos, but freedom to do exactly what the apostles did. Most of the practices your book promotes originated in American and European denominations that are now declining. Please don't bring their disease here!"

He took a step back from me, open mouthed, as if I'd struck him a blow. "They're declining because of unbelief, not because of their practices."

"I disagree. Many Bible-believing churches decline because they've gotten too sophisticated and institutional; believers go and listen passively to a sermon, watch a worship team perform, and give mainly to a building fund. Did Jesus tell His apostles to develop *that* kind of church?"

Leon did not reply, and I added, "Those declining churches use the Bible mainly for source material to teach and hardly at all to follow its guidelines to evangelize, organize, worship, and train leaders. Your book on standardized protocol neatly side-stepped New Testament protocols for these tasks."

Task 23–c.
MAINTAIN GENUINE UNITY IN CHRIST AND AVOID CULTURAL BULLYING

Leon stiffened and glared at me. What followed would show the need to **maintain genuine unity in Christ and avoid cultural bullying.** He snapped, "You lack the background to judge these things. The way you train lay pastors is woefully inadequate, Reverend Garcia. They lack . . . "

"You needn't call me 'Reverend.' I lack formal ordination too."

"Is that so? Well, *Mister* Garcia, you must apply for proper credentials, or else I'll recommend to the Alliance to withdraw you from the pastorate."

"Your threat does not frighten me. According to God's Word, my credentials are the folks I've edified. Urban pastors enacted your rule about ordination before these rural congregations had become part of the Alliance. The urban pastors I know respect us and will not let the Alliance force us to follow antiquated regulations that would strangle our work."

Leon's face turned red, but he did not answer. There was another small congregation in the hamlet for tribal people, and its pastor presented me with a beautifully hand-carved, mahogany plaque recognizing me as an honorary member of their tribe, in appreciation of my work with them. Leon asked the tribal pastor, "How many elders does your church have, brother?"

"Only me so far. Others are preparing."

"A church must have at least three elders. Our bylaws require it."

Not again! I argued, "A church is what it is, Reverend, with one elder or ten. God can give it any number He wants. In the New Testament, churches had more than one elder, but it never stated that as law. Most of our churches start with only one and later God adds more. In many new churches, such a law would disallow any leadership at all and result in neglecting Jesus' commands. He looks to see if a church is obeying, not to see if its number of elders fits men's bylaws! The crucial concern is that all believers in a flock receive effective pastoral care."

Chorcho told Leon, "I lead three village flocks that have no elders yet; I'm training them. But, they're true churches because they obey Jesus' commands."

Leon's narrow eyes and stiff clerical posture warned that he was in attack mode. "Just who are you, sir?"

"Ricardo Solórsano. Yes, the devil's assassin—transformed by Jesus' blood."

"*El Chorcho*?" Leon stammered and took a moment to recover. "Well, gentlemen, your unauthorized church procedures lead only to confusion. We who have proper theological preparation are the ones to order standardized protocol."

I clenched a fist in frustration. "We're on separate wavelengths, sir! The apostles respected different cultures, and biblical unity embraces variety. Cultural differences beautify the bride of Christ. Your book affirmed this. Have you forgotten how you pointed out in Revelation how all tribes and nations are present and recognizable with their different tongues and cultures before God's throne? You affirmed it on a cosmic scale; apply your rule now to this mountain village."

"God will do as He likes in heaven, but here on earth you will adhere to the protocols that the Alliance has laid down. You will do as I say."

To calm my anger, I stepped away and kicked rocks until I stubbed my toe painfully. I asked myself, *"Why do I let Leon irk me so? Is this about more than differences in church protocol?"* I argued with my conscience and it argued back, *"You're peeved because he asserts his ego over yours on your turf. Admit it! You haven't controlled your ego completely. Stop competing. Now smile at the man and show respect, or you'll only make thing worse."*

I invited Leon to have a private chat and told him quietly, "I have a question that might help us. Why do you think Paul scolded the Galatians so harshly?"

"Jews imposed rules on Gentiles that annulled grace. Why do you ask?"

"Paul complained that they were being circumcised, yet he circumcised Timothy so he could shepherd Jews in Lystra—two paths for two cultures, and Paul respected both. Does his principle apply here? Help me think this through."

"I'm not sure I know what you mean, Tiger."

"The two churches here have different music styles, different instruments, different clothes, and different prayer postures. Mixing two cultures annuls one of them. Is that unity or cruelty? We tried it here and most tribals quit attending. In your opinion, Reverend, should we heed Paul and *be all things to all men?*"

"I need to think about this." Leon calmed and watched from a distance as Chorcho served Communion.

Villagers joined us on our way back down the mountain, in order to arrive in town a day early for the festivities, to visit friends, and secure rooms. Three times as many passengers than Leon's Jeep would normally hold climbed on it. I expected him to complain, but he stepped to the roadside silently, facing the panoramic view of the town below. I remarked, "Beautiful, isn't it, sir?"

"Oh! My mind was elsewhere. Tiger, if you're right, then nearly everything I've dedicated my life to is wrong."

"Only if we assume there's just one right way, and that one of us has to be totally wrong. The answer is obvious: allow more than one path. Paul did."

We stood looking at the town below while Leon let the mountain air cool his face. During our bumpy ride down the steep road, I asked him about his church and family, and we chatted about his college achievements; he had been valedictorian, captain of the soccer team, and had a four-point grade average in seminary.

Back home, Leon studied a map showing our churches, and bowed his head for a long time. As he left our house, he motioned for me to join him outside and confessed, "I admire the scope of your work and apologize. Your departure from our norms shocked me and I acted imperiously. I'd assumed less educated leaders must follow our city churches' practices, but I admit now that God gives you the same right to develop your own protocols. Well, now I have a request. Will you help me revise my book where it assumes only one way is right?"

"I'm a poor writer, sir."

"You just point out the changes; I'll add them. Where would you start?"

"With the title. Change 'Leon's Standardized Church Protocol' to 'New Testament Church Protocol' and edit accordingly." He smiled, clasped my hand warmly, and stepped into the Jeep.

> ## Task 23–d.
> OFFER WHOLESOME ALTERNATIVES TO INDULGING IN VICES DURING PUBLIC FESTIVALS

That afternoon I'd see why caring leaders **offer wholesome alternatives to indulging in vices during public festivals.** The mayor called a meeting to coordinate the activities, and it irked me to see Panther enter Campos' office with Wanda. A young Catholic priest came, whom I'd not met, and Mayor Campos began. "Father Lozano, as in prior years, you will first preside over your church's traditional ceremonies. Then, Pastor Garcia, your children will recite as in the past, before I introduce the agronomist Stephen Reyes and you, Mr. Panther Jones, for your announcements. Mrs. Wanda Alvarez, you may play background music on your new sound equipment before and after these ceremonies; it'll add an elegant touch to our annual event."

Aaron Ortiz was whitewashing the patchy exterior walls of the courthouse; he no longer worked in the mine, as Mouse had fired him. He stopped outside a window, listening, and the mayor scolded, "Why such curiosity? Keep that brush moving. I want those walls looking sharp for tomorrow's festivities."

Panther advised, "I arranged with the military for jet planes to fly over at the moment we sign the document to transfer to me the land on the mountainside. We'll watch the time carefully; it'll be at three p.m. exactly, right to the second. I will announce officially that we've found uranium and that new mine excavations will bring profitable employment to many. Then I'll give beer to everyone."

Outside the mayor's office, Aaron boasted to me, "I'm commandant of the SRE in Los Vientos now, Tiger, and now I'm as good as Chuey with explosives."

"Congratulations for becoming as foolish as your predecessor."

"You'll regret you said that, Tiger. I'm going to . . . " Aaron saw Pacho approaching from his shop and resumed whitewashing without finishing his threat.

"Did you meet the new priest?" Pacho asked. "He graduated from a very traditional seminary in Spain. The bishop heard complaints about Father Camacho's reforms and reassigned him to a small parish out in nowhere."

Wanda approached in a buoyant mood, as things were going her way, and purred in an affected voice, "Tiger, can you carry my new sound speaker over and attach it to a tree here in the square? It's quite heavy. It's in my new house, in the side entryway. Come, I'll show you."

A painter was making final touches in the entryway when we arrived. Wanda pushed a button amid a tangle of wires and a tape recorder hummed. "Listen. I taped Anna's children's group to play for the festival tomorrow." The children sang Colombo's song *Come Quickly Dawn*.

"Such happy little voices!" I exclaimed. "And the words give me tingles."

"I hadn't noticed the words; I chose it for its harmony. My stereo sound equipment is the latest, Tiger, and this big speaker is extremely powerful. Yesterday I taped Mayor Campos' voice. Would you like to hear your voice?"

"Not now, ma'am. Thank you."

"Look at these handheld transmitters, Tiger. I press this one and the garage door opens. See? This other one opens my new curtains in the dining room, like those on an opera stage, so I can view the whole town square from my grand banquet room. Come in and see."

She pressed a button and I heard a buzz. Huge curtains slid open slowly in front of an enormous window framing a grand view of the town square. "Marvelous!" she squealed in delight and clapped her hands. "Now I can oversee everything that goes on in the heart of Bat Haven!"

"Impressive, ma'am! I admire this huge table; it's quite elegant."

She beamed. "I see you've finally acquired a bit of taste. It's an antique, three-hundred-year-old, royal banquet table. Kings and queens have dined at it with princes and dukes. I had it shipped from Madrid. Look at these works of art by famous painters. That mural you're admiring is called 'Scaling a French Alp.'"

"I wasn't exactly admiring it; I was trying to figure it out. Are those wiggly green smears supposed to be *trees*?"

"It's surrealist, the essence of refined culture! I bought it from Sebastian Milano. Relax your mind and its powerful impression will strike you."

"I'll have to take your word for that, ma'am."

An idea hit me, a way to trigger the Wasp's reaction. "I think they're going to dig up Mincho Medina."

"What?" she screeched. "Exhume his body? Why? When?"

"An autopsy, I guess, to verify the cause of death, probably early tomorrow."

"Oh, here comes Panther! Excuse me." She switched off the music and ran off shouting, "Simon! Simon!"

I started to lift the heavy speaker in the side entryway when I noticed the tape recorder and was curious. The controls were labeled in English—that jerky, abrupt-sounding language—so I simply pressed buttons. Nothing happened, so I hoisted the heavy speaker and staggered across the street to the town square.

As I learned later, after I left Simon's new house he had shouted heatedly, "We'll settle accounts right now, Panther. I fulfilled my side of our agreement."

"Partly."

"Completely, I tell you!" growled Simon and he repeated all that he'd done.

Mouse saw me struggling with the heavy speaker and came to help. He griped, "I told that ingrate Simon that the tunnel had extended beyond his mine property, and that his whole operation needed changes to make it safer. He got mad, cancelled my contract, and never paid me for last month's work."

"Let's go see him." We laid down the speaker, crossed the street, and rang a doorbell beside the new, ornate door—larger than the doors to Saint Muñoz. After a long wait, I heard a lock click and the door opened an inch. Mouse made his claim through the narrow gap, "Sir, you owe me for last month's excavations."

"I owe you nothing, I tell you," Simon growled. "Explosives are missing from my mine, for which you were responsible; that invalidates our contract."

"If someone stole your dynamite, you know it wasn't me. I . . . "

Simon slammed the door, and Mouse became livid. "He'll regret this, the lying miser! He'll pay for pushing me around! I'll let the town know! You'll see."

I'd never seen such fury, and warned, "Don't do anything rash. Let's keep our wits about us; if dynamite's missing, expect another attack soon by the SRE."

Back in the square, I connected the speaker's wires and Pacho hurried over from his shop. "Why take part in Saint Muñoz' Day, Tiger? We're not Catholics."

"We provide wholesome activities so that weak Christians can have fun without drinking. The mayor lets our children participate in the ceremonies, and the agronomist Stephen Reyes will reveal the mystery of the amazingly tall papaya."

"A client told me its radioactive fruit makes your teeth glow in the dark."

Children were kicking a ball nearby and heard us; one said, "The tree grew from a seed blessed by Saint Muñoz, and its fruit will cure you if you got worms."

"Tiger, listen. Torivio Ochoa, Chuey's brother, has a new cell group of SRE men who say they follow Jesus. I'm not so sure. They still look fierce to me."

"Only on the outside. Inside they're lambs; they're trying hard to follow the peace pact. So many have left the SRE that it's no longer influential and the few desperate ones that remain are becoming even more recklessly dangerous."

I'd find out later how true my words were. On one side of the square, Aaron at that moment was pointing to a large platform that workers had hastily constructed and told his comrades, "We'll show everyone that the SRE is still powerful. I heard their plans at the courthouse; Tiger will pray on that platform to end the ceremonies, so we'll hide the dynamite under it tonight and give the celebration a noisy climax! We can string the detonator wire alongside those temporary light wires, and no one will notice. Bring devils' masks to disguise yourselves."

Before dawn the next morning, Gadget took soldiers to the cemetery to exhume Mincho's body and they dug up the gravesite. "Empty! Someone took the body! We gotta find it! Search the town, Corporal. Quick!" Beady-Eyes shouted orders and soldiers ran toward every quarter of Bat Haven.

The big day had arrived, and Tino went out early to watch the devils. He returned yelling, "Papa! Soldiers are running around looking for a dead man, and devils are coming down our lane. Davey! Hide before they throw mud on us!"

Lucy and I later took the boys to the square where hundreds of villagers had already arrived. "Look, Tiger." Lucy pointed across the street." A wolf pack!"

Freckles, Fred, and Lorenzo Guzman in his neon blue, flaming shirt were observing the festivities from afar. I called, "Come, brothers. Enjoy the festival."

Fred snapped a photo of a "devil" before shouting back, "We take no part in your pagan orgies."

The devil approached with a handful of muddy ooze. "A little gift, kind sir."

"Give him a coin, Fred," warned Lorenzo, "or else . . . "

"Go, you greedy rogue!" hissed Fred. "I disapprove totally of your folly."

I motioned with my hand for the devil to wait, and told Fred, "Jesus took part in celebrations along with sinners, and we're to follow His example. We can't transform the holiday, but we can do our part to help weak believers avoid its excesses. They'll attend no matter what we say, so let's do damage control. I also want my son Tino to see me discern the good doings from the bad. We're the light of the world, and the holiday lets us shine. Now be courteous to the devil, or . . . "

"You compromise with the world! True Christians avoid joining with sinners."

"You're still overlooking what Jesus did; He partied with sinners, and you know why. We're to be *in* the world but not *of* it."

While Fred was sneering at me, the "devil" seized his camera and ran laughing into the square where he set it on the ground. "Come get it, sanctimonious *gringo*. You got to join us pagans here if you want your camera back."

The three wolves hurried to get the camera; the "devil" poured beer over Fred's head and announced to the crowd that he was drunk. Wanda hurried over to investigate, smelled the liquor, and rushed about publicizing it. Freckles began arguing heatedly with his father, but I did not hear their words. Fred and Lorenzo hurried from the town square, but Freckles stayed.

"How enchanting the typical dances!" Evita exclaimed. Trumpets, accordions, castanets, and marimba produced vivacious tunes as girls twirled in brilliantly colored dresses opposite mates clad in chic colonial garb. Their director had a playful sense of fun and matched the tallest fellow with the shortest girl; I couldn't stop laughing at the incongruity and energy with which they hopped around the platform. Tumblers evoked admiring cries, and to one side a juggler and fire-eater vied to attract spectators. Horses raced on the street, a booth held poker games, and others sold booze, tacos, fancy crucifixes, stuffed bats, miniature images of Saint Muñoz, and trinkets. A heavily muscled man had embedded a hook in the bare flesh of his body with a rope attached, and sadistic spectators tossed coins to watch him grimace in pain as he towed a car slowly down the street.

Gadget commented to Lucy and me, "If we'd had a murderer waiting in jail, I'd top off the entertainment with a good hanging."

"Stop that!" Lucy said. "So many bodies crowded together in this hot sun! I smell the sweat in the air! I'm feeling a bit apprehensive and don't know why."

Monotone chanting announced the return of the procession that had marched through the streets following Saint Muñoz. The "devils" fled, pretending to be terrified, except four who waited to one side with their detonator. Penitents followed the saint's life-sized image on their knees, hoping to earn merit. A pregnant woman pressed a candle against the saint and rubbed her belly with it. Another lady held a baby up, kissed the image's feet, and wept. The young priest strode to the platform in his flowing black robe and carried out the Catholic ceremonies.

Mayor Campos then announced, "Attention! The moment has arrived!" He had been eying his watch, counting the minutes to when the jet fighters would soar over the square. "Mr. Panther Jones will now legally purchase the Alvarez mine and the Evangelical church property. Come bring the property deeds, gentlemen." Panther, Simon, Arturo, and Amos Nuñez in his fancy white shoes marched onto the platform. Simon began, "Ladies and gentlemen, it's my proud privilege to introduce our town's benefactor, Mr. Panther Jones."

Panther looked at his watch and took the microphone. After a brief greeting, he said, "Miners happened to discover uranium, more lucrative than any meager veins of silver." He talked on about the money that would flow into the town.

"Where's cousin Mouse?" Lucy asked. "He's always loved this festival."

Mouse had ridden his mule up to the mine, as we'd learn later, toting the staff of Moses like a knight's lance, still fuming with irrational rage over Simon's accusations. He opened a storage shed, lugged boxes of explosives to the cliff's edge, and readied a blasting cap. He tried to set bushes on fire, but they were green, so he rolled out a fifty-gallon gasoline drum, opened its spigot, and lit the flow. He then hurried a safe distance away and aimed the staff of Moses at the celebrating throng in the square. "Behold the Lord's consuming fire! The Almighty's just revenge!" He pushed the detonator button.

The blast blew out the fire and burst the gasoline drum, propelling it down the slope, spewing its contents as it rolled. Mouse lit the gasoline again and flames followed the barrel down the mountainside toward the tethered mule, which brayed in panic. Underbrush under the trees was dry and the fire spread rapidly.

In the town square, the explosion interrupted Panther, and people looked up at the mountain; heavy black smoke billowed above the mine. Jet planes flew through it and swept steeply downward toward the town square.

"Bombers!" Pacho shouted. "They hit the mine and are coming for us!"

"No! No!" cried Panther. "I arranged the flights with military headquarters. Don't leave! Don't leave!" Nobody heard him in the din of the diving jets and people's screams as they ran in every direction.

Simon grabbed the microphone. "Men, let's extinguish that fire. Quickly, I tell you! To the mine!"

"We're not your slaves no more," shouted a miner whom Simon had fired. "Your blasted mine means nothing to us now. Go pee on your own fire!"

"But our peace covenant," Torivio Ochoa reminded the miner. "Let's obey Jesus. He told us to do good to those who have ill-treated us. Now's our chance." Several of us rode up to the mine in *The Caribbean*. The hungry flames were devouring the brush under the pines with the appetite of a starved dragon; I found a hose and began spraying water. Farther down, Mouse had untied the mule, but could not mount it, as it kept dancing around, terrified by the flames. He whacked its head with the staff of Moses and it stood still, dazed, long enough for him to climb on its back.

I heard pitiful braying and ran through the smoke toward the mule. It was refusing to go forward toward safety because it would have to pass near flames, and Mouse was beating it brutally with the staff. Suddenly, the panicked animal bolted. Maddened by pain and blinded by smoke, it hit a pine tree that knocked Mouse off. The crazed beast began trampling the body of its owner. I grabbed its bridle, but could not pull it away, and one of the miners shot it dead.

Colombo and I rushed Mouse to the health center, but the doctor was not there. We found him in the town square and told him what had happened. He sighed, "Your church doesn't need a pastor; it needs a squad of medics!" After examining Mouse, he told me, "Seven fractured ribs! It's the second time his ample flab has avoided sure death; it cushioned the mule's hooves. But he has severe internal injuries; it'll be some time before we can be sure of the outcome."

The men put the fire out, and Colombo drove them back to the square. It was dark, and Wanda sent a boy to her new mansion across the street to turn on the lights, which attracted a host of insects. The mayor resumed the ceremony and, while swatting bugs, called me to the platform. My clothes were filthy with soot, so I asked Colombo to take my place and initiate our congregation's participation.

"It's been our annual tradition," the deep baritone voice announced, "to present the banner, *Little Sunbeams,* to the Sunday School class that memorized the most Bible verses. We have changed our method of

Christian education. We now teach God's Word in home groups. Last years' winners, the primary class, will hand over the banner to the group that won it this year. Come up, children."

Grandma Anna climbed the platform, followed by tots who stretched out the large banner for all to see. Anna announced, "It's our honor to present the *Little Sunbeams* banner to this year's winners, the new group of Torivio Ochoa."

"Hallelujah!" shouted the former SRE men, leaping onto the platform.

Startled children hid behind Anna, while a roar of surprised laughter and congratulatory applause for the new "Little Sunbeams" rose in the square. Torivio Ochoa's face bore scars and he wore mended trousers. Another was missing an ear and a third wore a patch over one eye.

"Bandits!" jeered a familiar voice at my side. "What phonies!" I turned to find the elegantly clad Duke Reyes-Castillo standing nearby, the cattleman who had tried to rape Evita. I almost returned the wallop that he had given me, but I turned instead to watch the children hand the banner to the ragged men. They lifted it high with wide smiles, some lacking front teeth, and recited John 3:16.

"Comrades, look!" shouted Torivio, pointing. "Them devils are SRE and intend evil; I planted spies among them." He'd recognized Aaron and his goons in spite of the masks, waiting with the detonator. "Attack, 'Little Sunbeams'!"

They leaped from the platform, folks parted to make a path, and the "devils" fled. Torivio found the detonator and called for soldiers. The "Little Sunbeams" pursued the SRE goons to the street where men were bearing the image of Saint Muñoz into the church. The priest was scolding them for stopping during the distractions; the combatants accidentally jostled them, and Saint Muñoz tumbled into the dust.

"Papa," Tino laughed, "the idol's nose broke off! Isn't that funny! Tell the devils to knock Saint Muñoz down again!"

Beady-Eyes showed the explosives to Simon who stammered, "Those Communists were going to kill me! Take measures, Corporal! I tell you, the town needs a strong military defense now. Hop to it!" Beady-Eyes dashed away.

Mayor Campos took the microphone. "It's all okay, folks. Now, the mystery of the papaya. . . . Why'd it grow so tall? Is it a miracle of Saint Muñoz? Our agronomist Stephen Reyes has examined it and has a scientific answer for us."

Task 23–e.
PURSUE THE
NORMAL EXPANSION
OF CHRIST'S
KINGDOM

An apt illustration followed of the need to **pursue the normal expansion of Christ's kingdom.** The curly-haired agronomist explained, "The papaya's neither radioactive nor unnatural. Tended well, it simply grew to its natural potential by its innate power given to it by its Creator. It will grow no more; papayas have a short life. It has produced its fruit with seed that reproduces after its own kind. The only miracle is that these plants are so fruitful and reproductive. Our Creator has provided so many plants in abundance to feed us, clothe us, and provide wood and flowers to adorn our houses!"

The mayor then announced, "Pastor Tiger Garcia will pray to end the formal ceremonies. But first, Tiger, please explain another phenomenon of growth, that of so many evangelical churches all over our town and in the villages. They've taught the poorest among us to develop small industry and agriculture, and have halted violence and crime so effectively that our jail is empty!"

I felt ashamed of my sooty clothes, but Mayor Campos stepped down and thrust the microphone into my hand. What would I say? That churches can sustain a movement if they follow biblical guidelines? True, but folks didn't want a sermon. That it costs far less to start the kind of flock that multiplies than to start the kind that does not? Also true, but it wasn't the time for a lecture on strategy.

I stammered, "Good evening. Ah . . . The growth of our work is like what Stephen Reyes explained about the papaya: it's perfectly normal. Jesus Christ compared growth and reproduction in His kingdom to that of plants. God gives to an obedient congregation the power to grow, produce fruit, and multiply. We trust in the power of God and obey Jesus, that's all. Nothing special. Thank you, agronomist Reyes, for the most appropriate illustration. Now let's pray to close . . . "

"Wait!" Panther seized the microphone, rushed onto the platform, and announced, "The land transfer was interrupted. I'll now finalize it. Come, gentlemen." Simon, Arturo, and Dr. Nuñez joined him as he held up the property deed and continued, "The mine will employ two hundred workers and . . . "

A military truck roared into the square, honked to part the crowd, and jerked to a halt in the center of the square. Beady-Eyes and others leaped down with fixed bayonets and mounted a machine gun on the platform. "Quiet! Quiet!" Panther begged as he swatted insects with the document; he then waved his pen with a flourish before sitting at a small table to sign his check. As Arturo bent to add his signature, Nuñez orated, "Beloved citizens of Bat Haven who are groaning under a burden of poverty, soon glorious liberation and wealth will . . . "

Panther interrupted, "Time to celebrate, folks! Pass out the beer, Sebastian." Sebastian and Carmen had sniffed white powder and were too spaced out to react. Simon and Wanda held up between them the large mine progress chart for all to see; they had updated it show the "land acquisition" phase completed.

Alvarez Mining Co. "Rifle" Development Process Chart				
Research	**I**ncorporation	**F**inancing	**L**and acquisition	**E**xtraction of ore
➡	➡	➡	➡	

The mayor asked me again to pray to end the formalities, and I struggled to keep my voice from trembling with the sadness that had overcome me. I then told Lucy, "Panther has defeated us after all. It's over. Let's go home. Come, boys."

Arturo started to laugh, and I turned to see why. He was holding up the property deed, waving it in the air, and laughing hard, totally unlike him.

"He never laughs like that!" Lucy remarked. "What in the world?"

Nuñez grabbed the deed and examined it. "Fraud!" he cried. "This deed is worthless! It does not grant *dominio pleno* for full ownership, but merely *dominio útil*, right of use. Mineral rights remain with the state! Oh, surely Panther's lawyer told him this type of ownership is common in Latin America!"

Arturo continued to laugh. Panther grew red in the face, swore, and blurted, "Simon, you told my lawyer, Sebastian, that you had checked this out!"

"Impossible!" cried Simon. "Everyone knows they mined silver from the land that Olga Gomez' father donated to the church. The government knew he worked that mine, so it had to be *dominio pleno*, not *dominio útil*. It had to be, I tell you!"

Arturo came and asked Lucy and me, "Remember what Olga told us? Her father used that land above the chapel to graze mules. Like Simon, I assumed that he'd mined that upper terrain also, and never bothered to examine the deed."

Panther tore up his check and left the platform, cursing Sebastian who was sitting on the grass with blurred eyes and a vacant grin. Wanda stood nearby looking bewildered, and I told her, "Time for the background music again, ma'am."

"Oh!" She spoke to the young man who had turned on the lights. "Run quick. Start the tape recorder in the side entryway. Hurry! Hurry before anyone leaves!"

The harried youth turned the wrong switch and the lights in the town square went out. In a panic, he groped in the dark for the right switch. "Bats! Bats!" someone shouted. Those lovers of darkness were devouring a banquet, as the lights, unfortunately, had drawn swarms of insects. The young man managed to turn the tape recorder on, and Colombo's song resounded across the dark square:

Come quickly dawn! God's glory fills the skies!

Hail the new beginning when with Christ we rise.

Oh joyful hope! God's trumpet gives us wing!

Gaze on Jesus' face and with archangels sing.

Evita started singing it and soon everyone joined in. Wanda then eagerly leaned into the microphone. "Now everyone, you'll hear a grand surprise, a song I've been rehearsing for many days and . . . "

A click halted the music and the giant speaker boomed with Simon's raspy voice. "Let's settle accounts now, Panther. I fulfilled my side of our agreement."

"Partly," replied the heavy accent, amplified by the powerful speaker.

"Completely, I tell you!"

Oh, no! My fault! I had started the tape recorder the day before when I was flipping switches! The crowd roared with laughter and my face turned hot with embarrassment. Then suddenly everyone hushed, stunned, as Simon's voice thundered across the crowded square. "Didn't I arrange to eliminate that nosy dame that stumbled onto . . . ?"

"Stop your (*bleep*) whining!" bawled the ugly accent. "I took no part in that."

"And that brat who delivered the note I forged so the lawyer would leave . . . ?"

"Shut up, you fool!"

"Shut up, you fool!" scolded the parrot's voice in the background. Lucy was squeezing my arm, gasping, and we both rushed to steady Arturo who looked like he was about to faint.

"Did I not remove those people from the chapel?" continued Simon's voice. "And did I not eliminate that meddling Mincho Medina after he found out we were exchanging rifles for marijuana and buying off the SRE?"

"That was all your doing, Simon. I'll sign the (*bleep*) check to pay for everything tomorrow during the (*bleep*) ceremony. I'm going to my room."

We heard a door slam and Wanda's voice, "They're going to dig up Mincho early in the morning to examine it." She then swore as obscenely as Panther had.

"No, Wanda! They will not do it, I tell you. I'll prevent it."

"How?"

"Leave it to me. I know what to do. Nobody will ever see that body, I tell you."

The young man was trying frantically to turn off the tape recorder in the dark and hit the small transmitter that activated the huge curtains in the brightly lit banquet room. They opened slowly, revealing to the world the elegant interior.

"Look!" someone cried. "Alvarez' new house!" An enormous gasp came from a thousand throats, then horrified shrieks. On the royal banquet table in the elegant room, displayed for the world to see, lay the huge body of Mincho Medina.

For a minute, all was insane confusion. Beady-Eyes fired his rifle into the air to get order, which only stirred more chaos. The shots alerted Sergeant Perez at headquarters that something was amiss; he came running, sized up the situation, and told Beady-Eyes, "Remove that machine gun! Are you crazy?"

Simon had donned a devil's mask and disappeared into the darkness, but Wanda ran into the palatial house screaming incoherently. She seized a can of paint thinner the painters had left, poured it on the corpse, lit it, grabbed a knife, and began to slice the body, oblivious to flames searing her hands.

"Mrs. Alvarez, get away!" cried Campos, watching through the huge window.

He ran inside, and I followed. In the banquet room, Wanda was speaking not in her shrill voice but in a raspy, hollow tone like a bullfrog. "He joined my Enemy and turned the town against me. The cursed town believed him and now it persecutes me. But he's mine now. I'll slice the big liar up to fatten my pigs!"

I pulled the raving woman away from the pyre while the mayor found a fire extinguisher and covered Mincho's charred body with foam. He then looked at Wanda and shook his head. "Poor woman! She's lost her mind!"

The crowd, silent now, hurried from the square. Freckles found Roger and begged, "Let me come with you. My dad's mad at me; I told him I can't work with him anymore proselytizing, and the hotel's full. Let me sleep on your floor."

Roger and Freckles talked, and late that night Roger raised a question that challenges many budding pastors. "Are you seeking position, salary, and power, or a movement in which many follow Jesus? They're mutually incompatible."

Dr. Nuñez had been staying at the Alvarez' house and soldiers let him remove his belongings. He went to the chapel and tried to sleep on a hard bench; he finally dozed and did not hear the footsteps. Simon crept from the shadows to make a last defiant gesture; in morning's earliest gleam, he piled dry brush against the chapel, lit it, and fled into the hills. Smoke woke Nuñez; he escaped in his pajamas and stood barefoot watching the "House of Death" burn down, along with his beautiful white shoes, while a new dawn smiled on a changed town.

Freckles, his eyes reddened, told Roger and Lorena, "I couldn't sleep. You were right, Roger; I've been seeking a big salary and a position with power. He took a deep breath. "I want you to be my mentor." They embraced.

The new dawn also reached Mouse's heart. In the health center a week later, he told Lucy and me, "I was sure I'd die and I let Martha help me see the truth, just as Lucy had helped her. God uncovered ugly things in my heart; I asked Him to forgive my efforts to get attention, pretending to be a prophet like Ezekiel, making so many disturbances, and so much showy noise." Lucy clasped his hand and he wept. "As a child my mom whipped me when the people I preached to failed to give us large offerings; she said the Almighty was punishing me."

Martha sat by Mouse embroidering happy mountain samplers for the patients while his injuries slowly mended. When he recovered, Gadget drove him to the mine; he found the charred staff of Moses and broke it to bits. He returned the money to Lucy that she'd hidden in the hollow log and apologized to the church for his fanaticism. He still shouted at times, but for joy; even Pacho shouted joyful praises occasionally—a miracle almost as great as the Exodus! A legitimate mining company bought the mineral rights to the ore-rich slope from the government, installed safeguards, and hired Mouse to supervise excavations. His weight came down to nearly normal and he treated the miners as friends.

I asked Mouse to preach at an Easter sunrise celebration and told him I trusted him to control his passion. Our small groups gathered before sunrise in the square, and Martha asked me, "Why do folks call the town *Saint Muñoz* again?"

"You should know! You helped drive the bats out of the people's minds; residents now see the town as a cheerful place. They've all enjoyed your samplers; many have them, and no longer feel so adverse about the mountain looking down at them. Oh look! Dawn's earliest light is hitting its highest cliffs, and it's transformed! It's smiling, exactly as you embroidered it! Mouse's grand explosion on Saint Muñoz' Day must have shaken rocks loose to alter its expression, Martha."

"No, it's always been smiling. The cliff face hasn't changed—we have. We see it now from a different perspective, a happier outlook. Look for its frown and that's what you'll see; expect a smile and you'll see its true face."

Lucy hugged Martha and told her, "And just look at you! Some of the bulk Mouse lost, you gained. You look great!"

"At least folks have quit calling me 'Bones.'"

"Tiger!" Stephen Reyes was hurrying across the square from Saint Muñoz. "Can my life group join you? Can we celebrate Jesus' Resurrection together?"

"Wonderful!" I replied. "Will your new priest meet with us?"

"I'm afraid not." Those who disregard our new life groups prefer to stay inside, there in the dark."

The sun lit up the square then, and Mouse preached without theatrics, but with enough animation to satisfy those who liked to praise God with ample adrenalin.

Not everything turned out so rosy; a wire came from Sarah saying, "Thomas came upon a thief in our house who stabbed him, and he's with the Lord." The widow moved to Bat Haven to care for her aged parents. She and Lucy together taught homemaking to uneducated women, and a year later the impossible happened—Arturo wed Sarah!

After the ceremony, Lucy reminded me, "When Arturo first met Sarah in our house, he told her he'd never remarry, and I remember what she replied: 'We'll see about that!' Well, she did!"

By then Gadget and Evita were living in India; she wrote, "Folks love Gadget's story of the watchman who kept him from blowing himself up in a mine. You should hear his perfect speech now; learning Hindi made him aware of grammar. He trains leaders who multiply tiny flocks in villages and the city; the strategies Tiger taught him work well, with some adaptation to their worldview."

We wrote back telling our latest news, and Lucy added, "Where others put diplomas on the wall, Tiger has Jethro's ratty old black and white backpack hanging by its tail. He won't throw the ugly thing away."

Roger; however, wanted a real diploma. He enrolled in the seminary in the capital, and Lorena got a job designing dresses for a clothes factory, to her mother's dismay. Roger mentored Cy and Freckles who, after graduating from seminary, planted covert churches among Malayan Muslims. The faculty named Roger as Professor of Missions in Thomas' place, overlooking his youth because of his field experience and top grades. He made a promise to students that few professors make: "I'll mentor you until your flocks are multiplying. Don't hide stupid mistakes and setbacks from me, because that's when you'll need help."

By that time, authorities had given up searching for Simon and turned the new palatial house into a psychiatric asylum for severe mental cases, including Wanda. Lucy and I were on our way to visit her when Pacho, holding scissors and a comb, beckoned to us from his shop. He asked a man whose long hair he was cutting to tell us about the caveman. The man said, "Poor guy! My village is three days' hike to the north; a beggar with a hookarm lives there now, in a cave. We call him Batman because he sneaks out when it's dark, to scrounge for food."

Wanda received us graciously in the banquet room. "Tiger and Lucy! How kind of you! Sit and enjoy the music while I send a servant for tea."

That was the extent of any sane behavior; mumbling to herself, she strutted about in a purple velvet robe fringed with gold. She turned on the recorder with a scarred hand, and I recalled the flames of that fateful night as we endured her aria from "Aida." The royal banquet table that once held Mincho's body had been pushed against a wall and held old magazines and dirty cups. The coffee-stained *RIFLE* Mine Progress Chart served as a tablecloth covering the table's charred top. Wanda pointed to the chart's fifth and final phase, crudely shaded to indicate "Extraction of Ore." "My mine's in full operation now, earning me the vast profit I deserve, and I can keep up this grand palace. Simon's my foreign ambassador."

Alvarez Mining Co. "Rifle" Development Process Chart				
Research	**I**ncorporation	**F**inancing	**L**and acquisition	**E**xtraction of ore
➡	➡	➡	➡	

The paintings were gone, except the chaotic mural "Scaling a French Alp." A bearded man in an orange robe sat cross-legged gazing at it and I asked Wanda, "Is he a Buddhist monk?"

"Shh. Don't disturb him; he's transcending the world." I took a closer look; he was Panther's legal advisor, Sebastian. He'd scaled those surreal French Alps to the top and then some! Wanda took a notepad from a pocket, opened it, turned its pages, and eagerly whispered to us, "He left Carmen behind, so she married Panther Jones." She pushed the switch to open the elegant curtains and babbled, "Look at the glorious vista. I monitor all that goes on in the heart of my realm. The newspapers all print lies about me. That man out there doesn't know I reside here in the elegant, imperial citadel of the queen of Bat Haven."

I looked out the massive window; a man was wheeling crates of beer into the Alvarez' original, older house—now a hotel. "Look, Lucy." I pointed. "It's Beady-Eyes! Sergeant Perez told me his colonel had the corporal drummed out of the army for cruelty and forcing prisoners to pay 'protection fees.'"

"Shut up, you fool!" squawked a familiar voice from a cage in the corner.

I walked over to the bird and replied, "Your vocabulary hasn't changed a bit since the day I entered your former house seeking employment."

Lucy remarked as we left, "That day brought a lot of things into our lives!"

"It sure did! Long, dark nights, demonic attacks, harsh trips with brave co-workers, bundles of dynamite, flight from the law. But it's been worth it, right?"

"Yes, Tiger. God brought good out of evil and amazing peace out of havoc."

"Bittersweet memories! I shudder to think how many times my steps faltered as a leader—leader of a family, of a cell group, of newer leaders that I mentored, of a church, and finally of a movement with churches multiplying near and far."

"But your steps also led us all the right way and we both know why; those were the steps that you placed in the footprints of our Savior."

CHAPTER 23: CONFIRM THE GRASP AND THE PRACTICE OF LEADERS' TASKS

23–a. Deal more decisively with destructive addictions. Note what enslaves: *For by what a man is overcome, by this he is enslaved.* 2 Pet 2:19

Jaime's gambling made him lazy; note God's advice to one who yields to a sinful vice: *Do not be overcome by evil, but overcome evil with good.* Rom 12:21

23–b. Commission new leaders like the apostles did. Some churches claim "apostolic succession" through a line of bishops back to Peter. Find what true apostolic succession is: *The things which you have heard from me in the presence of many witnesses, entrust these to faithful men who will be able to teach others also.* 2 Tim 2:2

23–c. Maintain genuine unity in Christ and avoid cultural bullying. Find in Jesus' promise the kind of unity we have: *The glory which You have given Me I have given to them, that they may be one, just as We are one; I in them and You in Me, that they may be perfected in unity, so that the world may know that You sent Me.* John 17:22–23

23–d. Offer wholesome alternatives to indulging in vices during public festivals. Annual holidays impress children; some offer opportunities to exalt Christ. Notice what God commanded parents to do with children when He initiated Passover: *When your children say to you, "What does this rite mean to you?" you shall say, "It is a Passover sacrifice to the Lord who passed over the houses of the sons of Israel in Egypt when He smote the Egyptians, but spared our homes."* Ex 12:26–27

23–e. Pursue the normal expansion of Christ's kingdom. Leaders in Antioch sent workers to neglected fields (Acts 13–14). Note how far that movement spread from Ephesus, Acts 19:10: *This took place for two years, so that all who lived in Asia heard the word of the Lord . . .*

Church-planting Outreach in Asia Minor

Note: *Asia*, a Roman province in Asia Minor, had many cities and towns.

Verify who causes growth in God's kingdom. *I planted, Apollos watered, but God was causing the growth.* 1 Cor 3:6

Let believers and churches multiply "after their own kind" as Jesus' parables urged. Mentoring leaders the way Jesus and Paul did can sustain such a movement. Where will your church do this if it has not begun yet?

Mentoring Chains in the Bible

Jethro ⟶ Moses
   Moses ⟶ leaders of 1000s
      Leaders of 1000s ⟶ leaders of 100s
         Leaders of 100s ⟶ leaders of 10

Deborah ⟶ Barak

Eli ⟶ Samuel
   Samuel ⟶ Saul
      Samuel ⟶ Ahithophel and Nathan ⟶ David
         David ⟶ Solomon and many others
            Solomon ⟶ Queen of Sheba and others

Elijah ⟶ Ahab and Elisha
   Elisha ⟶ Joash and other kings

Daniel ⟶ Nebuchadnezzar and his officers

Mordecai ⟶ Esther
   Esther ⟶ King Ahasueras

Jesus ⟶ His twelve apostles and many more
   The Apostles ⟶ Barnabas and many other leaders
      Barnabas ⟶ Paul
         Paul ⟶ Titus, Timothy and many more
            Timothy ⟶ "faithful men" (Epaphras, et al)
               Faithful men ⟶ "Others also" (2 Timothy 2:2)

Philip ⟶ Ethiopian official who introduced the gospel in Africa

EVALUATE YOUR LEADERSHIP

1=Poor. 2=Planning to improve. 3=Doing well.

1-2-3   Deal decisively with destructive addictions.

1-2-3   Commission new leaders like the apostles did.

1-2-3   Maintain genuine unity in Christ and avoid cultural bullying.

1-2-3   During festivals, offer wholesome alternatives to indulging in vices.

1-2-3   Pursue the normal expansion of God's kingdom.

Dawn from on high will visit us to shine on those who dwell in darkness and the shadow of death, to guide our feet into the way of peace.
Luke 1:78–79

Appendix A: Vital Ministries Checklist

Locate a task by its number in the story and in the questions at chapter ends.
Note the date in the space following a task when you confirm its practice.
Download a similar menu and studies freely from www.Paul-Timothy.net.

Give Pastoral Care and Comfort to the Troubled

Correct offenses without condemning, *Gal 6:1–2; Matt 18:15–20; 1 Cor 5*

Remove roots of bitterness without delay, 06–g *(date, when practice is confirmed)* _____

Correct others' bad habits without grumbling, gossiping, or judging, 07–d _____

Provide caregiving for persons and families with problems or addictions, 08–c _____

Help the anguished and dejected to trust in Jesus' comforting power, 09–f _____

Reconcile enemies, 13–b _____

Restore those who stray without delay, 14–c _____

Assure the dying, console mourners, and help everyone think on eternity, 15–e _____

Follow the steps that Jesus prescribed to deal with offenders, 19–b _____

Agree on a peace pact to heal division, 21–b _____

Be a peacemaker, forgiving even one who has injured you painfully, 22–a _____

Stanch Satan's sneaky undercurrents of finicky criticism, 03–c _____

Advise and reconcile troubled people, *Phlm 1*

Deal decisively with crushing feelings of guilt, 05–a _____

Explain why our heavenly Father lets His beloved children suffer, 07–b _____

Let courage and faith override feelings, fear, and jealousies, 08–a _____

Face the world's hatred without letting it trigger despair and dismay, 09–d _____

Put to rest gnawing doubts that derive from defeat and fatigue, 09–e _____

Agree with one's spouse on prudent management of family finances, 15–b _____

Deal decisively with addictions, such as to gambling, 23–a _____

Watch over the flock, drive off "wolves," *Acts 20:28–31; Titus 3:10–11*

Drive off wolves that threaten a flock and shun all who cause division, 06–a _____

Heed Jesus' warning against apathy's deadly effect, 02–b _____

Pray, Intercede, Do Spiritual Warfare

Pray daily alone and with family, *1 Thess 17; Eph 6:10–18; Gen 18:20–33*

Detect Satan's treachery as he strives to stifle a church's revitalization, 04–b _____

Replace prayers to idols and images with prayer in Jesus' name, 09–g _____

Pray for the sick, needy, misled, and demonized, *Eph 6:10–18; Jas 5:13–18*

Pray with confidence in Jesus' name for the sick and oppressed, 14–d _____

Rely on the power of Jesus' name to discern and cast out evil spirits, 16–b _____

Detect and resist *demonic forces of darkness*, 21–c _____

Discern and expose false spiritual power, 22–e _____

Wage spiritual warfare strategically, prepared always for martyrdom, 03–e _____

Give and Be a Good Neighbor to the Needy

Serve the needy, be model citizens, *Luke 10:25–37; Acts 6:1–6; Gal 6:9–10*
Avoid using Satan's tools to extend Christ's kingdom on Earth, 05–d _____

Achieve social justice by using methods that also are just, 07–e _____

Deal with employers and employees with respect and fairness, 10–d _____

Instruct believers to do business in an honest way, 15–g _____

Help the poor advance economically without causing dependency, 16–a _____

In disaster's wake, deal with both spiritual and physical needs, 16–d _____

Integrate benevolent development work with other vital ministries, 16–e _____

Strive without rancor for social justice, 17–a _____

Train deacons to lead others caring for the needy and oppressed, 20–a _____

Be stewards of one's treasure, talent, and time, *Matt 25:14–30; Luke 6:38*
Practice Christian stewardship for the right motive, 13–a _____

Encourage believers to give cheerfully, 15–f _____

Instruct believers to do business in an honest way, 15–g _____

Verify a benevolence project before contributing to it; avoid frauds, 19–k _____

Take vacations as Jesus did, 20–d _____

Worship as a Body; Provide Time for Meaningful Fellowship

Worship, fellowship, break bread, *Matt 26:26–28; Heb 10:25; Acts 2:46,20:7*
Know the place of emotion in worship and a Christian's life, 05–j _____

Obey New Testament "one another" commands in small groups, 07–a _____

Let children take a serious part in worship and church life, 10–a _____

Maintain order during worship without discouraging spontaneity, 10–e _____

Experience the divine mystery of the bread and cup of Communion, 11–a _____

Build loving relationships between new and mature believers, 17–c _____

Include worship songs that one can recall and sing during the week, 11–f _____

Develop interaction in and between flocks, *Rom 12:3–21; 1 Cor 12*
Let believers prophesy in the way the New Testament prescribes, 06–e _____

Use spiritual gifts in small groups; heed "one another" commands, 07–a _____

Churches and cells help each other do vital ministries so that all are healthy, 12–b _____

Practice honest pastoral ethics, 17–d _____

Respect Christian leaders regardless of social and educational level, 18–b _____

Expose and shun false leaders without compromise or delay, 18–e _____

Cooperate closely with other congregations in the area, 22–b _____

Respect sincere Christians with differences in doctrine or practice, 22–d _____

Maintain true unity in Christ and avoid cultural bullying, 23–c _____

Be Transformed to the Image of God's Son

Be transformed and renewed daily by God's Holy Spirit, *Rom 12:1–2*

Resist deceptive alternatives to serving God in a fruitful way, 01–b _____

Resist the subtle lure to criticize too much, 04–g _____

Live by faith without seeking constant signs from God to bolster it, 08–d _____

Explain why the risen Christ is our only hope for pardon and immortality, 09–c _____

Resist fleshly temptations by slaying sinful passions, 12–e _____

Explain original sin and its consequence for all, 15–a _____

Discern God's will with certainty, 19–c _____

Cultivate fruit of the Spirit, *Gal 5:16–23*

Achieve holiness by nurturing the fruit of the Spirit, 06–d _____

Correct children, coworkers, and employees with patience and a cool head, 03–a _____

Detect and arrest gossip before its venom spreads, 05–b _____

Pound one's ego down daily with God's "hammer" and be a servant to all, 09–a _____

Evangelize, Make Disciples, and Start Churches or Cells

Tell of Jesus' death, resurrection, and how He's helped you, *Luke 24:46–48; 2 Tim 4:5*

Demonstrate how to evangelize entire families and networks of friends, 04–d _____

Let believers use the power that God promised, to spread the Good News, 05–c _____

Warn people of final judgment and God's just punishment in hell, 05–h _____

Provide easy ways for new believers to witness to friends and relatives, 05–i _____

Proclaim Jesus as one's only Savior and Mediator, 08–b _____

Help any who think their own good works save them to trust God's grace, 11–e _____

Be alert to God-given opportunities to witness for Jesus, 03–d _____

Evangelize a head of a family first or as soon as possible, 19–h _____

Offer wholesome alternatives to indulging in vices during public festivals, 23–d _____

Receive and baptize the repentant; avoid discouraging delay, *Acts 2:38–41*

Know baptism's original purpose and effect and practice it accordingly, 05–g _____

Respect the sensitivities of younger and new believers, 11–f _____

Train disciples to obey Jesus' orders, *Matt 7:24–29,28:18–20; John 14:15*

Provide separate cells for seekers and new believers, 06–b _____

Let Jesus be a congregation's top leader by obeying His commands, 01–d _____

Let older children lead younger, serving as role models, 10–b _____

Start daughter churches and cell groups at home and abroad, *Acts 13–14*

Keep congregations and cells multiplying in their normal, biblical way, 22–c _____

Multiply cells in larger urban churches, 19–i _____

Send workers who know how to multiply churches to neglected peoples, 18–a _____

Remove man-made barriers to the expansion of Christ's kingdom, 23–e _____

Respond by faith to questioning by hostile authorities, 21–a _____

Let a "sending church" hold its workers accountable, 21–e _____

Prepare workers to go to neglected fields and bond with people and culture, 21–e _____

Oversee and Organize

Agree with coworkers on objectives and plans, *Phil 2:2; Acts 15:22–31*
Take the first step to become a leader for Jesus: know him, 01–a _____

Provide a type of government that fits a flock's level of maturity, 04–e _____

Define short, easy steps to carry out projects large and small, 05–f _____

Identify thieves of valuable hours, 14–e _____

Discern levels of authority for what believers do to serve the Lord, 14–f _____

Become a leader of leaders by mobilizing and mentoring them, 19–f _____

Keep church bylaws general with freedom to adapt to new situations, 20–c _____

Agree on serious projects; let them be bound in heaven as Jesus said, 03–b _____

Develop cells that let all members use their spiritual gifts, *1 Cor 12*
Limit group size to enhance interaction and mobilize new leaders, 12–f _____

Let believers do tasks that fit their natural personality type, 14–a _____

Let folks use God-given gifts freely, not to do only what pleases leaders, 15–d _____

Organize different types of groups according to current, local needs, 18–g _____

Serve one another in practical ways, *1 Cor 12; Eph 4:11–16; Rom 12:3–16*
Let members of a group serve one another using their spiritual gifts, 07–a _____

Let believers in cell groups teach one another in some way, 12–c _____

Lead firmly as humble servants, not autocrats, *Matt 20:25–28; 1 Pet 5:1–4*
Examine one's motivation to lead and confess any self-importance, 07–c _____

Let willing believers help plan projects and do vital ministries, 01–c _____

Help your congregation make crucial decisions carefully, 04–c _____

Know when a shepherd should resign, and how, 04–h _____

Recognize limitations of democratic process in congregational meetings, 11–c _____

Exercise prayerful, decisive leadership without being bossy, 12–a _____

Unmask false friendship and deceptive diplomacy, 13–d _____

Avoid lording it over family, friends, or flock, 15–c _____

Prevent a clique secretly usurping control of a congregation, 19–a _____

Share pastoral responsibilities among several leaders, 19–d _____

Avoid making changes merely to please insistent people, 20–b _____

Assess progress in all tasks, *Acts 20:28; Eph 4:11–12,15; Jas 1:22–25*
Keep a fruitful ratio between diverse aspects of key tasks, 02–a _____

Develop and sustain all ministries that God requires of a congregation, 09–b _____

Evaluate results of service for the Lord, not merely efforts, 10–f _____

Focus on positive action, not squandering time on chronic problems, 18–c _____

Evaluate pastoral trainees' fieldwork frequently and frankly, 18–d _____

Avoid focusing too exclusively on a pet ministry; balance the body, 19–g _____

Train and Mobilize Shepherding Elders

Apply the Word to equip believers for edifying ministry, *2 Tim 3:16–17*

Disinfect a flock from the contagious, disheartening leaven of legalism, 05–e _____

Discern crucial differences between the Old and New Covenants, 06–c _____

Teach doctrine along with practical duty; let Bible stories clarify both, 10–c _____

Proclaim positive truths, avoiding excessive scolding, 11–d _____

Preach what is currently needed, not merely what fits one's homiletic style, 17–b _____

Serve as an example others can easily imitate, of a dutiful shepherd, 13–c _____

Let love rather than money motivate bi-vocational leaders and recruit many, 04–a _____

Train leaders of new flocks, *Mark 3:14; Titus 1:5; 2 Tim 2:2*

Mobilize all five kinds of God-given leaders, 12–g _____

Extend mentoring chains as Paul required, 06–f _____

Recognize conditions that call for extension training and mentoring, 04–f _____

Train new leaders the way Jesus and His apostles did, 12–d _____

Provide pastoral training at all economic and educational levels, 13–e _____

Interpret a Bible text according to its context, 14–g _____

Detect and avoid whatever hinders mobilizing many volunteer workers, 16–c _____

Name shepherding elders according to the qualities that God requires, 17–e _____

Discern the type of pastoral training that fits a field and its trainees, 18–f _____

Delegate a task to a pastoral trainee after doing it together to model it, 19–e _____

Let godly leaders who lack degrees serve where needed and wanted, 19–j _____

Discern and practice biblical commissioning of new leaders, 23–b _____

Follow God's order in the home, *Eph 5:21,6:4*

Correct children with positive and consistent discipline, without anger, 03–a _____

Advise couples with bumpy relationships and folks planning to wed, 11–b _____

Fulfill duties of husbands, wives, and children, 08–c _____

Evangelize entire families; avoid extracting isolated individuals, 05–i, 19–h _____

Manage family finances prudently, 14–b _____

Attain moral purity, 12–e _____

Put family before fame and fortune; don't be slaves of the urgent, 01–e, 14–b _____

Remove roots of bitterness quickly, 06–g _____

Appendix B: Index of Leaders' Tasks

Numbers refer to chapters, and letters to tasks and questions at each chapter's end.

Marriage

Prepare couples planning to wed, 11–b

Spouses' duties, 14–b

Martyrdom, be prepared for it, 03–e

Mediator, Christ the only one between God and man, 08–b

Mentor, Christian leaders, see *Theological education*

Mercy ministry, see *Humanitarian work*

Ministries

Balance, avoid doting on pet ministries, 19–g

Do what fits personality as well as gifts, 14–a

Evaluate by examining results, not efforts, 10–f

Evaluate progress in all vital ministries, 09–b

Missionaries

Sent to neglected fields, 18–a

Held accountable by a sending church, 21–d

Prepared to bond with a people and their culture, 21–e

Moses' law, Purpose and contrasts with the New Covenant, 06–c

Obedience

Obey God before man's tradition, 14–f

Obey Jesus' commands above all else, 01–d

Old Testament, key differences from NT, 06–c

"One another", commands, reciprocal service, 07–a

Order, kept without stifling spontaneity, 10–e

Organization (See also *Body life*)

Avoid overemphasizing a pet ministry, 19–g

Form diverse types of groups as needed, 18–g

Original sin, universal consequence, 15–a

Participation, by all in a small group, 12–c

Pastor

Authentic credentials, 23–b

Become leader of leaders by mentoring them, 19–f

Delegate a task to a trainee after modeling it, 19–e

Enable believers to carry out key ministries, 01–c

Enable believers to use God-given gifts, 15–d

Ethics in pastoral work, 17–d

Leaders lacking degrees serve where needed, 19–j

Mentor new leaders, a pastor's duty, 04–f

Resignation, when and how to do it, 04–h

Respect leaders regardless of social status, 18–b

Share responsibilities among several leaders, 19–d

Shepherds' required character qualities, 17–e

Train new leaders, a pastor's duty, 12–d

People group, workers sent to neglected people, 18–a

Persecution, Satan counterattacks the godly, 03–e

Perseverance, courage overrides feelings, fear, 08–a

Personality type, determines tasks one should do, 14–a